N

Published in the United States
by Myrmidude Press
P.O. Box 420731
San Francisco, California
94142-0731
www.myrmidude.com

Printed on recycled acid-free paper in the United States

Library of Congress Catalog Card Number 99-90529

PINS / Jim Provenzano
p. 288
ISBN 0-9672382-0-X (pbk.)

1. Fiction 2. Sports 3. Gay Interest
4. Young Adult 5. Wrestling
Provenzano, Jim

First Edition 1999 Second printing 2000
cover photo and design: Stan Grozniak

Tool, 'Forty-Six & 2' c. 1996 Volcano Entertainment

Hole, 'Violet' c. 1994 Mother May I Music/BMI/Geffen Records, Inc.

Nirvana, 'All Apologies' c. 1993 Virgin Songs/The End of Music/BMI/Geffen Records, Inc.

To James and Carol Rigney, Al and Maureen Provenzano, Paul Provenzano and Mary Perillo, Mike Salinas, Felice Picano, Michael Lowenthal, Bert Herrman, Richard Labonte of A Different Light Bookstore, Gene Dermody of Golden Gate Wrestling, and all the readers, writers and wrestlers too numerous to mention, thanks for holding.

Jim Provenzano's fiction has been published in a dozen anthologies. His produced plays include *Under the River* and *Bootless Cries.* He received a BFA in Dance from Ohio State University, fellowships from the National Endowment for the Arts and the New Jersey and Pennsylvania state arts councils. He writes "Sports Complex" for San Francisco's *Bay Area Reporter.*

PINS

a novel by
Jim Provenzano

Myrmidude Press
San Francisco

"Listen to my muscle memory."

Tool, 'Forty-Six & 2'

A defense attorney for one of five San Jose boys accused of torturing a 13-year-old classmate downplayed the incident, saying it may have stemmed from a shared enthusiasm for professional wrestling.

"All of these boys are very enamored apparently of the World Wrestling Federation ... and we all know what goes on at the World Wrestling Federation," attorney John Finkle said in a court hearing Monday.

The victim told investigators that the five boys had lowered his pants and thrown him to the ground before taking him to one of their homes. There, he said, he was handcuffed, beaten, kicked, forced to drink toilet water and shot in the torso with a pellet gun. The boys also stripped him.

The alleged assailants are charged with kidnapping, false imprisonment, assault with a deadly weapon, torture and committing a lewd act on a child.

A fifteen-year-old boy involved in an accident at a wrestling clinic has been flown to a private hospital in New Jersey after being mistakenly pronounced dead by emergency medical technicians.

According to one of three boys who witnessed the accident, the student was injured while an instructor demonstrated pins. "We could hear his spine snap," said fourteen-year-old Raul Klein of Little Falls. Klein and other boys claim that "insulting" words were exchanged between the injured boy and the instructor, and are calling his survival "a miracle."

Coaches at the clinic denied any intentional wrongdoing. Students at the clinic noted how safely it was run. The instructor involved in the accident refused comment, except to confirm statistics that wrestling injuries of this nature rarely occur.

Organizers of the clinic said that they were glad the boy survived. "Our prayers are with his family," said one coach.

The attorney for the parents of the injured boy offered no comment, pending an insurance settlement.

1

The boy's buzzcut swirled out like a tiny universe whose only limits were two stubby ears. For weeks Joey had been trying to stir up the bravery to say something to him, until his math teacher asked what was so distracting.

New school, new town, new home, new league. Pick one, lady.

"Wrestling, Ma'am. Tryouts start today."

The buzzcut turned around, smiled slyly, sized Joey up, whispered, "Whaddayou weigh?"

A month later, Joey got his first pin on his new team, the Little Falls Colts. He jumped in the air and the buzzcut, who was called Dink, caught all 126 pounds of him just like at the Olympics, except it was just an exhibition match with only about forty people watching, including all the other wrestlers, coaches, the ref, the mat maids, the janitor.

Anyone among the few dozen people in the stands was somebody's family, which included Joey's father and brother.

By the next Monday, which was the day after Halloween, his win was just history. Other guys had won. No big deal. Besides, it wasn't about wins, but the dailiness, the belonging. He'd chosen his group, or it had chosen him.

By the next Monday, which was All Saint's Day, Joey's leftover Halloween candy hangover continued to dull his senses.

While Joey Nicci the wrestler was a winner, Joey the boy hadn't done so much as a push-up since his victory. He'd basked in it all weekend; eating, lounging, getting phone calls from Grandmama and Aunt Lilla back in Newark, helping Sophia the angel grow wings and Mike the werewolf his fangs. Between hauling the kids around the neighborhood, his mom even made his favorite dinner on Sunday, lasagna.

He felt every extra pound when all the guys at practice, on some invisible cue he never saw, swooped around him in a circle.

Two of them grabbed him by the ankles. He nearly bit his tongue while being dragged to the center of the mat before he found himself suspended upside down like a newborn. Passed around from one guy to the next, hand over hand, one leg at a time, his crew of doctors seemed unsure what to do with such a big baby, until somebody dropped him. Dink fell on him, four more guys on top of them, then everybody else piled up on them, amid a flood of growls, roars, giggles, snorts.

Under it all, in the reddish darkness of the boy mound, Joey felt Dink being smashed atop him, but pressing up, pushing them back protectively, his chin stubble chafing Joey's neck.

His hands flattened by some other body, his arms pressed down by someone's fuzzy legs, he felt Dink hovering over him, humping him in a playful way. Joey let him. Dink was doing him a favor, taking more of the weight, after all. He opened his hips in the tiny crevice of space under the dogpile and let Dink cop a feel.

He grabbed for his shorts as someone else yanked. He wanted to thrash out, but remembered why they had all piled up on Dink a few weeks before.

He was the best in his weight class. He was in.

1.5

Panting, disheveled, the boys dispersed, playfully punched him, high-fived, stepped over him, barked.

Dink trotted off as if nothing had happened.

"Status?"

Joey lay on the mat, gazing up at Bennie, grabbed his ankle, pretending to knock him down. Bennie yanked his heel like a horse absentmindedly swatting a fly.

Bennie and Hunter hovered over him, the team's two biggest guys, not counting Mario "Buddha" Martinez, the heavyweight, who wasn't tall, just wide. Bennie and Hunter were full-time jocks. Wrestling just kept them busy after football, where both had been powerful linemen, and before spring; track for Bennie (pole vault, sprints, relays), baseball for Hunter (third base).

They did a lot of playing around in the locker room, had bodies that curved, bulged. Hunter was a little on the chunky side. Bennie was hairier than most other guys on the team, even the coaches. Joey'd noticed that. Being a smaller wrestler, he noticed other guys, where he fit; skinnier than most, but stronger than others his size.

In his impeccable Data voice, Hunter jerked his neck slightly, postulated, "I believe, Sir, sensors are accurate in verifying his state of varsitosity."

Bennie dropped his voice low, Worf-like. "It would appear the transformation is complete." They hovered over the spud, checking phasers.

A warm padded cell, moist, guy-scented, soft on the floor, walls, the last bastion for boys who cannot stop playing around, tubes of extra mats for matches lay on the side, rolled up like huge cushions in the practice room with no windows, not much ventilation. Sounds were muffled from outside. From the looks of kids who happened by the door, when open, it seemed to mystify them. Joey had never been asked what went on at practice. He did not make friends outside the team. Those that weren't in it didn't want to know, or were afraid to know. Joey was comfortable with that.

"I don't like Mondays," Dink grunted as they did neck-ups, bridging up on their heads and toes. Their eyes met as they rolled on the soft mat.

"You're ugly upside down," Joey said, as Dink counted off, his face blushing a weird pink.

"You're uglier," Dink blurted.

Joey tried not to laugh.

A lot of the guys ended up on the JV squad, including Joey, at first. Others started dropping out after they couldn't take the soreness, the exhaustion, the drills. For some, just the shock of regular bruises scared them off. Joey watched the departing novices, seeing failure in their eyes, unlike Jeff and Brett Shiver, who'd been telling tales about their summer week-long trip to Iowa where they actually wrestled with John Smith.

Jeff and Brett's name was pronounced Shy-ver, Joey learned, shortly after announcing a little too loudly, that no, his name was not Nitchey, but Nee-Chee, after which he was dubbed Neech.

After an hour watching videos from the previous week's match, Assistant Coach Fiasole paused on a shot of Joey's defense, how he waited as bottom man for the right opportunity to grab his opponent, instead of wasting energy.

Joey hadn't remembered it that way. On tape he didn't recognize himself, couldn't remember a thing, except that long part where nothing happened, then Joey got thrown. He definitely remembered that.

"Circle."

Assistant Coach Fiasole had Bennie Skaal sprawl out on the mat, told everyone to watch, as the hulking senior marked different arm and leg moves in Basic Defense Position. Joey enjoyed watching Bennie's technique, but also his glutes, which one JV inadvertently described as "cushy." The JV was thereafter dubbed Cushy, until he quit wrestling.

Dink muttered the word sarcastically, although everyone in the room acknowledged Bennie's amazing body. How they appreciated or accused each other of loving each other's bodies was the source of tension, constantly broken by small faked punches, blurted words, or in Dink's case, popped open by induced giggles.

Assistant Coach Fiasole looked up. "You gentlemen bored?"

Half a dozen "No sir"s, then silence.

"All right. Now, as I was saying, the spaces for your arms and legs are like hours. You gotta pick which hour to strike, you see?"

Below him, Bennie moved hands and legs like a four-handed clock composed of heaps of muscle. Fiasole hovered, lightly pressing against Bennie's back, while he grabbed at Bennie's hands. Joey and the others watched as they dodged, swatted each other's hands. While his coach explained, Bennie shifted his hips like a soldier burrowing down.

Above him, Fiasole rode Bennie, just surfed on his backside, occasionally spiking his hands down in a faked crossface, which Bennie dodged, then reached up behind himself, which was considered a weak defense, except that he flipped Fiasole, pinned him.

When being shown a move by an instructor, a wrestler is not supposed to do that. Bennie was hotdogging.

Fiasole recovered well, smiling, said, "And that's the defense!"

Everybody laughed, except Bennie. "Mister Skaal, why don't you show the upper weights. I'll take the little guys."

Bennie turned away, spreading his arms wide. "Pair up, brothers, the time is now."

"Congratulations, Joseph." Anthony jogged beside him as they finished their last laps of the day.

8

Joey panted, "Thanks," started slowing to keep pace. He'd wanted to sprint the last two laps, but that could wait.

"You should be very happy."

"You know, if you work at it, you could improve, you know."

"Don't flatter me."

Why's he always talking like that, Joey thought. *Snotty.*

The truth was, Anthony hadn't been doing very well, even if he was smart. He didn't get the fact that Joey didn't want to be friends with him anymore, at least not best buds, like Dink, who was starting to pay attention, finally.

"I was just tryn' to be nice," Joey muttered.

"Were you, really?"

Joey didn't know what to do about Anthony. Some survival instinct told him to stay away. He ran another two laps of sprints, scooped up his gear.

Amid the hiss of showers, the hoots, hollers, frank discussions of bodily functions with his toweled teammates passing by, after checking for zits, finger-combing his tight brown ringlets, stroking the newly-buzz-cut sections up the back of his neck, admiring the wisp of a mustache that almost needed shaving, he smiled for the mirror, beamed, muttered to no one in particular, "You fag."

2

He wanted to wait until dinner to tell–the varsity part. But his mother's smiling face, the smells of sauce cooking, Mike's pouncing on him as soon as he got through the door made him so happy, he burst out the news after he dropped his gym bag, limped into the kitchen. In the living room, Sophia sang a "Hi, Joo-eee," from a pile of Smurf toys.

"I made varsity!"

"You made a what? Michael, get off the floor." His mother seemed wired. He should have saved it until his dad came home.

"I made varsity. On the team." *You know what else?*

"But you're only a sophomore."

"I'm best in my weight. I wrestle varsity next match."

"Oh." His mother wiped her hands on a towel, his enthusiasm bringing some cheer into her eyes. "That's very good. Congratulations." She hugged him.

Joey felt a tension, pulled away after a moment, wondering what new problem bugged her that day. Little Falls was only a few miles north of Newark, but it might as well have been Long Island, with all the "foreign customs," she joked. Marie Nicci kept getting lost when they drove around for errands. There were too many trees, offramps.

"Your father should be very happy," she said.

Happy, like when his father carried her through the front door the day they moved into the new house, cradling her in his arms for a second honeymoon.

Sure, he'd be happy. His dad was gung ho, even though he'd never really wrestled, didn't know the rules. As Joey would lay on the floor while the family watched the tube, rolling through some of what his first coach at St. Augustine's called sphinx stretches, where he'd arch up like a cat, he thought his father was annoyed by his wrestling. He'd tell him to "Getchyer butt down," or "Stop humping the rug," as if it bothered him to watch his son bend his legs over his shoulders. After that, Joey only stretched at practice.

"Here, boys. Eat."

On the table, their mother had arranged a bowl of carrot slices, celery sticks, dip. Mike took one glance, headed for the cookie jar.

Joey went to the cabinet to look for peanut butter. "I gotta get a jacket," he said. "Everybody gets one."

"What kind of jacket?"

He opened the jar, dipped two carrot sticks in, stuck them in his mouth. "Vahshee jhacketh. I goaaa lhearr."

"Chew. Swallow. Then talk."

"Sorry." He gulped, redipped the carrots.

Mike winced. "Ew, spit in the peanut buttah."

He faked a punch to Mike. "End of season, I'm gonna get a letter. But first they got the mascot patch. Can you sew it on?"

Mike's revulsion switched to fascination. "Lemme see!"

Joey held the Colts patch high as Mike jumped for it.

"We'll have to talk to your father about it."

"But I have to get one. Stop it, Mikey!"

"Fine. Do me a favor. When your father comes home, I want you both in your rooms, doing homework, silent."

"But–"

"No buts."

Mike whined. "I wanna varsey jacket."

Joey obeyed, retreating to his room. He opened a book, his

notebook, set a pencil down, but instead got his little cassette player, put on his earphones, listened to his Pearl Jam tape, air-guitared around his room.

He hoped he wouldn't have to get a job to pay for the jacket, although he would if he had to. He didn't know how he could, since practices were every day after school until March. On those days he was usually so tired he fell right to sleep after dinner. Weekends maybe, but that wouldn't be enough.

He liked to think his dad supported his wrestling. In Newark, matches had been after school. His dad worked until six. He did come to a few weekend invitationals, but he usually seemed so tired, Joey's small weight class being early in the day, Dino Nicci sometimes couldn't remember whether his son had won or not.

His parents made a gesture of appreciating his wrestling. They got him a subscription to *Sports Illustrated*. What they didn't know, which Joey could have told them, was that the magazine rarely covered wrestling of any kind, except for the Olympics. It was all football, baseball, other games he could never play, not only because of his size, but because they weren't at all like wrestling. Too many sticks, balls. So much distance.

Sometimes he'd see championships on Saturday afternoon sports shows, state finals, nationals in Iowa or Oklahoma, fans stacked in auditoriums as high as silos.

He already had subscriptions to *USA Wrestler* and *Amateur Wrestling News,* saved every issue like a bible, leafing through the pages to read about winning boys from around the country, collegiates, even Olympians.

He liked to look at the few times he'd made it in the magazine, just his name in tiny print among a list of winners. He hadn't gotten a picture in yet, but hoped someday to see himself on the pages with other boys, so many of them handsome, with thick necks, confident smiles.

He was ten years old when he first saw wrestling. He never rolled around at home. Kids did not roll around at St. Augustine's.

But watching the 1988 Summer Olympics, inspired by the touching profiles of athletes overcoming difficult times, like when Greg Louganis hit his head on the diving board, how Americans had to work hard to raise money while athletes from other countries had all their expenses paid, he watched coverage of a few other sports, but he lay before the living room television, rapt as two by two, nearly naked men in shiny tights tumbled around on a circular mat

11

while thousands cheered.

Seeing the men grab each other, their bodies tense, close, Joey rose up on his front hands, then began trying moves. It seemed ridiculously easy, no sticks or lines. Besides, they were touching, wearing almost nothing. He could see everything, their broad thick backs, powerful legs, arms. Best of all, some of them were really short, but they still won.

At age thirteen he'd surprised his mother by handing her a form after school. "It's for a physical," he'd mumbled. "For what? You're not sick." "For sports. If you wanna try out for a team, you gotta get a physical."

He hadn't seen his mother look so shocked since the time she'd caught him in the bathroom. She'd sighed, signed the form. "We'll have to tell your father," as if it were something naughty.

Joey liked that feeling.

By the time try-outs began a few months later, Joey had already begged his father to give him money to buy special shoes, sweat pants, a sweatshirt, a jock strap. He'd almost taken a wicked pride in asking his father, saying "jock strap" aloud. He grinned with his dad. His father had put down his newspaper, dug in his pocket, gave him five twenties. "Keep the rest," he'd said. Joey wanted to hug his dad, who just patted him on the butt. "Don't tell your mother."

It was a secret at first, between Joey and his father, who'd come with him, waited outside, how he got on the team after a few days of tryouts.

"There's never been an athlete in the family," his mother had said at dinners with Grandmama, Aunt Lilla, everybody, who were all proud, but a bit unfamiliar with even the basic rules. The conversation usually switched to other topics, taller people.

"Well, he's our first," his father had said with a combination of quizzical pride and astonishment.

That first season, full of stumbling defeats, confused, exhausting practices, Joey knew he wouldn't quit, in spite of –or because– one of his 'former' friends back in Newark calling wrestling "a fag sport."

Joey didn't have to defend himself. He'd just ignore anyone who didn't appreciate it. He was becoming a jock on his terms. Other guys on the team, some of them real characters, knew they were a different breed. Even if some of them were ugly or smelled funny, he got to end his winter school days warmed by the burning tingle of contact. Learning how to clobber guys, if necessary, helped, too.

12

The garage door rumbled beneath the floor. Joey rose from the spread-out pile of schoolbooks, darted to his parent's bedroom window to watch his father's Bronco pull up, Dino Nicci walk up the driveway. His mood looked promising. Joey felt the gasp the house made as the kitchen door opened.

He listened from above, heard only soft muttering from downstairs between his parents, some rustling sounds, then his father's shout, "Yo, animals! Food's on!"

Joey's father waited patiently for Sophia's tale of "a princess and she went up some stairs and found a cat and it had a magic button and it took them to a balloon . . ." to dwindle down to something like an ending. Joey could watch Sophia for hours, fascinated by her animation. He'd watched Mike grow into The Pest. Sophia seemed different, enchanted.

"Very nice, Soph," his father said. "Now eat your dinner."

In a pause filled by the sound of gulping, forks on plates, Joey glanced at his father, who wiped a bit of food from his mustache. The rest of Dino Nicci's face followed close behind with a thick stubble that made Joey worry if he would someday be so hairy, but that hadn't gotten going yet.

Joey could manage a scribble of a goatee, but his mother always made him shave it by Monday morning, or Mass, if they went, which wasn't too often since they'd moved. Even though Mike went to St. Dominic's Prep, it seemed church lay unpacked in a box in the basement with votive candles, that picture of the Pope. That was one reason he feared his father sometimes. He had to keep his questions about church on a low flame. His dad didn't believe in it, so he never explained things. Joey just kept his prayers to himself.

Since they moved to a not-so Catholic, not-so Italian neighborhood, it seemed he wanted to push it all aside, act more like the regular people with names like Johnson, Ferguson.

"So." Joey's father looked at him. "I hear you have some good news for us." Joey liked the sound of his father's voice with everybody at the dinner table. It made him feel secure, with everything warm, this constant circle for him to come home to. Maybe his voice would someday sound as strong as his father's, if he practiced.

"I wanna jacket, too," Mike blurted.

Joey rolled his eyes. He longed to kick his brother under the table, but that didn't work anymore. Mike always told.

13

"What's this about jackets?" Joey could tell when his father pretended to not know what was up, like whenever he did anything wrong. His dad liked to drag it out of him, force him to report everything. Only then would he pass judgment.

Sophia gulped milk.

"I made varsity. You know, that pin I got at the match this week. I wish you'da been there, Mom." Wrong. Don't bring that up. "I got on varsity. I'm the best in my weight and it's an honor and but I gotta buy it, the jacket, 'cause I get to keep it. . ."

His father wiped his mouth. "Awright, awright. Can I congratulate my son before he talks me to sleep? We'll see about the jacket. Can't be too expensive."

"Two hunnerd-forty-nine."

"What?"

"Plus tax."

"What?"

"They make it to fit. They charge extra for the letter sewing, but Mom said she'd do that, but I gotta get my name embroiled on the chest like everybody else–"

"Embroidered."

"How much allowance ya got?"

Joey shot a glance at The Pest. He didn't want Mike to know about his money. He would find it for sure, always snooping in his room, nosing into his stuff, like his drawings; superheros, where sometimes he forgot to draw the tights. Joey rarely caught Mike, or noticed the remnants of his snooping. He'd become clever. "About thirty dollahs."

"Let's say you pay for the embroidering, and we make this an early Christmas present."

"Thanks, Dad." Joey couldn't help himself. He got up from the table, hugged, kissed his dad, liking the feel of his father's mustache on his face, then his mom, the soft moist feel of her skin. He smiled, felt as if he'd gotten away with something. They wouldn't dare get to Christmas and not give him anything else besides the jacket.

"So, I take it you're havin' a good time on your new team'?" his father asked as Joey sat.

A good time? It was his whole life, what kept him safe, what he loved. It kept his great secret, hidden away, right out front.

"Sure."

"Are they nice boys?" his mother asked.

"Sure."

14

"That boy from St. Dominic's, Anthony Lambros. You friends with him?"

Friends was not the right word for Anthony.

"Why you askin' about him?"

"Because I met his mother at Mass, she's in my St. Anne's group–"

"Yeah, right. Okay. I'm sorry."

"His mother told me he's having problems."

Problems being a geek? "He's on the team," Joey shrugged. "You know, he's at practice. He's awright. I dunno. He does okay. He's not great, but he just started this year."

Why was she bugging him about Anthony? Would she invite the Lambros family over for dinner? Did she want him to make friends with Anthony just because she met his mother? Didn't she know it didn't work that way?

Lambros.

They looked very much alike; thin, sallow-skinned, black-haired, eyes like brown pearls. But without his glasses, Lambros squinted like a baby rat with a big nose. He and Joey were the only sophomore Catholic Italian wrestlers in Joey's new school. Anthony thought that meant they should be friends.

Joey thought otherwise.

Draped in white and black vestments, the usually sullen Anthony glowed on Sunday when he assisted in Mass. Joey often had to be elbowed by his mother to stand, sit or kneel, his attention sometimes rapt on Anthony's almost superior stance. Anthony obviously enjoyed the power trip. Joey wanted to admire him, but at the same time wanted to see him fumble, one day drop the incense.

Anthony had cornered Joey at lunch since the first school day after recognizing him from church. Since Joey didn't have any friends before wrestling started, he pretty much allowed Anthony to eat with him.

Anthony delighted in telling secrets about Mass that Joey didn't want to hear. "It doesn't really turn into the body of Christ." "I chewed the host lots of times." Joey couldn't remember ever believing in Santa Claus, but he did believe in the Holy Virgin and Jesus and all the saints. Just because they were in public school didn't mean they had to turn everybody in.

Anthony liked telling Joey how that stuff was all made up, which

15

Joey didn't mind so much, except Anthony didn't tell it in a way that was funny, but more like a conspiracy.

Joey told him off then, saying that where he was from, in Newark, they had a better church and he shouldn't be talking that way about Mass in the first place, especially being an altar boy, and didn't he have any respect?

He didn't hear a peep from Anthony for weeks.

Until wrestling practice, where Anthony just showed up, not knowing a thing, not even knowing how to stretch, fumbling with his contact lenses. He got pummeled just like the others who'd quit, but he refused to give up.

He also refused to give up on Joey.

Two days into wrestling practice, Joey had approached Jock Row, a phalanx of tables full of athletes in varsity jackets. As Joey passed, guys mutely nodded while Anthony chattered away at his side. Joey had seen an empty seat beside that blonde buzzcut, the name that sounded like Donald Course. But then some other guy took that place, so Joey moved on, sitting with Anthony, some other geeks.

Along the walls, hoods relaxed. Babes hovered nearby, in packs. Guys and girls kissed. It was a system unfamiliar to him, having only dealt with boys, and not very well.

It was a Monday when it happened. Joey would never forget the way Anthony blurted it out, testing Joey, who sort of knew in the back of his cluttered mind the other thing in common between them.

Joey chewed on a last bite of Salisbury steak before catching Anthony's attempt at a joke about the cafeteria dessert for the day, canned fruit. He said, "Better to be a fruit than a vegetable."

"Huh?"

"A fruit. You know? Like me?"

Joey stopped chewing. He would remember the feeling of the meat lying inside his mouth, until he swallowed, hoping to choke on it. Then he squinted the squint he gave someone who tried to act tough with him before a match. He leaned in close to Anthony, as if hearing confession, absolving him. "Thanks for sharing."

"Joseph?"

"Yeah?"

"It's Donald?"

Joey and his dad were watching a rerun of *Who's the Boss.*

16

Sophia told stories next to him on the sofa, which he half-listened to while watching Tony Danza fumble through a shampoo commercial set in a shower, wearing only a bathing suit. Joey didn't want to get up, since he'd sprouted a boner, but tugged his t-shirt over his sweat pants as he walked to the kitchen.

Joey's mother held the phone a moment, her eyes saying, who is Donald?

Donald. Donald. Dink!

"Oh! Thanks."

Joey took the phone, retreated into the kitchen as his mother left him alone.

He heard Dink's mother in the background, "Who are you talking to, Don?" Dink refused to answer to Donald or anything else, so Joey never did, even just to tease. He didn't mock Dink's having a nosy mother. He knew that situation too well.

"It's Joey Nicci, from the team." Dink said his name perfectly.

Joey heard silence, Dink's hand covering the phone. He imagined Dink huddled over a kitchen wall phone, like him, pictured Dink moving to a bedroom, on the bed, on his belly, wearing only his underwear, white socks.

"Hey, what's up?" Joey asked. It was a little strange for Dink to call, since he never had before. They were just school, lunch, team friends. Joey figured that was about everything, so they must be best friends in training.

Dink sounded as if he were eating something. "I got some NCAA videos. Some Olympic stuff. My dad got our matches too, but just the ones he came to. Gotta warn ya, his camera work's a little shaky. Ya wanna come over an' watch 'em?"

It was definitely the varsity thing. Dink wanted Joey to dive into the team now with complete devotion. He wasn't sure how that was done. In Newark it wasn't such a big deal because they were a lousy team. As to dates, Joey rarely got bugged about not asking girls out. Not getting girls in trouble seemed to keep his parents satisfied, as if he were behaving. Talking with Dink felt like misbehaving.

"Sure," Joey said.

"What night, skeef?"

"What?"

"Skeef. You never heard–"

"What's it mean?"

"Aw, can't tell ya. You're too young. So when you coming over, my man?"

17

Joey couldn't think. If he knew what, then when would have been easier. Was this a date, or were they friends?

"Well, prolly Friday? Can't stay up on a weeknight."

"Okay."

"Yeah." Joey knew he'd have to ask. He thought Dink might be impressed if he didn't ask while on the phone.

"Lemme give you the address."

Joey didn't mention that he already knew where Dink lived, had memorized it the first day he and Dink walked home. He'd been waiting for Dink to want to be friends. On the mat, even though Dink was a weight class above him, they always partnered. Each of them had moves to share.

They fit together.

3

"What happens to them in the winter?"

In one of the sunken basement windows on the side of their new house, a foot-high wedge of corrugated metal arcing around the pane, some rocks and a few weeds had made a comfortable home for two sullen, brownish toads.

They'd never seen toads before, except on the tube or in *National Geographic*. Those were in a box in the basement, left by the people who'd moved out. Joey knew which issue had photos of Jacques Cousteau's crew with all the men in bikinis. He took that one to his room, along with about five other moldy ones.

In the basin of the dusty window pit, one of the toads jumped.

"Hold still," Joey yanked Mike's hand back.

"I wanna keep 'em."

"They'll stay here."

"What about when it snows?"

Joey wasn't sure. Weather wasn't something he thought much about in Newark, except as something to protect himself from with clothes between bus trips. He'd sometimes rode around with his dad in the plumbing pick-up, but the whole family gave up trying to fit into that years before.

The week before the Niccis moved out of Newark, their neighbors had been robbed. "Our final warning," their father had said. Out here, by their new house, with the evening sun cutting

18

golden slats through their new trees, in their new yard, he could feel the end of a season, the last bits of warmth touching their backs, and an incredible sense of safety. Maybe toads hibernated, dug in the ground. Maybe they hopped all the way back to the woods.

Maybe they just died.

"We can't take 'em inside."

"Sure, we can," Mike said. "There's a terrarium in the old boxes the people left."

The people. Whoever had lived in the house had left mysterious things like prizes. Mike and Joey foraged quickly, claiming old Matchbox cars, half a train set. Mike got more of them, because he seemed to need more toys. Joey could afford to be benevolent. Joey got a wooden box with a latch. He bought a lock, started keeping things in it.

When Mike said words like "terrarium," Joey had to smile in wonder. Only a few years ago, he had held Mike in his arms, or taught Mike how to hold Sophie when his mom was tired or his parents wanted to be alone. As a big brother, he had responsibilities, toads and such.

He'd said goodbyes to almost everyone from school and church at the St. Augustine Festival at the end of August, which, of course, was a big deal for a school named St. Augustine's. Joey imagined it as his own going away party. His mother even brought a camera, embarrassing everybody when she asked Father Scanlon, who only had one eye, to take a picture. Father Scanlon made a big joke about aiming with his patch eye, shouting, "Where are ya? Where the hell are ya?" He kept taking pictures as everybody barreled over laughing.

Joey thought of the move as his own gift, just in time for his fifteenth birthday, even though they moved weeks before September eighteenth. Mike and Sophia were going to go to the new Catholic school, but Joey graduated, switched to public school.

The matter of Joey's wrestling divided them.

St. Dominic's had no wrestling. Little Falls Public High School did. In the decisive words of Dino Nicci, who had become less than devout, "The boy wants to wrestle."

In an obvious show of gratitude, Joey helped with everything; making lists of box contents, running to the store for more packing tape, scouring liquor stores and groceries for boxes. The day they'd gone to see the big empty house, the kids had raced upstairs, claiming their own rooms as if they'd only been away for the summer.

19

In Little Falls, people said "hello" on the tree-lined streets with little shops and restaurants without bars over the windows. Nobody slept on the sidewalks. Banners hung across the tiny main street: "D.A.R.E. to Keep Kids Off Drugs!" and "Colts Pride is Citywide!"

Their new fifty-year-old but well-renovated house sat comfortably in a green yard, a big fat A-shaped roof, front gables pushing out over bedroom windows, flower beds in the back garden, a front and back porch.

"What are you boys doing?" Marie Nicci's hair swirled up in a just-get-it-out-of-the-way-while-cooking look. She wore jeans, an extra large Garfield T-shirt. The boys looked up at their mother on the porch, but remained crouched by the basement window.

"We found something," Mike blurted.

Joey nudged Mike to secrecy about the toads. He didn't want their mother to see them. She might want them killed. She'd insisted on hiring an exterminator before they moved so much as a box into the new house. His mom's favorite line became, "No more cockroaches," as if she were in a commercial.

The questions had come up more frequently as she arranged the contents of their new house "into some kind of order." The boxes were put away, finally, and now Joey was her project. "Don't you have any friends? Aren't there any nice kids at your school? Are there any Catholic boys you know?" were his mother's top three pop quiz questions. Every day it seemed as if he should file a report: *Have acquired one hello from boy in math. Two giggling 'Oh, I dropped my pencil again's from Miss Piggy in front of me in English. Religious background unverified.*

"We're lookin' at the winders," Joey said, moving to hide the toads.

"Windows." She'd been inspecting corners, shelves, still forming opinions about the house's details.

"I don't think anybody would break in," Joey said, exchanging silent "Are we in trouble yet?" glances. Mike crossed his arms, pulled back, stout and brown-eyed. He would definitely be short, Joey figured, just like all the Nicci men.

"Well, I suppose somebody could break in. Whaddayou boys think?" Marie stood, wiped her hands, pushed strands of hair behind her ears.

Joey assured her. "Forget about it. This kinda neighborhood, that just doesn't happen."

"Much," muttered Mike.

"You boys oughtta use that glass box in the basement."

"Terrarium," Mike announced.

"Right." She said, touching both their shoulders. "They'll probably sneak inside for the winter anyway." She ascended to the porch. "But I'm warnin' ya, I don't wanna be steppin' on frogs when I'm doin' laundry."

Before being elbowed by his brother, Mike shouted, "They're toads."

4

Over the sound of the ten o'clock news, Dino and Marie Nicci loudly discussed yet another bill that had managed to follow them all the way from Newark.

They'd just returned from a Colts Boosters dinner. Assisting the boys and the mat maids and coaches were the parents, who'd sold tickets at work or at church, each competing with every other charity and group fundraiser in the little town that Marie Nicci had already twice called Stepford Land.

Joey had convinced his dad to buy a Colts Boosters windbreaker, which looked hideous on just about anyone. The jackets were designed by the Shiver brothers' mom, who ran a gift boutique. Mrs. Shiver also designed ballet costumes. She was creative.

What nobody told her was the harsh orange slashes and white and black background made anyone who wore the jackets resemble what Dink called the Pumpkin Squad.

For the boys, other rituals united them. Spitting became a big thing again, along with new words to learn, like "paramilitary," "pickle-sniffers," "stoked," "sproing," a variation on "schwing" which Raul Klein the 140-pounder imitated with annoying frequency.

But spitting – that was serious business. Every drop counted for weight-cutting. Watery baptismals were hurled in every direction the moment the boys tumbled outside for running laps, especially from the protein powder set, who hurled big mucousy hockaloogies, scraped audibly from the throat, flipped up from boys' tongues to tile shower walls, where they clung like splayed tadpoles. Points were given for arc, parabola, viscosity.

Joey noticed how skinny he'd become after those first few weeks of shedding, and how he'd begun to tighten into what Assistant Coach Fiasole called "muscularity."

He checked himself in his bedroom mirror, compared himself to his heroes. He couldn't decide whether to cut the cover page of the November issue of *USA Wrestler* from the magazine and pin it on his wall with all the other pictures and drawings he'd made, or just put it on the pile with the other magazines on his bookshelf.

On the cover, Dennis Hall, a 125.5-pounder who'd recently won the bronze medal at the Greco-Roman World Championships in Finland, stretched his arms out, his hands in tight fists of victory. One nipple peeked out from the strap of his American flag Team USA singlet. His eyes were tight, wincing, his mouth open in a frozen shout.

Joey checked out the striation of muscles on his bare arms and shoulders. Knowing that Mike wouldn't barge in on him, probably still toying with his toads in the basement, he practiced what he did worst, talking.

"How ya doin'? What's that in the window?" he said to himself, trying to keep his voice low, give it some resonance. But it always came out flat, tinny, thick with the city accent he'd grown up hearing and speaking in 'Nerk,' which some guys mimicked with pointed accuracy.

Fewer of the kids in Little Falls talked with thicker Jersey accents. Some tried valley talk, but it sounded as if they were practicing? for Scarsdale? One kid in art class, Peter Hubbell, had talked with Joey a lot, until Joey got on the wrestling team. Then Peter treated him differently, looking at him in a way that made Joey nervous.

"So, you're a jock now?" he'd said, as if Joey had mutated, as if one couldn't draw superheros and also behave like them.

When boys reacted that way, he shut them off, even if they seemed to have romantic potential. Even blunt sex talk, though, led to nothing. Nobody ever taught him the difference.

"You got a worm. I got a helmet." Wiggling his own in comparison for a millisecond that Joey had expanded to hours of memory, Tommy O'Leary was only one of the boys from St. Augustine's he missed. Now he had a whole new team, better ranked, with bigger guys.

Moving to Little Falls also brought a feast of places to be alone; the garage, the basement, the woods only a few minutes' walk through some neighbors' yards. He and Mike had climbed four trees

22

in one afternoon.

Best of all, in his new room, he could wear clothes or not, play his music, leave his drawings all over the floor, smell his earwax, see how his lats were doing, feel the strain in his thickening neck, fiddle with his belly button, where little hairs grew in a trail.

With his door securely locked, he dropped his sweats and pranced around his room in only his white socks, silent, the bapping of his cock against his belly and his breathing the only sounds.

He let go of himself, calmed down, struck a few poses, punched air, then got excited again from the nervousness, the energy of working out again, of bumping bodies, of incredible changes.

Maybe he was as cute as girls said, or what he'd heard was said, what he wished boys like Peter would say. Maybe his thick lashes weren't too girlish. Maybe his brown eyes, so dark he had to lean in close to the mirror to see the little part at the center that moved like a camera, would charm somebody into falling in love. Maybe they already had.

He thought he had a big nose, but a girl once said it was sexy, how she liked that in Italian men.

Men. Like he was a man. Fifteen and never been Frenched. There were a few dates with girls at two dances at St. Augustine's, but that didn't count. That didn't count at all. The girls flirted, the girls talked, he talked, and they danced. That was it. They giggled a lot and were scented like Sophia's toys.

Joey looked at the shelf of little trophies and ribbons. His dad had helped him install the shelf, starting a new project every weekend, doling them out to both boys.

His two years on the St. Augustine's Knights really didn't count, according to some guys on his new team. They said Newark was a different ranked division, and considered him the bottom of the totem pole now that he was a sophomore. Still, it gave him a sense of pride to see the little brass figures crouching on the wooden stands, even if he'd had to start all over again. That made him want to work even harder.

In public school, a lot of kids seemed to pride themselves on acting stupid in class. Dink called it the Beavis and Butthead Pose. Dink became his filter, his informant, his best bud.

In math, Joey spent way too much time looking ahead, waiting for him to turn around. When Dink didn't, he watched the back of his buzzcut turn a dozen colors, depending on the light; copper, straw, even gold. As his hair grew out, the hair on the nape of his neck began to curl like a question mark. In practice, Joey got to hug in close to it, find answers. He began to resent anything that could interfere with this privilege.

He checked a list posted on the inside door of his closet, next to his calendar with little scribbles for practice days. Nitrogen loss. Water gain. He set a goal of five pounds of muscle before Thanksgiving. Every day he would weigh himself. Every meal would become a science project, each droplet of sweat a blessing.

5

"Gentlemen. Today, single leg takedowns and escapes so you can increase your versatility with some new technical moves. Go easy on your opponent's knees. Cartilage does not come cheap."

It was very scientific, the way Coach Cleshun talked.

He was a nice guy, but he was so "paramilitary," as Troy called it. Troy didn't like exercise. Troy just liked wrestling. Troy was undefeated.

With Coach Cleshun, though, everything had to be in a certain order. When Joey had approached Cleshun in his Chemistry Lab, saying how he looked forward to wrestling with a new team, Cleshun cut him off with, "Tryouts are next month, Mister, uh, how do say your name again?"

Assistant Coach Fiasole, on the other hand, attended to the boys like a mother hen. He tried to get everybody to dress up on match days. He was a local boy, but he'd been away in Manhattan, had some funny jokes.

Assistant Coach Fiasole did all the boosters stuff, like distributing the little orange and black signs for all the athletes' yards that read, "HOME of a COLT!" Fiasole made sure the guys filled out all their health forms, took care of sprains, cuts.

About a foot taller than Coach Cleshun, but younger, Coach Fiasole had a way of touching, joking with more sincerity. Because of his college classes, he wasn't at practice every day, but the days when he was, things were much better, not just Coach Cleshun the taskmaster drilling them.

Fiasole lined the boys up like chorus girls, had them all hop on one foot, the other legs stuck out in front of them. Guys held each other's shoulders, blasting out giggles while Fiasole clapped his hands. "I want one leg up. Keep it out. Keep hopping."

Fiasole picked Walt out, put his arm over his shoulder. "By hopping while your opponent tries to catch you off center," he announced while the boys backed off, watching in a loose circle, ". . .when he's got your leg. . ." Fiasole hopped shoulder to shoulder as Walt held his thigh like a Christmas turkey - "You need that one moment where you hop," –bounced– "to take" –lifted his free leg– "his leg" –kicked Walt down, swiveled over his chest, pinning him– "and get him down."

A few guys slapped the mat, admiring what they couldn't wait to learn, paired off.

"You hold my leg," Dink said. Joey took it, feeling the weight of his new friend. Dink's sparse blond hairs tickled his forearms. They hopped. Dink gripped his shoulder, then blurted "Hup!" kicked his leg back. Joey could have blocked it, but the point of the drill was to let the guy get it at first. It was like learning a dance. Dink fell on him, easily. They landed, chests pressed to each other, their faces inches apart.

"Think you can handle it?" Dink said as he hovered.

"Piece a cake," Joey challenged.

"Fruit cake."

"I got something to show ya."

They'd wolfed down another cafeteria lunch. Dink took him to the library, where he looked up the old yearbooks, secretively peered through the wrestling team photos, including one with senior Stephen Cleshun looking exceptionally dorky.

"What a geek!" Dink snorted a laugh as they flipped further back to older yearbooks to find other pictures of faculty members as teens. "Thank God we don't have to wear those stupid leggings."

They looked at yearbooks back to the fifties, when the school was in an older building, spotted some guys who'd gone on to become college champs. Some of them resembled nice guys he would have liked to have met. Most of them were just faces in pictures behind a glass case in the school's main entrance. They joked about their pictures gathering dust in a bookshelf long after an alien takeover which led to some other tall tale that got out of control and made them laugh so loud they got kicked out of the library.

25

Eleven blocks to Dink's house, he counted as he walked.

Through the week he'd felt a giddy rumbling in his stomach, a secret with Dink, who only had to mumble, "Friday," at the end of each practice to make him smile, look forward to their "date."

Practices had zoomed by that week. Classes were suddenly entertaining. He even got Mister Halprin, the usually grumbling history teacher, to smile when he made a joke about Christopher Columbus making the best wrong turn of his life.

Joey had listened intently to his teachers, even the boring ones. Even though he preferred to draw superheros, he'd drawn a still life of apples and a jug in Mrs. Bridges' art class with a newfound devotion.

Leafy avenues welcomed him as he trotted toward Dink's house. All was quiet, except for the rustle of his hard leather sleeves brushing against the softer fabric of his new varsity jacket, with his sweatshirt's hood hanging out the back. He silenced the noise by stuffing his hands in his pockets, even though his gloves kept him warm enough.

Front porches that weeks before hosted pumpkins and scarecrows now displayed clusters of corn husks with cardboard turkeys pinned to their doors. He passed homes with lights on, couldn't resist looking in, seeing the living rooms with pictures on the wall, old ladies sitting in chairs. He breathed in the smell of dying leaves, of peace. He wondered how people could be so calm, like they were pretending they couldn't hear the hum of New York just over the hill.

He liked this new town, but it was so quiet, as if they were all hiding something. Did anyone see him, see the big letters on his back, COLTS in orange on black, their school colors, how he walked so fast, knowing he was going to his friend's house? Did anyone see how he felt, as if he were walking in golden armor?

He rang the doorbell, ran his hands over his short curls once more.

"Well, hello, Joe. Come on in."

Mrs. Khors' hair was long, blond, but not real blond, more three or four blondes. She had a different sort of look than Joey's mom. She whisked in ahead of him as if she might be hosting a show.

"Lemme take your coat. Do you want something to drink? We've got some chips, stuff in the kitchen. You'll have to excuse the mess."

Joey wasn't sure what she meant. The house was spotless; no piles of Legos or stray coloring books. All the furniture looked new, sharp. He couldn't help but envy how Dink's house felt less stuffy, as if they should be living somewhere more sophisticated. He didn't see why a man would want to divorce Dink's mom. He noticed the way she held herself, relaxed yet self-assured. She'd been one of the realtors to help his parents find their new home, seemed to be making a good living at it.

"C'mon." Dink led Joey to his room. The back of Dink's T-shirt, one he'd worn before, read, in thick red and black letters:

I EAT WRESTLING
I SLEEP WRESTLING
I BREATHE WRESTLING
I AM WRESTLING

When Dink reached up for the banister, his T-shirt rode up. Joey had seen Dink naked every school day in the showers, had tumbled with him for hours more. That was a given. But seeing the small of his back, just that peek, teased him.

A muscle chart ruled Dink's far bedroom wall. "Hey, you got one, too!" Dink dug in a drawer for videos. "Yeah, you got one? Makes it easier to figure out what muscle I broke."

"Ya can't break a muscle. It's either a sprain or a strain. . ."

"I know. I'm joking." Dink plopped down on his bed. Joey stood, looking at the other wall stuff; a poster of Nirvana hung over Dink's dresser, framed newspaper clippings of Dink wrestling, posters of wrestlers, including one with a drawing in black with white pencil of a white guy giving a black guy a tight Nelson: Below the picture it read: BO DON'T KNOW GRAPPLIN'.

Above a pile of clothes spilling from the closet onto the floor, a full length mirror hung on the inside door. Above that hung a poster of Marky Mark, shirtless, with several inches of underwear showing. Joey wanted a closer look, but didn't want to go nosing around in Dink's stuff, at least not with him there.

There weren't any chairs. He wanted to lie down next to Dink. He didn't. It was in front of his thoughts but he never mentioned it and didn't know where or how he could. He wanted to be in Dink's room all night. It smelled almost like him.

He looked at Dink's CD collection. "Man, that's a lot."

"Not so much. How many you got?"

"Zip."

"No."

"Got a Walkman, about a dozen tapes."

"We gotta get you into the '90s, my boy." Dink stood close to Joey as he thumbed through the stack.

"Soundgarden," Joey said. "I heard them on the radio."

"Yeah. Bring me some tapes. I'll make dubs for you."

"Really? Cool. Hey," Joey held the CD. "This guy looks like you, if you didn't have your buzz cut." He pointed to a cute blond guy standing in a purple shirt, jeans.

"Who, him?" Dink smiled. "He's the drummer."

"Hmm." He looked at one of the song titles. "'Jesus Christ Pose'?"

"Aw, man, you should see the video. They don't show it anymore, 'cause a bunch of religious assholes got it banned. The singer is on this cross, then he like flashes to all these different creatures being crucified, like even Terminator."

"What, Schwarzenegger?"

"No, the machine, the robot part."

"Severe."

Dink stood by him as he picked out a few others. "You like metal?"

"Well. . ."

"You'll like them."

"What's this? Tool?"

"You know." Dink grabbed his crotch suggestively. "Tool. They got one song called 'Prison Sex.'"

"That is sick."

Dink went back to his drawer, held the three videotapes he'd fished out of the pile. "So, c'mon. Showtime."

They went downstairs. While Dink fiddled with the VCR, his mother came in with her coat on.

"I'm going out, so keep it down," she said. "I don't want the neighbors calling the police on you boys. I'll be back by ten. That's when I should get you home."

"Awright, Mom," Dink said.

As the tape started, Joey watched her car lights pan across the wall through the living room window.

"Jeez, your mom let's you have people over and goes out?"

"Well, sure. She's got a life, too. Ya wanna beer?"

"You sure it's okay?"

"Sure it's okay."

He scanned Dink's living room. A big stereo, VCR, even modern paintings on the wall, not like the corny landscapes that were in his house.

"Nice place," he said as Dink handed him a bottle.

Dink hit his bottle against his, said, "To a season of pins."

Joey'd never been toasted before, except at Christmas or New Year's when he stayed up late with his parents. This was different, this was somebody special, a guy, a new friend.

The beer tasted like salty soda.

"It likes you," Dink said.

"Huh?"

Joey's beer spilled foam down the neck.

"Oh shit. I'm sorry."

"No prob." Dink went to the kitchen, grabbed a few paper towels. As he wiped up, he said, "Moved here after the divorce. Mom's cool. Makin' some bucks with her real estate gig. Plus Dad sends alimony and. . ." he pointed the bottle at himself, "child support." He sipped more beer.

They did a bit of battling burps, watched their own matches first, cringing at fumbles, slams, cheering smart moves, escapes, all caught on video by Dink's father, who lived in Passaic, but came to all of the matches. Joey wondered how it felt, not having a father all the time, but it didn't seem polite to ask. Instead he merely grooved on the buzzy beer feeling.

"Shoulda tried a whizzer," Dink advised as they watched an earlier match. They'd both lost, but Dink was still a better wrestler, so Joey listened, all the while admiring his own image. It was one of Dink's gifts, seeing how impressive the team looked, black singlets with thick orange and white stripes down the sides.

The side piping made them look somehow thicker, he wanted to say, but didn't think Dink would get it. He was still getting used to the Colts as his. As much as he enjoyed the strange thrill of being next to naked in public, he was glad the body of their singlets was black. Some teams had light-colored or even white singlets, which left nothing to his imagination. He could even tell who wore a jock strap or Lycra shorts, or even detect the shifting positions of a wrestler's gonads.

Watching himself on video for the first time up close, Joey couldn't help but compare his own body with his teammates. He fit on the ascending scale of weights, bigger than Anthony and the others below him; smaller, of course, than the upperclassmen. He liked the way Dink was smaller, yet thicker than him, the way their

29

butts were different. Seeing himself wrestling, he realized he wasn't a muscle-bound hulk, but he wasn't the bean pole he saw in the mirror. *I'm goodlooking, I have a very nice body.*

"So, you had Fiasole last year, too?"

"Max? Naw."

"Max? That's his name?"

"You didn't know?"

"I . . . I never asked."

"The guy is so cool." Dink told him Assistant Coach Fiasole was getting a Masters Degree in Kinesiology at Montclair State, so Coach Cleshun was working him too, coaching him on how to coach. Fiasole had almost gone to state championships as an undergraduate at Trenton State.

They watched some other matches, ate some chips (a total no-no), then turkey sandwiches (a not-so-bad no-no), then some Häagen-Dazs (a total, complete absolute Nein!). A Greek guy and a Japanese guy butted heads. The Greek guy was getting creamed.

"They got tiny dicks," Dink blurted.

"Who?"

"Japs."

"So?"

Dink kind of grunted.

"How do you know?"

"Look at 'em."

Joey did, then said, embarrassed to blurt it out, "They always get small when you wrestle. It's self-defense of the body."

"Who said that?"

"I dunno. I read it somewheres."

Dink grunted out some fake Japanese, "hoojiga boojiga!" piled on top. They rolled around on the floor for a bit, fake stuff.

While Dink straddled his back, Joey lay on his belly. They settled that way, feeling each other's warmth through their sweats. Dink's groin pressed against his butt. Joey pretended not to notice, hoping Dink wouldn't pry him over, since his penis began to stiffen between his hips and the carpet. He folded his arms under his chin, content. He could have stayed there longer, if Dink had only chilled, let the moment be, before whispering in his ear, "J'ever get a boner from wrestling?"

He tried to shrug Dink off, but Joey found his hands clamped down like Spidey under the Octoguy. Dink held him down. He put his arm around Joey's neck, arms, held fast.

"Get off me!"

"C'mon, Neech. You can tell me."

Joey might have told him if he'd just let go. Dink rubbed against his butt, insisting. Joey feared Dink was trying to trap him somehow, But then, how could Dink fake a boner if he wasn't a homo, too? Dink rolled off.

"Geez, Dink."

Joey sighed, put his head under his arms to hide his embarrassment. But under his armpit, he spied Dink's body, his belly exposed with his shirt up, his boner pressing his sweats into a soft tent. Everybody called him Dink because his penis was small - Dinky Dick - but the way it pushed up in his sweat pants, Joey figured that wasn't always true.

A long moment passed. The people on the the tube roared.

Dink said, "Sorry."

"S'okay."

They continued watching the video, touching every now and then, bumping shoulders or kicking their feet.

Joey couldn't help but feel relieved and comforted from just watching, not just discussing ace moves or dopey fumbles, but that he could see the match from the outside, not under the knot of sweat and limbs that often hurled by like hours crammed into six minutes. He could let his eyes linger on a guy's spread butt, the little descending bulge.

Both boys had settled down to watching the tapes without comments or jokes, their first truce.

"I got some other stuff, too."

"What stuff?"

"You know, different stuff. Movies. Pro stuff, Van Damme."

"Cool."

"And some other kinda wrestling."

"Like what?"

"Like no holds barred."

"Mmm. Pancreeze, whatever they call it." Joey looked around the room, trying to find his other shoe.

"You can take this one home, or I'll make a copy for you."

"We ain't got a VCR."

"You're kidding."

"No."

"You're not poor, are ya?"

"No, it broke on the move. And Dad keeps sayin' he's savin'

31

gettin' a new one till Christmas. Made a total fuss over buying my jacket." He lied, but it sounded good. He'd worn the jacket every day since then, even on weekends.

"You keep wrestlin' good, you get a scholarship. Free college."

"Yeah, well, maybe."

"Don't maybe. You go all over the country, fly in planes."

"Gee, real planes?" Joey gasped in mock wonder. Actually, he'd never been in a plane. The idea sounded terrific. He imagined hotel rooms in there somewhere, too. Maybe they'd be like the time his family went to Point Pleasant Beach in South Jersey for a whole weekend. He'd slept between Mike and his father for two nights since his mom got sunburned and had to lay all over the other bed with cream on and the sheets off.

About ten-thirty, Mrs. Khor's car pulled up. She greeted them, said there was "no rush" to take Joey home, even though she kept her coat on.

Joey tied the laces of his Avias when Dink said, "Hey, I got it. Tell your dad Coach wants us to study tapes."

"Yeah, so?"

"So, Christmas is comin'."

"Yeah, so what?"

"And my birthday."

"Double so what."

"You freak."

During the short ride home –Mrs. Khors insisted– the boys sat in the back. Even though his mom was being really polite, talking about the school, the team, Joey felt nervous, because Dink kept pressing his thigh against him, silently saying, isn't she a bore. Maybe that was all Dink meant by it.

"See ya Monday."

"Adios, amoeba."

Joey laughed as Dink closed the car door. He watched Mrs. Khors pull the car out of the driveway, disappear down the quiet tree-crowded street. Their street. He was still getting used to that concept. He looked up at his new house, with the wide porch, a night breeze rustling through tree branches under a sky he could see, not smell.

The house sat in silence, dark except for one light in the living room. He walked in, having drunk his first beer, having felt the nudging boner of his best bud. Altogether, it had been a good night.

32

After almost interrupting what appeared to be a successful attempt to create another Nicci, Joey bid his parents goodnight and retreated to the lower level of his big new house.

His mom had ordered cable, herself. Apparently the argument over that had inspired his father's apologies and passion, with the usual results.

He had homework, to be sure, but not in the books. They may have been strict at St. Augustine's, but because of it, he was miles ahead of the other kids, especially with reading. Besides, it was Friday night. He had culture studies. Nine years of Catholic school and no cable had warped him.

Joey foraged in the fridge in preparation for the surf session, about to gulp the last of the milk from its carton, when his father came downstairs in his bathrobe, flicked on the kitchen light.

"Use a glass."

"Sorry." He went to the cabinet.

"It's late."

"Not too late, right?"

"No, I guess not. You have a good time?"

"Yeah, we watched wrestling tapes. These college guys."

"That's a different style, isn't it?"

Joey gulped. His father taking an interest in sports? "Yeah, but still, it was nice to watch 'em. Learn stuff."

He almost asked his dad about the VCR, but then his father just said "G'night."

He drank in silence, burped, washed the glass, ate a bunch more stuff while channel-surfing for two hours, then went upstairs, brushed his teeth, stripped down to just his sweats, tissues nearby, recreated every touch of Dink that night, quietly humping his mattress, then went further, brought Assistant Coach –Max!– into it, flipped over on his back, legs over his shoulders, let fly.

He woke up in a fog. The chain of his crucifix had caught on his pillowcase, lightly choking his neck. He felt drained, weird. He'd actually imagined sex with Dink and his coach. He knew what he wanted. He ached from the pain of knowing it might never happen.

He extracted his Saint Sebastian prayer card from the little bedside table that made him miss his cramped bedroom back in Newark just a bit. It wasn't forgiveness for his sins he asked for, but relief from a strain in his back. He was taught to pray to his patron saint for healing. He figured he might as well keep in touch.

Saint Sebastian's body looked strange to him, not a modern body at all. He needed to work on his shoulders, abs. Joey had always been oddly fascinated by the light shining down on him while tied to the tree, the arrow in his neck, all of it arranged for eternity. The saints always looked as if they knew all along they would suffer, like they had appointments with God, who was detained, and would they mind waiting?

6

The best thing about invitationals; guys from a lot of different schools competed. The worst thing; weigh-ins started at dawn. On Saturdays.

Fair Lawn was less than half an hour away, but Coach Cleshun had made a six a.m. call for the bus, just to be sure.

Due to the new job and all its unspoken pressures, Dino Nicci worked Saturdays. "Leaky sinks never take weekends off," he'd said too many times, so Joey didn't even ask him to come. He knew the real reason. He'd heard his father say something about having to impress his new boss, "being in debt up to our asses," then grinning like it was beyond hopeless.

His mom had packed a lunch, given him money "just in case," even though Mr. Khors had called the night before to ask if it was all right if he "took the boys out to dinner" after the invitational. Of course he would pay for it. Parents always paid.

She also tried to get him to eat the eggs and toast she'd made appear out of nowhere, but he had to explain weigh-ins again while fishing through his gym bag to make sure he hadn't forgotten anything; jock strap, extra singlet, fingernail clippers, towel, lock, with the combination secretly written inside his worn-out wrestling shoes.

"I'm just barely over twenny-eight, Ma. I gotta be one-twenny-six. I'll eat after."

"Have some juice at least."

"Okay," he relented, knowing he'd have to sweat every ounce off before weigh-ins.

"I still don't understand why this weight thing is so important. Can't you–"

"You know how we don't have breakfast on Sunday until after

34

Mass? After we take communion?"

"Yeah." She looked confused.

"It's like that."

"Joseph!"

The doorbell rang. Joey gulped his juice down. "I'll get it," he raced past his mother to the foyer, embarrassed that Dink would see her in a nightgown.

"C'mon," Dink said, shivered on the porch, his hands in his pockets.

"Just a sec." He dashed back in the kitchen, grabbed his lunch, stuffed it in his gym bag.

"Do well," his mother said.

"Thanks," he muttered, then turned back, gave her a kiss.

Joey got in the back with Dink, buckled up. The man at the wheel reached over, shook hands. "Hi, Mr. Khors."

"Good morning, Joseph."

Dink's father wore glasses, had hair the color of Dink's, but not much of it. "You boys ready for today?"

"Better be," Joey said.

"I'll drop you off at the bus, then I'll see you in Fair Lawn."

Then he got it. This was what divorced dads did, had weekends with kids. He thought it was special, but then realized how awful it must be to get dropped off in both directions. He felt a sense of camaraderie that Dink was sharing this time.

Parked in the nearly vacant school lot, the driver chatted by the bus door with Assistant Coach Fiasole, waiting. Fiasole waved to Dink's dad as he drove off.

Dink hopped up the steps of the bus, called out, "Window seat," but Joey didn't mind.

"Neech!"

"The Dinkster!"

They high- and low-fived. Some guys were still trying to doze, despite the uncomfortable seats, the morning sun glaring through smudged windows. Most others chatted away expectantly, bursting out with jokes, laughter, grunts, hoots.

Bennie and Hunter took the two back rows, laid out flat, faking sleep. Buddha Martinez sat behind little Lamar, the team's only African-American kid. Guys sometimes called them Laurel and Hardy. Stevens curled up, half asleep. Buddha Martinez stuck his finger in Lamar's ear, who swatted him away. Dustin and Raul pulled their hoods up over their heads, pulling the drawstrings out to do the by-now overdone impersonation of Killer Ants. Troy hummed along to a song in his cassette player, fending off the Ants. The Shiver brothers sat together, talking their own secrets. They were nearly twins. Everybody made jokes about them being boyfriends. Brett Shiver had a stutter, so he didn't talk much. The Shiver brothers were experts at making odds. They'd tally up other school's points from wins, losses, tabulate what they considered would be the probable point spreads. It was a crazy system, but it sometimes worked.

Others chuckled, talked with Chrissie Wright and Kimberly Holbrook, the two mat maids who volunteered to assist on scorekeeping, timing, stats. Guys liked to flirt with them. Everybody had a pal or someone to talk to.

Except Anthony. Sitting alone in a seat up front, his head buried in a book, Joey gave him a glance, was about to say at least "Hey," but Dink called for him, waving him to a seat, where they would spend the morning staring out the window, goofing off, getting nervous about the day to come.

LITTLE FALLS COLTS
103 - Dustin Ely
112 - Anthony Lambros
119 - Lamar Stevens
126 - Joseph Nucci
130 - Donald Khors
135 - Troy Hilas
140 - Raul Klein
145 - Walter Cryzinski
152 - Jeff Shiver
160 - Brett Shiver
171 - Andrew Hunter
189 - Benjamin Skaal
275/HW - Mario Martinez

They'd misspelled his name again. He stuffed the program in his bag, tried to forget about it, get ready.

Invitationals were more relaxed than duals, since five or six teams competed. It dispersed the tension. Three mats were rolled out in the gymnasium with competitions going on like a quiet circus. Clusters of guys herded around the outskirts in teams, shouting suggested moves, sitting, stretching, jumping rope.

There were few outside people at tournaments. Half-filled with parents, family, wrestlers who weren't competing, the bleachers were also cluttered with gym bags, coats, coolers, crumpled bags of bagels, half-empty plastic soda bottles, assorted headgear. People walked up and down the aisles, across the three mats with a casual comfort while boys twisted and turned amid them. Boys leaned or lay on the extra rolled mat along the wall of receded bleachers.

At each table, a timer, statistician and scorekeeper, mostly boys either not competing, or mat maids, watched the matches, took notes.

Joey's headgear dangled from the shoulder strap of his pulled-down singlet. Over that he wore one of his usual baggy sweat shirts, his favorite from St. Augustine's.

Joey and most of the Colts lounged around one corner of the gym floor, gear half-spilled out of their gym bags. Raul and Troy did push-ups. Anthony passed them, considered sitting with the rest of the team, then darted his glance away, sat in a corner.

"Damn. That loser is bringin' us down," grumbled Hunter.

"Aw, give him a break," Raul said, huffing between push-ups. "Even if he's lousy, you gotta give him points for trying."

"There is no try. There is only do." Hunter blurted out the quote from Yoda. Coach Cleshun did it better, though.

"Mercy is for the weak," Bennie added as he stuck his earphones in, deposited Megadeth's latest into his small CD player, walking off to the bleachers. Only after he was well out of range did Joey see Raul swirl his finger toward his own temple, as if silently saying, "Certified Nut Job."

At another mat, Coach Cleshun barked out commands to Walt, who seemed to be doing pretty well against a kid from Haledon.

Over the loudspeaker, a voice announced, "All one-twenty-six, cadet. Please report."

Joey trotted to the table on the other side of the mats, away from the bleachers. A cluster of boys hovered about, waiting for the slip of paper that they were to take to one of the three mats. It was also where they got to see their opponents. Joey's, however, didn't make eye contact. He saw that as a good thing. From across the mat, amid the relaxed traffic of others, they watched each other get ready.

When his match came up, Assistant Coach Fiasole rubbed Joey's back while he bent over. He massaged Joey's muscles, digging his big hands into the boy's lats and traps.

"He's a rookie," Fiasole whispered into his headgear. "Be nice. Think of it as a warm-up. This'll be an easy one."

Then Fiasole said the secret word, one that he probably said to the other boys, because it sounded like the team's name. Since they were both Italian, Joey liked to think of it as their secret code, a word that meant "cultured."

"*Colto.*"

Joey sprang out onto the mat, hyped yet calm inside, tingling from Fiasole's touch, relieved to see the fear in the darting eyes of his smaller opponent from Hackensack, a curly-haired redhead who kept glancing back to his own coach, a burly black guy. Help me, the kid's eyes said.

Two strips of fabric, red and green, with Velcro attachments, lay in the center of the mat. Joey attached one around his ankle while his opponent knelt with his back to him, putting on the other.

Assistant Coach Fiasole didn't need to shout more than a few cues. It was like a rehearsal for a more important match. "Fireman's!" he yelled. Joey did it, tossing the kid over him like a bag of leaves.

"Hold it!" Fiasole barked. Joey did, until the ref blew his whistle. The Hackensack kid fumbled under him in the center, Joey's hands carefully placed below the kid's belly, the other at his elbow.

After a warning for passivity, generally flopping around like the untrained guy he was, Joey got him down with his first sprawl like a bird picking at a dying turtle. He plied him one way, tried to grab his arms. At least the kid knew how to hold a position, but moved too slow to manage an escape.

After the ref raised his arm, Joey shook the kid's hand, the other coach's. As he returned to his side, Fiasole patted his butt.

Joey had barely broken a sweat, wondered if it was too soon to break into his lunch.

"Good job," Dink said, having just wrestled. They dug into their bags. He offered Dink half his sandwich. Mr. Khors leaned down from a bleacher seat behind them. "Watch my backpack. I'll get some more food."

"What's in it?" Joey asked Dink.

"Duh! What were you, Neech, raised in a cave?" Dink picked up the square bag, more of a purse than a backpack to Joey, compared to their gym bags and all the junk they hauled around.

"The camera," Dink said.

"Oh. I never seen one up close."

Joey pushed aside a burning feeling Dink gave him, especially when it came to not having things. Dink seemed to have no picture

38

of people unlike himself; spoiled, rich, lucky.

"You want up close?" Dink opened the bag, fitted the little machine in his hands, pressed a button, aimed it at Joey. He jumped into a nasal announcer guy voice. "We're here with Mister Joseph "Newark Newboy" Nicci, a top contender in the one-twenny-six cadet level, who's literally taken over the landscape of Northern New Jersey. Mistah Nicci, what is your secret?"

"Well, Bob, I'd say it's the support of my teammates and the love of my fans. All. . . kazillion of them."

Dink sputtered into laughter. Joey saw Dink's dad walking along the bleachers toward them.

"Hey, your dad," he warned. But Dink turned, got a shot of his dad coming toward them, a paper plate in each hand.

"Hungry, boys? I know you've got to keep your weight, but since you've got some time before your next match. Donnie, don't waste the batteries." He'd bought them hot dogs and potato salad from the concession stand. They ate the potato salad.

"You gonna tape Dink's match?" Joey asked.

"And yours, if you like. Make a copy for you."

"Oh, thank you, Sir."

Dink glared over to Joey. "Sir?"

Joey didn't like Dink making fun of him, or maybe making fun of his dad. Maybe he should give them some quality time. "Well, I gotta go see when I'm up."

"Later."

"Have a good match, Joseph."

"Thanks."

Taped up along a wall were the result sheets for Qualifying, Prelims, Consolation rounds and Finals, each name on a line narrowed toward the single line for Champions.

"So, you gonna bust ass today?"

Pauly Somebody, from . . . "Irvington?"

"Kearny." Pauly pulled up his T-shirt to show his singlet, which bore his school name.

"What exit?"

"The first one. North."

"That's right." Joey remembered the match quite well. He'd been screwed into the ground in twenty seconds, a sprained finger his souvenir. He hadn't drawn for weeks afterward, and wasn't about to let that happen again.

They didn't give each other's names, didn't want to make it

seem as if they forgot, or cared if they forgot. It was cool.

But there was something new, along with what looked like several more pounds of muscle. On his shoulder he had a small tattoo of Wile E. Coyote. Joey wanted to touch it, compliment him. He did neither.

"Man, I'm psyched," Pauly said as Joey pulled his gaze from the guy's shoulder.

"Really?"

"Oh, man, not you?"

Joey grinned. "I'm not even awake yet and I already flattened a guy."

"What school?"

"Hackensack."

"They are so gay."

"Whatever." They looked at each other, not speaking, then he returned his gaze to the wall. The line-ups came out printed from a computer that one of the coaches had brought.

Joey could feel the guy still glancing at him. "Ya get nervous when it gets down to the wire?" Pauly asked.

"Naw," Joey said, pointing at the chart like an art critic. "It's kinda like lookin' at the Empire State Building, only sideways, so it's more relaxed than like, just one match, more . . . . linear."

"You're weird."

Then Joey figured it out. His eyes followed the rows of his name, Pauly, oh, that's it. Tucci. They would spar later that day. He was trying to psyche Joey out.

"Well, good luck," Joey said, lightly smacking Pauly exactly on that tattoo.

He retreated to Camp Little Falls. Hunter, the Shiver brothers, Lamar, Raul Klein, Tommy Infranca, a JV gunning for varsity, sat in a lazy circle. Joey parked himself down. They were talking about football. Joey didn't say anything until Dink approached, stretched out, laying his feet on Joey's shins like a human foot rest. Toying with Dink's shoelaces, he even began to untie them and relace them together, but Dink didn't protest.

"When you up?"

"Two more on mat three."

"Good. You got time to massage my back."

"What, is he your slave?" Hunter sneered.

"And my massss-ter!" Dink said in a prissy way that made everybody laugh.

40

Hunter looked shocked.

"Didn't you ever see *Kids in the Hall?*"

"No." Hunter said, still waiting for an explanation.

But apparently Raul and the Shivers and even Eddie Whitehirst and a few other JVs who just came to the match to watch had seen the show. The boys started imitating the "I'm crushing your haid" guy, pinching their fingers at each other, until Raul crawled over, actually grabbed Tommy's head, hooking his arm around the boy while another guy plucked off his shoes. All Joey could see was Tommy's crewcut getting noogied by Raul, then a few others. Tommy ripped himself out of it, chuckling, his face flushed.

Hunter said to Joey, "Hey, go talk to Chrissie. She wants you."

What for, he wanted to ask. He didn't want to move, wanted to lie there, retain his post as Dink's sofa.

Chrissie and Kimberly were busy with the score keeping. With their hair hidden under baseball caps, not all done up like in school, from behind they almost looked like boys.

A guy from one of the other schools stood from the table, conferred with the girls, stepped out onto the mat, tapping the ref's back with a taped-up towel, the time clock in his other hand noting when each period ended. When Joey had defeated the Hackensack kid, his timer had tossed the towel, which sometimes happened. He remembered dodging it when the kid's aim missed. Sometimes the towel would bop the ref in the head or back. People would laugh.

"Go 'head." Hunter shoved him.

"Naw. They're busy."

"Well, go tell Bennie he's up soon."

He obeyed. He didn't know why. He just wanted to hang with Dink. He liked Hunter well enough, even though he and Bennie kind of scared him.

Bennie had moved to the bleachers, munching on something, his NO FEAR T-shirt showing spots of sweat. He lay on the foot rest of a bleacher. Joey approached Bennie cautiously, watching him through the side guard rail as if observing some large creature in a cage.

Bennie tapped his finger lightly on his own chest to the beat of the music hissing from his earphones. Joey didn't say anything at first, but then Bennie looked up, as if sensing him. His arm rose. Hands slapped low fives, fingers hooked, parted. Bennie pulled one ear free. "Good match, Neech."

Joey brushed it aside, climbed around. Bennie sat up. Joey

41

joined him. A bagel was offered. They munched. "He was out of it. Too easy," Joey shrugged off his victory, but he still felt a surge of pride. One of the big guys rooted for him. He'd noticed.

Two rows below them sat two large older people, a man and woman Joey assumed to be Bennie's parents. They didn't look it. They were both overweight, really large, quiet. Occasionally the man leaned back to make a comment about a guy's moves. They both nodded a silent greeting. Bennie introduced them. They nodded hello.

Joey tapped Bennie's arm. Bennie plucked his other ear free. "Hunter says you're up soon."

Bennie replaced one earphone, continued to watch the match before them. "Aw, I got time. Besides, I always beat that fag."

The word hit like a little misguided splash of venom. He wanted to go talk to someone else. Paul E again? No. They were opponents. Not that there was any real animosity. Wrestling wasn't like that, mostly.

Who would he talk to, if he did? Introduce himself to the kid he beat? He figured he'd get along well enough with any of them, but he didn't know what to say. He'd sure acted stupid with Paul E. Coyote. Staying on the bleachers with Bennie felt safer, venom or not. They watched Dink wrestle a kid from Passaic.

"C'mon, Dink! Take 'im down!" he shouted. Bennie clapped a few times.

Joey tried to believe that he got caught up with Dink's matches because in duals, with just two teams, Joey always competed before Dink. He was already fired up.

But it was really about smaller things; how Dink's buzzcut felt like bristles, the way Dink grabbed his ears when they played. He could almost see Dink considering which move to try, which one he'd fumble.

Bennie and Joey shouted encouragement, filling in the gaps between Coach's yells and Dink's dad, who sat down in front, videotaping.

Dink had nearly been pinned a few times. That always got people going, especially a takedown. Most people were watching as Dink and his opponent went at it. The match to the left had finished, and the one to the right had just begun, so almost everybody watched center ring.

Breaking the 7-7 tie, Dink escaped an almost fumbled reversal, The kid at the scorekeeping table tossed the towel to end the period, but the ref, even though he stood only a foot away, didn't see Dink get the reversal until after he saw the towel, so Dink didn't get the two points.

Dink's father jumped up, stepped to the mat, still holding the video camera, yelling at the ref like a baseball coach.

The ref twice said, "Off the mat," but a few people began yelling, booing, including Bennie, who'd ripped his earphones off to stand, mutter a curse.

The other guy's coach and teammates stood around sheepishly, preparing to defend, as if to say, well, it happened. Too bad.

The match went to the other guy. A few people booed. That irked the ref, but with such an obvious blunder, even opposing teams' parents agreed, chattering away in the bleachers at the injustice.

"I'll go cheer him up." Joey left Bennie at the bleachers to sit with Dink on the rolled mat in the back of the gym. Dink peeled his singlet down to his waist, tossed his headgear into a corner. Joey retrieved it, put his hand sympathetically on the sheen of sweat on Dink's back. "Shoulda won that," Joey consoled. He retracted his hand, but did not wipe it off.

"I did."

"Yeah."

They sat together, Joey looking around, trying not to stare at the heaving, glistening torso of his buddy, Dink's milky skin spotted with light shoulder freckles. A mole poked out of his skin near his right latissimus.

"Could you get my bag?" Dink asked.

"Sure."

Joey retrieved it, feeling a special privilege as he crossed the mat between circles.

He watched Dink's dad talk calmly with the ref over by the official's table, then walk over, crouch before the two.

"He even admitted it," Mr. Khors said, apologetic. "It was a bad call. But they can't use video to determine that. They never do."

"He can't just change his mind, Dad. It doesn't work that way."

"I'm real sorry, Donnie. You know you won."

"Fuck it. It's just an invitational. I'll get my stats up before the season's out."

Dink's father put his arm around his son. Joey turned away, felt a strange ache not incurred on the mat, as if he wasn't part of that, a closeness his own father didn't share. Sure, his dad was nice enough, gave him money for equipment. But he wasn't there. He had to work.

Dink spoke a few words into his father's ear. Mr. Khors went off to get something for him. He'd called him Donnie. How would Dink feel if he called him that?

Lamar came up to try to cheer the two. "Hey, what's this?" He placed the hood of his sweatshirt up over his head, then pulled it down from the bottom so it fell away from his bald head.

"I dunno," Dink said.

"It's Neech gettin' a boner! Ha Ha!" Lamar ran off to the practice mats. Joey jumped up after him, but he didn't feel like completing it. Stevens could get away with jokes like that because anybody could pummel him, so nobody did. His sense of humor protected him.

Joey wanted to stay with Dink, not let the wicked joke keep them smirking. Stevens had cheered them up, for a minute. But then he felt weird, comparing how he should feel if it were a girl coming up, saying a pussy joke to a guy. When guys talked about girls, they were outside, something over there. The way they talked about women according to their body parts annoyed him.

He didn't want to think of Dink as either somebody to have sex with or a friend. He didn't know how they could be combined. How could he think about him like that, separate, when his whole life was immersed in what he loved? Dink was part of him, not someone he caught, the way guys talked about girls but never hung out with them unless they were going steady. He didn't have to ask someone else to ask if Dink liked him. He knew what Dink smelled like. He knew every inch of his body.

Several boys, knocked out of the running for the day, lay on rows of bleachers, resting, flat out, rows of bodies. All around the gymnasium, all the people, families supporting their kids, other kids from different teams, most in gray sweats with emblems, the names of their schools, all of them stirred in Joey a feeling of incredible belonging.

But would he belong if he was honest about himself?

He'd read news stories. They said all kinds of confusing things; gays had bigger brains, lesbians got cancer more often, then all that Christian stuff, the Pope not being much better, calling homosexuality an "intrinsic evil." He reminded himself to look up that word.

When summers came, he saw stories about the parades, with rainbow everything - like the DNA model in Coach Cleshun's classroom - balloon links floating skyward, hopeful.

One thing didn't confuse him; the number, one in ten. That meant there was somebody else like him in the gym, at that moment, another Joseph Nicci on every team, with another Dink, Bennie, everybody. He just couldn't see which one. Why couldn't it be like Ash Wednesday when all the Catholic kids had smudges on their foreheads, like a club?

A voice over the loudspeakers: "All one-twenty-six, cadet, please report."

"What's the plan, Mister Nicci?" Cleshun asked, rubbing Joey's arms.

"I'm gonna try a single into a takedown."

"Try?" Cleshun switched to Yoda voice. His hands patted Joey's back. "There is no try. There is do or not do."

"Right," Joey smirked.

Coach slapped his ass.

Joey's eyes got distracted by Pauly's little tattoo, or maybe his equally cartoon-like grin as he stood out on the mat, waiting.

Paul E. Coyote crouched, arms in the perfect stance. His yellow singlet with black stripes displayed his angles and bulges to perfection. He wore knee pads, which could have meant an injury, but Joey wouldn't take advantage of that. The moment after the whistle, Pauly dove between Joey's legs, grabbed his thigh. Joey went down.

Not a good sign. He struggled through a difficult escape, grabbed around to catch Pauly's arm as the two locked shoulders, fighting for top position. They ended up hip to hip, Pauly sitting almost on top of Joey, trying to get Joey over, but he resisted. They'd both become stronger since their bout the previous year. They kept surprising each other.

Joey tugged his way to his stomach, he the turtle this time, took a breather while Pauly attempted to pry him over. His shoulders? Erg. His head? No. His hips? No. He released Joey just long enough for him to scoot out from under him to standing.

Flubbing a half-assed fireman's throw, which should have landed Pauly on his shoulders, Joey scrambled to get his hips over, or his arm around Pauly's neck. He at least got Pauly down, got his turn on top. It felt good to be there, just consider his options, the hours of the clock, but Coach Cleshun yelled alongside Fiasole. He couldn't hear what they were saying, until Fiasole bumped his hips up against

45

Cleshun, showing him. He caught an image outside the circle: Assistant Coach Fiasole's T-shirt: ACTIONS SPEAK LOUDER THAN COACHES.

Behind him he heard Bennie yelling, "Getcher leg out!"

Joey crossed his legs, spreading them out wide for support, his hip becoming the third point of his tripod as he shoved into Pauly's ribs. Keeping his grip on Pauly's shoulders, he shoved again, slowly, methodically. Pauly resisted, grabbing Joey's neck. Joey wrapped his forearm around Pauly and yanked, desperately. He almost got him, but Pauly hip-heisted, forcing Joey's head down, closer to his shoulder, to that funny tattoo, the sharp smell of his armpit.

The whistle blew. End of period. The two boys rose. Joey retreated toward his coaches, sucking in breath. Fiasole gritted his teeth, showed a hand lock, what Joey had tried to do. Coach Cleshun said, "Keep yer butt down. Watch his hips."

Joey grabbed the back of his thigh, which began to throb from some shove or strain. When did that happen, he wondered. He didn't have time to think about that. Choose: which position? He signaled neutral, forgetting to check what Cleshun was signaling, glanced back once, didn't see any look of disapproval.

They faced off again, but this time Joey went for the double leg. Pauly jumped back. Joey only got one ankle, but he got a takedown, refusing to let go. *He's hairy down there, just like me,* Joey thought with a sliver of pleasure, noticing a few blue-green thigh bruises Pauly must have gotten from previous matches or practices.

Before lunging further up Pauly's body to go for a cross-face, they were out of the mat. The ref stopped them to come back to center.

Pauly dropped down to bottom position. Joey placed his hands on Pauly's back, ready. He expected the quick escape, but he got hold of Pauly's torso. They gripped, tugged, figuring each other out, panting, his heart jabbing against his ribs, his thigh jolting with shards of pain.

There weren't any more ace moves, no outstanding throws. They were equally matched and exhausted. Neither could overpower the other. Their indecision, their stalemate, seemed to bore the onlookers, who were screaming about some other match beside them, maybe one of the Shivers. Joey concentrated on thinking of an escape, just getting through the period, then just breathing.

Pauly's body pressed down the length of Joey's, twisting sideways around Joey's waist, gripping, torquing, his other hand forcing Joey's head down to the mat sideways. Joey's nose flattened against the mat. Pauly's hips ground against his back. Drips of Pauly's sweat fell onto Joey's neck as Pauly pried him –using his own arm, slowly, almost tearing a few shoulder muscles– open like a clam.

Like the other boys, he tried to be nonchalant about being up on the winner's stand, the little steps with 1st, 2nd and 3rd painted below their levels. He'd put his ice bag away, but his shoulder still felt cold.

Joey watched a moment as Pauly, at Second, raised his hand. Dink's father stood right in front, videotaping it. Joey realized he felt glad he could at least see a tape of Pauly anytime he wanted, if he could just convince his dad to add a working VCR to the pile of necessities.

While he shook hands with some kid from Wayne, then Pauly, he heard scattered applause. "Good match, man," Joey said.

"You too." Pauly jumped down, but then some guy waved him back, they all posed again.

Stepping down, Pauly gave Joey a pat on the back. "See ya next time, huh?"

"Sure." As he walked off, Joey muttered to himself, "When?"

Kids and parents milled about, eager to go home. They knew who'd won. It was no surprise. People cheered for the team scores. Little Falls came in fourth. This was just a formality. Besides, getting wins like these were similar to the results board; lateral. It was moving on, not up.

Even so, he received his small ribbon for Third Place, wrapped it in his empty sandwich bag, just to make sure it wouldn't get wet or smelly from his wrestling clothes. He would put it with the other awards, on the shelf in his room, where his mother sometimes dusted, keeping his little shrine to himself clean. He took a breath in as the final awards, hubbub of team points, best player, other trophies went to other boys.

He took it in, the humming, laughing families trundling down bleachers, the hugs, the last of the Gatorade. Caught in a bar of light that angled through the upper windows of the gymnasium, even floating dust shimmered like particles of gold.

7

"My stomach is eating itself."

Joey received merely a scowl from Dink, who'd warned him about attempting humor without trained supervision.

Driven to a nice restaurant in Fair Lawn, Mr. Khors kept trying to cheer up his pouting son. It wasn't working. Dink's father kept talking while Dink didn't, so Mr. Khors quizzed Joey about school, about wrestling, what his plans were.

"College, maybe," Joey shrugged.

"Maybe? Smart kid like you? You could get a scholarship."

"Yeah. Coach says a few schools are good for that. Trenton's top in the division."

"So, you hope to get a scholarship?"

"Yeah, maybe in art if not for wrestling, but if not, then Rutgers or Montclair. Course my mom wants me to go to Montclair so I'll be close to home."

Plane trips. Hotel rooms. Outta here.

"Rutgers is a fine school. Lovely campus."

"You went there?"

"Um, Columbia, actually, but I visited. Some protest, I think. Back in my radical days."

"Dad, he doesn't wanna hear about that," Dink muttered.

"He speaks."

Joey felt awkward, caught with Dink on one side, his father on the other. Mr. Khors let it go, but the silence seemed too much for him. He kept talking.

"Got any girlfriends? Come to the matches to see you guys compete?"

Around the restaurant, passing waitresses whooshed by. Old people huddled in booths. Joey searched for an excuse, another lie.

He considered Chrissie and Kimberly, the faithful mat maids. They were about the only girls who ever came to a match, if any. Chrissie seemed sweet enough. Joey couldn't understand why she was so cheerful all the time. Kimberly seemed more genuinely into the sport, tolerated such cheerfulness with a sense of humor. Maybe he could date her. She didn't seem like she'd expect much.

"In my day all the girls went for jocks, didn't even look at geeks like me, of course . . ."

"Dad. We aren't dating, okay?"

Joey nearly spilled his soda at that. But then Dink said, "Besides, most girls don't like guys who wrestle. They don't get it." Dink couldn't have really meant it the way it sounded.

"What about this Melissa girl? Your mother told me she's very nice."

"Yeah, well, don't believe everything she tells you."

"Okay then." Mr. Khors put his napkin on his plate. Joey figured it meant dinner was over. He'd seen that in movies. He glanced at Mr. Khors, wondering if he and Dink would still be friends when they were Mr. Khors's age.

"I'm tired," Dink said.

"Why don't you boys sit in the back, get some rest."

"And you sit up front like a chauffeur?"

"That's what I'm here for."

Mr. Khors went to pay the bill. Crumbs, spilled things, forks, napkins cluttered the table. Dink slouched in his chair. "I was beginning to wonder."

Joey sunk the last bit of apple pie into a pool of melted ice cream. His belly felt like a bowling ball. His neck twinged with a sliver of pain. Every muscle had begun to stiffen. He had to pee again.

"Hey, whyncha stay over?" Dink sat up.

"What, your house?"

"Naw, my dad's."

"In Passaic?" Dink nodded. "I shoulda asked before."

"Call 'em. My dad's got a car phone."

"No, my parents . . . He didn't meet them yet."

"So?"

"It's–" A tightness blocked his throat. His head flooded with possibilities. Stay over. Would he and Dink sleep in the same bed? Joey knew he wouldn't have a problem with the sex, if it happened. He knew it would be fun. But the afterward worried him. Would Dink treat him the same way he treated Anthony when he found out? Toss him away, ashamed, or bored after they'd done it?

"It's an Italian thing."

"What is?" Dink asked.

"Your dad's gotta meet my parents." Why resist? Why be so scared? If he'd known that morning that Dink would ask him this wonderful thing, that this would be the night, maybe he would have

49

asked Mr. Khors inside to meet his dad, gotten approval, received some shred of the respect that straight kids who dated got to have, some measure of allowance.

But then Dink would have seen his mother in her bathrobe, his dad probably half-awake, looking like a slob. Maybe he was embarrassed by his parents. Dink's dad turned his kid into a movie star with his video camera, but his own dad couldn't even go to all his matches. That would change, his dad promised. "Besides," he lied. "I gotta go to Mass in the morning."

"You still go to Mass?" Dink asked, amazed.

"Well, yeah," he lied again. He'd actually skipped a few weeks.

Dink looked like he wanted to say "Why?" but instead just sighed, "Oh well, that's okay."

"Sorry."

Mr. Khors returned, pocketing his wallet, a toothpick in his mouth. "You boys ready to rock?"

Once they got on I-80, the drowse of the big meal settled in. Mr. Khors turned the radio down low, soft music, violins.

Dink spoke softly, inches from Joey's ear. "Hey, what was it like in Newark? Were the brothers awful?"

"No, they were okay."

"Yeah. They were pretty good here," Dink said as he flipped the lock button with his foot. His other thigh pressed against Joey's. "Until we left."

"Huh?"

Dink mouthed the word so his father couldn't hear up front. Divorce.

"Oh."

He wasn't sure if Dink meant they quit going to church afterward, or if they quit being Catholic because his parents got divorced. He didn't want to ask. He could feel Mr. Khors listening through the violin music.

"So, what's your confirmation name?" Joey whispered.

"Nicholas."

"Oh, that's nice. Mine's Sebastian."

"I know. That card is so cool, the way he's tied to a tree with the arrows in him."

"Actually he didn't die from them. That was later."

"Still, it's cool. Gothic."

He'd never thought of St. Sebastian as cool. Maybe he was, if Dink said so.

The dinner in his belly, the soft music, the soreness of getting through seven hours of on-again, off-again exertion in a gym full of jocks, the dream of sleeping with Dink hovering sometime soon finally hit. The boys fell silent.

The rhythm of the highway bumped under the wheels. Dink began to nod off. Joey felt his head fall, jerk up slowly a few times before he scooted over closer, let Dink's head rest on his shoulder. Dink nudged him, moving in tighter, until they were touching all along their bodies. An erection crept up, subsided. Otherwise, Joey didn't move.

Mr. Khors glanced back once through the mirror with something Joey read as approval. He prayed for it.

He closed his eyes, feeling Dink's breath on his neck, Dink's nose occasionally grazing his earlobe, Dink's arm reaching closer on his thigh, Joey not at all minding. He thought about how his parents spent every night together, no matter what; his dad's snoring, his mom's health problems, being pregnant. They always slept together, always.

8

When Joey strained his hamstring some guys called him a wuss, wimp, the usual stuff.

Injuries didn't fit into "paramilitary" training. Fortunately, Assistant Coach Fiasole wasn't paramilitary, and recommended Joey take a day off.

He didn't mind staying at home, except for his mom, who started up about him "hurting his young body like that," as if she had proof that wrestling wasn't good for him.

After doting on him for a bit, she instructed him to stir the sauce at least once, "if you can manage to get up to the kitchen," then took off to pick Sophia up from kindergarten. "Adios, amoebas," he called out, tickled to be alone in the new house for the first time.

After his mother left, he scarfed some leftover coffee. His pile of homework lay untouched on the dining room table since breakfast. Joey scanned the book. Math. Squiggles. Bars. Forget that. What would he use hypotenuse stuff for, except maybe in college? What would he do in college? What would he do after high school?

He flipped through the channels.

$100,000 Pyramid. "These are things associated with skiing."

Nine Broadcast Plaza. "What we are saying is that's killing unborn babies and–"

Home Shopping Channel. "I'm so glad you dialed in today. A big honk for you–"

"–not fully clean unless you're Zest-fully clean!"

Sally Oprahue. Men. Stripping. Big muscled men with long hair stripping. He dug his hand into his sweat pants, grew hard in a few seconds, trying to finish off the moment a stripper ground his butt into the camera, did a half split on the stage floor. Joey spilled onto his hand as the show cut to a floor wax commercial.

At school, once, Joey felt like a naked guy on a Greek vase.

Mrs. Bridges the art teacher was a lot nicer than the prim old nun at St. Augustine's who coveted paper as if it were money. Mrs. Bridges wanted color, still lifes, figure studies, cartoons. "Experiment!" she announced.

Sometimes kids got up on the big tables. Everyone would make a few jokes, but then get down to working, making the classmate's form come to life on pencil and paper. So when Mrs. Bridges asked him to wear his singlet and shoes, he got teased for it, but it felt great with all the different versions of himself pinned up on a bulletin board for weeks.

He lay on his carpeted bedroom floor, working on a few wrestling poses, positions he'd borrowed from the instruction books Coach Cleshun gave out. Mrs. Bridges said it was okay to "borrow" an image every now and then. He made the outlines, then decided to not draw the singlets.

His pencil drew erections between the wrestlers' legs. His eraser censored them. He used his own spit to smudge the lines, making the bodies seem to press out of the paper, sometimes even buckling out from the dampness.

His drawing shoved safely away, images came tumbling into his head, interrupted by fascinated glances at his own cock. He felt so joyously lucky to have one right there on his own body.

The remembered smells from practice came to him, then Coach Fiasole's voice, softly, like the times he'd come in close, showing a move. Fiasole wasn't married. Coach Cleshun had a wife, but no kids. That could mean something. He'd heard about married guys being gay or getting caught, then divorcing.

He had to hold back just a few more moments, grabbed one arm around himself, licking, biting his tight biceps as if it were Dink's or Bennie's, then Dink's again, then Paul E. Coyote's legs, for a moment Dink's father, a crazy image of himself as a little sperm, then Coach again, the guy in *Return to the Blue Lagoon,* then the kid who played Sara Gilbert's boyfriend on *Roseanne,* but then back to Dink, it always came back to Dink, rolling with him, gripping, tangled in him.

He started up to what sounded like the garage door opening, but relaxed a moment, then got up to wash off. False alarm.

Joey hid his drawings in a spiral-bound pad high up in the farthest reaches of his clothes closet. He knew better than to hide things under his bed, the first place Mike the Pest would look, the first place his mother hit during one of her Search and Destroy cleaning missions. The comfortable smell of his own body would be wiped away. His dirty clothes would disappear, then reappear, folded on his bed for him to put away. He wondered if his mother noticed the stains. She must have, because she never said anything.

"Uh, this is Joseph Nicci from the Gotyou Collection Agency, calling for a Mister Donald Khors. Sir, it's about your overdue credit charges. Please call me back."

He knew both Dink and his mom would laugh. Mrs. Khors once complained that regardless of the credit card's name, she could never discover what she spent it on. Dink would laugh, so Joey would laugh, but he wondered if maybe Dink's family was rich, but in a different way.

By the time his mother and Sophia got home, Ricki Lake's guests were discussing the ramifications of being a straight edge teen mom in a punk rock world.

Sophia had ripped a coloring book to pages on the floor, with all the blank sides up, swirling with three crayons at once in each of her fists.

"That's it. Very nice. You're gettin' it," Joey said as he knelt on his knees, watching her crayons rotate.

"We did a song and I got a bird in da book an we played on the swings and I fell. Ya wanna see my boo-boo? It's disgusting."

"Sure." Her adventures never ceased to amaze him.

The phone rang. His mother got it.

Sophia showed her knee, where barely a trace of a scrape had reddened her soft skin. Joey tried not to laugh at Sophia's concern. His own knees had been scraped, his legs bruised, arms chafed in so many places since starting up wrestling again, they blended together to cover his whole body. He didn't mind the pain so much. It told him he was there, a person, in his body, unlike the other times where he could feel invisible, nobody, alone. The pain was a dent, a reminder.

Joey played with Sophia awhile, then distracted her while he switched channels to the Smurfs. She abandoned him quickly. Joey took up her crayons, turning her little bubble creatures into Itchy and Scratchy.

During a break between commercials, one of those awkward gaps where some dozing guy in the production room forgot to put in a tape, he heard his mother in the kitchen talking on the phone to some other mother, by the sound of it. But her words were hushed, and he heard just one sentence: "If he became one of those, I'd kill myself."

Joey cringed on the floor, stilled. It must have meant what he thought it meant. No way could he tell her. No way.

Sophia blithely watched the tube, waiting for it to continue its barrage of cartoon images.

Waiting until he heard his mother finish on the phone, he limped to the kitchen, sat at the table, helped her unpack the groceries, prepare dinner. She placed a big chicken on the counter, began running it under water in the sink. It dropped down with a heavy plop. She was always working, cooking, running the kids from one place to another. Maybe that was why she never had time to look nice like Mrs. Khors, who was always "showing a home" or "going out."

"You stir my sauce?" She inspected a box of something, unsure where to put it, or why she bought it.

"Yeah."

She put the box down. "Chicken and shells. And salad. I hope that meets with your approval."

"Sounds fine."

"You want something now?"

"No, Ma." It would be a good time to ask her, tell her, before she got to the point of really meaning what he thought she'd said. As she cooked, he helped put stuff away. That would work. "Who ya talkin' to?"

"No one. You bein' nosy?"

"No, I just—"

"Mrs. Gambardello. You know her from church. She's got that

54

nice daughter, Cara. She's in your grade, isn't she?"

"Yeah." She's also good at dropping her pencil a lot to get my attention.

Mike marched to the kitchen doorway, halted to attention like a king's guard. "I demand seven cookies, Madam, to pay your taxes."

"You can have two."

Mike dropped the military stance, moved the stool, leaning over the kitchen counter to tug the ceramic teddy bear closer. "We got ants."

"Here." She gave Mike a bottle of Windex. He took cookies out with one hand, shot ants with the other.

Joey's mother continued talking about Mrs. Gambardello and her daughter "and the car they just bought had something wrong with the transmission." Her only new friends were other Italian women, like their neighbor Mrs. DeStefano, who sometimes babysat Sophia and Mike. The few women in town she'd come to know were all Italian, as if they all spoke a secret language nobody else knew and she wouldn't dare befriend anyone else. "You hungry? Are you allowed to eat tonight?"

He smiled. "Yeah."

"So here, eat." Carrot sticks again. He nibbled one just to please her.

"How did you meet Dad?"

"Why you wanna know?" She cut tomatoes on the counter. It must have been for the salad, because the sauce bubbled slowly in the immense pot that rarely left the stove.

The smells made his stomach growl. He got up, grabbed a piece of bread, dipped it in sauce. "I dunno. Jus' curious." The sauce almost burned his tongue, but it tasted good; salty, sweet, everything he loved about food. He got another piece of bread.

"Well, it's not a very romantic story," she said. "Your father was with a bunch of his buddies at a school dance and he just walked right up to me and said, 'I'm Dino. You want a soda?' and we started dating."

"Dating," Mike mimicked, pointing the spray gun at his brother. "Don't even."

"Michael, put that down. Go inside."

Mike dropped his weapon, marching out in retreat.

"When was that?"

"What?" His mother kept chopping.

"So, when did you meet Dad?"

"In the fall, in seventy-seven, our senior year in high school."

The year before his birth. He imagined the young version of his father picking his mother out in front of his friends like a dare. "So, you got married pretty soon, huh?"

She scooted him away from the stove, giving him a suspicious glance. "You wanna know if you were conceived before we were married."

"I'm not. . ." He tried to block the image of his father and mother having sex out of his mind, even though it seemed nice. They must still love each other, since they didn't fight. They argued about things, but they always settled it by laughing or going off together to their bedroom. She lowered her voice to a whisper. "You have to promise never to tell him, but yes."

"So I guess I'm a bast–"

"No." She held the knife up, put it down, folded her arms. "I don't wanna hear that talk in my house. I love him and we love you. I love all my children."

"Awright. Awright." He watched her resume chopping, then dump the tomato bits into a bowl. "Were you in love with him?"

For a moment he could see the same woman in the picture albums, the young girl with the sweet face empty of worries.

"Of course I was in love with him."

That's great. You know what? I'm in love too!

She stood still, a bit dreamy-eyed, not seeing where he hoped to lead her. She said, "He told me it didn't matter. He would have married me anyway."

"That's nice."

"What are you asking me all this for? What, you got a sweetheart you not tellin' us about?"

Sure. He weighs 130, most days. We're a perfect match.

Ever since a seventh grade coatroom epiphany with Giovanni Rodriguez, who was a bit of an exhibitionist, Joey had a rather complicated idea about desire, if not anatomy. Some of what he heard or read seemed so misinformed he didn't like to think about it. The news articles were good for facts, or what people argued as facts, but he had so few real pictures, including an image of a guy in a leather jacket, with a handlebar mustache, a pink tutu. He'd seen it in a card shop in Newark. All they showed on the tube were guys in dresses or people screaming in the streets or dying of AIDS, or else it was cartoons, screaming fags. Hated it.

Of course he did have his Melissa Etheridge tape, and the k.d. lang tape. They were nice, and there was Martina, and Madonna, who was called a lot of things, but she was definitely on his side.

That guy on *Melrose Place* was a bit of a dope, he heard, but the one time Joey got to watch the show, he wasn't on it much. "Too much sex and violence," his mother said. "You should be studying." He'd heard about Pedro Zamora on *The Real World*. Joey had swiped a picture of him, another of Dean Cain from a magazine before his mom threw it out. It lay in his little box with some other pictures, souvenirs.

Wrestling magazines, comics and his drawings were all he had to look at when looking at himself wasn't enough. Joey ripped out pages from a pile of magazines in the bathroom at Dink's, a page with a picture of Marky Mark in his underpants on a stage. In the article he said something about performing at gay clubs, sayin' "It was cool." Joey thought his music was cool too, remembering the Saturday he spent with Dink, learning the moves from the "Good Vibration" video. He could even do the move of bridging backward, flipping his legs up to land standing, but after they knocked over a lamp Mrs. Khors told them they had to do that in the yard.

Joey was fourteen when he saw two men really kiss.

A news story on AIDS or gay rights or something. Fortunately Joey sat in the living room in Newark, with Aunt Lilla asleep at her babysitting post, so he could watch closely. He saw crowds of them, like at a party. It confused him. Why did they go in clusters like that? Why did they all live across the Hudson and over the bridge?

He'd seen a news story showing athletes preparing for a sports event like an Olympics, but not. Women ran a marathon, guys played basketball, swam, played soccer. Drag queens flashed pompoms.

The voiceover blabbed away, but Joey heard himself gasp. Two men finished wrestling. A ref held up the winner's hand. The two men hugged, which wasn't unusual.

But then they kissed—smack—right on the lips. The two men waved at the audience like they were Mickey Mouse and Pluto at Disneyland. He had to hold back a laugh, a warm feeling in his chest, not embarrassed, but hopeful. Someday, he was going to get a ticket, go there.

He chewed on carrots, a fingernail, watching his mother prepare dinner, waiting for a light to come in from the kitchen window, give him a vision of how to tell her why she shouldn't be expecting grandchildren any time too soon. Although nervous about it, he felt as if he'd accomplished something with Dink. Something was going to happen. He wanted to share the feeling, but ended up talking about anything else.

They talked about his finicky diet changes since he'd begun wrestling again. She was bewildered when he pushed away cookies. "I never thought I'd have a son who asks for more spinach," she joked.

Mike's pouncing Glob Monsters entered. He waved them off. "I need carbohydrates, too, like in pasta, but I can't have fat stuff, and sugar just. . . um, it depletes me."

"Depletes you," she echoed.

"Yeah."

"Systems depleted," Mike said in a robot voice.

"Okay. No sugar." She made a mental note.

She seemed content, talked while she cooked, filling him in on her latest version of terror and scandal, how bad things were in the city. "Aren't we lucky we moved out here to Little Falls, before anything bad happened, what with all those awful things going on in Paterson, Newark and, God forbid, New York, with all those sick people, homeless bums, maniacs shooting people dead on trains? I used to get so worried about you kids."

Even after a bath, the leg spasm had switched to a single tight knot. His body told him to stretch, even if he was missing practice. He checked the source of his lingering injury by comparing it with the muscle chart on his wall by his closet.

"Semitendinosus muscle." Pulling down his sweat pants, he fingered his right hamstring, as if by finding the particular muscle he might poke out the shred of pain. He looked down at his thighs, which had thickened in the last few years. When had they become so hairy, like he was another person down there?

His hand crept further up, groinward, when Mike barged in, growling like an old werewolf.

"Because, Brother, when you cross that line from my world–"

"What the hell are you–"

In his own voice, "It's Hulk Hogan," then, "When you cross that line from my world, brothah, the dark side of visionaries, you're gonna get beat up real, real bad."

Joey yanked up his sweats. "Get out."

"No." Mike jumped on his bed, rapt by the presence of his older

58

brother, but feigning disinterest.

Joey walked over to his desk, thinking once again about what he might do someday, showing Mike a thing or two, what he probably really wanted to catch him doing. He'd been almost caught too many times.

On the nights when Mike slept with him, in the old house in Newark, while quietly massaging himself off under the covers, Joey had wanted to simply flop it out in the dark bedroom, as if he didn't care what Mike saw. What was the mystery? He must have known. He should just show him.

But then he got a sick feeling low in his gut, figured Mike would probably tell on him a minute after he did it. It felt weird to think of Mike like that, since he looked so much like just a smaller version of himself, the dark wavy hair, the thin face, the brown eyes "the girls went wild over."

"You rip something?" Mike mocked.

"Strained my hamstring."

"I'm gonna see you wrestle next time."

"No, you can't. It's past your bedtime, wiener."

"Da said I could."

"How you know he's even goin'?"

"Said so."

"We'll see about that."

"I'm goin'."

"Next time, wiener."

"Show me a pin."

"No."

"Come on."

"No."

"I'll tell."

"Tell what?"

"I know something."

What could it be? That he had his pants down? The way Mike snuck up on him, always spying, it could have been anything. It was probably the drawings. But how could his little brother get up inside his closet to find them? He'd have to check later. He didn't want to know what it was.

"Sure you know somethin'. Assume the position."

Mike jumped off the bed to the small carpeted floor, waited. Joey stood over him, ready to start. He lightly grabbed Mike's arm, careful not to bump his groin against Mike's butt.

"Readeeee, wrestle!" He put so little pressure on the frail limbs, yet he held him down. Mike grunted below him.

He gently showed him some moves, gave him a few pointers for when he would start Kids Wrestling, then the two lay on the floor as Mike tried prying him over, to no avail. Joey reached over, tweaked Mike's nose, then tickled his belly. The squeaky laughter made him feel good, almost a man.

"Hey, what's that? You made a mess." Mike pointed to a wet line dribbling down Joey's dresser to the floor.

So that's where that first blast went. "Uh, I sneezed." Joey stood.

"You gotta cold?"

"It's pecker snot."

"What's that?"

Mike was shoved to, through, out the door. "You'll find out in a few years."

9

Hunter tugged his WRESTLING OR MY GIRLFRIEND? T-shirt up, wiped off a faceful of sweat, watched, waited, then threw his hands up at the lost cause before him.

"Ely, just. . .take his arm down. Lambros, at least try to bridge."

Unlike other sports, with a hard wooden floor for basketball or the bitter cold and rain of football fields, a sense of comfort filled the wrestling room. Sounds were absorbed in the private sanctum.

People rarely came to watch, except maybe the yearbook photographer every now and then. He was almost invisible. The principal came by a few times to talk to Coach Cleshun and Assistant Coach Fiasole, watch the team's progress, until he got uncomfortable in his suit. Basically the wrestlers were a clan unto themselves. Other people didn't know the way it worked. Other people didn't know.

Except the quitters. The banner hung high along the walls of the wrestling room, displaying the Colts insignia, a leaping young horse. But what never left the practice room was a long white banner with a list of the 1993-4 names, including those who dropped out. Little lines cut through their names. Unlike the plaques and trophies, this was a list no team player ignored. It hung as a warning; Quit and everyone will remember you.

So when Anthony had been out for a few days (stomach flu, he'd said) dragged in practice upon his return, guys razzed him. Wimp.

Pussy. Fag. The usual stuff.

Coach Cleshun shouted another demand that all the guys wear clean T-shirts for practice. The reek factor was rising.

Some wore shorts with jock straps, others the little Lycra shorts they all had to wear under their singlets in competition. Some wore kneepads. Brett Shiver wore the Jason mask since he had a cut on his eyebrow.

The boys had divided into groups of four. Everybody was supposed to go through short sit-outs into reversals, with the bottom guy going for an escape. Joey watched as Dustin flattened Anthony.

"Lemme show ya," Hunter hissed. "Neech, get on me."

Joey knelt down, wrapped his arm in a similar position. Hunter lay on his back. Joey nestled his head over Hunter's shoulder, heard his voice next to his ear, humming into his chest. "Ya gotta press up from your hips. . ." Hunter's gut shoved up against Joey, pulling him up off the mat. "Arch on your feet and your head–"

Hunter slow-motioned a bridge, poured Joey around his stout column of an arm until Joey lay shoulders down, legs high, his arms folded like a pretzel around his face, Hunter's tie with his legs threatening to crunch Joey's knee in just a hint toward permanent injury.

But there wasn't pain. Hunter carefully restrained his weight, the other boys having watched them move with exhausted fascination. Pulling away, Joey secretly felt the warm trade of sweat, how it clung to his shirt after they moved apart, smelled of chicken soup.

For wrestle-offs, which took place last, if there was time, Joey immediately went to Dink, even though he knew Dink would win. He waited beside him, sitting outside the circle, while other guys stretched and watched the smaller weights go first.

"Here we go again," Dink muttered.

Joey couldn't help but feel sorry for Anthony when he competed against Lamar Stevens. They bounced around the mat like two rubber bands, then got caught up in holds like one tightly bound pretzel, Lamar's dark brown legs entwined with Anthony's pale limbs. It hurt just to watch his legs get twisted in such strange positions. No wonder he always got hurt. Anthony got one of his legs caught around the grip of Lamar's leg, his other leg pulled back under Lamar's arm, his ass up high, exposed.

"Stack Attack!" Raul Klein yelled. It was their joke term for a stack, the position which left the loser butt up, arms pretzeled, most important, shoulders to the mat.

"Hey, we're up."

Joey fought all he could, thinking, not exhausting himself. It took Dink longer to pin him. Joey was getting better.

Cleshun and Fiasole went light on the guys, since it was still early December, told them to do only five laps around the school. Most of the football guys had become thick, overweight actually. Their bodies needed to be heavy for self-defense. But for wrestling, they had to get all the padding off. Even Buddha Martinez had to lose enough pounds so he could at least get down to some sense of what Coach Fiasole called "muscularity."

Joey loved the sound of the word, how Coach Fiasole led them around the weight room, showed them how to think of their bodies as machines.

Joey had drawn a cartoon of the biology chart of the human body, like his own muscle chart at home. Muscue Larry, a guy with exposed body parts, veins, showed off his temporals, lats, deltoids like a new suit, a map of body parts, pink and purplish muscles the countries, tendons the border crossings.

Coach Cleshun asked a few guys to stay after practice, those that were being ranked. Joey relaxed. He wasn't in such a rush to get out of there, without all the guys yakking, hooting. He padded naked across the clammy floors, his towel in his hand.

Bennie stood alone in the shower room, his wide V of a back shiny under the water that fell off the round shelf of his butt. Joey at first went to a far shower, then decided he could handle it. He turned on a nozzle one to Bennie's left. Bennie turned to face him, grinned.

"Hey."

"Neecheroonie. Gettin' good."

"Thanks."

As they talked, Bennie turned, as if testing Joey, held his head under the water, arching back, turning to reveal his cock slowly peeking around the corner of his hips. Joey had to see it, the way Bennie's stomach hairs quivered like river moss under the water that rolled over the ridges of his abs and off his body like a muscled waterfall. Bennie brought his hand down for a quick scrub with soap, tugging It a few times longer than usual.

Joey turned away, smiled inside.

HOSTILE? DESTRUCTIVE? PRONE TO VIOLENCE?
HAVE WE GOT THE SHOE FOR YOU.

Below the Asics poster, other posters of Gable, Smith, Baumgartner, Schultz, Ventura –all the greats– covered the walls. Off to the side, Coach Cleshun had hung a team photo of himself from his college wrestling at Penn State.

Guys liked to joke about how geeky he looked, his glasses covering up most of his face, his little head nearly hidden by another guy in the row in front of him. Cleshun liked to take the ribbing, Joey thought, to help the little guys like him believe even they could succeed.

Walt, Bennie, the Shiver brothers, Hunter, Dink and Joey crowded into Coach's tiny office or leaned in his doorway. Coach had posted the results of the previous week's seeding meeting. Coaches from around the region had met to vote on each others' players, determine the boys' rankings, which were not only an often accurate estimate of a wrestler's previous and potential record of where the boys were considered for that season, but who to beat, where they would go. Rankings had a powerful effect on serious athletes and a big ego boost to the hot dogs.

The boys listened while Coach stood, paced, telling tall tales of the other coaches' bragging. Fiasole rocked back and forth on the two back legs of the desk chair.

"So then, so then, the Paterson coach says, 'My one-seventy-seven can lift an ox. He grew up on a farm and gets up at dawn to bench press oxes.'"

Everybody laughed.

"Oxen," Dink corrected.

"Smartass." Coach smiled, beaming. "Then the Wayne coach goes, 'Well, my boy can bench press a gorilla. He is a gorilla. Mattera fact, we got him imported from Africa!'"

The boys blasted out in laughter again, hanging on Coach's every word.

"So I said, 'Well, my heavyweight recently visited Japan, where he beat Godzilla twice in Sumo!' Man, it was such a bunch of, 'I got bigger balls 'an you, my team's better 'an yours,' I tell ya, the testosterone was so thick you could cut it with a knife. And this little spaghetti man," Coach nodded to Joey. "Once I brought out his records from the tough-fightin' city of Nerk. . ." A few more chuckles. Dink tugged Joey's ear. "I tole them you were a hit man with the Mafia, and they better rank you, or else," Coach made his hands into guns, "Ba-da-bing, ba-da-bang!"

Guys shoved each other, chuckling. Joey didn't mind that they made fun of his being Italian. That was how they said he was theirs.

"I don't want you men to get all high and mighty with the other guys. They're still your teammates, even the first year guys. I want you to teach them what you've learned. Got it?"

Heads all nodded, obedient, silent.

"Now, I want you all to remember. I don't want any of that stupid weight-cutting action. You boys wanna move up or down, you do it natural. If you feel you're growing out of your weight class, you can, at any time, challenge your teammate in your chosen weight class for a varsity duals position."

More silence. Through the wonders of the order of wrestling, the weight classes, the pecking order seemed to have been achieved, for the time being. Joey didn't even move.

Gaining weight meant moving up.

Moving up meant challenging Dink.

He would never do that. He would starve first.

10

Bennie's large hands slapped down on their shoulders. "So brothers, do you feel proud to be so good?" He escorted Joey and Dink out of the school. Their gym bags kept banging against their backs.

"Fuckin' A," Dink said.

"Feels great," Joey beamed.

"Pride," Bennie scolded. "The greatest sin."

"What?" Dink tried to shrug off Bennie's grip, but he steered them toward the parking lot.

"Don't let your heads get big."

"Aw, c'mon, Bennie," Dink pulled away. "We're just happy, you know? Can't a person be happy about something without suffering eternal damnation?"

"That's right. You Catholic boys get to sin over and over again." Bennie stopped by his dingy blue-gray Mustang, the car's body a mottled map of gray primer, a giant burnt Hot Wheel. Joey could see himself and Dink reflected in the windows. Were they going to get a ride home? He found himself feeling giddy, as if another gift were being presented.

Bennie jingled his car keys. "Just pop into the booth, presto-change-o, start from scratch. You know, I wish I'da been raised a Catholic."

"Well, it's never too late," Dink smirked as he stood by the door.

"Oh, I'm sorry." Bennie pretended to be confused. "Did you boys want a ride?"

"Yeah, I mean, if it's. . . we thought you were. . ."

"So sorry to have misled you."

"Come on Bennie, we're beat. Just this once."

"Soon, brethren. Not today. But remember, we wrestle not against flesh and blood, but against powers, against the rulers of the darkness of the world, against spiritual wickedness in high places."

"What?" Joey blurted.

"Ephesians, six twelve." Bennie's grin disappeared as he sat down in his car, shut the door, gunned the motor, ambled carefully out of the parking lot, Guns and Roses blasting from inside the Mustang.

Dink turned away, shaking his head. Joey didn't know what to make of Bennie. "What was that about?"

"That," Dink said, "was Bennie's way of fucking with our heads."

"Well, it worked."

Dink adjusted the strap of his gym bag over his shoulder. "Yeah. Well, let's get going, before my legs give out."

"Ba-da-bing, ba-da-bang," Dink shot Joey with his fingers as they walked home. Joey dropped his gym bag, fell to the ground, and Dink fell atop him.

In the briefest moment, Joey stole a glance at Dink's ear, the one that wasn't thick from a beginning cauliflower. The sun shone through Dink's skin, turning the thinnest part a bright crimson. Veins and capillaries fanned out like a tiny river. Joey impulsively reached up, grabbed for it. He wanted to touch it before wrestling thickened it up forever.

Dink grabbed his arm, headlocked him, released him. They jumped up as if nothing had happened.

They could be so up, hyped, stoked, but as soon as they got home, wolfed down some food, they'd crash out like zombies.

"Hey, I got some other videos," Dink said.

"What, any college stuff?"

"Yeah, and more school tapes."

"What, yer dad's?"

"Naw."

"Coach's?"

"Naw. This guy comes to matches. Goes to other matches too, all over. He's a real fan. Came up to me once, asked me to make a video. He's got his basement all set up with mats."

"What, then he sells 'em?"

"What? No way, Jose. I dunno. Maybe. He just like, gets these guys to wrestle. I think he sells 'em. Gave me a hundred dollars."

Joey half-sang what had become one of their private jokes. "Fruit cake."

Dink never said yes or no. He just sang a line from a Nirvana song: "What else should I say. Everyone is gay!"

He sang it so loud Joey had to swat him. "Shut up, man."

"Y'oughtta come with me, man. Lives in Paramus. He's got all these tapes, all these guys. . ."

"I don't think so." He was actually curious, and interested, but it sounded like Dink was trying to set him up again, as if he needed an excuse to have sex with him. Why didn't he just say it?

"Whatever. Those shoes a yours are gettin' pretty skanky. I did not get my Asics International Lyte from allowance money."

Dink's shoes were top of the line. But just the idea made Joey feel creepy. "I ain't lettin' some old guy make videos of me."

"They come to the matches anyway."

Joey didn't say anything. He just wanted to drop it. How did Dink know all these things? Why did he hang them in front of him like bait? Dink didn't need the money. Why would he do something like that? Guys like that came to matches? Their matches? He wanted to ask Dink all sorts of questions, but he didn't want to scare him off. He didn't want to be like Anthony, getting too close to the truth, ending up alone because of it.

Dink said nothing for a while. They walked.

"My mom's goin' to Willowbrook Saturday. Ya wanna go with me?"

"Sure."

"Okay. Cool."

When he asked his mother if he could go, she said, "You're going where?"

He had a hard time explaining, since when Dink invited him, Joey didn't know that Willowbrook was a shopping mall. His mother thought he meant the insane asylum of the same name.

Joey didn't care what it was. He was going with Dink, away,

anywhere that little girls didn't need the answer to "Why is My Little Pony pink?" explained in endless detail, where no runts would spy on him, where his buddy's every touch made him think sexy thoughts, where no one made something as dumb as shopping sound like a sin.

Mrs. Khors said, "See you in an hour at the fountain." They sped off on a quiet spree, downing coffees at a cafe, since they had to cut weight. Joey learned quickly that he should only drink coffee in the morning, even then on weekends only, or else he'd be up all night drawing.

Joey followed Dink through every shop in the mall, including both sporting goods stores, where they laughed at the dorky salesmen dressed like refs, scanned through the circled racks of T-shirts, knowing they didn't even have wrestling shirts, let alone the wild ones from the catalogs.

"This is all junk. Come on." Dink led him to a vintage store with a lot of old stuff, already worn, everything half as much as the fake grunge in the mall.

They clicked through CD racks. Joey told Dink which ones he liked. Dink took him to the bookstore where they had planned to spend the extra cash on comic books, until Dink dared him to steal something.

The first thing Joey wanted was the Marky Mark book, which he'd already looked at while Dink scanned the shelves in Sci Fi/Horror.

His heart thudded from the glances at the pages where Mark Wahlberg's shirtless torso stuck out like a wet muscle version of some pop-up book. He wanted to see something like that at night. He wanted more pictures of men he worshiped. He couldn't draw everything.

Joey walked to the back, checked for circular mirrors up in the corners, then stuffed the book under his jacket, under his sweat shirt, against his belly, down his pants.

He saw Dink standing out in the lobby of the mall, but then he considered a scarier way to make sure he didn't get caught. He went to the newsstand and grabbed a fitness magazine with even more nearly naked muscular guys in it, bought it. The bald guy at the cash register smiled ever so nice.

Joey trotted out to meet up with Dink, who tried hard to hide the dopiest of grins.

"Whadja get?"

"Hold on. Not till we're home."

"Show me."

"It'll fall out. Come on."

They snuck into the men's room. Dink pulled out a paperback copy of a Clive Barker book. Joey yanked out the Marky Mark book. It peeled off his skin like a bandage.

"Cool."

They marveled quietly at each other's catch until somebody in one of the toilet stalls emitted a disgusting sound. They shoved the books in the bags with the other stuff, rushed out giggling.

Ten minutes later, Mrs. Khors found them waiting at the fountain with the smiles of angels.

11

Proudly showing off his front lawn fort from the first day, his brother had already made a few friends with some boys his age, who'd come by on little bicycles. Mike doled out empty boxes, becoming instantly popular with a casualness Joey secretly envied.

He'd helped unpack with his father and the movers, occasionally glancing down the street to see if anyone his age might also come by to introduce himself. No such luck.

He'd been wiping his face with his T-shirt when a chubby lady with big bosoms under a flowery blouse and tight pants that showed a bit too much of her wide hips smiled benevolently with a tray in her hands. "Your mother's inside?" Joey nodded.

She called herself the Tuscan Welcome Wagon. That first September day with the huge moving truck taking up half the street, Irene DeStefano walked right through the open front door with a fresh-baked lasagna and a bundt cake, as if she had always been his mother's closest friend.

A widow with kids in college, content to live alone in the smaller house next door, Irena "Call me Irene" DeStefano seemed to move into their lives to fill up her own. But his mother liked her. Even so, every time he came home, it became a signal for her to wrap up the chit chat, let her "get dinner on the table."

He tried not to resent his mother's times with her friend, but so often he had good news, or wanted to spout off about something someone said, or rehearse his day's events before repeating them for his father at dinner, or after, or not at all. He sure wasn't going to tell anything in front of Mrs. DeStefano, even though his mother probably discussed every cold or report card or ear infection.

"Well, Hello, Joseph. How are you?" Mrs. DeStefano's arms were out, demanding, so he hugged her.

"Okay. Hey, Ma." He bent down to kiss her. "I got a shirt, like you said." He pulled the wrapped shirt from the bag.

He wouldn't tell his mother he'd taken all of three seconds picking it out from the bargain bin. He just knew what her idea of "a good shirt" meant, so he got one, as promised, stuffed with cardboard, about a dozen pins, one of which always seemed to stay hidden until Sunday.

"What else did you get?"

"Oh, a book, another shirt. See?"

"That's nice. Is that flannel?"

"Yeah."

"Keep him warm," Mrs. DeStefano said.

"It'll definitely keep me warm," Joey grinned as he raced upstairs. He didn't mean the shirt.

He'd already scanned the Marky Mark book, saw the third nipple with a little arrow, and the wet shot, with his soaked jeans down so low, his skin taut like a cream-colored dolphin. Joey clutched the growing contents of his pants. Oh man. Save it for later.

He read the page where Marky's brother Donnie, from New Kids on the Block, told about his relationship with his brother. Joey had two NKOB cassettes, plus Marky's too, which he'd scrubbed his Aunt Lilla's stove to pay for.

In the Marky Mark book, Donnie Wahlberg explained how close he and Marky were: *Whenever I'm leaving Marky or he's going away, or like even when he finishes in the studio and is takin' off, we always kiss goodbye.*

It wasn't sexy to Joey, just a reminder of how to love your family, even if he sometimes didn't like them. He hadn't kissed his brother in years. Mike never held still long enough for him to try. Of course, if his brother were Marky Mark, he'd probably have a hard time not kissing him.

Restless, anxious, starving, not knowing whether to beat off or say a prayer for the contorted heat in him, Joey crept back to the top of the stairs to listen to the women talk. He didn't want to pig out with Mrs. DeStefano there, so he perched, listening from above.

"It's very nice, give him a little responsibility."

"But you know, the mother is divorced."

"What does she do?"

"Do?"

"Her job."

"She's a secretary at some real estate company."

No, Ma, he wanted to shout down the stairs. She sells houses.

"Well, it's good he's making friends," his mother said.

"And in sports. That's so good for a boy his age, to let off steam. The girls love an athletic boy."

A silence, then his mother shifted to talking about Sophia, then Mike, then Mrs. DeStefano said that no, Gwendolyn's cancer had not gone into remission and Burt had yet to return from Cairo but it wasn't until they said something about maybe next week that Joey realized they were talking about people on the tube.

12

"You don't know what goes into makin' a toilet. They gotta do a lot of work to make a pot to piss in."

Joey did not want to hear about the wonderful world of plumbing. He was set to wrestle a junior with a 27-8 record and wanted to keep cool for the next night's match. He'd looked the guy up in a copy of *Amateur Wrestling News* in the Cadet section. He thought it would be a good idea to get more information on his competition. It made him more nervous, with facts.

His father sat opposite him, his mother hovering, so she could be closer to the counter, since there was always something to get, more water, more cheese, the pepper, another fork. Sophia kept dropping hers.

"What, no plumbing?" his father grabbed another piece of garlic bread. "Plumbing paid for the food you're eating."

"We know, Dad." Joey sliced a piece of romaine lettuce, trying to make his salad at least seem like a full meal, but the smell of his mother's sauce made his stomach rumble.

"It's like sculpture. Those fancy ones? They make 'em one at a time." Joey tried to show his disinterest, looking over at Sophia, who pulled a string of pasta, holding it high above her open mouth. "Sophia, stop that." His father turned back to his oldest son. "It's

70

good work. You'll like it. You don't gotta wear a shirt, it's so warm in there. I'll take you out to the plant."

"Dad, I don't wanna make toilets."

"It starts at seven bucks an hour. That's good pay for an apprentice. You got better?"

His mother tried to change the subject. "Let's talk about this later. Joseph, eat."

"Ma, I tole ya, I'm up in my weight. I gotta float a pound."

"Why this craziness, this diet thing? The boys on football don't do this. Irene told me."

"Football season's over. Besides, they train them like bulls. They just have a trough for them in the cafeteria."

Mike snorted a laugh. Joey felt better.

"What about basketball?"

His father dropped his fork against his plate. "Marie, the kid's five-foot-four. He's a midget."

"That's because he don't eat!" She shoveled a glop of steaming pasta onto his plate. Sophia and Mike giggled, repeating, "Midget, midget."

Joey ignored them, looked down at the swirl of noodles, the blood red sauce tempting him. A pang of hunger flamed up from his belly.

He wanted to eat it all, but reached for the glass, gulped milk instead. "Ma, I gotta float a pound or I gotta change weight class. And I can't change my weight class 'cause I'm already ranked this season in this weight class."

"I don't understand."

"If you came to a match."

"I can't watch that. See you get beat up by some other boy, just like that time. . ."

Instead of listening for the fourteenth time about some kid in California who broke his neck, Joey decided to talk over her. "We don't beat each other up. It's a world-renowned sport."

He pushed his plate toward himself, picked up his fork. "Look, one big mouthful, okay?" Shoving it in his mouth, he savored it like an entire meal. He chewed. Everyone watched, until Sophia, bored more than full, squirmed out of her seat with an "I'm done." Dinner seemed to have been adjourned, or dismantled.

Joey sat at the table watching his parents take the dishes. "Save some for tomorrow, okay? Then I'll pig out." The look in her eye wavered between suspicion and flirtation. "You coming, Dad?"

71

As his father hesitated, Joey shook his foot nervously under the table, making a piece of glassware ching against a bowl. He glanced up at the clock on the wall. Five-thirty. He would have half an hour to get there. If his dad drove, he could make it early. If not, he had to jog. The gulp of pasta burned in his stomach, warm, delicious. He wanted so much more.

"I think I might make it." He paused.

"What?"

His father's sly grin reassured him, kidding. "If you promise to come to the factory and see about a job."

"Why do I gotta apply for a job I don't need till June?"

"Because you already got about a thousand outta work guys in line ahead of ya, but if I get you in now, you'll have a job then."

"Joseph, give me your plate, No more job talk."

"What's a matter? He's got a problem with it? It's very artistic, you know. Clay, glaze, makin' molds. You oughtta like that, being the artistic type."

Joey scowled, burned with embarrassment. He knew exactly what his father meant.

"Dino," his mother scolded her husband.

Sophia paraded through the kitchen, piped in a mimicking "Dino" that made everybody laugh.

"Well, the kid says he don't got a summer job. I'm just tryin' to help out. You said you don't wanna be a plumber."

"It's not for everyone," his mother said.

"It's good enough to put this food on the table."

"Mamma put da food onna table," Sophia said.

"But daddy paid for it." He pointed a thick finger at her tiny doll face, until she grabbed it, after which he scooped her up. "Paid for by all those crazy people who don't know how to take care of their plumbing. I tell them all that old saying what the chamber pot said."

Oh, not again, Joey agonized.

"'Use me well and keep me clean, and I'll not tell what I have seen.'"

"Ya got that right," Mike agreed, glancing at Joey, showing his spite. Dad likes me better, he said with his smile. Joey wondered how a ten-year-old could get so good at sucking up.

"You don't wanna make good money, that's fine with me." His father shoveled a last forkful of pasta into his mouth, chewed, dropped the plate in the sink, continued with his mouth half-full, "Just don't expect us to pay for all your expenses. You gotta save up

72

for college. This ain't no free loading zone."

"Fine, Dad."

"Yeah," Mike chimed in. "And I get your room the minute you're gone."

"Don't hold your breath. Porky."

13

The weekend after Thanksgiving it snowed four inches. Joey made angels on the yard with Sophia after shoveling the sidewalk and driveway clean. Everybody was happy, not just because of the snow, but because of December and all that it promises.

He'd remembered Dink's birthday. The night before, he'd made a card with a hand-drawn Spidey and dropped it in the Khors' mailbox. The next day Dink invited Joey over again to watch more videos. They had a great time. Nobody got boners. Boners were not up for discussion.

By Monday everybody heard the news that Lamar Stevens broke his arm sledding, so Anthony got moved up to wrestle in Stevens' weight, 119, for the rest of the season. Dustin moved up to 112. Tommy Infranca, the best of the JV runts, won the practice wrestle-off, got to start at 103.

Most of the guys who'd already heard about Lamar's accident expected the change in the line-up. Nobody seemed especially thrilled with the news, except Tommy Infranca.

Joey lay on his back, stretching his legs. Coach Cleshun walked over him to hand Dustin, Tommy and Anthony copies of diet plans, nutritional information.

"We get to pig out again!" Dustin bragged.

"No, just build up," Cleshun said.

Dustin held his stomach, lording it over the team as best a five-foot-two boy could. "I'm gonna have my mom make spaghetti and sausages and a big apple pie for dessert and cheesecake!"

Anthony squinted as he scanned the copied papers, adding up his intake like an accountant. He looked up at Joey. "Guess I'm next to you now, huh?"

Joey squirmed, pretended like he didn't care; Anthony sitting next to him at duals for the rest of the season. Make nice-nice with the runt.

Rolling over on his hands and knees, Joey crawled toward Anthony. "You better bring me luck, Lam-bee Boy." Anthony dropped his papers, tumbled under Joey. They pulled apart when Coach Cleshun blew his whistle for everybody to start warm-ups.

After drills, which included crab walks, push-ups, going up and down the pegs, Coach split the team up in twos. Assistant Coach Fiasole was gone that day, so Hunter and Bennie led some drills.

"Ow, hey, watch my hamstring. It's still sore." Joey rubbed it, stopping a moment, amid the couplings of boys practicing moves.

Dink rolled off him. "Coach'll be pissed if he finds out you're back in practice with a ripped-up leg."

Joey watched Dink pant, inches away, a sheen of sweat brightening his face. He noticed Dink lick the salt around his lips. Joey wiped his arm across his face, and while watching Dink, licked his own arm, but he made it look as if he just wiped himself.

"Yeah? Well, I'll be pissed if I find my name on The List."

It loomed, higher on the wall than all the awards, like a sentence served from on high. Two more JVs had dropped out the previous week. One chipped a tooth after falling on his head.

Dink assured him. "You're not like Whiner." Dink nodded his head toward Anthony, who desperately fumbled under Dustin. "He's a total loser."

"At least he's having fun," Joey scolded like an old school-teacher. "Besides, it's only his first year."

"That's just it. He don't know shit, not like us. We been wrestling since cataclysm."

"You gotta give him a chance."

"This is competition. You don't get charity."

"'Move it or lose it,'" Joey echoed Coach's catchphrase.

"Yeah, move it–" Dink lunged for Joey, his arm suddenly around his waist, his head digging into the back of Joey's neck. Joey clenched his leg back around Dink's, to no avail.

"–or lose it," Dink grunted from behind his ear. The moment Dink had Joey flat down on the mat, pressed against Joey's butt, Joey played his little interior game, Snapshot. He blinked, stored the sensation. But now, with a match in two days, he had to work, get his fireman's down, sharpen his crossface and peel his new best friend off his back.

It started out like any other dogpile. Some guys just got stupid, ended up deserving a whipping. Joey got his, didn't scream much.

Dink got his when he got lettered. He griped about it for a while, had a few bruises, but that was just part of it. Part of the fun. Everybody had it done to them.

When Joey wrestled in Newark, the thing was snuggies. He couldn't count how many times he had a chafed butt from the pranks the upperclassmen played. Guys could ruin a good pair of shorts with one yank. "Why do you always need new ones?" His mother had quizzed. He couldn't tell her. She wouldn't understand it wasn't a big deal in a world where tokens of friendship included blown snot.

So dogpiles were no big deal. You take your punches and scream and yell and it's over with. It was how everybody said, "You're one of us."

But Anthony never went for that. Anthony had a way of complaining or questioning the rules, as if he could somehow argue his way out of getting flattened. Everybody started calling him new names, first "Lambrusco," then "The Wine Man," then just "Whiner."

A few times he'd get to leave practice early, or go off, sit in a corner, breathing from a little inhaler, or else it was his contacts. Joey wondered if Anthony felt chest pains from just walking down the halls. He didn't understand what asthma could do, how someone's lungs could do that, become pain-filled.

Practice wound down to a sputter. Coach got a phone call, left them to drills, with Hunter leading. Then things got silly.

When they heard everybody else running, dogpiling, Joey and Dink pried themselves away from each other and just jumped on top. They had no idea who lay on the bottom, but they were all growling and yapping and yelling when one of the voices became high-pitched, weird, like somebody on the bottom was getting an arm gnawed off.

"Let him up," somebody said. They pulled apart. Under it all, flushed and panicked, his eyes livid with hatred, Anthony flung his arms about, hitting at anybody nearby. Guys kept backing away, just watching him hurl himself about in defiant fury.

"Fuck you! Fuck you! I hate you all! You fucking morons!"

"Calm down, gentlemen, calm down." Coach Cleshun ran in to see what the problem was.

"These fucking animals just attacked me!"

"It was just a dogpile," Hunter said.

"Somebody was punching me!"

75

Coach Cleshun led Anthony away, while the rest of the team had to do twenty laps around the school, outside. Afterward, everybody panted, wheezed, made grunting jokes.

"Circle."

They grouped, sat, settled down, as Cleshun stood, waiting for what became several minutes.

"I can't leave you alone for a moment without you turning into animals, is that it?" Coach's face flushed crimson. "You need a babysitter, is that it?" The strap of his whistle tightly bound around his fist, Joey thought Coach might punch something, or someone, but he just kept lecturing.

"This is a team sport. Even though it's just you against another man once you're out there, you still have to. . .you've got to support your teammates. You think you're gonna get it from out there?" He pointed to a door. "From the people who wanna cut our funding because we don't bring in the crowds like the B-ball boys? From the people who wanna replace us with a girl's lacrosse team?"

Silently, the circle of boys either stared down to the floor, or at each other.

"Evolve. Go. Now."

The briefest utterance of moans was silenced by Cleshun's bark, "Mister Skaal, Mister Hunter, I'd like to have a word."

The boys rose, their muscles stiffening already.

Troy shouted after they'd trotted to the locker room, "I think the word is 'ass-reaming!'"

Joey laughed with them, knew that Coach had tried to sway the team's energy back in line. But he also knew the truth.

Whosoever didn't already hate Anthony did by now.

14

As the Giant Hohos, also known as Tubers, were carefully unrolled by the JVs under his and Raul's watchful supervision, behind him Joey heard a snapping sound.

"Hi, Joey." Chrissie Wright grinned, giving her gum a moment's rest. She wore jeans and a Little Falls Wrestling Boosters T-shirt. Her hair frizzed out like an exploded cat.

"Howdy," Joey smiled at her, then turned away, busying himself with unrolling the mat that came toward them like a slow bulldozer sprinkled with monkey-like mimicked, "Howdy"s.

"Um, they're coming this way." She hopped back.

The mat shoved them apart. Joey went back to work. He half-heard "stuck up" come from her direction, but ignored it when a couple guys tried to roll Tommy Infranca under the mat.

"Neech! Laps Land!"

Dink grabbed Joey as they rounded the back court of the gym, which the boys had been granted only out of the graciousness of the "grand high" basketball team, which was in Clifton, about to lose, Joey hoped.

The basketball team always caused problems when the wrestling team had tournaments: late practices, alumni matches. They didn't like the wrestlers dragging mats over their precious floor. That's how Dink explained it to Joey, who took it as common turf action. As one of Brett Shiver's T-shirts read; THE SIGHT I ADORE ON A BASKETBALL FLOOR IS WRESTLING MATS FROM DOOR TO DOOR.

"Whyncha go talk to her?" Hunter shoved him as they finished with the mats and began jogging around the gym perimeter.

"Because I'm busy."

Dink jogged circles around the others.

Hunter quizzed him. "Why, you don't go out with south-mores?"

"Naw, too skinny." Joey always had an excuse ready.

"Yeah, guess yer right. Go for the older girls."

Dink cut in. "I like 'em with big tits."

Hunter said, "Whadda you know, you haven't even–"

"I know, awright."

"When was the last time you had a date?"

"Last summer. Melissa Hutchins."

"Ja get any?"

"It's all pink inside."

"You perv."

Hunter jogged on, laughing. As he and Dink looped around again, Chrissie glanced at him, then turned away in a huff. Sure, he could fake it, but he wasn't about to. Forget that. Besides, it wouldn't be nice or fun to lie to Chrissie.

As they passed her, Dink bellowed out loud, "Well, Neech, it's sure better than layin' in bed an' beatin' off into a sock!"

Dink slapped Joey on the back, nearly making him trip.

He'd never thought of doing it that way.

Coach barked a few orders, silenced the herd, all hooded under sweat shirts like monks.

"Mister Skaal, will you honor us with a prayer?"

Bennie stood, nodded to Lamar, who held a small boombox, his other arm in a scribble-coated cast, then headed out to the gym.

The team went to their knees in the damp quiet of the locker room. Joey bowed his head, glancing at a crack in the cement floor before shutting his eyes. There was no request, no demand. They simply went to their knees in prayer. That was how it was done. It was a rare moment, when Joey actually felt as if he might be talking to God and Jesus and everybody.

Silently, secretively, Joey slipped his crucifix, which he had removed from around his neck, dropped it between his right sock and ankle.

Bennie paused a moment, surveying the sight of all his teammates kneeling below him.

"Lord, please help us in our mission tonight to defeat our enemies from Bayonne. Give us strength that we may be victorious and not cause great harm to our foes. Let us bring honor to our school, our team and our teammates, who are our brothers, and our friends, for a man that hath friends must show himself friendly, and there is a friend that sticks closer than a brother. Amen."

After the mumbled Amens, the Catholic boys –Tommy, Dustin, Anthony, Joey, and Dink– crossed themselves. Everybody opened their eyes, slowly stood, as if waking from a nap.

Coach said softly, "Remember gentlemen; it's on the mat that counts. Let's go."

The rumble of the boys standing was followed by a low growl

that rose higher and higher as they huddled in a tight circle, each with an arm extended to the center. Joey loved the moment, feeling his arm as only a part of another creature. They gripped their fists tightly, aiming them low, layered, a tight chrysanthemum of teen rage.

As their growl became a medium yell, then a high howl, the arms rose and rose high to the ceiling. Their singular howl dispersed into a round of doglike hoots reverberating into the lockers.

Joey kept his hood up, as did the others through their opening entrance and run-around. They jogged around the circle while the mat maids clapped to the music, leading the crowd in the chant, "Colts! Colts! Colts! Colts!"

Tommy Infranca led them. The team marched in by weight, growing in size as each boy trotted out. Lamar sat proudly by the tape recorder at the announcer's mike. Music blasted the gym.

The basketball team had the whole stage band to pump up their entrances through a big paper banner emblazoned with a life-size drawing of a Colt. At the Homecoming football game, they even had a real horse that some guy rode around the playing field.

The wrestlers had a Panasonic and guts.

The boys had convinced their coaches it was a very healthy psych-up, since other schools did it too, with other music, even on the PA sometime. "Eye of the Tiger" was called "way eighties" by Dink. Walt had suggested "Lunatic Fringe," from *Vision Quest*, but that was considered sacred. They didn't tell Coach Cleshun the name of the Stone Temple Pilots song that Bennie chose: "Sin."

Joey shot a dopey pretending-to-flirt grin at Chrissie, showing off how easy their little dance was, even though it had taken Assistant Coach Fiasole hours of practice to get them all in sync.

Joey's favorite part was sidesteps, because it reminded him of the ride at Great Adventure that spun around until the floor dropped out. The boys whirled about the perimeter of the circle, facing in. Across from him, Joey grinned to Hunter, who spotted him between darted glances to each side. With Anthony to his left, Dink on his right, Joey maintained the space. The faces and bodies of his teammates, the twelve chosen, remained focused. Behind them, outside the circle, the gym walls, the bleachers, opponents, scorekeepers, coaches whirled by in a blur.

Usually Assistant Coach Fiasole turned down the tape at the right moment, but he let Lamar have the honor. The team ended their warm-ups standing in a row, pointing across the mat, shouting the chorus lyrics once, loudly to their opponents, "Down You Go!"

Assistant Coach Fiasole had edited the music to cut to the song's end. Their opponents, who stood or sat, slightly stunned by the display, watched as the Colts bowed reverently like young Samurai warriors.

Despite their roar of adrenaline, the small yet appreciative crowd brought them down to reality. Despite the mat maids' posters in the halls, kids didn't want to go out on a cold night just to go back to school. Despite the bake sales, T-shirts, Booster Club meetings, some parents had jobs, or other kids to feed, pick up, drop off. The gym echoed, near-empty.

The coaches often told Joey it didn't matter so much who showed up. "Wait till finals," Hunter had said. "It's on the mat that counts," Coach had said. But Joey had too often tasted victory with near-empty bleachers as his witness. In the wrestling room, the practice mats covered the floors, comforting and soft. But in the gym, with the polished wood floor spreading out and shiny as a lake, the mat was a lonely island.

Sitting by themselves, expectant, Joey's father and Mike sat amid the sparse audience. Mike waved. Joey grinned wide, baring his teeth. Fine, they'd showed up. Now he had to win.

Tommy Infranca got pinned, more nervous than unskilled. Dustin did well, winning by a technical fall. Just before Anthony stepped out, Assistant Coach Fiasole whispered something to him, and he took off.

"Come on, Anthony!" Joey yelled. Along the bench, a few Colts gave him a strange glance. He kept his attention on Anthony, but from the side, he half-saw, half-felt their glare, even Dink's.

Anthony got pinned before Joey even took his sweats off. The shock of seeing Anthony slumping back to his seat so soon distracted him.

"What a fish." Troy made his lips pop open and shut like a trout.

Joey had seen movies with silent slow motion sports scenes, the hero making the snap decision at the moment, all the voices fading away into a muffled silence, followed by music rising to the roar of victory at the last moment.

This was not his experience.

When he saw the pair-up, he tried his best to keep his eyes off the opponent, Bradsomething, a blond with a sleek nose and blue eyes. Joey tried not to think too much about him, see him, or else he'd see him as a person, humanize him, and then all would be lost. He sought out his opponent's glance, seeking a trace of innocence, a hint of respect or fear or arrogance, something to start with.

Bayonne had an average record, and their lower weight guys were giving a good fight. Joey waited for Coach Fiasole's pat on the butt and the magic word, "*Colto*," then stepped over the line and into the circle for his three two-minute battles.

"Take charge right off," Coach had said a hundred times. Joey half heard it through his headgear, his ears muffled from most sounds.

He thought his upper body weakness would peg him, since the Bayonne guy was a bit buff. The guy nestled his head under Joey's armpit, shoving through his arm lock. Then he used his head like a battering ram, shoving him back. Joey looked to the guy's feet, distracted while trying to get a takedown, an arm slapped over the side of his head, clutching, grabbing. Joey responded by ripping away, shifting around him, back in again.

He grabbed the arm, twisted, dropped with a small yank, the guy's body hurled over his shoulder. He sprawled, his body sprung taut over his opponent. Get him on his back, get him on his back.

"C'mon, Joey-eee!" a high-pitched voice. Chrissie. Suddenly she was all for him.

He got distracted again. The school photographer, out of nowhere, lay sprawled at the rim of the mat, elbows up, clicking a shot of Joey gritting his teeth. *Cool. Hope it gets in the yearboo–*

Wham! A crossface nearly punched him. Joey pressed up, pushing himself up on one elbow, yanking away an attempted arm bar. He pressed away from the floor. The ref whipped into his sight, whistle at his mouth, palm poised over the mat. No, he was not going just yet. Joey released a thick grunt, reaching under, pulling his arm free.

A tweet and they released. Choosing ref's position, Joey knelt. He saw his dad out in the audience. Think, think, not about him, not about what he thinks. Win for you, not him.

"Flank!" Coach shouted. Joey felt weight descend behind him as the hands were set in place, the back of his opponent warm, pressing against his butt.

He felt the Bayonne guy edge to the left, thought it might be a fake-out to get him to twist left. Joey faked a nudge left, twisted right, lunging his left leg out, digging the heel of his shoe deep into the mat. He pivoted on it, wriggled out of the arm lock to break free, face off, lock up once again.

Great, he was fine at squeezing out, now how about dealing with the guy? How about getting a pin instead of just points?

Joey glanced a brief moment at the blue glint in his opponent's eyes, then down. Watch the hands. He dove, shooting down, grabbing for torso, exhaling as he went down, grabbing a leg, tying it, thinking of wrapping it with a hand, grunting up the strength to keep him down.

Twisting out of his hold, the blond backsided over him, took one arm around Joey's neck, another to the crotch in a near-nutpull.

Don't you dare.

Joey wriggled about, his arms useless, his hamstring spasming in a frenzy, his throat wheezing, sweat stinging his eyes, his headgear mashed against his temples at a wrong angle. His opponent squeezed, shoved. Joey's face flattened sideways against the mat, his cheek smashed against his teeth. He gasped, gulping air, feeding his little heart.

Looking at the gymnasium sideways, his arm feeling like a chicken wing about to be dismembered, Joey could see each light of the ceiling reflected in the glasses of someone's mother. Nearly all the bleachers were empty, the long rows of warm blond wood. Chrissie and Kimberly kept their seats, cheering him on from behind the scorecards. 11-8. What color was he again?

Somewhere behind them his dad must have been cheering. He heard his name sprinkled in among the shouts. Coach Cleshun paced over to face him. "Get out of there!" he screamed. Yeah, easy for you to say. He twisted his head to try another grip, then bit his lip.

Tasting his own blood, he swallowed, took a deep breath in, then relaxed a tiny moment. So did his opponent, as if they were both agreeing: This is crazy, who are we doing this for? The guy's grip on him loosened, the ref stood back, not thumping around, Cleshun stood silent. As often happened in matches, where not a lot of people attended, nobody cheered.

A fraction of near-silence filled the gym.

Joey's opponent broke it as he let out a little sigh. Nobody heard it but the two boys, the grunt lost under the tangle of their bodies. Joey wriggled out of his opponent's hold, noticed a faint smell of deodorant.

Almost charmed, instead of weakening, as he usually did when a sliver of desire forced its way into a match, he made it the other guy's weakness, his fault. He could win, even if he liked this guy. He drew breath in, sucking in another trace of sweetness from the guy's armpit. It fueled his last lunge in what he sensed as his few remaining seconds of energy. He fully tensed every muscle, let out an anguished bellow, imagined himself exploding.

The noise of the gym rose with him as he twisted out, grabbed the guy in a cradle, picked him up fully off the mat for a small moment, squeezed in. Joey shoved his chest into him, pushing, digging with his feet, pushing like a snow shovel, until he ground his torso up, over, shoving his belly against the guy's crotch, clamping his arm under a knee, forcing the leg up, the Bayonne guy onto his back, until he locked in, groin to groin, between the guy's upraised legs.

The ref spun around in his range of vision, arm raised, then slammed his palm onto the mat.

He'd done it.

Joey glanced up at the ref to see a slight nod of assurance, then released the guy, pulling his arms out from the tangle of their bodies. He crawled up to standing, turning away, looked out to see who was cheering. The hooting and applause rose.

His posse was on its feet, high-fiving, his coaches strutting away in satisfaction.

Yes.

They crouched before the ref, whose belly nearly poked out under the striped shirt. They both shook hands, glanced at each other. More hoorays. He looked out, too exhausted to manage a grin. His dad stood, clapping. Good. That'll shut him up for a while.

They shared a glance between pants for air, when the Bayonne guy leaned in, gave him the briefest hug, a pat on the back.

As he returned to the bench, hands high-fived him. Coach Cleshun patted his butt, then Assistant Coach Fiasole too, the double seal of approval.

"Good goin', dude," Bennie patted him.

"Awright, Neech, my man." Hunter chucked him on the arm. Joey sat on the bench, dropped his headgear between his legs. He licked his lips, the salt of his blood and sweat mixing.

Joey merely high-fived Dink, who was up next, always after him. He hoped the energy of his win would magically pass over into Dink's body from their brief touch.

As he sat in a dizzy state, wiping down, his sweats clung to his skin and singlet. He sucked in air as the spasms and quivers in his muscles calmed, his own and his opponent's sweat drying on his skin.

His hamstring throbbed. Somewhere in there his wrist got crunched a bit.

Sitting to his left, Anthony hadn't said a word, but sat with his arms crossed, furious.

Joey tried to reassure him. "Hey, man, I lost my whole first season."

"You did not."

"How do you know?"

"You brag about your record all the time, like it's some kind of–"

"Stow it."

"Hey."

"Me?" The photographer seemed frightened for a moment, but became slightly more relaxed as Joey talked with him. He wore a too-long flannel shirt. The strap of his camera made it bunch up.

"You got some pictures a me, huh?"

"Yeah, some pretty good ones, I think."

"How's about makin' me some copies?"

"Want some prints?"

"Sure, if it's not, I mean if they let ya."

"Sure. No problem. No problem at all." The photographer adjusted his glasses, awkwardly fumbling with his square-shaped photo pack.

"I'm Joe."

"I know. Tom."

"Nice ta meetcha."

"We're in History together."

"Oh, really?" Joey'd never noticed him. He didn't even remember the guy ever speaking in class. "Oh, yeah, in the back."

Anthony approached the photographer. Did he want photos to remember his pathetic loss?

"Right," Tom said. Seeing Anthony, he blurted a soft, "Hi," as if they were friends. "Well, I should have the photos done in a few days."

"No rush. Just thought I'd ask. Good for the ego, ya know." Joey backed away.

"Sure."

Joey saw his father and brother waiting by the bleachers. "Well, gotta go. See ya in class."

"Right."

"Hey, kid, good job." His father's arm came around him, patted his back while hugging him.

Mike jumped off a bleacher, landing on the floor, eying two other young boys who were already playing on the mat.

"Take your shoes off."

"We gotta go," their dad said.

"It's awright," Joey said as a few other younger kids rolled around, terrorizing each other while the coaches chatted with parents, shaking hands. Chrissie Wright walked by. "Hello, Mister Nicci."

They both watched her go by, then Joey watched his father watch her. "I'll just be a few minutes." Joey said.

"Okay," his dad, said, turning back. "We'll be out in the parking lot."

"Go talk to my coaches." Joey steered his father to other side of the gym.

"Awright, awright."

Walt asked one of the Shiver brothers a question in the showers. Joey crossed between them, and because of the conversation bouncing back and forth, he got to steal a few choice glances at his buddies. In previous years, Joey would count what he called Sightings, which were merely seeing another guy's dick. That got replaced with Maybe Bigger than Last Time, which got replaced by Butt Shots.

But Joey felt less than amiable scoping his teammates' bodies when he realized what their conversation was about.

"No, it's a part of their brains."

"What's that called again?"

"The fag part."

Everybody laughed, but then shut up when Brett Shiver said, without stuttering at all, "The Hypothalamus!"

Hunter broke the silence with, "Hypothalamoose." Everybody started making what they thought were moose calls.

He'd already memorized every detail of their bodies, the way soap suds slid down their muscled curves, the freckles on Walt's back, Raul Klein's appendix scar where his oblique met his hip bone. None of that felt very sexy when he figured they'd hate him if they knew he could do a better moose call. Joey padded back to his locker when he saw Anthony sneak out quickly. Joey dressed in a rush to catch up to him.

"Nine-ish. Saturday," Bennie said with a fake British sneer. He dropped his gym bag on the bench next to Joey, began combing his wet tangle of hair into the look of an AWOL marine.

"What?" Joey fumbled with his laces, tied them in front of Bennie, who stood before the mirror. Joey stole a long glance at Bennie's dick. Bennie never raced through the showers like other guys, but stood, slowly rinsed off, back to the wall. He was very comfortable watching guys notice him, notice It. When he put his pants on, he stood up on the bench, claiming it prevented his pants from getting wet, but everyone knew. He showed off like the statue he thought should be made in his honor.

"Saturday. Party at Hunter's." It began swaying as Bennie toweled his back.

Joey had to look up, Bennie's cock at his eye level. Bennie caught him looking. "Hunter's havin' a party?"

"Firm grasp of the obvious. Bring brews."

"As if! I'm fifteen."

"So bring munchies."

"I gotta ask my parents."

"Sure."

It excited him, getting together with them, but he couldn't help wondering why Hunter hadn't invited him. "The guys on the team coming?"

Bennie re-wrapped his towel. "Not all brethren."

Weird. Bennie was weird.

Joey raced to the parking lot. His dad wasn't there yet. He scanned for Anthony's junker of a Pinto. Once when it stalled in the street on the way out, a bunch of guys laughed at him. Nobody offered to help except Joey and Dink, and even Dink had to be coaxed.

He found the Pinto parked at a curb half a block down the street. Anthony sat inside, holding his hands to his face. At first Joey thought he was praying, but when he saw his breath steam through his fingers, he figured he was just warming his hands.

He knocked on the window. Startled for a moment, Anthony unrolled it.

"What, you got no heat?"

"No." Anthony looked up, smiling. "You need a ride?"

"No. I. . ." Joey looked back to the lot. "My dad's here somewheres."

"Oh. Then, what?"

"You know that photographer guy?"

"Tom? Yeah."

"He said he'd get me some pictures. He ever give you any?"

"Yeah."

"Oh. That's good."

Silence.

"So you don't need a ride?"

"Naw."

"So?" Anthony wanted to leave.

"Look, I just wanna, you gotta keep tryin'. I know it's tough." Joey felt awkward talking through the window, like he should be in confession or taking an order for cheeseburgers. "You tried, right? That's what counts. I know you can do better."

"You are so clueless, Joseph."

"I just thought I could help you–"

"What do you care?" Anthony's eyes burned with a new anger. "When have you ever cared?"

"Whaddaya want? I should ask you to the prom?"

Anthony tightened his grip on his steering wheel, shifted into reverse. Joey jumped back, but grabbed the door as his gym bag slid off his arm. He tripped. One foot landed in a puddle of half-frozen water.

"Shit." He pulled his sopping shoe back onto the curb. "Look. I, hey, come on, man. Stop the car."

Anthony put it in park, dropped his hands from the wheel.

"Just 'cause I don't hang out with you. . . That dogpile thing was nothin'. I just don't– You know, I thought you were okay with that."

"That's it?" Anthony hissed. "You think I'm afraida you tellin' everybody? I got news for you. Everybody knows."

"That's not it. What I'm tryna tell ya is you gotta lighten up. This thing is not–"

"Don't you tell me what is not. You're the one with the problem. I am just biding my time. You know what that means? I go to a group, and I talk to people. I told my parents. I even told Coach. But that don't mean you can go around tellin' people."

"What? I don't. You think I told?"

"Yeah. And you know what else? Coach is okay with it." Anthony fumbled with his clutch, yanking the stick a few times. "Which is what you are not." His clutch slipped into gear, almost by accident, it seemed. "I got a bit of advice for you, Joseph. If I were you, I wouldn't hang out with those goons."

"They are not goons. Where the fuck do you get off–"

"You know, I really thought we could be friends. I really thought that."

"But. . . so you go out for the team just to–" Joey sputtered a moment, letting the depth of Anthony's attachment to him sink in. "Look, you tryin' to wrestle is not going to make us friends. I mean, jeez."

"I'll do what I do, okay, whether we're friends or not."

"But, Anthony–"

"I gotta go now, so will you step back, please?"

Anthony tooled his Pinto down the street in a gurgling cloud of exhaust. Joey stood at the curb, dazed, panting, not even noticing as Troy and some other boys walked by. As Joey tried to ignore them, search out his dad, Troy reached out, brushed his hand over Joey's frozen spikes of hair, dubbed them "wopsicles."

15

"Well, you saw what he did to his nephew in the ring, the son of his dead brother. By what he did to him, he has now shown us he is the lowest form of human life! He is out to utterly destroy him!"

With the advent of cable, peer pressure, lack of porno, Joey finally got into professional wrestling, but drew the line at the soap opera.

Raul Klein collected the action figures. Lamar Stevens collected the magazines with Ken Shamrock, Ravishing Rick Rude in hot pink tights, Babes of Wrestling.

The Shiver brothers, Troy, Raul and Buddha Martinez even got on pay-per-view once, when they got shots of them in the stands of the Meadowlands Arena, waving signs somebody gave them, their bellies painted C O L T S.

It was good clean fun.

After Dink lent him about a dozen tapes, he grew to appreciate it, particularly in slow motion for some guys, certain positions. Joey had to admit that pile drivers, flying leaps, huge musclebutts did intrigue him after all.

As they watched one ham-faced ringside guy barrel off on another about the ridiculous grudges that justified such silly violence, Joey excused himself to pee, ducked into Dink's room.

It looked the same, just a bit messier. He scanned, snooped, stole a brief glance at the Marky Mark poster. He saw books he should read. He knew he'd only have a few minutes before Bennie or Dink would drag him back to enjoy one more piledrive or chair whack before heading to Hunter's party.

"Ooh, a drop kick right to the head!"

"Oh, I love that!"

"Down he goes!"

Hunter's place was rumored to be on the large size. Dink had hinted about a walk in some nearby woods. In case that didn't happen, he wanted a souvenir.

"–and sent him all the way out of the ring–"

"Dat has gotta hoit."

"Ooh, not the chair!"

He quickly dug his hand under Dink's mattress, the side against the wall, he figured, felt under the mattress, found a sock.

His hand went quickly to his varsity jacket pocket as he shoved it in. In a bounce on the rumpled bedspread, he stood, darted to Dink's bookshelf, looking for nothing, when he heard someone behind him.

"Whadda ya doin'?"

Bennie stood in the door, wearing the T-shirt Coach said he couldn't wear in practice, since it was "in poor taste." A cartoon grim reaper hovered over a skeleton wrestling a guy, with the word NEXT!

"Looking through the Dinky's CDs. He's gonna make some tapes for me."

"That's sweet. Think fast."

A beer can flew into his arms.

Dink seemed comfortable having the guys over, even though Joey knew he really wasn't allowed. Maybe that one beer the few times he'd been over, but a party for the party? No way.

"Yer mom out on a date?" Joey muttered as he caught Dink alone in the kitchen. Dink's hair lay flat, darker in wetness, so Joey figured it must have been the shower water that made his eyes so red.

"What do you care?"

His remark stunned Joey. Weren't they friends? Didn't they tell each other stuff? What was with him? Or was he just nervous because Bennie was there? What did he expect?

Joey decided to let it pass, let the evening move on its own. Dink played a Helmet CD. Metal guitar thuds blasted the room, making things vibrate.

Bennie stood in the middle of the room, taking in the sounds. Dink danced with his beer can, in jeans and a Columbia University sweat shirt. Joey sat on the floor, sipping, afraid the thuds he heard were neighbors banging on the walls, afraid they'd notice him watching Dink's hips buck as he danced. Dink turned the volume down a little after a few minutes so they could talk.

They'd made jokes about Helmet's name, which led to war, which got Bennie talking about his dad. "Killin' gooks was his profession. Blew into Danang with his buddies an' tore it up. Won the Congressional Medal of Honor."

"He must have been old," Joey thought. "My grandfather went to Vietnam, but he was only fifty when he died."

Bennie's glance implied that he was not to be interrupted. "My dad, my real dad, was in Nam. I kept his name, though. Skaal. Know what that means?" No one offered a guess. "It's the name of the wolf in a Norse myth, Skaal the wolf that eats the world come the Armageddon. 'Cept I think it's spelled different."

"So why'd it change?" Joey said.

"Same reason your grandparents prob'ly were named Niccerello or something. Got chopped off in Ellis Island."

"Like a tail."

Bennie and Dink laughed. Joey didn't.

"So anyway," Bennie continued.

It seemed Dink had heard the story before, but he sat silent, reverent. Bennie was a little weird, that much was obvious, but it was his benevolence, his being friends with Dink and Joey, that made them like him; that and it being a pretty unsafe proposition not to.

"My mom took up with this other guy, a lot younger, total asshole who I fought with. Me, ten years old and startin' fights with this weasel. A stoner. They gave me up. Then I got dumped into the house of holy hell, but now I'm with Pattie and Lee. They're nice. They taught me a lot. They don't hit. Ja ever get strapped with a belt, Neech?"

"Huh? Naw, my dad don't hit me." He couldn't remember doing anything to make his dad hit him. He was the oldest. Joey had been good, real good. He had to be.

"Maybe you'll deserve it if you don't keep winning. A little corporal punishment never hurt a guy!" Bennie went for him. Joey giggled as Bennie lifted him up from the floor, grabbing him around the torso, swinging him around.

"Hey, hey, watch the lamp!" Dink yelled. Bennie let Joey down halfway, holding him sideways like a suitcase.

Bennie would never hurt him. Besides, Joey liked it, the feeling of being toyed with by this big crazy guy. Joey worried more about Dink's sock falling out of his pocket.

Bennie dropped Joey, who landed silent as a cat, then stood. "For Joseph was Benjamin's brother and his bowels did yearn upon his brother."

Joey gave him a look. "You toss me around like that again and my bowels'll do somethin', brother."

Bennie laughed, so everybody else did.

"So, are we goin', or are we gonna play Neech Toss all night?" Dink stood, impatient.

"I thought a little art appreciation would be in order."

"Huh?" Dink looked confused. "I thought it was babe party. House o' Babes."

"You draw, right?" Bennie asked Joey.

"Yeah."

"Like what?"

"Like anything." Even you, dude.

"Can you draw horses?"

"Possibly."

"Like colts?"

"What, like the mascot?"

Bennie's eyes glimmered. "Possibly."

16

"It's the Doritoes."

"No, it's not. Sniggaz is." Hunter, up in shotgun, countered Bennie's joke.

"Sniggaz fo' life," Dink echoed, dumped in the back next to Joey. They would never ride shotgun. It was hard to lean forward in Bennie's Mustang. The seats were so low they could feel the asphalt grumbling away under their butts.

They were debating over who made New York City the worst. They'd crossed off homeless people, dubbed "moving garbage." They knew about New York, since they'd all been there a few times.

"Doritoe Sniggah half-breeds," Joey added, grinning at Dink, since he'd outdone him.

Dink shouted, too close to Joey. "No, no, Doritoe Sniggah half-breed hookers!"

"Doritoe Sniggah half-breed drag queen hookers!" Joey shouted and immediately blushed. Even though the cassette player in Bennie's car blasted the Meat Puppets, the way everybody reacted, it felt like silence.

"Whadda you know from drag queens, pissant?" Hunter turned to Joey from the shotgun seat. Bennie glared at him from behind the wheel, his eyes framed in the rear view mirror as he steered his Mustang along the offramp leaving the Jersey Turnpike Northbound. They were in Teaneck. Enemy territory.

"Yeah, whaddaya know 'bout drag queens?" Bennie asked.

"'Cause that's all he gets a blow job offa!" Dink bellowed from the back, elbowing Joey.

"Ha!" Everybody laughed, except Joey, who scowled. How dare Dink make such a crack, especially after that night watching wrestling tapes, what Joey secretly called The Boner Incident. He landed a punch on Dink's shoulder, thinking maybe it was cool for Dink to make that joke, to get him off the hook.

Joey only said such words in the company of Bennie and Hunter. Joey never said "pussy" or "muthahfucker" or "fagityassbitch" or any of the new words he learned from the posse. His parents never said them. His brother tried "muthahfucker" once, but never twice.

Joey had pored over the pages of his Marky Mark book, the solemn faces of the Funky Bunch, comparing his own thick lips to that of the black band members. They were handsome guys, strong and cool.

They all liked Lamar Stevens. They even dressed like black guys, with their baggy pants, long shirts, baseball caps and angled buzzcuts. It was as if they dissed anybody who was different, but first they stole what they liked about them.

"Hey! Fag." Dink punched back, light though.

"Shut up, Dink."

"Shut up, Neech."

"Dinky Dick."

"Neech the Leech, he'll suck ya till ya screech!"

Joey punched him again. Dink punched him back, but it didn't hurt. His fist bapped the leather sleeve of Joey's jacket. Dink was being such an asshole. Joey knew the reason why, the same as his own behavior, to act tough in front of Bennie and Hunter, who probably didn't care about either of them.

Even if they didn't, Joey felt honored to go out with them. At first they went to a Sylvester Stallone movie, which Joey was excited about, but they got there late since Willowbrook's parking lot was jam-packed, but he wasn't about to tell Bennie to hurry up so he could catch a peek of Stallone's butt.

They got kicked out when Bennie and Hunter started making noises, throwing popcorn. Joey wanted to watch Wesley Snipes have fun, but walking home didn't seem like a good idea. So they drove around, played music.

Bennie drove them back toward Little Falls to his home, a tiny rundown split-level in Meadow Village. A pile of stuff lay next to the garage. Bennie didn't invite them in.

"What's he doin?" Joey asked as he watched Bennie disappear into the garage.

"I dunno," Hunter said. "Think I can see through walls or something?"

"He could butt his head through a wall," Dink said.

"Huh?"

Hunter's face locked, as if he couldn't decide whether Dink was complimenting or insulting him.

"Of course he's modest about it, aren't ya, Hunt?"

"You weasel." Hunter turned to change a cassette on the tape player, ignoring the other two.

Bennie came outside through the garage door with a small cardboard box, which he put into the trunk, then returned to the driver's seat. "The wicked have waited for me." He backed the Mustang out of the driveway as Hunter's tape blasted, some hard metal Joey'd never heard.

"So, what's the mystery?" Dink shouted.

"Art Class," Bennie shouted back.

They headed into Paterson, home of Washington High, where the team would compete in two weeks. Bennie said he wanted to "get a little turf encroachment going." Hunter had made a stupid joke about there being a St. Joseph's and a St. Anthony's school in Paterson. Joey ignored it, but then the question popped up.

"You go to church with Lambros, doncha?" Hunter asked.

"Yeah."

"Are you friends?"

"No."

"Hung out with him, dincha?"

Joey didn't have to answer. Bennie cut the engine off. "Out."

Orange, black and white, with fire red for the eyes.

Joey stood before an old brick wall of a parking lot somewhere in Paterson. Bennie shook the spray cans, laid them out as Joey surveyed his color choices. Hunter and Dink were about ten yards off in either direction, watching for passing cop cars.

Joey had drawn on notepads, book covers, construction paper, even plastic once, but that didn't work. He only had a few tablets of real drawing paper. He was shy about asking for more supplies from his parents, since they always bought him wrestling gear when he asked.

But he'd never drawn on a building. It seemed too huge, not just some little scribble.

He'd tossed his jacket in the car. Bennie even brought little rubber gloves so Joey wouldn't get paint on his hands. "I don't know where to start," Joey sputtered as he held a can of black paint.

"Start where Coach tells us not to."

"Huh?"

Bennie pointed to his eye.

"Oh." Joey switched to a red can and sprayed a dot, then surrounded it with black. "Here." Bennie held the front of his own jacket close for Joey's inspection.

Once the copied outlines were done, Bennie stepped back. Joey filled the body in with white, then shaded the lower flanks with orange, making the horse look creamy, a sherbet sunset burning under its belly. He redid the legs, which were a bit off, then striated the mane in black and orange and white. It was sloppy. The cans sputtered out of paint, but he felt so fluid, drunk on the beers, wild with the action of painting. He stripped off his gloves while Bennie stowed the box. Dink and Hunter came running at the sound of Bennie's trunk slamming shut.

"Man, that is so cool."

Hunter added, "Fuckin' A."

"Awesome," Bennie said.

"What?"

"'Awesome is this place. It is the house of God and the gate of heaven.'" Joey's beer buzz or the paint fumes almost made him see something. His mural shimmered, grown from his hand, caught mid-stride, still wet on the brick wall.

94

"That looked so cool," Dink said as they drove away. "Hey, we shoulda brought a camera!" Dink shouted.

Bennie said, "There'll be more, boys. We got a busy season after New Year's."

"Leonardo da Nicci!" Dink joked as he shoved closer to Joey.

It was all a rush, a joke, something special, ridiculous, yet immensely fun, something Joey'd become privileged to be a part of, cooler than anything.

The orange and black. Wearing masks like it's always Halloween. But Dink had said it differently. "Like, it's *always* Halloween."

Now he wore those colors, shoving playfully with Dink in the same soft armor.

"Shut up, the both a yas," Bennie growled. He pulled into the parking lot of a 7-11. "Bucks for brews." He shut off the engine and held out his hand while his three passengers dug in their pockets for money under the glare of the store's lights.

"Rocks or Heinies?"

"Rocks."

"Get bottles. They smash better."

"Fine, you vandals." Bennie twisted his keys out of the ignition. The radio went silent.

"Hey! The tunes!" Hunter whined.

"So sing as angels," Bennie quipped before slamming the car door.

But Hunter followed. Dink got antsy, saying he wanted some chips, but Joey felt Dink feared being alone with him in the back seat, not like back in his home, where it was warm, and they shared, settled, got along so well.

Joey sat alone for a few minutes, watching his buddies ghost about under the 7-11's fluorescent haze. His pride about the painted colt drained as he wondered if he'd have to keep drinking to be their friends. He was smaller. He couldn't keep up. He saw them as friends long before he arrived, how if he'd never been a wrestler they would never have noticed him. They would do this whether he were there or not.

17

Bennie started calling their Saturday nights "Bible Study." Joey thought it was a little odd, although he did like Dink's joke about him and Joey being "Laps Catholics." Dink and Joey would jump into fake Swedish accents and yak about the Laps Lands, where Frozen Catholics come from. Bennie didn't get it. Neither did Dink or Joey.

But the day of the Jehovah's Witnesses clinched their pact. The four boys had been walking out of practice, laughing loudly about that day's drills in "penetration," "the high crotch," and the high single takedown, also referred to as "the snatch."

They came upon a pair of men in suits and ties, standing on the corner across the street from the school, doling out tiny books as if they were candy or crack.

Bennie did it first. He approached the tie guys calmly, then slowly started shaking, feigning an electric shock, the Lord jolting through his body. The other three looked confused a moment, then Hunter started too, then of course Dink and Joey followed along. They wiggled around on the sidewalk, the two born-again/Jehovah Witnesses looking confused, when suddenly Bennie jumped up, grabbed one of the mini-Bibles out of their hands and roared into their faces.

The boys had kept the mini-Bible after the guys ran off, twisting passages into revised versions:

"Is any pingie too hard for the Lord?"

"And she danced for him, and he was risen."

"And Obed begat Jesse, and Jesse begat David, and David befucked Queeny and they begot a duplex in Whippany, Amen."

"So Hunter an' Bennie, they gonna go out on Saturday. Ya wanna come?" Dink asked Joey just after practice on a Friday; two glorious days without the coaches on their backs. Dink dressed the way he always did, putting his hooded sweat shirt on first. It bothered Joey. He got too long a moment to steal a look at Dink's body as he stretched up into the arms of the cozy sweats, his lower torso bare. Dink didn't seem to mind Joey's glances, or he wouldn't have asked him to come along, would he?

After four times, the spray-painting got boring. Bennie said it was time to move on to other amusements.

When he had a date with a girl whose name was "Nona Yabizness," that left the three others to scrounge a bus ride for a movie or some aimless music store shopping. One such night, Joey invited Dink and Hunter over for pizza. Joey's parents were extra friendly, gave them space in the living room to channel surf. After they'd left, his mom had mentioned how nice his new friends were. Joey noticed how Hunter and Dink behaved like Stepford kids, since his parents were in their faces the whole time.

Since Bennie and Hunter politely introduced themselves to Joey's dad at the matches, Joey merely had to say he was going out with his teammates, and his dad would slip him a ten dollar bill. Before they headed out that night, a week before Christmas, with one more match before break, Joey trod the blocks to Dink's house and caught him still getting dressed.

He lay on Dink's bed, watching him walk around his room in his shorts, picking out T-shirts four at a time before deciding on one.

"So, how come Bennie's always makin' Bible wisecracks?"

"That's 'cause we didn't do that. He was a born-again. We got our own version, much more aesthetic."

"Athletic."

"No, dummy, aesthetic. You should know that."

"Whaddayou mean?"

"Bennie's father, or like his first foster father, jeez, this preacher who adopted him, nearly sent him off with the born-again shit. You shoulda seen him in junior high, man. Like, pen pockets, glasses, stern as a board, total geek. Only played football."

"So what happened?"

"I dunno. His dad kept beatin' him. Then he went back to foster program or somethin'. He's livin' with these other people now. Big guy and his wife. You met 'em at the matches. Works in a linoleum place on the One and Nine. Then he got into wrestling. That's when he started talking," Dink shrugged, then leapt onto Joey in a surprise move, shouting as he fell on him in the bed, cinching him in a not-at-all-legal nelson in two seconds, "and he used the power of Gawd ta rassle thu Angel!!"

Joey's kept giggling even after Dink conquered, then abandoned him.

Rassle the Angel.

Joey wondered how hard it must have been for a guy like Bennie to grow up, having his family fall apart. Maybe that was why he was so driven, so crazed to lift weights, slaughter guys on the mat. Dink didn't seem to have such a hard time, though, even though his parents were divorced. Dink seemed to groove on it.

That night, they did not drive aimlessly. Bennie had a plan.

The Mustang zoomed south on the Garden State Parkway, a Stone Temple Pilots tune blasting away. At one point, everybody sang along. Bennie rolled down his window, shouting the lyrics, "We are aaaall God's children! We will survive!"

They came down from the high of speeding when they turned off the freeway into East Orange.

Hunter changed the cassette. "We get the Whiner off the team, then we'll do okay."

"Whaddaya mean, get him off the team?" Joey asked. Dink gave him a glare.

Bennie turned back while driving, which made Joey nervous. "Because, dipshit, he is a loser, a total fish, and me and Hunter–" Bennie faced front, but his glare continued through the rearview mirror. "–and your sorry asses are never gonna get recruited to no colleges with scholarships if you're on a loser team, no matter how hard you try."

"That's bullshit," Joey blurted. "It's not a team sport. You're gonna be judged on your record, not–"

"Or how well you suck up to coaches," Dink blurted.

But Bennie had already slowed the Mustang down, cut the tunes and opened his door, as if waiting for them to get out of his car for disagreeing.

Joey looked down at the triangle of asphalt. Leave now, a voice said. He made a move, but Dink grabbed him.

Bennie waited a half a minute. Everyone sat silent, listening to the glug of the Mustang's guts beneath them. The cold air brushed their faces.

Bennie gave Joey a rear view mirror glare, waited, carefully closed the door. "As I was saying, they read our record, no scouts come by, and it's community college. That is not in my plan."

"Jeez, awright." Joey wanted to say how Bennie was full of shit, how he just liked to pick on guys, just lord it over.

Instead, he just kept quiet. It did sort of make sense.

The windshield didn't shatter. It crumpled.

Joey remembered that most after they zoomed away.

Bennie had driven by a porno shop near the overpass, while Hunter made jokes about the store selling videos of women "with tits out to here, I swear."

Then Bennie drove by a bar a few times where he said fags went. "Prepare yourselves for some wrath."

"I don't feel good about this," Joey muttered to Dink. He wanted to ask what they knew about gay bars, like the time they'd quizzed him about his drag queen hooker joke, but he didn't feel too snappy after the three beers he'd drunk, so he didn't want to start anything.

"C'mon. It's just a joke," Dink said as they tooled around the block the last time.

But it wasn't a joke when Bennie drove into the parking lot. Hunter spotted two guys standing close together by a car. Bennie lurched the car to a halt. He and Hunter, who had the bat, jumped out, running toward the men, who ran off.

Dink had hopped out of the car too. Joey followed.

"Come on, faggots, come on!" Hunter yelled. But they had run back into the bar. Then Hunter swung his bat around a few times, considering his options. He slammed it along the front windshield of the car they'd been leaning on, not even caring whose it was.

The windshield broke into a thousand pieces, but held together, like candy or as if it were glued together. It just clung there. Joey found that odd. He also found it odd that the music from Bennie's car still blasted away.

Part of him wanted to just tear off, run into the bar, but then they were all running back to Bennie's car, with Hunter sitting shotgun, holding his seat forward for him. He and Dink piled inside. Bennie took off before Hunter even had the door shut.

"I'm gettin' out."

"You don't even know where we are. Just let them drive us home."

The glare of the gas station lights where Bennie finally parked the Mustang almost burned. Bennie left Hunter to fill the tank while he went into the little booth of a store.

In the car, Dink hummed a song, drumming his fingers on the back of Bennie's bucket seat. Joey looked out the window, looking for any excuse to leave or say something, but he didn't know where he was. He pointed to the sign on the wall of the cashier hut. A flat disc of neon five feet high glowed a dull white. Inside the circle, a red winged horse took flight.

"Pegasus," he said.

"Huh?"

Joey pointed until Dink saw it.

"Corporate logo."

"So?"

"So, nothin.'"

"Are you stoned?"

"Just drunk, tonight."

Joey had to think about that.

Dink started drumming to Joey's silence, but stopped. "Look, I didn't wanna do that, okay? Don't worry about it."

Joey kept his eyes on anything outside the car, anything not Dink. He had to let it out, but he still found himself pointing at Dink, repointing for emphasis, just like his dad when he was beyond pissed. "Man, I spent my whole muthah-fuckin' life in Newark–"

"Dude. Don't snap at me."

"My whole life, an' I been clean the whole time."

"Neech."

"I did nothin'. I kept my nose clean. Mistah Khors, I am not up for this shit."

The back seat thunked beneath them as Hunter pulled the hose from the tank.

Dink glared back. "We won't get caught."

Hunter got in, then Bennie tossed them each a bag of nachos. Joey was starving, so kept quiet, ate with them while Bennie mucked up some break bread brother quote from Ephezius or whoever. Joey put aside what he wanted to say, that getting caught was not the point.

18

"It was the oldest school they'd ever been to. It was so old, the walls had wrinkles."

Dink narrated their tour with a serious tone which he only maintained at intervals between forced giggles.

Washington High was an inner city school that Bennie and Hunter had a dozen names for, even though they had a good wrestling record. Despite all their boasting, Joey knew they were all nervous. Being the visitor didn't make it any better. For Joey, he hadn't made morning weigh-ins. He was over by three pounds. At lunch, he'd wolfed down two peanut butter sandwiches, thinking eating faster would maybe help him digest it better.

He'd tried to cut back the days before the match, skipping dinner, but with his stomach gnawing, aching, he couldn't sleep, had snuck down to the kitchen for a late snack which became a very large snack, which ended up almost cleaning out the fridge.

Ducking into the bathroom, he spit between classes to get the water weight out. If Joey was still too far overweight, he might have to just run a few laps.

At Washington High, there were no bulletin boards with colorful posters under glass like at Little Falls, no painted murals, no modern lockers neatly clunking open and closed. It reminded him of the opera house that became a theater Joey had been to when his parents took him to see *Dumbo*. He couldn't remember where, or if it had happened. There was no Mike or Sophia then. Maybe he'd dreamt it.

He felt sad for the kids who had to go the dilapidated school. There were so many worn edges. The lockers were beaten, the walls marked, the floors sunken under cracked floors. He didn't say that, though, but tolerated the whispered jokes, Dink darting them into his ear at close range, his lips bumping Joey's earlobe.

Joey had felt great while being drunk, but all his old injuries moved up to his head and parked. He'd been drinking a lot of water to get the alcohol out, advice he read in a magazine Dink let him take home.

Since the Paterson boys' basketball team played on the same day of the wrestling matches, the teams competed in the girls' gym, a smaller, cavernous place with dark walls, cloudy high-arched windows.

Dink announced, "Diana Ross in *The Wiz, Part Three: Back to School.*"

Joey scowled. His friends didn't seem so funny anymore.

The ref was late, but Joey could have waited. Three pounds over. Wearing extra sweats on the bus ride to Paterson hadn't cut it. He stood in line with all the others in the large locker room. On one side were all the Little Falls guys, all white except for Buddha Martinez, Lamar Stevens, and Raul Klein (Jewish-Latino, he called himself "a person of not-that-much color"). They watched Fiasole and the ref check off everybody's weight on a chart.

Across from them, in an opposite line, the Washington team was all black guys, except one white kid. Some guys made jokes about it, the Washington guys blurting out "cracker," and "White boy, you gonna be flattened," little insults, boastful threats, but Joey didn't make jokes. He kept telling himself he wasn't uncomfortable standing in line in just his underpants with two dozen other guys, while the ref, who'd finally showed up, checked them in on the scales.

"You're still overweight, young man."

But Bennie cut ahead in line. "Give him a minute." Then he took Joey by the arm, signaled to Hunter, who followed them back to the lockers.

"What, you got some Ex-Lax or something?" Joey asked, crossing his arms, nervous, chilly in the clammy locker room.

"Better." Bennie sat on a bench and removed a small box from his gym bag. "Come on." He steered Joey back to the toilet stalls.

"Did Coach tell you to–"

"Coach's got nothing to do with this."

Hunter stood by the doorway in his shorts, keeping guard. Bennie stood before the sink, poured out the contents of a box. Inside the box a plastic bottle with an attachment wrapped in clear plastic fell on the counter. Bennie poured a bluish liquid out, filled the tube with tap water. "If it's warm, it feels better."

Joey read the box label for a woman's douche kit.

"You want me to. . . oh no. Aw, Jesus."

"He's got nothin' to do with it, either."

". . . I can't. . . I can't."

"You gonna forfeit to that punk 'cause a two pounds a shit?" Bennie growled, his face so close Joey could smell his anger.

Joey held his stomach to his belly.

"You shove it up. Wait. Squirt it out. It'll work."

102

"But–" There was no stall door.

"Just do it. And if that don't work, I'm stickin' my fingers down yer throat."

Joey obeyed. He parked his butt on the cold porcelain. Joey took the hose, slowly aimed it near, then at his butt. The rush of water flooded his insides.

With Bennie standing nearby, hearing every squish, it made him wonder if fucking would be anything like this. He hoped not. He pulled the tip from his ass. Immediately, water splatted out. Hunter snorted a stifled laugh.

Joey flushed the toilet. He felt further humiliated, but at least Bennie and Hunter turned their heads, even though they were both giggling as Joey crouched. Another blast plopped into the toilet. Joey felt like his insides had fallen out. He felt like the guys had pulled the worst stunt on him, but then realized a sick truth; he felt lighter already.

Hunter mumbled, "His water broke," giggling until Bennie hushed him, approached the stall. "You okay?"

"Yeah." He grimaced, leaned forward on the toilet to hide his dick.

"Okay. We'll see you out there." Bennie and Hunter left.

He felt queasy, more than just the usual.

Another chunk slid out. Joey's body relaxed. He felt dizzy, didn't know if he could stand up. He looked at the stall walls coated in scribbles of graffiti. 'Got AIDS Yet?' and 'Die Fags.'

The ref called out, "Nickey, one-twenty-six pounds. Last call!"

A few kids gabbed away in the balcony above the gym. Having them up and far away made Joey feel like the teams were in a pen.

Joey looked around at the gym, wondering how many years of kids had played in the space. Washington was a huge school but the girl's gym didn't even have a score board. He just felt sorry for them, how the mat was connected with used tape, uneven, curling up at the ends. They probably had no money in their program. They didn't even have sweat pants, just hooded sweat shirts that simply read WASHINGTON WRESTLING.

Visiting teams always had the mat first for warm-ups, so the Colts didn't have the luxury of their well-rehearsed dramatic entrance like the home team, who jogged out in formation as they ran from the locker room to trot down around the mat in a circle.

Joey and the rest of the Colts had retreated to their side of the mat. Joey didn't feel like warming up more, afraid he would leak. He'd had to run to the bathroom again, even though he'd already made weight.

He lay down a moment, just trying to get himself back in order, get ready. He tried to meditate, imagine himself winning, what moves he would use, envisioning a swift single leg takedown. He looked up at the gym ceiling. The only light was a diffused white through three looming arced windows like St. Augustine's, except there were no saints in colored glass. Metal webbing made the gym resemble a prison.

Joey returned to the team, ignoring their gassy sound effects, foraged in his bag for his water bottle. Fiasole and Cleshun headed off to the tables to go over the line-up, chat with the other coaches.

Anthony sat by the wall, pouting. Joey gave him a glance that might have turned into some sort of show of support, but then Bennie strolled up to him, kicking Anthony's gym bag away from his own.

"Hey, who touched my clothes?" Bennie looked around. "Whiner?"

Anthony shrugged.

Joey stood, shrugged his shoulders. Other guys just ignored Bennie, something Joey wished he could do. How could Bennie make helping out feel so cruel?

"Hey, I'm talkin' to you, pee wee."

Joey turned away.

"Don't call me pee wee," he heard Anthony say.

"That's what you are. You got a dick the size of a noodle."

"Oh, you lookin' at my dick?"

"Fuck you." Sounds, grunting.

"Go ahead."

"You better win this time." Bennie loomed over Anthony, almost ready to kick. Anthony's head aimed down, four inches from the floor. From five feet away anyone would think Bennie was merely showing a move to another pal.

"Hey, go easy on him, Bennie. He's gotta make it through his match."

Bennie relented, let Anthony up. His face flushed, he blinked, wiped off his neck, then said, "Why don't you just worry about your own match?"

"I don't have to worry," Bennie said. "I worry about you."

"Well, I worry about you guys. I know you go out drinkin'. I

know somebody's been doing a little extracurricular art project."
Anthony glared at Joey.

Joey's jaw dropped. How could he know?

"What are you, playin' snoop?" Bennie was on Anthony again,
feigning arm grabs that kept hitting closer and closer to Anthony's
head. Anthony couldn't get out from either side, so Joey said,
"Duck."

Anthony did. Bennie halted himself from chasing after the boy.

Joey looked for Coach Fiasole.

Fiasole's eyes across the gym caught Joey's, then beyond him,
where he could see Bennie shoving Anthony.

Fiasole barked out a "Hey!" then was upon him, argued quietly,
intensely. Bennie received a telling off. Joey moved in to see
Anthony, whom Fiasole had pulled away. Bennie blurted something
that enraged Fiasole.

"Oh yeah?" Fiasole seethed. "The meek shall inherit the earth.
Love of your brother. Love of your fellow man. What happened to
that, Mister Skaal? Are you in there, Mister Skaal?"

Joey kept his distance, watching Bennie stand silently, nodding
occasionally. Fiasole twice thudded a pointed finger into Bennie's
chest. Joey turned around, pretended not to be listening, but other
kids paced, staring, until Cleshun got into it, separated Bennie from
Fiasole. Walt ambled by with two oranges. He offered one to Joey.
"Thanks."

"You see what Bennie did?"

"Sort of."

"Why's Coach screamin' at him?"

"He was pickin' on Lambros."

"Well," Walt said. "That's why we're all starin.' Everybody likes
seein' the big guy get dressed down. We all been there, but seein'
the big guys fall is just more fun."

Walt wandered off to hang with the other guys and eat. Joey dug
down into his bag. His water bottle had spilled all over his street
clothes.

The ref finally arrived. Anthony, obviously still upset, waited for
the signal to take the mat. He kept tapping his foot in a way that
annoyed Joey. "Why'd you bait Bennie like that?" he asked.

"I was not baiting him. I was telling the truth."

"So? Same difference."

"Coach said he could smell beer on your sweat every Monday.
You're gonna get caught."

"You're a liar."

The ref walked out onto the mat.

Anthony stood. "Joseph." He struggled with his headgear, nearly tripped on his sweat pants, but finally got out on the mat, after saying, "I am not the liar here."

At first everybody figured Anthony was just wimping out as usual. But then he fell down in the second period, collapsed. Coach yelled for somebody to get his inhaler from his gym bag. Joey and a few others stood but Joey found it first.

Assistant Coach Fiasole and the Washington coach hovered over his prone body as he thrashed about, trying to breathe. Joey handed the inhaler to Cleshun, who tried to aim it over Anthony's mouth, but the boy couldn't even muster the strength to bring his head up.

Joey used his T-shirt to fan the air above Anthony, but it didn't do any good. "Go sit down," Assistant Coach Fiasole said. Joey obeyed.

The men hovered over Anthony a while, then Fiasole left the gym. The other opponent, a skinny black kid, sat in the middle of the mat, bending over his seated frame, stretching, waiting patiently.

"You hungry?" Dink took a bite out of a sandwich he'd plucked from his bag.

"Naw." Then he looked back accusingly at Dink. "How can you eat?"

"I'm hungry. He gets better or not, I'm still hungry."

"You are one considerate guy."

"Come on, just a bite." Dink held the sandwich out to Joey.

"Get that outta my face."

He did want to take a bite, almost exactly where Dink had bitten would have been nice, but he was up next, whenever next would be. He could just imagine coughing up a chunk of peanut butter and butter sandwich.

"Look at that," Dink said.

Coach Fiasole led two men in long black coats with yellow stripes. One held a toolbox full of medical supplies. The coaches parted, giving the firemen room to examine Anthony. All Joey could see were Anthony's legs sticking out of the cluster of men, bending over, discussing, concerned.

Some of the Washington kids began tousling about, just joke wrestling. All the coaches were bent over Anthony, not at all paying attention. Other Washington kids walked around, impatient with the interruption from the match.

Anthony was brought up to sitting, was breathing, at least.

Joey wasn't upset or concerned for Anthony so much anymore, but almost jealous. But he sat with his teammates on the bench, hoods up, waiting. Joey saw a few school kids in jeans climb down from the low balcony, drop their backpacks, coats, just play. They had no inhibitions, while he and his clan perched, obedient. Their attitude looked like more fun.

But then he thought about that day, the dogpile, and those times where they'd all done stuff like that, and it was good that a coach was there to keep them all calm, or Anthony or him or any other guy would get dogpiled all the time. It wears on a guy.

"He'll be okay," Coach Cleshun said.

No one said, "Oh boy, am I relieved," or "We were so concerned." They just sat, Dink eating, Bennie plugged into his thrash tunes, Hunter clenching and unclenching his fists, tapping his feet, Walt Cryzinski picking a scab, while Coach shouted technical advice with a bit more strain than usual.

The rest of the match finally got going, but by then Joey felt cold, his legs stiffened taffy. He tried to use the first half of the period to just get warm again, fake a few single legs, just top the guy, but the other guy grabbed all over him, bendable, quick.

At one point, he had Joey's head in both his hands, and he pulled, and something in Joey's neck ripped. He yanked himself out in an escape.

He'd never felt his back on the mat so much since his first year. Fortunately the ref was slow. Once, the timer, a chubby girl with long tresses of black hair, forgot to start the clock, so they got some leeway, a long breather when the ref had to check a two-point takedown. Joey felt like he was going to pass out, too.

Commands and cheers tumbled around in his ears. The wash of shouts banged against those old walls, until he only heard a ringing, then sometime later, it was over, his arm was grabbed, raised.

Joey had caught his breath, shaken hands with his opponent, the opposing coach, retreated behind the bench to peel his singlet down to his waist. He tucked his headgear into his bag, pulled his shirt out to let it dry off. He'd probably have to wear his sweats home.

"Get some ice on that neck," Coach Fiasole called out to Joey before crossing back to the scorekeeping table. Joey dutifully went over to the cooler full of ice Fiasole had put into little plastic bags.

Since his opponent was a no-show, Dink won by default, jokingly raising his hands in victory, as if he'd had to work for it. Some of the other guys won. A few lost. Joey wasn't paying attention. His neck began its little twinge response. His guts felt weird. Where had they taken Anthony?

Hunter was up to his usual tactics, and got a warning when he shoved a guy who he had down after the ref blew the whistle for time. A player was supposed to help a guy up. It was supposed to be all in fun. But Hunter seemed determined to pummel the guy who so easily held on to his defensive moves. He never got Hunter in more than one good hold, but Hunter still scowled, even after his victory. When he was supposed to shake, he just slapped the guy's hand. The black kid smiled, showing for all how childish Hunter behaved.

By then, a crowd had drawn, all of them Washington kids.

Bennie had been skipping rope, slapping his legs and face all through Hunter's match. He came bursting out onto the mat, determined to attack from the beginning. The Washington guy had a sharp angled cut. His muscles pressed out in all directions. They faced off. The floor rumbled with their first throws.

At one point Bennie had his opponent in his arms. He stood, lifting him off the mat, about to slam the guy down to the floor, but the ref said, "Easy."

Bennie slowed, then more politely lay the guy down before cross-facing him.

"Like spreadin' pizza dough," Dink said. Joey saw. Bennie could reserve his power, like driving his Mustang. He worked on half-capacity. What was scary was what Bennie didn't do.

Coach Fiasole argued with the ref in the locker room doorway, something about insurance. Everybody rushed to get in and out of the showers. Fiasole kept yellin' "Hustle! Hustle!" clapping his hands. There would be no victorious anything, except the numbers.

"Hey, how's Anthony?" Joey rushed up to Fiasole, who seemed a bit wired.

"He'll be okay. Just go get changed and let's get outta here."

"But–"

"Go." A smack on the butt. That worked.

A few guys tried to repeat the hypothalamoose call, but it wasn't very funny after a few times. It still had a useful charm when wrestlers met up, but with the draft of a broken window making the room extra cold, the joke fell flat. Few showered.

By the time Joey finished changing, Bennie walked by.

"Hey man, what did Anthony say to you?"

"What?" Bennie stopped, turned, his bag over one shoulder.

"What you did, what'd you say to Anthony?"

Bennie dropped his bag, loomed over Joey in a way that made him want to back away. But Bennie stopped.

"What did I say? Like you think I got him all upset and it's my fault he doesn't know how to breathe?"

"I'm just sayin' why you gotta be that way with your own team member?"

"Team member?" Bennie's neck muscles flexed. Joey wondered how long it took him to shave that neck every morning. At the same time, he wondered if Bennie was going to punch him. "Listen, little man. I been on this team three years. You don't know how we do things here. It's not like Saint Ingratius or wherever you come from. You don't tell me squat."

"I'm sorry, I was just–"

"If he can't cut it, he's out. There's better JVs in Paramus."

"No, there isn't. Tommy's a spaz, but he tries, and Lamar's out."

"Dude, he broke his arm."

"That's not the point."

Bennie grabbed Joey's shoulder before he could turn away. "You don't seem to get it, bro. This is hard work. This is not recess. There has to be a sacrifice."

"What?"

Bennie's fingers clutched Joey's biceps, his fingers filing through the striations of muscle, checking Joey's growth. Bennie softened his grip, blinked a few times, as if he didn't understand what he'd said. "We have to sacrifice for our team, right?"

"Yeah. . ." Flooded with embarrassment, lust, fear, Joey stood as Bennie steamed down a bit, retracted himself from Joey, picked up his bag. His expression changed gears into a false look of fatherly concern. "Just. . .do your best. We all . . . just gotta do our best."

"Yeah. Right."

As he dressed, Joey wanted to turn around, see if Bennie was still looking at him, what mood he might try next.

As they tumbled onto the bus, Fiasole stood at the door, counting them, glaring each boy to silence. Everybody settled down, the losses or wins replayed in their heads. Behind him Joey heard Walt and Hunter whispering something about Anthony.

With Cleshun off to the hospital, Fiasole didn't even have to say anything, just sat up front staring out the window with the driver. Nobody even coughed.

Dink didn't say much in the seat behind him. Joey had to sit sideways against the window, but it scraped his back, so he turned around. He looked at the guys sitting in front of him, like little monks in a chapel on wheels, all hoods up, except Buddha Martinez, his hair so black. Joey wanted to touch Buddha, but he only stared, then staring became exhausting. He closed his eyes, feigning sleep the whole ride back to the school parking lot.

He didn't relax until after dinner, some tube, the tub. He made sure everybody else had finished first, assuring his parents that a good hot bath would restore not only his muscle fiber and accelerate the healing of injuries but boost his post-dinner carb build-up and rejuvenate his endocrine system. He wasn't sure what it all meant, but it sounded impressive.

"Just don't fall asleep in there again," his mother joked. "I don't want you drowning in my new bathroom."

To be invoked for healing from both physical and spiritual wounds, the card read. Tonight was definitely the neck. He read a prayer, figuring it was a good idea to say one for Anthony. He considered saying one for Bennie, asking him for patience, but then he remembered Bennie being so weird, yet incredibly sexy. He lay under the covers, wishing he'd taken care of business in the tub while he had a chance.

19
MEGAZOID's EVIL PEGASAURUS
DON'T JUST BUILD 'EM! BRING 'EM TO LIFE!™

Amid the boxes of Grobots, Star Trek ship models and other "age 6 and up" toys, Mike pointed to a two-by-three foot box. On the box cover, a photo of a four-legged beast in shiny black plastic held him transfixed. Its forelegs glistened, silvery, its body a red and black cluster of sharp angles. At its hind quarters rockets and blades jutted out. Red wings hovered over a mane of black blades. Its silver eyes glared with a cold fury.

Joey had come to the Willowbrook Mall with his father on Saturday, which was Christmas Eve, to buy presents for anybody he'd "forgotten." Mike wanted to tag along, so he had to help him get presents, too. Their dad said he'd meet them at the hardware department of Sears, giving them an hour to shop.

"So, are we getting a new VCR?" Mike had asked.

Joey had mentioned it in the car, but his father scoffed at the idea. "That's all we need, you watching wrestling tapes all day and Sophie wanting to sing some Barney song for the hundredth time."

Then Joey felt guilty, not even thinking that Anthony might end up spending Christmas in bed. He'd called Coach Cleshun to find out, but all he got was "Steve and Anne aren't in, but if you leave a message. . ." over "O Night Divine." He'd left a message.

"Are we?"

"I dunno." Joey didn't want to worry about VCRs. That Washington kid had left what he hoped wasn't a permanent dent in his spine. Even though he took three aspirin with breakfast, he walked carefully, not turning his neck too fast or bending over for anything, worried some crazed shopper might bump into him again. The entire mall bustled like an anthill after somebody kicked it.

Maybe his mother would like a new pair of earrings, small ones. Joey picked out a pair while Mike stared under the counter at the rows of bottles, holding his nose amid the heavily perfumed women's department. The moment the counter girl, who kept smiling at Joey, put the little box in a bag, Mike said, "Come on. I wanna show you something."

He'd led Joey to a toy store, "so we can get Soph's presents," but Joey knew Mike couldn't be so enthused about getting something for their sister.

His instincts were right.

"You put it together." Mike said, holding the Pegasaurus box. "It moves and shoots these rockets, see?"

Joey thwapped his finger at the corner of the box. "It's forty dollars." But it wasn't the price that made him frown. As creepy as it was, Joey considered getting one for Bennie to put on the hood of his car. "I ain't gettin' you that."

"No, stupid," Mike sighed. "You tell Dad to get it for me." He clutched the box as if he already owned it.

"I don't think so. And don't call me stupid."

"You get stupid stuff. Your dumb wrestling shit."

"My equipment is not dumb. Stow it or you're gettin' squat."

"I'm leaving."

"We're getting our sister's presents, remember?"

Mike stormed off to Mermaid Land, abandoning him. A mother with a herd of kids gave Joey a glance. He turned away, his neck twinging with a shard of pain. He caught up with Mike, who'd grabbed a mermaid doll.

"Do you have enough money?" Joey said as they stood at the counter behind about two dozen people.

"Duh. I can count."

When they finished, Joey said, "Okay, I gotta go get something else. You gotta stay somewhere."

"The toy place."

"That's where I'm getting your present."

"Oh. Bookstore."

"Okay. Ten minutes."

Mike saluted in mock obedience. Joey sort of smiled, as if maybe they'd reached a truce. He wanted not to care for just a few minutes.

Rushing back to the toy store, he grabbed an X-Men action figure he didn't think Mike had. He walked back to the department store, through Men's Clothing, trying not to think about how Wolverine and the Pegawhatsit both reminded him of Bennie. He was supposed to have a crush on Dink. Wasn't that enough of a problem?

In the Men's Department, rows, stacks of ties, shirts, suits hung in neat rows. He soaked in the smell of leather wallets, belts, the swirling patterns in the ties, the shirts layered like a dad factory. He knew better than picking a tie for Dino, who only wore ties when he went to church, which was close to never.

Joey moved to a display with fancy underwear, boxers, silk paisleys, even one with a bright yellow smiley face, its tongue sticking out in a silent Yum. He thought it might be a funny gift, but then blushed. *Underwear. I want to buy something that's gonna be right next to his . . .*

Almost touching a pair of shorts, a thin clerk appeared out of nowhere, scared him off with a lisping, "Can I help you find something?"

Mike, surprisingly, was actually in the bookstore, poring over a book on female sexuality. So much for that question.

"Come on. Let's go to the hardware place," he said to Mike, leading him out of the same place where he'd swiped the Marky

112

Mark book. He felt relaxed there, as if stealing something there had made it his turf.

"But Dad'll be there!"

"Not yet," he said as he tugged Mike along. "That was his way of sayin' he wants somethin' from there. We gotta figure out what it is."

It wasn't easy. He put his father's workbench, neat and orderly down in the basement, in his head. His dad had everything from his years of plumbing. Maybe some new gadget, a drill or a level? No, it had to be special.

"If we go in together, we can both get him one thing," Joey offered, trying to erase the option of stealing something again. But Dink wasn't around to dare him.

"What? Whaddawe get him?"

A new toolbox would wipe them both out.

"Look at this!" Mike pointed. Among the plumbing tools hung a plaque. It was a joke gift, stupid maybe, but just stupid enough to make his father laugh. The plaque featured a man lying in a tub with his bare feet up, a smile on his face, smoking a cigar. Around him were a dozen tangled pipes, a cartoon effort to stop a leaky pipe. Below the cartoon it said, "World's Greatest Plumber."

"We got you something really funny," Mike teased when they met up with their father.

"Hey, don't give it away." Joey had made his purchases quickly, relieved to forget about the whole thing. It wasn't that he'd spent a lot of time thinking about the gifts. He'd already had Dink's present hidden away in his room, and he didn't have to buy anything.

"Hey. Merry etceteras!" Dink sang into the phone.

"I'm dreaming of a gray Christmas!" They laughed at Joey's joke about the traditional New Jersey holiday drizzle.

"Mind if I stop by?"

"Sure, man. I gotta warn ya, though. My mom's got about a ton of cookies. She's been force feeding anyone who comes by."

"Ooh, I'm scared. I think my mom's gonna make me bring over some monster cake thing."

"As long as it's not a fruit."

"Cake."

The canopy of crossed arms, the flex in the legs, the effort; he'd captured it. He almost wanted to keep it, but then knew. He'd made this drawing of the two wrestlers just for Dink. It was a picture of the two of them.

Using a piece of cardboard and some brightly colored paper, he carefully wrapped his first masterpiece, which he'd labored over for days.

When Joey heard the doorbell, he deliberately waited upstairs, shoving away the scissors, tape, savoring Dink's arrival. He tingled with anticipation, heard the cheerful chatter below, then waited for the thud of steps bounding up the stairs.

"Hey."

"Hey."

"Ta da." Dink held out a little gift-wrapped square box. His face and varsity coat glistened with droplets of melted snow.

"Gee, I wonder what it is."

"Can't open it till tomorrow."

"You too." He handed Dink the gift. Dink's look was one of curiosity, as if he hadn't expected anything.

"Hey man, thanks."

"It's nothing." It was everything.

They were inches apart, alone. The moment where they could have shared a first kiss passed like a toy train.

"So! You into some Grinchness?"

"Sure. Not." Then Dink fell back on Joey's bed, his varsity jacket and sweatshirt slid up, showing a peek of belly. Joey wanted to tumble down on top of him, just playing. He didn't. He satisfied himself in knowing that the sock he'd stolen lay under the mattress, once again inches from its owner.

"So, you havin' all the relatives over?" Then Joey cut if off. "Oh, sorry."

"It's okay. Really, it's okay." Dink sat up, peeled off his coat, tossing it on the floor. "Actually, I'm doin' Christmas early with Mom, then Dad's pickin' me up for the afternoon. Lucky for me, her parents are back in Michigan and Dad's mom is makin' dinner so we don't have to cook and she's so old she falls asleep. Then Dad an' me drink a glass of brandy."

"Where's she live?"

"Metuchen."

"Hell of a ride."

"Yeah, but it's neat. Streets are like empty. We zoom. We'll be back day after tomorrow."

"We're goin' to my grandmama's in Newark. They're havin' this huge-oid dinner like always."

"The big Eye-talian fambly."

"Whaddayou, makin' fun of me again?"

"No, man, chill, I just–"

"It's okay. I was jokin'."

There followed a predictable pause that Dink knew to break. "How old is she, your Gramma?"

"Actually she's my great-grandmother. 'Bout eighty."

"Grampas all gone?"

"Yeah."

"The men always die sooner."

"Where'd you hear that?"

"It's a medical fact."

"Is not."

"Is so."

"You're so weird sometimes."

"Don't call me weird."

"What?"

"I'm not weird, dude. I'm like, just elsewhere sometimes."

"Like when you're stoned."

"Look, I don't. . . shit." Dink sat up. "Do I push it on you? Do I? No, I respect your space, awright? What I know, and what Coach don' know, and what you better not tell him, is remember those pins I got, those times I was so relaxed, all the times I won?"

"Yeah."

"I was slightly stoned then, okay? I say it works, that mellows me, an' I don't hurt, which is okay."

While waiting for Dink to unhurl, to toss off the words he needed to say, Joey stared at a corner of his desk, wondering if any stains showed, if there was anything Dink could do to make him stop hurting for loving a guy so messed up. Joey's face and ears burned the way his whole body burned after practice. Troy once said that it was the team's germs burrowing into him.

Dink tried to shrug off the silence, but he was up, walking around Joey's room. "So, when all the 'family' time's done, we could go out, y'know. With Bennie and Hunter."

Joey tried to hide his surge of, what? He didn't know. Fear? Jealousy? He just wanted to spend time with Dink. "I dunno. Those guys are buggin'."

"You don't like doin' that punk stuff, do ya?" Dink's face fell slack, without a trace of teasing. "Aw, don't sweat it. They just like, get dopey. Besides, once wrestling's over, they'll forget we existed."

"So why we go out with them?"

"You got a car? Or a driver's license, even? Can you go out an' buy a six-pack? Can you get into an R movie ever?"

"Well, no, but–"

"So, let's just have fun with them while it's fun, okay?"

Joey could have argued, but he didn't want to. If Dink had said, let's go jump in a pile of mud, he'd have done it. So he just growled a line from a Nirvana song, "Forever in debt to your priceless advice." That got Dink grinning again, but he stood up, grabbed his coat.

"Be real nice to your parents now, so when you ask to go out, they let you outta the cage."

"Right."

"So, what's this you said about Ton 'o Cookies?"

Dink thanked Joey's parents graciously, his gifts secured in a plastic bag. His mom once again said what a nice friend he had. Joey agreed.

Before Sophia and Mike were sent to bed, Joey helped them set a little plate of cookies and a glass of milk on the dining room table. It was really for Sophia that they were doing it, since Mike kept making wisecracks about "the fat guy getting stuck in the chimney."

Sophie peeked up, her chin just shy of the table. "You gotta leave him something too, Joeeo."

"Well, Sophio, I'd leave him a protein smoothie but it would get all gloppy by the time he gets here."

"Joey, don't be obnoxious."

"Whoah. Where'd you get that one?"

On TV, Bing Crosby sang with David Bowie. His parents lay at opposite ends of the sofa, their legs entwined in the middle, Marie the recipient of a long-promised foot massage.

"Didn't we see him at the Meadowlands?" Dino asked.

"That was Bob Seger," she corrected.

"Oh, right."

"How could you confuse Bob Seger with David Bowie?"

"Who did I see Bowie with?"

"Sharon Kelly." She kicked him. "Who he dated twice before he met me."

"Oh, yeah," his dad said. "Wonder what happened to her?"

"I took you off her hands and she lived happily ever after."

Sitting across the room from them, Joey tried to see his parents as the kind of kids who did things like that. Joey wondered if they'd partied, if that little nudge his mother gave his father said, Don't talk about that. That was when we were wild.

Sensing another rampant heterosexual display of affection, Joey kissed his parents goodnight, hightailed it up to his room, ripped the wrapping paper open to see what he knew Dink's present was.

Four cassettes, each one a special music mix. Dink had even listed the songs on the inside and used pictures from wrestling magazines to decorate the outside of the cassettes. There were four titles: GRAPPLE!, AAURGGH!, PSYCH UP! and one called ZONE OUT, all written in Dink's neat handwriting, the tapes full of different tunes Joey had heard at Dink's place, music Dink knew he'd like.

He'd tried to listen to them all before he fell asleep around midnight, but ended up listening to ZONE OUT, which had all slow songs, love songs, sad songs that had nothing to do with Christmas, but made him feel a warm joy that took him off to a half-dream where he and Dink were competing for the world federation championship, cheered on by a crowd, both winners, which he knew was impossible, since he'd never done tag team.

20

"Drops your cocks and grab yer socks! It's Chr-r-ristmas, sold-juh!!"

Joey woke up with his earphone wires wrapped around his neck, his batteries dead, a pajama-ed Mike bouncing off his bed, a bell-ringing Sophia doing a jig up and down the hall.

Under the tree, little and middle-sized gifts wrapped in reindeer-striped paper surrounded a big box in the middle of the room.

After too many mornings of sweaters, stockings full of Pez, stick and ball sports equipment, he'd learned to make lists, get what he wanted, within reason, be happy to watch Mike and Soph do the screaming while his father took pictures. Stuff didn't matter much to Joey.

But the big box sat in the middle. Even though everybody knew what it was, his dad said, "Wait, that's for everybody, from Santa."

His mother was appreciative, happy with her presents: clothes his father had picked out secretly, on his own, wrapped in a quartet of matching different-sized boxes. His mother had gotten him nice clothes.

Sophia's toys were all pink and plastic girl stuff. Mike made a point of showing his disapproval, making her whine a bit, until Joey promised to play Little Mermaid games with her later. Sophia had made paper angels for everybody.

Mike didn't get his Evil Pegasaurus, but with all the other toys and stocking candy, he must have forgotten about it.

Ankle-deep in wrapping paper, by the blinking tinsel and ornament-encrusted tree, Joey sat content before his new pair of white Converse shoes wrapped in virginal plastic, his new sweater, a pair of jeans he could actually wear to school, since his mother "found out they were supposed to be baggy, even though I did not understand, this lovely boy at the store said all the kids were wearing them like that, so anyway, if they don't fit, you can take them back."

"No, Ma, I'm sure they'll fit. Thank you."

His father laughed at the plaque, said he would hang it up over his workbench, exactly where Joey had imagined it.

"We gotta open the big box!" Mike insisted.

"First, everybody gets a little something else." Dino, in a show of theatricality he only made at Christmas, wedding anniversaries, maybe a birthday, pulled a quartet of similarly shaped boxes from behind the sofa. He doled them out like playing cards, and had everyone open them at the same time.

Sophia, of course, shrieked with joy upon unwrapping her copy of *The Little Mermaid.* Mike howled with glee at his own *Batman,* which he would immediately memorize and quote constantly. Marie got *The Sound of Music,* and Joey *Olympic Highlights.*

Only then did his father allow Mike to shred the wrapping paper open to reveal what Joey knew was inside, a new VCR. Everybody clapped, hooted. Showtime.

Mike became more interested in the Styrofoam packing for a while. Joey was intent on plugging it all in ASAP. The sooner they got bored, the sooner he could study his real homework: matches.

Then his father said, "Marie, did we forget something?"

His mother tried to act confused, but as she arched her eyebrows too high Joey knew something was up. What was it this time, a car? A dog? Probably something so overblown it would surely be a disappointment, like the time they led him out to the driveway in Newark blindfolded. He was supposed to be excited about a new bike, but it was totally wrong for him, more the kind Mike would have wanted, did and quickly inherited.

Instead it was a box. Inside, his already broken-in varsity jacket lay neatly folded. Joey got it. They were reminding him that they had paid for the coat. He would definitely have to get a job after wrestling. He owed them.

"Thanks."

He was about to get up for the round of thank-you kisses, but his mother said, "Wait, wait. Inside."

He looked down under the folds of his jacket. Nestled deep inside like twin babies lay a pair of new black suede Asics International Lyte wrestling shoes, with orange laces already entwined through the holes.

"Those old ones you wear were really getting smelly," his mother said.

"Yer mother went crazy tryin' to find them."

"Well, I had to go all over with Irene. Why don't they sell them in stores? Maybe the size number's different than your regular shoes, I thought, and the number was all faded away. . ."

"She went while we were shopping."

"Besides, I figured these would look better with your uniform."

Dit. Dit. Dit. The sound of his tears christening the shoes.

So very embarrassed about it, he got up, hiding his eyes behind his parents' faces, letting the gush pass while he hugged them. He wanted this moment to last for a long time, so he even posed for extra pictures to finish the roll so they could drop them off at the Photo Hut on the way back to Newark.

21

"A priest and a nun are riding through the desert on a camel."

"Where are they going?"

Laughter.

"I dunno. They're, they're escaping the Philistines."

"Why didn't they take a horse?"

A little less laughter.

"That's not the point. They're going into the desert. It's very dry. The camel passes out from lack of water."

"That's impossible–"

"Shhh."

"So the nun says, 'What are we gonna do?' The priest says, 'Pray.' So they pray, but the camel's getting worse. Finally the priest turns to the nun and says, 'You know, Mother Superior, we might die out here. Is there anything you've always wanted to do before dying?' The nun says, 'No.' The priest says, 'Before I die I would like to make love to a woman just once.' The nun says, 'What'll that do?" and the priest is flustered, totally desperate, so he says, 'It'll give us eternal life.' So the nun says, 'Forget about me, go fuck the camel!'"

Grampa Nicci got away with telling that joke at the dinner table only once. Joey never forgot it, because it was the only time he ever blew milk threw his nose. Years later, Joey's father told him that Grampa Nicci dragged out the joke so that everybody would laugh the moment Joey gulped his milk.

Grampa Nicci was a funny guy.

He usually sat engulfed by the great red chair that cushioned him from his increasingly frequent hacking coughs. By then, he was not so funny.

Grampa Nicci died messy.

Joey still feared his memory. Moving away had made it less scary, simply mysterious.

With all the war pictures of Grampa in Vietnam, Grandpapa in World War II, Grandma in Newark, Grandmama as a girl in Milan, then in New York with her new husband, mementos hanging, looming, the den was more fascinating this time.

The initial reason for his fear was also a family joke. As a young child, Joey was afraid to go in the room when he heard Grampa Nicci say that "Grandpapa was killed in our den."

Joey didn't remember misunderstanding that his great grandfather, then only twenty, with a pregnant wife back in the states, was an infantryman in World War II, killed in the Ardennes, the dense forest in Belgium. It was one of those non-memories that relatives told him he experienced. Someone might mention it on a visit to Grandmama or Aunt Lilla's little home in Nutley. It was just another repeated bit of conversation between people who were very close, but really had nothing much to say to each other. It filled the time, reminded them why they loved each other.

Sophia and Mike had each been allowed to bring a toy to Grandmama Nicci's to keep them occupied for the drive down to Newark. Sophia sat her Little Mermaid doll in her lap, the hem of her best dress peeking out from under her coat. Mike occasionally made pre-emptive strikes on Joey's head with his new Wolverine. Joey couldn't exactly bring his new Asics, so he wore his varsity jacket over his suit, which felt dumb, so he left it in the car. Joey hoped he'd see some of his old friends. Part of him didn't want to see them, though. He didn't understand that fear.

He could tell how nervous his mother was by the way she and his father were quietly arguing in the front seat, or else not speaking at all, except to Sophia or Mike, telling them how nice everything would be if they would just behave. It was as if his parents talked to each other through their children when they didn't want to talk to each other.

His mother was more nervous, since it was his father's relatives they were visiting, like she had something to prove, to show how happy they were, now that they'd moved away from "the rest of the family."

The house was as he remembered it: dark, musty, but with sweet smells of cooking food, furniture polish, every table filled with knick-knacks. Grandmama liked the radio, couldn't see a television well enough even if she had one, so the kids had to find something better to do.

Other relatives crowded the kitchen, talking loud, frightening him off with fawning adulation every time he entered. Aunt Joyce's husband, Uncle Harry, who wasn't Italian, was being especially nice, as if still seeking approval, even though he was a rich executive with some accounting firm in Elizabeth. Joey and Mike secretly called him Uncle Boring.

Joey's father's brother, Rico Nicci, had moved with his family to Atlanta years before to make a mint in hospital management. He acquired a large house they had yet to visit, but had seen pictures of. They were called to the phone to be nice with the relatives they rarely saw. Mike got shy all of a sudden, his eyes dull, saying only "Uh-huh," and "yeah," reciting his list of gifts into the receiver. Joey made a face while Mike held a finger to his ear.

When it was Joey's turn, he talked with his Aunt Alicia, being polite, wondering if she remembered what he looked like. Then his Uncle Rico got on the phone, asked how his wrestling was doing.

"Pretty good."

"You gonna be a champion, ah?"

"Sure."

"Like Hulk Hogan, ah?"

"Actually, I'm more the Kendall Cross type."

"Who?"

"Or Terry Brands."

"What?"

"Tom, on a good day."

"You have a nice Christmas, ah? Putcha father back on the phone."

"Dad." Joey handed it over, relieved of another duty, eavesdropped on his father's brotherly talk, realized his father was the Mike of his family.

Everybody talked, chatted, eating, drinking. Joey wanted a beer, but he knew he wouldn't be able to find one. Sneaking wine was OOTQ, which was pronounced "Ooty-cue." It stood for Out Of The Question, a term Dink taught him.

Maybe just one beer after dinner, if he asked.

After hiding outside until it was too cold, he found his father in the den, standing with—how convenient!—a beer in his hand, talking with Uncle Boring, who was smoking a cigar. Joey tried to dodge the cloud, but his father caught his eye.

"There he is." He collared him with one arm. His dad would make something up, as they did sometimes, instant secret jokes.

"So, how long have you been wrestling, Joe?" Uncle Boring seemed interested, for the moment.

"This my third year." He squinted through smoke.

"You're getting pretty good, I hear." He nudged Dino's elbow, spilling a bit of his beer.

"I'll get you another," Joey said.

"No, no, it's fine."

"Nineteen-two," Dino said. Joey noticed his father was a tad drunk. Marie, with the women in the living room, the desserts and lots of coffee, would be driving.

"Scuse me?" Uncle Boring cocked his ear.

"His record. Nineteen wins, two losses."

"Twenny," Joey corrected.

"Oh, sorry," his dad patted him.

"Our boy's on the football squad," Uncle Boring said, then, "Right Guard."

Joey often wondered if he had some sort of allergy to the sport. His eyes went glassy anytime someone mentioned football. He did not get it, couldn't follow the rules, could admire the butts, but in more situations, found the need to at least pretend to listen to the men gossip about certain players' private lives, stats. He heard there was a gay one, tried to think of his name, figure out where to find out, drew a blank.

All the while, through the stiff shoulder of his jacket, he felt his father's hand, felt a warmth, a pride of ownership.

Napkins delicately cradled silverware in little china holders that were taken out once a year. He heard the rattle of his cousins in the hall, the mumbles of over-friendly relatives pretending to enjoy each others' company, even though after every gathering his parents would sigh with relief once they were in the car, away, or his dad would fart and his mother would roll down the window in disgust while the kids all laughed. He longed to be gone, finished with this show. He knew the script. He craved Dink. Dink was unwritten.

A steaming bowl of glazed carrots preceded his mother. She set them on the side table. "Why don't you go be with your cousins?"

"Be? Be with?"

"Don't get smart." She headed back to the kitchen. "Just go."

"Awright."

But adult talk was dumb, and the other kids silly. Bratty Matty and Theresa, snooty since they went to a private school, sat in the living room with Grandmama, probably hoping to get some extra presents for good behavior. Joey had gotten a tie and shirt. His mother got a sweater. Uncle Boring gave his father a bottle of whiskey in a fancy box, which may have explained why they were being so nice to each other.

Joey wound his way around the old house back to the Our Den.

His glanced at the more recent family portrait of Sophia's christening. A little bundle in her mother's arms, his father beside her, proud, beaming, Joey and his brother stood stiff in suits, dwarfish sentries to their parents.

In the baby pictures, the young portrait photos of his father's high school graduation next to another of his Uncle Rico, who was thicker around the face, Joey saw his father, then maybe eighteen, and saw part of himself.

Joey looked along a small bookshelf, spied a few photo albums. He took one out, an old one he remembered seeing once, years ago. He flipped through the black paper pages. The photos had wavy edges snug in little corner frames. Some of them had fallen out, leaving ghostlike squares.

People stood in front of row houses, like the one where he'd spent the first fourteen years growing up in Newark. There was a succession of children who became mothers, soldiers, plumbers, lawyers. Aunt Nina, who died before he was born, somewhere in a group photo at a factory in Linden, had made planes in World War II. She'd moved to Arizona.

He felt glad his father never had to be a soldier, but a slight longing came over him. Where would he be on the wall if he didn't come up with a wife, babies? Would they still include him if he never did any of that? Would the pictures just stop?

Joey nearly dropped the album. Photos fell to the floor as he turned to see Grandmama Nicci standing in the door. Bratty Matty and Theresa guarded either side of her.

"You like to see old times, eh?"

"Yes, Grandmama."

"You gotta siddown," Matty said.

"Go eat someting. *Andate.*" She waved them off like servants. Joey bent down to retrieve the fallen photos, stole a glance at his Grandmama's feet as she delicately stepped into the room. Her shoes were dark black. Her hose sagged a bit at her ankles.

He stood. She smiled, her skin crinkling around her eyes. He could see the curve of her skull under the wisps of white hair.

"I'll put these back in."

"Sokay. I do later. Lemme see."

He held out the photos, found one of his Grandpapa.

"You see. You look just like him. *Bello.*"

She pointed a bony finger at the photo, then put her frail hand to his face. Joey blushed, returned his gaze to the picture. His great-grandfather grinned, no more than a teenager, standing in the snow, a tarp over his shoulders, a gun strapped to his shoulder pointed upward from behind his back. Joey peered into the blurry image, let out a little sigh.

"Some boy, *un compagno,* took dat. He send it when my Giuseppe, he froze in da woods waiting out da goddamn Nazis. Dint find him until de snow gone. Many month. We come all way here to have him go back there and die. A crime, no?"

Joey wanted to laugh, hearing his Grandmama swear, but he knew she still hurt after all these years.

"You take." She pushed the photo toward him.

"Huh? Oh, no Grandmama, I couldn't."

"I gonna die some day. They all take, take," she nodded toward the door. "I give you now. For Christmas, extra, ah?"

He couldn't refuse the link, the fragile bond from one generation to the next, the lost pieces, the lost men. "Thank you." He hugged her, delicately. He put the album away, carefully placing the photo in his suit pocket.

They had set the table, the kids were running around, getting excited. Everyone sat to eat, Joey at the far end of the big table, no longer at the little folding card table with the kids. He didn't have to talk. He just ate and ate, forgetting Coach's warning about "overindulging during the holidays." He would sweat it off.

22

"Bitchin' drawin', dude."

"Thanks."

"I'm getting it framed."

"Great."

"Hangin' it right over my bed."

Joey wished he could work some sort of spell, like in a movie, where he could peer out from the drawing, watch Dink all night long.

Dink hadn't called for three days. Joey decided he wouldn't call first. That would make him seem like he was itching for a compliment about the drawing, or like he was a grabby girlfriend. He did not want that. He'd waited.

"So, you like the tapes?"

"Like 'em?" Joey said. "Man, they are awesome. I got my ears plugged up all day."

"And?" Dink hinted.

"And what?"

"Something else?"

Joey didn't want to tell him about the Asics. He wanted to show them off in school, but he told Dink anyway.

"I called your mom about them," Dink giggled.

"You did that?"

"Well, I didn't think they'd know to do it, so–"

"You're like my fairy godmother."

"Hey, I'm not your godmother."

Joey just laughed, nervous, giddy. "So, look, I'm like sorry about the other night. It's like I just don't–"

125

"Forget about it, awright? You don't wanna. I'm not askin' you to. I'm just like–"

"I know it's like, really."

"Fine. Fine. Whatever."

In that pause, they came together again, like when they locked up on the mat, tested the waters. Joey realized they hadn't touched in over a week. He craved it.

"So, ya wanna get together for New Year's?" Dink asked.

If Dink tried to hump him this time, he knew he wouldn't push him off. He imagined their first kiss starting off 1994 with a real bang.

"Saturday night?"

"Sure."

"Be at my house at eight. Bennie's pickin' us up at nine."

Damn. "The posse?" Joey whined.

"What?"

"I just–Dink, I don't like those guys. Do you . . . do like Bennie and Hunter get stoned?"

"Hunter? Hell, he's so dumb he'd catch fire if he tried. Naw, man. And Bennie? Naw, but I think he tried juice."

"Oh. Juice?"

"Roids."

"Oh." Then, "Let's be friends with some other guys."

"Who? Walt and the twins are like those Simpsons neighbors–"

"Who?"

"You know, 'Hide-el-ee Ho!'"

"Oh, yeah–"

"The Flanders, fer chrissake, and, I mean Buddha and the little guys are nice, but I mean they're totally–"

"What?"

"Dweebs."

"So?"

"And the others are either the God Squad or JVs who can't even tie their own shoes–"

"They ain't that bad–"

"Okay, but–"

"I mean other guys too."

"What? Guys who don't wrestle? Forget it."

"Whaddayou mean, forget it?"

"They don't have a clue of what we're going through."

Joey was silenced by the truth. If they weren't brothers, they weren't friends. Wrestling wasn't just something they did. It was a different world, a different language.

"The thing is, Neech, we already picked our friends for the year, you know? I mean, wasn't it the same way in Newark, except they call them, uh, gangs?"

"You are such the jerk."

"And you love it."

Joey waited, hearing Dink's breath catching up. He couldn't say anything. It wasn't that he didn't believe Dink. He knew the ranks, the barriers, how he had moved away from boys who in younger grades he'd befriended but eventually pulled away from; geeks, fags, wimps. Wrestling had pulled him out of that. He was now a proud geek, or a fag jock, or something.

"Neech?"

He had new shoes, a best friend who might put out. He was gonna rock the mat once school got back in session. Even those muscleheads couldn't mess things up.

23

The "huge-ass party" Hunter boasted about turned out to be a private affair in Alpine with a bunch of rich college kids. The guy who invited Hunter was nowhere to be found. They didn't know anybody else, and no one else was wearing a varsity jacket, so the four of them stood out like re-painted lawn jockeys. Joey wanted to escape immediately and just walk home.

He would have explained it to Dink later. But even Bennie relented, promised other amusements.

Since he sat in the back seat, didn't have a door, he had to ride along. Besides, Bennie drove them. Bennie always drove.

They kept drinking beers. Hunter produced a bottle of holiday peppermint schnapps he'd swiped from the party. They goaded Joey into gulping a shot, then another.

"Aulgh. Tastes like cough syrup."

They laughed, each took a swig. Joey felt more than drunk. He was getting dizzy, not saying much. His gut rumbled as if it might fall through the low seats down to the ground below. Joey tried not to think of moving things, but the car kept hitting bumps. Bennie kept gunning the motor, making Joey's stomach lurch. Where were they? Weren't they going home? He saw a large lake to his right. A sign. Cedar Grove Reservoir.

"Where are we?" Joey moaned.

"Are we there yet?" Hunter mocked him. Dink's eyes were glazed. Maybe he felt as awful about bashing the car window as Joey did. Maybe he didn't feel anything.

"Near home, Neech. Hold tight."

"I gotta piss," Joey mumbled.

"Let it flow." Bennie scanned his right, then veered off. The Mustang gurgled low. Hunter pulled his seat forward. Joey stumbled out, momentarily afraid they might leave him on the roadside as a sick joke. Then he figured that might not be so bad.

"Hurry up," Hunter shouted.

He couldn't just do it in the middle of the road with the guys watching. He found a shrub, ambled over to it, his vision blurred. He looked out at the water, saw his breath escape in cold whirls, fished out his dick. After a few sputters, it gushed for minutes. He kept swaying, having to right himself.

He tried to trot back to the car, but had to steady himself, moving slowly to stumble into the back seat. "Man, you musta had a whole gallon in there," Dink said, still sipping his beer.

Joey said nothing.

Hunter pointed ahead at a pair of passing headlights. A white subcompact slowed as it passed. The driver glanced at them, accelerated, sped off.

"Hey, look at that car."

"Which one?" Bennie asked.

"The Pinto!"

"Pinto?"

"Could it be?"

"Our little Whiner?"

"C'mon."

Bennie wheeled the car around on the road. Joey felt his guts slide sideways. Dink spilled beer on his coat. "Shit, man."

"Sorry."

The Pinto kept up a steady pace. Bennie soon caught up, tailing from about fifty feet behind.

"Don't rear-end him." Hunter laughed, then made an exploding sound.

They followed the Pinto up the northwest edge of the Reservoir, where it turned on Ridge Road.

"Where's he goin'?" Dink asked.

Hunter said, "I think home."

"Naw," Bennie said. "He's on the prowl."

"This is so dumb," Dink said. "We don't even like the guy and we're following him on New Year's Eve. If you hadn't been such an asshole we'd still be at that party-"

"Patience, brother," Bennie said.

"Bullshit," Dink muttered.

"What?" Joey mumbled. Why were they following Anthony?

"He's gonna pull off."

"See?" The Pinto turned right, up the onramp.

Bennie sighed, as if bored but determined to follow through, as if he knew what he was doing. He floored the gas, veered away from another car, then up and onto the highway.

Bennie gunned the motor to catch up, until the Pinto burned white from his headlights.

"You're too close!"

Hunter poked half his body out the window, reaching, lunging for Anthony's window.

Anthony once again pulled back, gripping his steering wheel. He braked, but then so did Bennie. The two cars edged close together, then scraped in a moment of metallic ripping that made Joey scream.

"Shit! My fuckin' car!"

"Fuck this. Slow down, Bennie!"

Joey watched from the tiny rear window as Anthony veered right, getting smaller and smaller, then braking slowly, disappearing behind them.

Bennie pulled on the brakes.

Anthony loomed forward again, steering right.

"What the fuck are you doing!" Dink screamed.

Bennie's eyes seethed in the rear view. He pulled right, ending in front of Anthony, who pulled back, then zoomed forward. Hunter twisted back from shotgun, hoisted a bottle. Dink and Joey both jerked their heads back to see beer foam coat Anthony's windshield.

That was when the Pinto went off the road.

For the briefest moment, Dink and Joey looked at each other, frozen, afraid to move, to say anything.

Hunter blurted, "Holy shit."

Anthony's car weaved over to the gutter.

Bennie slowed down, pulled over. "Aw fuck him, he's just gotta wipe it off. Look, he even turned his blinkers on."

Bennie did not turn back. He merely glanced at his rear view mirror. Joey saw the red from Anthony's Pinto flashing on his forehead before Bennie ripped himself out of the driver's seat. He heard Bennie's heavy clomping steps as he walked down the road, away.

Hunter followed, leaving the door ajar.

Dink kept darting his head back and forth, looking to Joey, along the road. Joey couldn't move his head. He was afraid of what would happen if he moved. He crept his eyes toward Dink, who peered out the rear window. "Oh, shit, no. Stay here."

"Huh?"

Heat escaped the car. Joey shivered. Was Anthony okay? Were they getting an ambulance? Were the cops there yet? The red light continued to blink. No cars came by. What was happening?

Joey slowly, carefully peeled himself out of the back seat, trudged down the roadside over gravel.

Were they doing something with Anthony? Maybe helping him, like the time he passed out at the match in Paterson?

No.

They were doing something to Anthony.

Bennie had him in his car, holding him down. When he saw Joey approach, he said, "C'mon, Neech. Get your punches in."

Hunter held Dink back with an armbar that verged on permanent injury. "Get back in the fuckin' car!" he shouted. Joey wasn't listening. Dink couldn't help.

Joey leaned against the Pinto, his legs giving way. He had to bend over. Bennie's feet stuck out of the back seat door. Joey heard sounds, like Anthony gasping.

Anthony was getting fucked, or killed, or both.

Joey had to hurl.

He heard Bennie say, "We'll fill that little mouth up so it doesn't talk. A fool's mouth is his destruction." He heard the clink, the sound of a belt knocking against the buckle, the sound of a zipper.

The last part of Anthony that Joey saw alive was his hand. It clutched the tip of the driver's seat, almost ripping the fabric, his small fingers gripping it like a claw, before it fell out of view.

Joey leaned against the Pinto's bumper, coughing, spitting, then falling to all fours. Little pieces of gravel bit into his palms and knees.

Dink started bawling, yelling, "Stop it! Stop it!" Hunter twisted his arm more until Dink was down to the ground, as low as Joey, whose guts were about to roll out like a carpet.

A gurgling force swirled around in his belly, punched its way up through his throat, mouth, nose. He lost the beers, dinner, Christmas cookies, lunch, even, it seemed, the last bitter mucousy gasps of breakfast. He kept crawling, backing away as the small lake of steaming barf spread before him. He heard Bennie retreating from the car, Hunter groaning in revulsion.

Hunter said, "Shit, he's puking' and the other one's havin' an asthma attack."

"Let's go."

Joey felt someone's arms grabbing him. They were screaming at each other. All Joey heard above Hunter and Dink was Bennie threatening.

He thought he was next.

He'd made it a good distance away from the guys, felt like he was running, but by the time he figured out which direction was towards the car, the ground fell up to meet his face.

Some arms held him up. He unraveled inside, coughing, expecting another bucket of acid to jump out of his gut. He tried to snort a burning chunk out of his nose.

Dink whispered into his ear, "Come on, Neech, we gotta go now," pushing him down the road, lifting him up and in. Joey tried to hold on, but his jacket got caught on a sharp edge of Bennie's car door. He didn't even get to say anything before they dropped him in the back seat, Dink not even holding him up or letting him lay in his lap, just pushing his head down to the floor as he coughed, sputtered.

Nothing came out, even though the smell of the dirty floor runners mixed in with the burning in his nose made him want to be sick again. He could only feel relieved. His body quivered. Blood pounded in his head.

A few inches away he noticed that one of Dink's shoes was untied.

Above them, Joey heard Bennie mutter, "We have to meet up again."

"In jail, mutherfucker!" Dink shouted.

"Man, just shut up–" Hunter's voice above him.

"No, you shut up!"

"You faggots narc on me and you are all dead, you hear me?!?" Bennie's monstrous shout silenced them all. His voice almost made the Mustang itself vibrate. "I don't care how long it takes, but you narc on me and I will eat you alive!!"

"Shit, man, what the−"

Joey tried to say something, but it came out garbled.

"He's passed out," Dink said, as Joey felt his hand pressing down, holding him down.

No one spoke for miles.

"We're gonna meet up," Bennie said.

"When? It's already one. We gotta get him home. I gotta go home."

"Tomorrow." Bennie commanded. "I'll call everybody. Now just shut the fuck up about it."

Joey found his hand had crept down to his stomach, clutching it, holding, but really, his hand wanted to be close to his chest, as if he could push his ribs down to slow his heart from thumping.

Dink began muttering something familiar to him as breathing. Joey heard Bennie try to catch up to their words. He started to join in while automatically reaching inside his varsity jacket, under his sweatshirt to find, along the thin metal string, his crucifix, ". . . is with thee. Blessed art thou among women. Blessed is the fruit of thy womb, Jesus. Holy Mary, Mother of God, pray for us sinners, now and at the hour of our death. Amen."

They dumped him off in front of his house. He told himself he didn't know what happened. No, he wasn't considering that. He was considering the distance from the sidewalk through the door, from the door to the downstairs bathroom, if there might be interference.

He coughed out a ghost of a hurl, washed his face, rinsed off bits of barf and asphalt from his jacket. He found some old mouthwash under the sink, gargled, sat, his shorts around his ankles, on the toilet, when he heard a knock. "Yeah."

"Are you okay?" his father whispered.

"Yeah." He finished, flushed the toilet. Opening the door, the glare of the bathroom painted his father's face a ghastly color. He hadn't been sleeping.

"Were you drinking?"

"Yeah."

Joey waited. Come on. Hit me. Knock me out. Please.

"I take it this was your first time being shitfaced?"

"Ungh. Dad. I'm sorry."

"Firing squad at dawn. Happy New Year."

His father scowled, padded away, barefoot, bathrobed, back upstairs.

24

"Why are they hangin' the flag at half mast?"

"That kid what got killed."

"I heard he was in a car wreck."

"What was his name?"

"No, he got beat up or mugged."

"Lambrusci something."

"For a guy like that? He wasn't even popular."

Dink? Absent.

Hunter? Unknown.

Bennie? Mustang not spotted by lunchtime.

He couldn't remember where he got that new knuckle scab, but pretending to be fascinated by it helped him dodge the glances around his desk. Kids in class wanted to see him break down, cry. He could almost feel them waiting for it. They knew he knew Anthony, was of the same tribe.

In the halls, his jacket off, they didn't know:

"Did you hear the joke?"

"What?"

"Why'd Anthony get stoned the night he died?"

"Why?"

"'Cause he wanted to die a Lambros-co on the rocks."

"That's stupid."

While eating, or giving the impression that he was:

"I heard he was up at the graveyard, 'cause that's where all the fags go."

"Hey, you know what gay stands for?"

"Guys, guys, he was on our team. Let's not–"

"Oh, come on, Klein, we're just having some fun."

"Did you get on the tube?"

"Naw, they left before I got to say anything. I think I got my face in, though."

Over the loudspeakers: ". . .that our uh counselors will be coming to homerooms throughout the week to uh talk about this tragedy. Any students who feel they need to talk with them sooner uh can come to the Assistant Principal's office to uh make an appointment. . ."

He grew a headache in second period, stopped into the Nurse's office, not for "crisis counseling," but for an aspirin. He saw Hunter down one hallway, dodged him. The guys were starting to ask him about Dink.

Frozen clumps of mud trimmed the streets outside. He'd spent all Sunday trying to find the nerve to just tell his parents everything, spill it out. But everything held, waiting. He was told to rake leaves in the rain.

Maybe Anthony was okay. Maybe somebody found him, took him to the hospital.

When he would have to act surprised, could he act as sorry as he was? Could he do it then? Would that be mistaken for genuine innocent sorrow? If he bawled like people expected, he knew his feelings for Anthony, the real ones, the loving, wish-I'd-been his friend, wish-I'd-told-him, wish-I'd-kissed-him feelings would roll out like a flood.

In the hall, huddled in groups, sharing rumors, he could see some girls crying, or acting as if they were crying. They didn't even know Anthony.

But Chrissie Wright did. She huddled next to Kimberly Holbrook, the other mat maid. He considering turning around, maybe ducking all the way around the school to avoid them, but he'd been doing that all day, dodging some football guy who resembled Bennie from fifty yards.

"Oh, Joe, my God, isn't it awful?" Chrissie's thin arms were around him, her sweet perfume surrounding him, her light combed-out hair in his face. He brought his right arm around her back, clamping his hand down on his raised books. His biceps twitched.

Almost landing on the strap of her bra under her sweater, he darted his palm down, then tried to release her, but she started crying, his chin parked on her shoulder as if it were a chopping block. Kids passing by stopped, or slowed, some of them, their eyes welling up. It was contagious.

Behind Chrissie, Kimberly crossed her arms, obviously over the sobbing phase. Kimberly was already medicated. "Yeah, it's terrible. I can't even think. Is this sick or what?"

Chrissie sobbed. "I mean, he was so good, he was just tryin' his best, but who could have done it?"

He almost said it, but it got caught on the way out. The flood came up, choking him in the throat. He hugged closer to Chrissie, closing his eyes, letting the drops fall on her shoulder.

The bell rang.

"What are we gonna do?"

He released Chrissie, wiped her tears off with his fingers. "Pray for his soul." He walked on to class, leaving them both, stuck his finger in his mouth long enough to taste her salt. "Among others."

A strip of the list where Anthony's name had been was cut off. The piece had been put on the banner wall, in a frame.

Coach Cleshun stood in the middle of the mat with his arms crossed in a knotted bundle. Assistant Coach Fiasole stood nearby, but never said a word. His eyes were bloodshot. Beside him, Dink stood in street clothes.

Hunter looked freaked as the others silently entered the practice room. Joey could tell. Their shared glances shot around the room like lasers, silently asking, 'Where's Bennie?'

"Circle," Coach Cleshun said.

Colts crouched or kneeled.

Coach announced, "We will have a talk."

Just that one sentence kept them silent. Hunter stood at opposite corners from Joey and Dink, pieces of a broken compass.

The talk turned out to be few words, all of them Cleshun's.

"I know it's already been going around the school all day, that one of our team members, Anthony Lambros, was found dead yesterday. Despite the rumors and the talk I want to hear none of that coming from a team member. We will honor and respect Anthony Lambros in memory."

Cleshun sort of choked on the last part. "Any of you. . . who might be having. . . personal problems . . . I wish you would . . . I want you to please talk to me or your parents or anyone you can trust. No matter what you are feeling, no matter what your problems are, nothing is worth. . . doing something that could hurt yourself or someone else."

He kept tripping over his words, but it was understood. A few guys were trying to hide their tears. Fiasole would not even look at him or anyone, but kept his head bowed, hands over his face.

Coach waited for someone to bring up a topic, to ask a question. "There will be no practice today. Go home and think about that."

"But we got a match against Montclair tomorrow," Hunter blurted.

"Go! Now!"

The team flew apart. Boys ran off toward the lockers, some directly out the door.

Across what was the circle, Hunter stood apart, on the other side, doing anything not to look at anyone.

Joey had to tell. He had to tell.

Guide of Pilgrims, direct my steps in the straight path.

He hoped one of the men could reassure him, talk to him, but he couldn't bring it up. Dink signalled with a nod. *Outside.*

Hunter kept lingering at the door, the potential stranglehold he could apply looming behind his glare. Fiasole had begun pacing, just walking away. Cleshun stood, staring at nothing.

A few guys puttered in the locker room, bouncing their voices off the walls, which were oddly dry, the echoes quiet.

"Jeez, at least he could have told us not to suit up," Troy grumbled.

"That was the point," Buddha Martinez said.

It felt as if Hunter had gone. He must have gone.

But when Hunter appeared behind him, Joey turned, afraid of anything. Hunter only stared down at him, sang softly in a voice like the guy in Pearl Jam, "Anthony spoke in. . . cla-a-ass today."

He wanted to punch him, scream, but he sat, relacing his new shoes, again.

Hunter walked away.

Some lockers slammed. Some guys came by, patted his back.

Dink whipped around a corner.

"What did you say?"

"Hold your mud, Neech. We're gonna get out of this."

"What, are you gonna steal a car now?"

"No man, we have got to be together on this." Dink's hand gripped his shoulder. "We were not even there."

"No way."

"Are we gonna stick together on this?" Dink asked.

"Not with those goons."

"No, not them. You and me. We did not do it. You didn't do

136

anything. I didn't do anything. You hurled. I got punched."

"Did you tell? I'm tellin'."

"I say you didn't. You say I didn't. We're fifteen. We'll get off. Believe me. I know. Max told–"

"How does he know?"

"Just–" Dink released his grip on his shoulder. "No matter what, we gotta stick together."

He wanted to hug Dink right there, just grab him.

"Dink?"

"Yeah." He tucked his shirt in, got frustrated, yanked it back out.

"This is some heavy shit."

"You got that. Oh, you gotta come to my house, get some tapes, before they bust me."

"What?"

"Neech, just–"

"Could you, could you not call me Neech anymore?"

"Whaddayou talkin' about?"

"Dink. . . Donald."

Dink winced.

"We're maybe gonna have to keep our mouths shut and go to court and wear suits and ties and then tell everything."

"Dude, I am so reamed. I got priors."

"What?"

Dink held two pinched fingers to his lips.

"Look, if they do and even if they don't you are no longer Dink to me. Dya unnastand what I'm sayin'? What you said, about Orange and Black."

"What?"

"It's always Halloween."

Dink leaned in, put his hand on his shoulder as if knighting him. "Joseph most just. Joseph most chaste. Joseph most cute."

They were staring eye to eye like they had never done before. He was obliged to do it now.

He leaned in, kissed Dink, just once, on the side of his face, expecting a shove or a push, something that would help him do what he knew he might have to do, narc on the boy he loved.

But Dink moved his face toward Joey's lips. His lips parted just a moment to where it was wet and their tongues met. He wanted to think of it as a sexy love kiss, but even a dumb jock Laps Catholic knew about kisses.

137

Joey stared, blinked, slightly amazed. They pulled apart at the crunch of a distant locker. Dink hovered close, whispered, "We got about an hour."

"Till what?"

"Till your dad or my mom figure out we're MIA. Till the end of the world. Alone. In my house."

He waited, gulped.

Dink pressed his partner's nose, transforming him. "Are you with me?"

They knew all the moves, they'd just never done them naked, but they knew each other's bodies, knew their limits, how far to pull a leg and grip an elbow and how long it can last before another shift exposes slowly with no whistles to stop a visit along an underarm always too rushed past by a mouth or nose. Now he could see that mole on a left lat, an island in a milky muscle sea. Instead of grabbing, he licked. No more secret stolen drops. He could lick long and slow, remain inside and over every corner and curve. He grabbed tight, holding him, humping him, until he peeled him off, muttering, "Stop." "What?" "Stop wrestling." He grabbed his wrists, held him, kissed him again, as if pouring a slow wet love into him, to slow him down, hold back the rush. He straddled him, humped his cock up along the crevice of his butt. He let his cock bap up and down with every one of his thrusts, until he grabbed it, tugging it closer to him. He jerked his neck up from the pillows, opening his mouth in a wet silent shout. He aimed for teeth and got tongue. He caught the first glop like a grape. They laughed as it happened. He felt a flood of relief as jets of him exploded on his face, his neck, licking it up, pulling him down, sucking his face, gluing himself closer. Entangled, encrusted with each other's fluids, they dozed for what felt a night, a lifetime, as if they levitated over fields and plains. Half-awake, he feared movement, for it would initiate departure. The light was gray, half-night as they lay in silence. He was asked if he wanted to shower. "No," he whispered, holding his sticky belly like an unfinished painting, a souvenir for the ache inside. "I love your back muscles," he said as he kissed his back. "Latissimus dorsi." "I love your nose. It's so horsey." "Horsey? Fuck you." "Next time." He nestled closer. "You know, your nose muscles flare when you come." "Nose muscles?" He kissed them. "Snortissimus dorsi." They slurped more and coughed and shared spit and extracted hairs from between their teeth and swallowed and dry-kissed each other. They traded clothes.

Led to the door, holding hands as they descended the steps, he remembered the first time he'd been in this room, wondered about all this. He remembered climbing these stairs months ago, his partner's skin peeking from his sweats. What would it have been like if they'd been able to just fuck like straight kids? There never would have been a care about anyone else and no one would have been hurt, no one would. They kissed again, clutched dicks, the skin around lips and helmets chafed. Walking backwards as the sidewalk took him further and further from the house, he tried not to cry, but joy and pain formed tears too wondrous to halt, too wondrous not to crave rushing back up for more.

"I'll see ya tomorrow."

"Maybe."

"It'll be okay."

"No, Don. It won't ever."

1

"Oh my god, did you hear?"

"Yup."

She went to hug him. Joseph pulled away, afraid she'd smell Dink on him. He didn't know what she knew, what would come out if he started bawling.

"You're all wet. Why are you still sweating? Were you just running?"

"Yeah. I, uh, gotta take a shower."

"Where you been?" his father's voice commanded from the kitchen.

"Go and eat first."

The cloud of steam, signifying the pasta's readiness, had long before settled over the kitchen. He was that late.

But that was not the bother. The bother was trying to pretend nothing had happened when less than an hour ago he'd been splooging all over his best friend and accomplice.

"You hot? Open a window," his dad suggested.

"It's freezing outside."

"Take something off. Take off your sweat shirt."

"I'm okay." Maybe it was the sweat shirt, or the pasta burning his throat, or the third glass of water. He wasn't concerned about the sweat droplets falling onto his plate. They came out of him. They could just as well go back in. He wondered how long before those particles of Dink he'd licked would become a part of him. Would he taste more like Dink?

Food, he reminded himself. You are sitting at the table. Pick up your fork.

"Wipe your face."

"Your napkin."

He used his sleeve.

"It's Sophia's turn to say grace."

"Dear Lord. . ." she started.

From the living room, the tube answered. "An altar boy's bizarre murder leaves a New Jersey town in shock. Coming up on Eyewitness News."

"Hey, that's about Anthony."

"I need some water." He bolted from the table.

"I'll get it." His mother scooted her chair out. "Sit. Sit."

"I'll get it!" He darted out of the kitchen, pulled off his sweatshirt, tossing it on a chair.

"It is difficult to understand the logic of murder, but in this it is simple to understand the pain the Lambros family is feeling tonight. In Totowa, New Jersey, John Soto tells the story."

The reporter stood solemnly a moment, the mike poised near his chin. A car alarm went off a few blocks away, on the tube or outside.

He grabbed the remote. POWER OFF.

"Why did you do that?" his mother yelled.

"I'm sick of news while I eat."

"I want to hear about that."

"Well, I don't, not while I'm eating," his father said. "Leave it off." He agreed with his father, but for all the wrong reasons.

"Dino, this was one of his–"

"I wanna watch it!" Mike yelped.

"It'll still be on when we're done eating. You. Sit. Let's calm down here."

Everyone returned to the table, but his mother wouldn't let up. "What do you know about this?"

Her look pierced him. He dropped his head, paced around the living room, considered escape. No. OOTQ.

He headed back to the table, sat. "I heard about it. We had a talk in practice. The principal made announcements and everything."

"Why didn't you tell us?"

"I didn't want to talk about it." Everyone at school did, though.

"Why not?"

"Because I'm upset! Okay?"

"Keep your voice down."

Forks clattered against plates and teeth. Gulps. He hung his head, staring at the patterns in the plate. Was Dink taking a shower now? Was Dink lying to his mother now? Was Dink ever going to do any of that fun stuff with him ever again? His ears were ringing. He felt as if they could see his blood pulsing.

He looked up. His entire family stared at him in the sort of silence that precedes an earthquake.

"He was a fag." Mike blurted.

In response, the entire contents of his plate landed with a thup sound in the middle of Mike's chest.

His mother's gasp matched Mike's. She leaned forward, smacked

143

his head. The entire table rumbled, a smash of dishes, liquids, arms.

"Don't you ever say that again!"

He shut his eyes as the sting of his mother's slap set in.

When he opened them, Mike's chair had fallen over, Mike himself hung by the scruff of his sauce-spattered neck from his father's grip. Sophie's tiny mouth ripped open, winding up for a really big howl.

"Dino!" Marie shrieked while Mike milked a choking sound. Dino dropped Mike, who fell to the floor.

"Pick it up!" he commanded.

Mike pulled his chair up meekly, rubbing his throat for sympathy.

"It's true." Mike muttered, then glared at his brother with the pure hatred a ten-year-old never hides.

His father shook Mike again, then shoved him down. "Shut up. Eat."

"I can't eat."

"Then go to your room! Sophie! Stop crying."

Mike darted to the living room. Marie extracted Sophia from her chair, held her close. Her little legs clamped around her mother like a starfish. Her cries became muffled in her mother's arms. He and Dino followed them into the living room to see on the tube, that sad little beat-up Pinto.

That's when he lost it.

He bawled all the way back into the kitchen, howling like a cub in a trap, almost out the door, before his father grabbed him, yanked him back. He collapsed to the floor, shoved off his father's attempt of a hug. He was unworthy, untouchable.

Doors upstairs closed, muffling a tandem crying jag. He leaned forward, grabbed paper towels from the roll under the sink, snorted a blast of tear-filled snot.

"You were there?"

"Yessir."

"You're telling me everything right now."

"Yessir."

Before they were done, his father told him to make the phone call. While they waited, his mother goaded him into eating. He did, but more in the motion of comfort than comfort itself, fuel for his trip to the realm of minors and major miracles.

He didn't finish dinner.

The cops show up a lot faster in Little Falls.

2

"You said that after you all attacked him—"

"I didn't attack him!"

"Sorry, after they attacked him." Another man entered the room. They murmured something.

"Will you excuse me a second, Joe? Sergeant, come with me a moment."

He looked at the hard blank walls of the room the policemen brought him to, where he'd spent two hours spilling his guts, telling them everything. He wondered if he would now spend his days in jail. He wondered what his dad thought about while he waited in the hallway, waiting to smack him, ground him for the rest of his life. Maybe a police van awaited him, then prison and a career as butt boy for guys with tattoos up to their armpits.

The men at the police station were bigger than his father, thick in the face and belly, looked as if they'd never laughed at a joke in their lives.

One of the detectives twirled a set of keys in his hand.

"C'mon, Joe. We're going for a ride."

The way he said it sounded a lot like Bennie.

They took him into a police car, sat him in the back again, behind the caged front seat. When he figured out where they were taking him, he got a sick feeling in his stomach.

"The site" was being dutifully, meticulously inspected, searched under bright lights by a dozen men on their hands and knees with magnifying glasses looking sideways across the ground. One of them, who had been trained in the Marines before joining the police force, he heard, had made a joke about looking for tiny land mines.

They had him point to the area where it happened. Police cars guarded the surrounding area, a little piece of offramp.

The roar of traffic blocked words in the darkness and harsh floodlights. The POLICE LINE DO NOT CROSS tape glowed a sick yellow, fluttering in the breeze. Above the main road back toward home, a restaurant sign beaconed: Anthony's.

He looked down to a stain in the gravel, felt ridiculous having to identify his own barf.

"You see, what we're trying to determine here, Joe," the detective said as he patted his shoulder, "is what you, your friends did or didn't do. We're telling only what we know, not what just you remember. We're pretty sure it is, but we want to be really sure. Now, go over again what you said."

He looked around, trying to remember this patch of road through drunken eyes. Beyond it, he could see sprinkled lights in the darkness, under hills. Somewhere across that highway sat his new home, where he felt he should want to be.

"You said you're not from here?" one of the detectives said.

"Newark."

"And Italy before that?"

He nodded, couldn't tell if he was being pumped for more information or if the detective was just making conversation.

"Mine are from Italy and France, Germany and Spokane," the detective smiled.

"Spokane? How'd that get in there?"

"We get around. We're all pilgrims."

"They tell you?" the boy asked.

"You gave a statement."

"Um, yeah, um."

"Did you sign it?"

"Oh." He didn't know what to say, except, "I'm sorry. Yeah. Was I not sposed to?"

His father took that in, sighed, turned onto a main thoroughfare through town. He had that lost look in his eyes. Maybe it was just the events, being confused.

Finally, his father said, "Can we start with why?"

"Why."

"Why you were out with them."

"We hang out. They're on the team. You met them."

"Who killed him?"

"Bennie."

"But you did something, in the car."

"I didn't do anything except get sick."

"But they did."

"Yeah."

"Why?"

146

"I dunno."

"Why would they do something like this?"

"I tole ya, I dunno!"

That's when the smack came.

He almost forgot he was definitely going to get one, so his slouch was especially slack, his mouth hung open a bit, when the callused palm of his father caught him about the jaw and upper neck. He kept his eyes shut until he'd scooted further away in the seat, almost ready to fall out the door. He couldn't believe how his father could hit him so hard and not even swerve the car.

They drove in silence for a while. He realized that his father was driving south, too far south. He didn't say anything. This was not the time for corrections.

After several more minutes, Dino said, "Did you do it?"

"What?"

"Kill him?"

"No, Da, I'm tellin' ya, we went out–"

"Who?"

"Bennie and Hunter and Dink and me. We went out had some beers and Bennie gets this idea to go out driving I don't know, I think to a party but we left there then they saw Anthony and followed him and like you know ran along beside him and they were just jokin' but then it got outta hand and then Hunter threw the bottle, then Bennie–"

"What do you mean, outta hand? The one 'at threw the bottle? Did you throw anything at this kid, I swear, if you–"

"No! I was so sick by then, I'm sorry, I am so sorry–"

"Stop it, stop it. Here. Take this. Wipe your nose. So, what, what did you guys do after that?"

"What, they tole you?"

"Yes."

"Oh, well, then you know."

"Know what?"

"They did it 'cause he's a total runt on the team, everybody hates him. He's gay. Was."

"What? How do you know that?"

"I am, too."

He figured it best to toss that in while the other fusillades landed, distract him.

Instead Dino pulled over in the middle of traffic.

Joseph yanked his neck around, looking in back at a honking

car. He felt a shred of pain from his last injury. Cars behind them veered off, away. His father's face twisted into a knot of confusion. He pointed his finger three times while saying, "Tell me. . . everything. . . now."

"Um, they just hated him 'cause he's, you know a, and. . . and. . .and I think I'm. . . I mean, we talked about it, but we knew, I mean we just. . . knew."

"What, you like read each other's minds?"

"I was. . . No."

He wanted to hit the radio, the wipers, anything, just not be inside a machine, feeling so bad about being in so much trouble. He could smell his father's spilt coffee mixed with Sophie's bag of Cheerios under the seat. He hadn't scheduled this conversation, not today, while he could still feel Dink's bites and chafes.

His father looked out the windshield at nothing, trying to add it up. "But you're jus' tellin' me that you're. . . Then, why do you wanna go do that? Why would you be a part of that?"

"I dunno. Maybe. . . maybe I was tryin' to prove somethin', tryin' to make myself not like that. I don't know. They're my friends, but I mean, we say fag alla time. You don't know what it's like. When they say let's go out, I go out. It's, it's. . ."

"It's stupid, is what it is. I knew this would get you into trouble."

"What? Wrestling? This got nothing to do with—"

The next smack missed him, but it was just a fake. He dodged anyway.

Cars zoomed by. The blinkers blinked. He wanted to hear music, to soften this closeness, but his father was still taking it all in, what to tell his mom, the kids, Grandmama, everybody else, that and what not to tell. Then there would be the Official Version, which would most certainly exclude his personal revelation. He tried to reason. "I thought you knew about me."

"What?"

"You know."

His father shrugged, nodded, rolled his eyes.

"I mean, didn't you think there was something funny since I never really went on a date with a girl?"

"What?"

"I said—"

"I heard what you said. I wanna know what makes you know?"

"I know."

"You don't know. . ." He muttered at a passing truck that

honked at them, "Son of a bitch." The emergency blinkers made Joseph think they were on a timer.

"I know," Joseph said with a shred of conviction. "And about stayin' Catholic–"

"That we discuss later, awright?"

A dozen more cars went by.

"So. You've done it, you've had sex?"

"Yeah." Hours ago, my father.

"With who?"

"Wed–"

"Who?"

"We'd–a guy. Not on the team, just a guy, in school. He's nice."

"Whaddaya mean, he's nice?"

"I mean, don't go looking to beat up his dad or something. I'm telling you, it's okay. That is the least of my problems right now."

"Did you use a rubber?"

He stopped. Discussing that with his father, in a car, was too much. Ever since Little Falls, his whole life was falling apart in cars. He needed a good long stinky bus ride to erase everything.

"So you're okay with that?"

He wasn't, but he wanted to be. He had to be strong, for now. "Yeah."

Silence. Sniffles. Cars zoomed by. The hazard blinker clicked, clicked, clicked, clicked.

"Well." His father sighed. "Okay. We will talk more about this. Right now, we gotta go home. Your mother's prob'ly out of her skin by now."

Dino shut the blinkers off, checked behind him, pulled onto the road, accelerated, drove on a few blocks before Joseph said, fighting back a smirk, "Um, Dad? Could you turn around? We passed home a few miles back."

"Where the hell are we?"

"Um, I think, Verona."

"What?"

Parked in their new driveway, his father talked softly to sort of cheer them both up before they faced Marie Nicci, who stood sentinel on the porch.

"So I still gotta go to jail?"

"No. I will not let that happen."

Joseph knew not to ask anything else. "I narced on my buddies."

149

His father got out, said, "They ain't your buddies no more," slammed the door.

"I really don't think that's our main problem here, Marie."

"But he just said. . ."

"Look, we gotta get a lawyer. He's got to watch himself until these other boys are arrested."

"But they didn't all–"

"Wait–"

"He has to go to confession tomorrow."

"Marie."

"I don't care, school, or no school, he goes to conf–"

"Can we worry about his eternal soul a little later and just try to keep him out of jail right now?"

She sat, finally. His father stood, checking for visitors, peeping Mike.

As Joseph sat on the sofa, his parents conducted the "discussion" before him. He had to answer a lot of questions. He couldn't cry again. It wasn't in him. He still felt numb, watching his parents take in the fact that their first-born had just gone bad.

"Will you be okay if you go to school tomorrow?" she asked.

"Yes. I already–" he stopped himself from saying 'narced.' "I already told. They can't do anything to me in school." He really just wanted to see Dink, to explain.

"And you wanna go to your match tomorrow," she said, as if he were asking to skydive.

"Yeah. Please? They're gonna do a thing for him at the match."

"You have homework?"

"Naw, it's . . . nothing."

"Get some rest."

"I wanna watch the news. See what else they got."

"Joseph–"

"Please?"

"You go to bed right after," his father said.

His parents continued their discussion upstairs, but softly. They kept the upstairs phone off the hook, or were talking on it. He'd already tried to sneak a call to Dink's house.

Visiting Mike and Soph in their rooms, explaining some lie to tell them, Joseph heard his mother walk about above him. He tried to warn her the kids were both supplied with a foolproof Fib-ometer. He'd have to compare stories again if she didn't tell the truth.

"Whatcha watchin?" Mike had snuck downstairs for more cookies, obviously dissatisfied with their mother's version of things. Joseph watched him walk into the kitchen, return. It didn't look like he was going to get rid of that baby fat anytime soon.

A special local edition of some teen show spilled into the living room. Girls who never looked twice at Anthony sobbed openly for cameras. He wanted more news, to see what they found out. Nothing but that detective taking credit for Joey's spillage.

"Fuck. I am so dead."

Mike smiled, as if given a present to use against him later.

He imagined himself out on parole, a renowned tattoo artist, Curt Gowdy doing a voice-over: "Overcoming the tragic events of his school years, in which he was tied to the death of a fellow teammate, Joseph Netchie, the avowed homosexual, after spending ten years in federal prison, returns to the sport he loved. . ."

"What's so funny?" Mike muttered, half a cookie falling out of his hand.

"Nothing."

Mike picked up the broken cookie, ate it. "So, what did you do?"

Joseph looked up to his brother. "I messed up big time."

"I'm sorry. Here."

"Thanks." He took one.

Mike watched him eat, stood over him, viewing the body.

3

The boys on the team had joked about the extras in movies, how crowds like that never came to their matches, especially cheerleaders, especially in January, in the dead of winter, on a weeknight.

The next night half the school and a hundred other people and three dozen members of the press awaited entry before they'd even unrolled the mats.

Bennie and Hunter had been plucked by the cops the night before, and with footage on the tube. They appeared somber in cuffs, but Lamar Stevens, whose cousin was a policeman, told them, "Hunter was bawling his eyes out, tried to hide in his daddy's garage before they caught him."

Tommy Infranca fumed. "How come they only come now that

151

one of us died?"

"It's morbid, is what it is," Coach Cleshun muttered as the boys huddled in the locker room. Joseph had to agree. The gloomy look Dink gave him confirmed it.

While the boys from Montclair warmed up out on the mat, their busloads of fans filled the bleachers. They'd even brought extra cheerleaders, as if to ward off the implied taint of their opponents.

Coach Cleshun called out to nobody in particular. "I want you all to forget about this when you're out there. Just do your best. I want you wrestling one hundred percent!"

"A hundred per cent of what?" Troy muttered as he laced a shoe.

With three forfeits on the blocks, Troy and the Shivers had been all over the practice mat, pouring hints into the eager if not inept JVers Eddie Whiteherst and Ricky Ponzell, who'd volunteered to fill the weight slots of their "alleged killer" teammates. They'd shut it out, or acted as if they had, focusing on moves and technique, which was good. The principal and a few other guys in suits had "just stopped by to see how things were going before the tribute." They hadn't left the vicinity, which was not so good.

Once the crowd filled in, the cameras took perches ringside, the boys all gradually found things they needed to do, in the locker room, away from the glare.

Joseph said nothing. He had no idea how to behave, so he opted for sullen, wary. It took less energy than upset, crying.

Dink hadn't said more than a few words since practice, wondering why he hadn't been arrested yet. It loomed, though.

At practice, Coach Cleshun had them all sit down for a talk about drinking, and "anger management." Cleshun began to make announcements about who would fill in for the three missing slots.

"Okay, so, um, since so many people are here tonight for this, it seems, I'm sorry to you one-twelve guys who feel like you're missing an opportunity, but we are going to forfeit that weight category, and the visiting coach and player have agreed to give that victory to our, your slain teammate, Anthony, uh. Anthony Lambros."

Nobody dared a word of protest.

By that point Joseph needed contact bad. Dink turned to him. They held hands, shared a long silent hug that nobody dared joke about, not even when they banged against a locker, still hugging, Dink almost trying to smother the sobs out of his sparring partner.

152

The opening music: cut.

The fancy moves: cut.

Nobody complained. Inside Joseph knew they all felt odd, strange. They just walked in silently, hoods up, solemn, until Walt tripped on Jeff Shiver's leg.

By the time they got seated, Dink still hadn't more than glanced at him. But when they sat side by side, Dink pressed his leg against Joseph's. They stuck that way, unmoving, until he had to get up to stretch.

Few people in the bleachers looked familiar. Cameras, little ones, were everywhere, held by strangers, Dink's dad, Buddha's dad, Dustin's older brother. A bunch of other people kept taking pictures. They pointed at the bench, the mat, scanning.

Beside his mom and Soph, Aunt Lilla sat with Grandmama, who looked like a ghost to Joseph. She was said to be praying for him.

Mike stood up, waving at him like it was a party, until his father yanked him down behind someone else's dad. His father's look was not one of concern, but a glare that said, If you freak out, I'm right here. His mother smiled to another woman up the aisle, then darted back down as if checking for snipers. Joseph felt he ought to check the exit doors.

The principal and some students, actually Chrissie and Kimberly, put together a little cluster of announcements and speeches about "letting the healing begin." The principal spent a lot of time talking, as did another man from the school, the superintendent, some teachers. It took longer than anyone figured. Cameras rolled, stopped, rolled again.

At an awkward moment where even his coach sounded apologetic, Cleshun turned behind him. "These gentlemen have asked me to simply let them play the sport they love, for a teammate they'll miss."

The ref and a kid from the other school, in street clothes, shoes off, walked out on the mat. Instead of holding up the hand of Anthony's opponent, as would happen with a forfeit, the ref signaled to his left. People stared at the empty space where Anthony should have been.

Everyone else realized, or some of them did, because the quiet in the gym was only interrupted by someone who snapped a flash picture, as if Anthony might show up later on film.

Dustin lost.

Tommy lost.

"You're up, Neech."

He peeled off his sweats.

He shook hands with his opponent, Somebody Guerrero, whose wisp of a mustache, and possibly the sweetest baby face Joseph would ever bump against, crushed him enough without the added announcement of his being a two-time county champion.

As they shook hands, the kid smiled, disarmingly.

Yanked down by a swift single leg grab, on his belly in the first ten seconds, Joseph let the kid ride him, try a bulldozer after half a minute of near-crossfaces. It wasn't like the kid couldn't do it. He was enjoying just humping Joseph's butt, racking up points as Joseph twisted about beneath him.

His skin still tender from Dink's love only a day before, he found each nudge from the beautiful boy burned him. His was a different body, his skin still raw with desire. He tensed a moment, tried a move, but then figured, why?

The ref called a stalemate.

The boys stood. Joseph reminded himself to keep his face toward the cameras. That would be all he needed, not only pegged, but his ass all over the nightly news.

Come on, Guerrero said with a nudge of his chin, bouncing around Joseph like a boxer, faking Joseph out with little hand grabs before they got down to it. Joseph looked into his eyes, charmed by his smile, then felt the floor smack his back as he collapsed under the blow of a takedown. Joseph rolled over, grasping for basic defense position, unmoving, arms at ten and two, a stilled clock.

He was pried from all sides, until he felt himself grabbed around the waist, coming up off the floor, flipped over. His nose met the mat first.

By the time he recovered after the ref's whistle, he wiped a bit of snot—wait—blood.

Coach Fiasole appeared, wiped his face with a towel. When Coach took it away from Joseph's face, it was splotched dark red.

"Easy, head back."

"I'm okay."

Fiasole shoved a swab up his nose, wiped his face again.

Joseph looked over, saw the other coach wiping Guerrero's shoulder, then he knew. It was the same as the day a bunch of guys coated their arms and legs in a foamy antiseptic.

They couldn't touch a known fag without freaking about germs.

His win going down the tube on the tube, a cherub about to flatten him, he looked to Dink for support, but all he saw was a little hooded boy, bent over, tapping his feet.

He turned back to Fiasole. "Say it." *Colto.*

"What?" Coach Fiasole asked, holding the bloody towel, looking a little too nervous about it.

"Say it!"

But the ref was calling him back. Coach Fiasole just held his hands out, like, what can I do? His minute was up.

"Come on, son." The ref signaled him back.

Coach Cleshun yelled, showed a little move, but Joseph returned, alone. Nothing Cleshun or Fiasole or his dad or Dink or anybody could yell or say would help.

Joseph got into position, the two lines marked for knees, hands. After the whistle, the rest was a blur. He tried to mouth-breathe so he wouldn't blow the swab out of his nostril. His arm was yanked from behind. He got flipped, his neck hit the mat. For a brief eternity of pain and tightness, Guerrero's hard hip bone pressed into his backbone, one arm cranking his elbow.

As the ref dropped beside them, his palm waving back, forth, signaling no, not yet, Joseph shoved his right shoulder up. The kid pressed down on top of him, tugging, grabbing him like hard clay, forcing him down. Joseph pressed his torso up, crunching his spine in a bridge, the top of his head, his heels pressed into the mat, all the pain darting into the ends of his body, his face contorted, staring out as the upside down world looked on. If he could only roll over, find a last shred of strength, he could escape.

But Joseph was gone, his breath gone, there was no way out, except to wait for a moment, a breath of air to give him a sliver of hope.

The timer cranked off.

He didn't even stand upright, just kneeled to catch his breath, look at no one while the ref raised Guerrero's arm. People clapped, hooted, shouted, roared, stood up, cheering. Guerrero tapped his shoulder, pulled him into a hug, muttered, "I'm real sorry, guy."

All he could do was try to clear his dizzy vision long enough to find his chair, just get away, just sit down, breathe.

He felt Dink's hand on his back. Joseph flinched, not wanting Dink to touch him, to jinx him, but he let Dink do it before he walked to the mat. The announcer bellowed names.

Joseph kept his head bowed, couldn't look up, but he had to, he had to see. Please, Dink, please don't let him get you. Put it away for just a bit.

Another hand on his back. Assistant Coach Fiasole leaned low over his shoulder, offering another paper towel. The whistle blew, people were screaming, so Joseph didn't hear what Fiasole said. It didn't matter. He'd brushed his face against the side of Joseph's neck, stayed standing behind him, hand on his shoulder for a whole period, guarding him, empty chairs on either side. Joseph leaned down to the wrinkled pile of Dink's sweats, placed them on Dink's chair, looked back behind him to where a lot of people in the bleachers were looking.

At the gymnasium doors, four policemen had entered, stood against the wall, failing miserably at being inconspicuous. Joseph's glance turned back to Dink.

He touched Dink's sweats again, held his hand there, witnessed his longer, more painful loss, tied for two periods, then only a one point loss, but then, Dink was distracted by flashing cameras. He tried a grab behind, a mistake. The opponent hooked Dink's arm around, drove in, had him on his back in a slow painful pin.

Dink came back, sat. Joseph offered him water. Dink gulped it down. Cleshun looked at the two of them with a glare. Dink grabbed for his sweats, covered up. They huddled close as the others won, lost. Joseph wasn't watching. His eyes were on the drops of sweat that fell from Dink's chin to his knee.

His parents seemed to be watching only him, even though Joseph hardly moved. Dink settled down, gave Joseph a nudge. The two exchanged a glance. Dink muttered into his ear, under the sudden quiet, "I think my chauffeurs have arrived."

"We gotta talk."

But Dink just gulped down water, let the empty bottle drop to the floor. He leaned in to Joseph's side, said softly, his hand on his thigh, "Whatever happens, man, I love you."

They more nuzzled faces than kissed. Dink licking his neck was what made some gasp. An affront to them all, its power sent a shiver that radiated outward. He heard whispered comments, but the pain and shame in Joseph's body fell away to nothing. He floated inside a crust of sweat.

As Buddha Martinez's match came to a thunderous halt, the cameras had already swarmed around Coach Cleshun, the school principal, people craving their moment. A cluster of kids stood behind them, waving or glaring into cameras.

Joseph was half-way into the locker room with Dink when a hand grabbed him by the scruff of his neck.

"Come on," his father barked, dragging him off down the school hallway, but not to the front door, where the parking lot was.

"Where we goin'?"

"Adios, amoeba." Dink thrust a hand out. They barely grazed fingers.

"Donnie?"

But his father said nothing, only shoved Joseph out and through a side door he'd never used before.

Mike and Sophia smashed their faces against the back window of the Bronco, giggles under glass.

"Get in." His father shoved him past the back seat. Gramma and Aunt Lilla sat in the back with his mother.

"Sorry you lost," Lilla offered. Dino pulled out of the back driveway, avoiding the street in front of the school. For a moment, before they turned away, Joseph looked back, saw two police cars parked at the front entrance of the school.

"What is going on?" he screamed.

"It's alright," his dad said.

The front entrance to the school was ablaze in swirling silent sirens, shifting camera high beams.

"Stop the car, Da! Stop the car!" Road zoomed by beneath him as he opened the door, but he was ready to tumble. He had to see what was happening to Dink, but his mother lunged forward from behind, grabbed his hand, slammed the door shut.

"Jesus!" His father shouted, grabbing his son's arm while steering with his left. Sophia shrieked. Joseph lunged closer to his father to get away from the door, expecting a smack on the back of his head from his mother. It didn't happen. Grandmama began to babble the rosary in Italian.

"You wanna kill yourself?" his father barked.

Nobody spoke for three blocks until Mike called out, "Hey, I got a Colts banner. Look." He wagged it up to the front seat. The felt edge tickled his ear until his mother swatted it away.

His mother tried quieting Sophia by showing her how to make hand prints in the frosted windows. It wasn't working.

Aunt Lilla finally exhaled, then said, "Well, thank God we got out of that."

Grandmama Nicci and Aunt Lilla stayed the night, for support, for spells, to cook, to get in the way. As the boys knew with a small shred of joy, at least what used to be joy, this visit meant they got to sleep downstairs.

Joseph brought the team videotape Dink had given him weeks before. He would use the blank half to tape the news. He'd missed that night's footage, wasn't sure if he was relieved to have missed it.

Joseph set down the rules: "Volume down. I got the remote." Mike agreed under the threat of a headlock.

After all the trips to the bathroom above them dwindled down to silence, Joseph lay on the living room sofa to tape his friends getting arrested. As he expected, it was the top story.

"Local police arrested three teammates of the alleged murder victim. Police would not reveal why they questioned one team member and released him, but sources say that each of the arrested boys, aged eighteen, seventeen and fifteen, were at the scene of the Lambros boy's death."

A shot of Bennie, Hunter outside their homes, and Dink being led down the front steps of the school, looked frightful under the harsh glare of the lights.

He tried to recall their warmth on him, compared to the cold video image, ended up crying in silence. With Mike once again sleeping nearby, it didn't hurt so bad.

Inside the Peter Pan sleeping bag shaped like the large green fuzzy alligator who'd swallowed a clock, his little brother turned over as he lay in its jaws.

Remembering Uncle Boring's bottle his father got for Christmas, Joseph snuck into the kitchen, took a sip, then a gulp, then a chug.

DOG-PILING
NOOGIES
SNUGGIES
PARAMILITARY

The next night, their own private rituals were spelled out in terrific graphics. Their jokes were twisted into the terms of "a cult-like ritual" by one reporter. She was the one who got her hands on a catalog with Bennie's banned Grim Reaper "NEXT!" T-shirt, among others.

Joseph couldn't help but smirk at seeing noogies defined on the local news by a reporter, that same chubby Latino guy. He'd flipped to the other channels, watching three or four versions at once, flipped more channels, recording bits and pieces until his father yelled for him to stop.

"The atmosphere was tense, and as the forfeit in honor of Anthony Lambros came up, a hush fell over the crowd."

A shot of the ref with the other kid, standing, dopey, ignited a jab of pain that slid through Joseph's stomach. He felt a weird sense of disappointment when they cut away from the match to some guy sitting behind a desk in an office: "We had to wait until evidence was substantiated to make our arrests."

Other repeated shots showed Bennie, Hunter, Dink led out, handcuffed, Dink with his varsity jacket over his head, Bennie and Hunter with their sweatshirt hoods up.

Cleshun talked nervously about how he'd taught his players "to respect other people's rights and treat them with kindness and understanding."

The reporter outside the school: "Prosecutors neither confirmed nor denied the rumor of a confession by another team member. . ."

A shot of Joey walking away in defeat, his face blurred out, electronically erased. He looked like an alien with a human body in a singlet, above the neck, a cluster of square-shaped blurs. What remained of his face looked obscene. Just blocking him off like that made him look guilty. Anybody from school would know him.

"Oh, shit." He dropped the remote.

"Joseph, watch your mouth."

". . . whose name is being withheld, since he is a minor. . ."

"Oh, triple shit." He paced around the living room.

"I'm warning you!"

". . . who may have been in the car that rammed the Lambros car the night of his death. . ."

"Whaddaya– Dad, whad' they? Aw, shit."

"Joseph Nicci, you shut your mouth!!"

". . .but the court would not reveal more on the minor. In Little Falls, this is John Soto."

"More on the minor? The hell with you, dickweed."

"Joseph!" His mother's face flushed, steamed red, brought him to pleading.

"Ma. They got me. I'm a dead man."

"Siddown."

He walked away from the television, pacing around the dining room, looking for something to grab. There were only plates, glasses, baskets, useless things he couldn't hurl to absorb his rage. Everything seemed stupid, every bit of his home a reminder of how dumb life was, how things were just going to sit there while he was fading, not even there.

"Joey, calm down."

"Siddown."

"They got me."

"Joseph, calm down."

"Why don't you eat something."

"I'm not hungry."

"Just. Sit. Down."

He sat. One knee refused to stop tapping.

"Now. They are not gonna know that was you, and even if they did, they are under arrest now. They can't hurt you. Awright?"

"Yeah, but what about everybody else? What about at school? What about Bennie's parents, or Hunter's?"

"They are not going to hurt you. I will not let them."

He didn't feel convinced, and his father didn't look convincing. His father wore out any argument with a look, a glare that said, trust me. He wanted to believe him. He always wanted to believe.

Mike hovered outside his bedroom door. He felt him. Joseph darted to it, opened it, waited. But Mike didn't flinch, merely gazed at his brother with a curious upward glance as he walked in.

"Did you see him?"

"Who?"

"You know." Mike waited, then, like saying boo: "Anthony."

"No, I didn't. Leave me alone." He started to shut the door, but Mike had scooted in. The interrogation wasn't over.

"Was he all bloody?"

"No." Joseph knew he was supposed to shut up about everything. But with Mike, it felt easy, as if they were discussing something gruesome, but outside themselves.

He closed the door, put on some music, low so nobody else could hear, swore Mike to complete, utter secrecy, omerta. "And if you don't–"

"Okay," Mike said, as if he were preparing for a science project. They sat on opposite ends of the bed, cross-legged. They squared off, eye to eye.

160

"Bennie did it. Hunter threw a bottle that almost made him wreck. Dink was fighting with Hunter, and I was. . . Bennie like, was like strangling him, I think, in the car."

"Did you see him dead?"

"No. You know he had asthma."

"No."

"You know what that is?"

"Yeah. When you don't breathe good."

"Close enough. So Anthony got scared and went off the road. He might have even had an attack. Maybe even Bennie was. . .no, I mean, no, it. . . But I seen that, he did that at the match in Paterson. He like passed out. Remember? I told you when that happened."

"No. You don't talk to me at all."

"I'm sorry."

"Okay. So why'd you do it?"

"Me?"

"No, yeah, alla youse."

"Don't say that. They don't talk like that here."

"All of you'all. Why, bro?"

"Because we. . .the other guys were yelling things at him."

"Why?"

"Well, Bennie I think is like a psycho, basically."

"So why are you friends with him?"

"Because I am a total jerk." *Because Dink is,* he started to say. He didn't want to choke up in front of Mike, so he forced a cough until it pushed the tears back. "Bennie's got a car. He would drive us around, buy us beers. He has a fake ID, looks twenny-one."

Mike understood. "How much can you drink?" he asked, as if conducting a survey.

A pang in his stomach echoed the memory of their binge. "A couple, that's all."

"But. . ." Mike was bursting with questions. "But what happened?"

"I know, it was . . . Look, I was really sick. I passed out. I wasn't even . . . I really don't think he knew what he was doing but he was like beating up Anthony in his car and he like lost his breath and died."

"Huh." Mike looked at him, curious. "Are you gonna go to jail?"

"I dunno."

"Dad says you won't."

"When did he say that?"

"I got ears. My room's next to theirs."

"Can you hear everything?"

"Except when they whisper, or when they're bumping around."

"Do they do that a lot?"

"Sometimes."

"You know what they're doing, doncha?"

"Oh, gross, stop it."

Mike paced aimlessly around his brother's room, almost window-shopping for what he would claim if his big brother wound up in the slammer.

Joseph really didn't care. It could go, all of it. Where he was going they don't take luggage.

5

Miss Rita Pooley, Joseph's assigned Case Worker for Family Court Case number 4567blablabla, had hair pulled back in that intricate braided style that made Joseph think she ought to be on a throne in Africa being served wine in gold cups. Instead, she typed and talked from behind her desk, getting information and reports from Marie and Dino with what his mother would later describe in the car as "a great deal of authority." In her presence, even his dad shut up.

Dino Nicci seemed relieved that Miss Pooley laid it down clear for them. "You just moved here. He's squeaky clean, and from what St. Augustine tells me, a top athlete."

He choked on a laugh.

"What you seem to be suffering from, Joe, is a lot of peer pressure from jumping into the wrong group of buddies, am I right?"

He would not be sent up the river, not even across the skyway to the Paterson Youth Authority, where–while his father and mother sued each other for custody–Dink was probably wearing his jeans.

"He'll get a suspended sentence, most probably."

'Probably' kept him up nights.

"Unless you do something again," Miss Pooley stated very clearly. This woman would take no hooey.

"Straight up front; a swift negotiation to turn state's evidence would almost assuredly relieve him of any duty such as community service, which I strongly recommend you start him on now as a show of faith."

She tried to joke, smiled, but seemed distracted by the dozen other kids she had to see that day. Her office was neat but there were papers everywhere, files in stacks. She wore a jacket that looked like a man's jacket, only made different. Joseph didn't know what it was about her, but something under her methodical behavior and calm eyes made him like her. She took to him immediately, especially when she told him he was a Person In Need of Supervision, or PINS.

Another choked blast. He was asked if he was okay, but when he explained his reason, she smiled. "You might have to show up for a few days, in one of the other boys' cases, or trials, if it comes to that. But from what I hear, they are going to seek a plea, in um, one case."

Joseph looked at his file on her desk, trying to read it upside down. His father's knee, to his left, kept tapping.

"So, he's gotta do what?" his dad insisted.

"Hold on." She looked at the forms. "He might perhaps get a suspended sentence for conspiracy, since he waited a day to tell about the incident, but that could be excused because of his intoxication. I'd like to recommend an Ala–Teen group. It's right in your area."

Although his parents didn't speak much, it seemed they understood. Joseph understood, too. They were not being punished for the perceived lack of control over their son, just made to feel that way. She suggested his parents go get a soda while Miss Pooley talked with Joseph alone.

"I'll be getting the transcript of your sworn statement, but right now you need to tell me a few things, Joseph, things you may not be comfortable telling your parents, but I may tell them anyway."

"So, their leaving is. . ?"

"Tell me about this posse, Benjamin and. . ."

"Bennie and Hunter and Dink."

"Dink? That would be. . ." she looked at a piece of paper atop a very thick pile of papers. ". . . Donald Nicholas Khors?"

"Yeah."

"Donnie Khors?"

"Uh, sometimes." Joseph had a very strange feeling. He watched Miss Pooley fuss around with his file. "You know him?"

"We've crossed paths."

So Dink wasn't bullshitting.

"How did he get that name? Dink?"

"You don't wanna know."

163

"Okay."

"Do you know. . . how is he?"

"I'm sorry, he's not mine. But I can try to find out." It seemed there was a moment where Joseph almost spilled everything about Dink, and Miss Pooley saw it, but tactfully put it aside. "Now, can we talk about the night of Anthony's death?"

"What, like facts?"

"No. Feelings."

"You got a tape recorder in here or something?"

"No, why?"

"Cause I'm getting tired of telling this, y'know."

The tears didn't start up again, though. He didn't need to repeat his attempts to cough, hold his mud. He felt thirsty, sleepy. Telling the first few times had drained him. The formality of the office, the hum of her computer and harsh lights, the buzz of other people outside her office lulled him, that and the fact that he hadn't slept in two days.

This time he left out the part about Anthony's hand. Every time he told it, that night got colder, as if it were a movie he heard while half-sleeping on the living room floor. Maybe someday he would convince himself of that.

She left Joseph in the room alone for a minute. Then he heard Miss Pooley talking with his parents, then they all returned. Something was up.

"What is it?"

His father sat beside him while Miss Pooley watched. It seemed to humiliate his father. Dino Nicci sat facing his son. "I'm only gonna ask you this once, because I know you are never going to lie to me about this kinda thing again, right?"

"Yes, sir."

"Okay. Aside from the drinking, did you do any drugs with those guys?"

"No."

"Any pot?"

"No."

"Any supplements or pills or shoot anything?"

"No, no, no. I told you."

"Okay, okay, stay calm." He patted his son's back. "Miss, I'm sorry–"

"Pooley."

"Pooley. Sorry, but I think, that, that is good enough for me."

Miss Pooley sighed in a resigned way, filled out another form. "Unfortunately, it may not be good enough for Family Court, so what I'm suggesting, Joseph. . ." She stopped writing, gave him another one of those looks, ". . . is that you undergo a voluntary urinalysis to prove this."

"A what?"

She explained what, then why. "They searched Bennie's duffel bag and found steroids. And when they apprehended Donald, they found some marijuana at his home."

"But, they never said anything about that." His voice came out high and tinny, in a way the boy now trying to act like a man didn't, or couldn't understand could be very grating. "They never did any of that! Dink wasn't the one who tried to run him down! Bennie did it! I tole you! Hunter was the one 'at threw a bottle! Dink didn't do anything! Where is he? Am I ever gonna be allowed to–"

"Joseph," his mother warned.

"He never even said anything about that, I mean sure they acted funny, but Bennie's the one, Bennie's the one 'at–"

"Joe!" his father barked.

"Yessir."

"Stop."

Looks, glances all around. He felt his parents being silently checked by Miss Pooley. He saw how they felt more embarrassed by him, how they were being observed by Miss Pooley as a possible cause.

He was going to get it so bad when he got home.

"I'd like to meet with you again next week, Joseph, and one of your parents. You two can trade off. I know how crazy it is with three kids."

"Oh, you have children?" Marie's face brightened as she scanned Miss Pooley's wall for pictures. Marie turned back to her son. See? Babies. Family. Just try it.

But Joseph was reading Miss Pooley as another sort of woman, just before she said, "Oh, my sisters do."

It was then that Joseph found an ally in Miss Pooley.

As she stood, showed off a few pictures, Joseph reached into his backpack to get out the little 1994 appointment book his mother bought him. His old wall calendar had been filled with weight changes, carb intake, workout times, exercise schedules. Now scribbled in were: *Health Report on Drunk Driving, due Monday. Miss Pooley, Case Worker, Second floor, Tuesday. School*

165

Guidance Counselor, Wednesday, 3 p.m. Bring list of goals.

"Come on." His mother was already out the door Miss Pooley held open.

They all shook hands as Miss Pooley reminded them of their next meeting. He trailed his parents through the hallway. One kid, a white boy skatepunk, sat alone. The other three boys were all African-American, all with their mothers, a sister maybe.

Before they headed down a larger echoey hall of the County Family Court door, Joseph looked back. Miss Pooley had already moved on to another group, welcoming the next fractured family.

"Sup," one boy said. Joseph nodded, realizing that Dink's baggies were hanging on him excellently. Even if he was a mess inside, at least he was fly.

6

As Mister Clutter defined "fallout," Joseph cracked a tiny grin nobody else could see, his gaze intent on his left hand. Like one of last semester's lab experiments that had failed to die, his third knuckle erratically twitched.

Although the smallest, it was the more fascinating of his injuries from the previous week, including his ear, which had inflated and been drained of blood. A very colorful shin bruise had flattened to a dull yellow. His neck injury, or, more accurately, re-injury, was fine, with a daily five hundred milligrams of Motrin, courtesy of Mom.

The day's science class discussion had shifted from energy to atoms to bombs to Nagasaki to anti-war protests and on, anything but Anthony-rama. That, apparently, had been discussed the day Joseph had to leave early to donate a test tube of his pee.

His absence created opportunities for conversations about him. He quickly mastered the trick of ducking through halls quickly enough to get in class early, thus avoiding the wall of eyes and whispers he got after being late for English. Keeping his head down at about a forty-five degree angle kept the false "Hi"s away. He looked at kids' chests, hunching down.

The comments bounced off the halls, another version of locker room swipes one of the JV runts sputtered about someone "losing all his butt buddies."

It could have been during his Family Court hearing that just had to happen on Wednesday, the day of the match at Haledon, his first forfeit.

He'd become what Dink had termed a Zone Case, kids like Russ Hershler, who returned from a drug rehab program with short hair and speech like a zombie, or Stacey Andress, rumored to have received an abortion for Christmas. There were kids at school with magenta hair, two with nose piercings. They seemed disappointed that no one thought of them as radical, so they just pouted. They were all Zone Cases, and he could feel himself shifting. He didn't need pot or speed or mascara like the stoners, the skatepunks, the other world that didn't wear varsity jackets, the kids who walked down the halls trying to be invisible or freakish. He saw them all for the first time and they saw him. They understood each other in brief wary glances.

As Clutter rambled about radioactive particles, Joseph kept his arm over his notebook while he converted a swirly doodle into the shape of a boy's body rising from a box. He didn't notice it was really a drawing of Anthony's spirit rising up to heaven until Greg Fletcher leaned over to peek.

He turned to a blank page, looked up, thought back to a day at St. Augustine's, one of the few times he'd asked a question, "Where do souls go? Are they like atoms?" Brother Jonathan had burned with anger, saying science had nothing to do with faith. He then explained why, for the next week. The other boys blamed him for the lectures. Joseph learned to shut up after that.

Ahead of him, the tips of Sharon Falconi's brown hair barely grazed his desk top. Why do I not like that, he wondered. Why do I like guys' heads, short with ears sticking out? Was it because he'd spent so many years rolling around with guys? Then why didn't it make all the other guys gay, like Walt or the Shivers? Maybe they were, but didn't say anything.

As if.

Six o'clock and ten o'clock became the dreaded hours when everybody in the northern tri-state area got updates on the condition of "the Lambros killing," "the teen assault," or the more popular "varsity murder."

Thursday night's news included the fact that Anthony's body was still at the morgue, pending an autopsy to determine the cause of death. Bennie's public defender, it was said, wanted to consider the possibility of death by asthma attack.

"Yeah, right." Joseph took up the habit of talking back to the television.

By Friday, practice continued to creep him. Everybody had finished patting his shoulder, pulling him aside to say how sorry they were about everything, and they were glad he'd stuck it out, done the right thing.

Some had been interviewed in the parking lot, supporting him without naming him; Raul, Dustin, Walt.

What shocked him were the students interviewed who claimed they "didn't see how Ben would do something like that," how he was a "prize athlete," one administrator said, a guy Joseph had never even seen at a match.

Before warm-ups, a few guys rolled around, playing, doing everything in their power to ignore the four invisible teammates, how no one was about to add them to The Quitters List.

Joseph wasn't paying attention while he tried to pry Walt's arm up to turn him. Walt tousled with Joseph a bit, accidentally elbowing him in the nose. Walt apologized profusely. Joseph waved him off, ignored the pain, relieved he wasn't bleeding.

Coach Cleshun clapped his hands, bringing everyone to order. "Start stretching. Stop horsing around."

"But we're Colts," a Shiver brother joked.

Cleshun glared them to silence, except for a few grunts and groans as the boys were led through stretches. Joseph noticed how much more space surrounded him.

Brett Shiver had said that Cleshun had been "put through the wringer" at a special meeting of the school board. Troy Hilas used more colorful terms. "He got his ass totally reamed. They're this close from cutting the team," Troy hissed, pinching his fingers close just like the "crushing your haid" guy.

When Troy later offered to show Raul and Joseph a cradle, Joseph felt wary. He couldn't tell sometimes with Troy.

"So, you miss him?"

"Who?"

"Khors."

"Yeah."

"You were close."

"Huh?"

"I heard you were really. . . close."

He just found himself grabbing Troy in a headlock, holding it pretty well, until Coach Cleshun pried him off, dragged him to his feet. Troy lay on the mat, flushed, overdoing it. "What a psycho!"

"Shut it," Cleshun barked. "Hilas. Twenty laps. The rest, showers."

Cleshun took Joseph into his office. At some point shortly after the new year, the "Destructive? Prone to Violence? Have we got the shoe for you!" Asics ad had mysteriously disappeared from its honored place on the wall.

"Sit down, Mister Nicci."

"Yes, sir."

"Are you okay?"

"Yes. I just, he was—"

"Look, I don't care about that, or what he said. You have a lot of pressure now goin' on, and I understand that, but you are going to have to behave like a regular person. You can't just blow up with whosever tickin' you off or don't understand what you're goin' through."

The boy nodded, gaze to the floor.

"If you're feeling pressured to keep some kind of normalcy, maybe it's just time to relax. Maybe you want to take a break, when you feel pressure isn't so hard. Do you want to just maybe take a break?"

He felt a shudder. He would have nothing, no one. His face began to cringe. He couldn't cry in front of Coach, he couldn't. "No, sir. Please don't."

"Awright. Then you will behave. You will obey. You will take all that negative energy and you will convert it to attacking your opponent and only your opponent. Can you do that?"

"Yes, sir. I'll try."

Cleshun sighed in Yoda voice. "Do or not do."

He had to smile as he returned to the practice room just to sit and stretch, let those who didn't want to see him get a head start. Cleshun slowly passed behind him, then pressed his arms against Joseph's back as he stretched over his legs. Joseph soaked up the warmth and silent sort of hug his coach gave him, the ripping tingles down his legs, the feeling of relief to be touched without the intention of doing damage.

He held out until the showers. By then he was so tired he could feel relieved doing it. It worked. And if he might stay a little late, nobody would notice how red his eyes were. It was the soap, he would say. Just the soap.

When the date of the funeral was announced, kids at school waited in line for passes to get the afternoon off. Joseph stormed past them, brooded outside, awaiting his ten-block escort.

His after–school daycare, should Marie Nicci be foraging out in the hinterlands, Irene DeStefano always had food ready, and Joseph was ready. Without Dink around, the 130 slot was open. Big Woop.

But he didn't talk shop with Mrs. DeStefano, whom he suspected of being quite the gossip. He bottled up telling her or anyone else about the day's troubles. To avoid future punishment, he would continue this tactic.

Her idle afternoon gossip proved useful, though, connected to some invisible network he decided he'd better not inquire about. He just compared facts with those on the tube and in the papers.

He learned that while the Khors parents continued their custody battle, Dink was shuttled off to juvenile hall somewhere in Paterson. Irene's version: "The mother drinks a little. She'll lose."

Bennie had been "remanded into custody in Paterson County for attempted sexual assault, attempted manslaughter, reckless endangerment with intent to harm, plus drunk driving charges," the news said. What the defense was still going off about was determining if Bennie had even killed Anthony.

The steroid issue hadn't been mentioned, but Irene knew more. "The step-parents are trying to sue the guy who sold Bennie the steroids, like it wasn't his fault, since he was on drugs, which I find ridiculous."

Hunter's father's lawyer sprung him on bail, was remanded to the custody of his parents, until some "domestic situation" flared up. Irene's version sounded more colorful: "The boy and his younger brother were fighting and the older one, Andy, he knocked the lights out of him, so his own parents called the cops on him. Apparently the father is a big development honcho, really rich, that sort of thing."

Joseph spent the first Saturday after Anthony's death in what Dino Nicci joked as "being under the remainder of your father," helping him work in Cedar Village on a new development of ranch houses with nightmare bathroom configurations. He jokingly threatened to complain to his father's union, until his father half-smiled and threatened to smack him with a wrench.

The thing was, he liked doing it, working with his dad. He forgot everything for a few hours. At home, he'd always had chores. Now he got to do the dishes, and the laundry, forever.

Actually, it was supposed to be until he graduated from high school, but he figured if things went well, he might be able to take a few weeks off sometime around his senior prom, where he'd bring Dink, and they'd both wear tuxes, then just leave, forever.

Sometimes he had hopeful wishes amid the desperation, but mostly it was trying not to think again about the moments that led to Anthony's death. Different imagined possibilities kept ending up the same way.

Then Joseph would hear his own breathing, a panting, and he'd find something, anything else to distract him: the headphones, the tube, some food, anything to stop wondering if Anthony had started to turn green or if some creepy guy was injecting him with fluids on a slab somewhere, poking around for microscopic bits of Bennie.

"I'm going over to Irene's," his mother said. Dino was upstairs giving Sophia a bath. "I'll be right back."

"Awright." He tossed the remote to Mike.

"Don't answer the phone."

"Huh?" Mike clicked channels.

"Just let the machine pick up."

"Shields Up!" Mike called out, settling on Nick at Nite.

"Mikey, get your PJs on and get up to bed!"

She slapped the kitchen door shut. Mike yanked his shirt off and began a strange sort of hip-swaying strip tease. Joseph watched, dumbfounded.

"Get upstairs."

Mike mooned him as he tripped up the stairs.

The phone rang. He didn't wait for the machine to pick up. He unplugged it. They'd been calling again. The news people. The principal's assistant. A bill collector or three.

Watching through the window, he saw his mother cross the driveway, stand under the back door porch light, saw Irene DeStefano's arm extending out, holding the screen door open, sweeping her in.

He sat on the couch, leafing through the latest bundle of forwarded mail: magazines, *People's Most Beautiful People*, a *Catholic Digest*. "Is It a Sin? Improve Your Confession." "Pilgrimage to Lourdes: One Man's Story."

Maybe that was what he needed, a pilgrimage. He thought that might do something for him, remind him what it was all about. Then he saw an ad for the Pope John Paul II doll, a tiny potato-faced

171

version of the pope dressed in a tiny miter, chasuble. "Six convenient monthly installments of $29."

He tossed the magazine back onto the coffee table, replugged the kitchen phone, turned pages in the phone book to look up the Lambros' number.

There were seven. He picked one.

An older woman answered.

"I'm really sorry about what happened," he said.

"Thank you. Who's calling please?"

"Joseph. Nicci."

A hand covered the phone. He heard mumbles.

"Was that you on the news the other day?"

"Um, I think, yeah. I mean, I don't know about that."

"Well, thank you very much for your condolences. The funeral is at eleven." The phone clunked down.

Their house must be even worse than mine, he thought, with people moaning and crying. Anthony would never graduate, never become the person he was supposed to be, okay with it, Tony.

7

"Are we going to the cemeterrarium?"

"No, Soph, we don't have to go to the cemetery."

"But why?" Mike was obviously disappointed.

"I'm a scared. I don't wanna go."

"Hush. We're not." By the time they were in the car, Joseph gave up arguing with his mother about bringing Sophia after she gave the glance that said, If it weren't for you, we wouldn't be going to this funeral, so keep your mouth shut.

He knew where Anthony would be buried, since the news showed it like a movie opening; Cedar Grove Cemetery. A statue near his family plot stood proudly, a stag in bronze with the words around its square base, among other phrases, BROTHERLY LOVE.

He got that one on tape, planned to visit someday.

Mike was told that he didn't have to go if he didn't want to. He countered, "Are you kidding?" It was later discovered that he had smuggled in a disposable camera.

Dino had to park so far away from St. Dominic's they could have walked, if it hadn't been five degrees above freezing.

Joseph thought about lying to his mom again, saying he was sick, but she was too busy squeezing into a black dress that she'd been trying to find time to press since dawn.

Anthony. The contents of that thing in the aisle.

He stopped at the entrance just long enough to let his eyes adjust. A copied program was handed him by someone. They stepped down the aisle. He was about to sit down, but then knelt on his way in the pew, ten feet from the casket. It seemed too large, a shiny black sandwich with gold handles and a funny skirt below, as if little puppets might pop out.

Behind him, rows of familiar faces; three rows up, Chrissie Wright turned back. Joseph dropped his head, dodged stares but heard the whispers.

Everybody on the team, everybody from his school, it seemed, people showed up who never spoke to Anthony, never looked at or even touched Anthony, just to get the afternoon off from school.

He was spoken of as a model of perfection. Every time a pair of eyes met his, Joseph gazed down. The program curled in his hand. He unfolded it. The words began to swirl in his vision as he looked down, waiting for a tear to drop onto the paper. Then he folded it neatly, placed it inside his jacket pocket, next to his wallet, which, he remembered, had about four dollars inside. He wanted to take a train somewhere, buy something. He felt in his breast pocket, found the picture of Giuseppe of the Our Den.

Joseph kept his head bowed, his lips tightly shut, as he heard one after another person or priest talk in wonder, justifying why a young boy should be taken, a good boy, a devout Catholic, a loved boy, an athlete. Joseph squeezed a hand from his parents, who bookended him for support.

Anthony's brother stepped up to the podium. His hair slicked back, his brown and bloodshot eyes darting around, he sought familiar faces.

With one vindictive bleary glance, he brought the rustling, fluttering audience to silence.

"I don't know why you're all here. Most of you didn't know my little brother," he said into a microphone. "At least the way I did." And there his throat choked, but he held back. He was magnificent, what Anthony might have become if thicker, tougher, better off.

"He wasn't what everybody wanted him to be." The brother sniffed. Joseph wondered, *Is he saying what I think he's saying?*

"Sometimes he wasn't what he wanted to be, but he was trying.

173

He was really moving forward." He looked out over them for a moment, checking, looking for some consensus. "He was. . . he was learning how to become himself, but he was killed. I love him and will miss him. . . every hour. . . of every day of my life."

He then folded up his speech, half of which it seemed he could not read. "This is a song he loved, so we're gonna play it. And I appreciate Father Thomas for allowing us this favor. This is one of those songs my brother used to play a lot and it's The Cure and he taped if off the radio so I apologize but for those who don't know it, if you could just think about the part where it says, 'To Heaven, forever,' and just wish my bro a safe trip."

Anthony's brother pressed a button on a small cassette player. Priests and parents clicked their ears in wonderment while the girls in black sweaters, the boys in baggy jeans and perfect buzzcuts lost it, their faces burning crimson, eyes wet, souls dented. The song filled the church. They sang it in their heads, kids who had expected a mere freak show on their day off from school.

It was decided that Dino would bring the car around, since Marie needed more time to display her son to her friends as a fine upstanding boy, despite evidence to the contrary.

Joseph hung with the team a bit, savoring the only time being seen crying with his teammates would be allowed. They didn't talk much at all; the scrutiny of parents, cameras, strangers scattered their once-comfortable herding.

Joseph dodged stares from kids he'd met once or twice at school. They filed past, looked down, stared silently, or whispered to each other, blended in with older versions of the Lambros family, who disappeared into a stretch limo that could barely navigate the small corners of the tiny town. Some kids had retreated toward Farnese's Bakery, where the cameras gathered across the street. Sister Emilia and Sister Bernadine had to keep shooing them off church property.

"I'm gonna go check to see where the car is," he said.

"Don't go far."

"Right."

He walked down the slush-clotted yard of St. Dominic's. At the foot of the church lawn, behind the brick edifice that housed a small statue of Mary, a few reporters had snuck up.

He scanned the street for that chubby Latino guy, when a woman emerged from the camera cluster, approached him, her brassy blond hair immobile in the wind. She held a microphone, the wire trailing behind her, attached to a man with a black camera for a head. Joseph wanted to escape her, but it was too late. Some other kid, after giving his two cents, pointed right at him. He couldn't duck behind a car. He'd seen guys do that. He was trapped, but it almost felt good, relieving, like he could stop running.

"Aren't you a member of the Little Falls wrestling team?"

"Yes."

"How do you feel about the death of Anthony Lambros?"

The women's microphone aimed for his face, closing in like a snubnose. The camera jostled around behind her. He looked at it a moment, then at the woman. Her makeup was so thick, like his Aunt Lilla. He waited for the camera guy to settle down.

"Uh, I'm very sad. It was very unfortunate, the thing what happened."

"Have you talked to the family members?"

"No." They hung up on me. Joseph shook his head at nothing, bit his lips in. "I miss him. We all miss him a lot." The tears started, welling up in the back of his eyes. He looked up so they would stay in there. "Can I go now?"

"Thank you." The woman pulled back with a sigh of well-rehearsed sympathy. Joseph backed up as two other crews spotted him, then he walked briskly away.

He'd get hell for that. Everybody was gonna see it. He retreated back to his mother in time to see the cameras all shift and jostle towards the door.

It came out, held by larger versions of Anthony: brothers, cousins, uncles. Even that photographer kid from school, all of them aimed at it, as if the lenses could see through it, through the wood and through the lining and the satin-pillowed stuffing and through the sewn-up three-piece suit with a seam along the back and through the stiffening body no bigger than his, a boy's body that probably shifted when they walked it down the stairs and through the drying skin and down to the bones like an X-ray. That's what's gonna be on the tube. Sliding X-rays.

He'd lost his family in a flock of black coats. The sun shone bright in the freezing afternoon, glaring over bits of frozen ice, flat snow. He kept hoping someone would just take him in, let him back in there, let him cry, weep, howl to the Holy Spirit for forgiveness, plead for mercy so as not to be swept down into hell or its many dark waiting rooms.

175

But he couldn't change what would really send him to hell. He could be forgiven for letting a guy die. But kiss him?

In the car, he felt no obligation to speak, nor did anyone else. His nose thawed, dripped. His father's handkerchief appeared. He took it.

At a stoplight, softly muffled from inside both their closed windows, Joseph turned to see a gloriously handsome man gripping his steering wheel. The man didn't turn, just sang along to a song the boy couldn't hear. Joseph wondered if he had just become invisible.

And then the man turned, saw him, winked.

The light changed.

The number on the mike. Nine. Yeah, he liked nine. Nine was a good number. He was born in the ninth month. His dad won three hundred dollars playing Lotto on a few nines. That was about the only good thing he could think of to keep his feet in the car, the door locked, his body contained.

8

He never went in through the front door anymore, where Chrissie Wright and some other girls put an eight-by-ten photo of Saint Anthony surrounded by flowers in the display case. More flowers appeared daily, cards, tiny teddy bears, scribbled notes.

Joseph wondered why the principal let them do that. Had he read it out of some instruction manual on Grief Counseling for Adolescents? He didn't care. He couldn't see Anthony's picture when he had a math quiz or worse, lunch, where entire conversations were a dodge effort. Every day another wrestler found a reason to skip lunch or split off.

What had protected him had fallen away. The very air around him felt colder, despite the once-golden armor of a varsity jacket. Even that seemed too heavy to wear on rainier days.

He dodged their glances, where once there were close nudges or quiet jokes between his friends. The looks now said, He was one of Them.

Some of the other guys on the team talked with him outside of practice, but only briefly, hesitantly, or at lunch with fellow Colts, other jocks he didn't know, like Brandon Miller, a basketball goon about six feet high. One day Miller made a crack about fags. Joseph got up, left his tray. He was later told that Miller got a complete chewing out from the wrestling team, but he wasn't sure what was said. He got conflicting stories about who was defended as a fag.

After school, gatherings were held, chaperoned parties with fruit drinks. Introduced to a girl who told him he looked really cute on the news, all he could do was smile, walk away.

After-practice events, prayer groups, even the wholesome pasta parties at Tommy Infranca's, then Raul Klein's birthday party, wore on him. He told them he was grounded. He wanted to give them time off from him.

At the dual match in Clifton, Joseph competed with an inexperienced boy for a few minutes, letting him get some points in before simply grabbing the boy's arm, which had hung too close and too long not to grab. As Joseph had been trained, the head followed, leaving Joseph flattening, then forgetting him.

Tommy Infranca sat to his left. On his right, Ricky Ponzell, a soft-spoken JV, shucked off his sweats. He'd tried really hard through his first bouts, but he was a bit of a fish.

Joseph learned something from Bennie, after it all. When falling apart, retreat into headphones. From Dink he still had PSYCH UP. GRAPPLE. AURGH.

Joseph didn't take the team bus home. The whole family drove that night for team spirit, that or just as a security measure.

In the Bronco, good things were said. Chat was made. He counted the minutes until he could escape to the tub or his bedroom for ZONE OUT.

It was like the time Ronny Boyer's brother died in a car crash, how everyone treated him delicately, as if misery were contagious.

Since the "fag" incident with Miller, Joseph usually found an empty table during lunch. Buddha Martinez or Lamar could usually be trusted to stop by or sit with him when Jock Row was too much.

He heard it once, a joke over his shoulder, "Nitch the Snitch," but he didn't respond.

Then he smelled someone approaching, sweet girl perfume. He looked up from his cafeteria tray, where he'd been toying with his creamed corn. Chrissie Wright smiled like an animal trainer; cautious.

"Can I sit with you, Joey? Kimberly's skipping today, the hood that she is, and I don't know any of these people except those dogs

177

on the team. Thanks. How are you?"

"Fine." How am I. That was just something people said, just a motion. He concentrated intently on swirling his spoon around in the creamed corn.

Chrissie's chatter dodged any mention of the team or Anthony. Maybe some guidance counselor had corralled her into doing it. It seemed the thing for her to do, like all those mornings at invitationals, afternoons spent volunteering for the team, suffering for a cause. "So whaddaya think?"

"Huh?" He was busy checking his creamed corn, which had begun to resemble old teeth in pus.

"Going out with us this weekend."

"Naw, I can't." He didn't bother to ask who "us" was. "I'm grounded forever."

"I think you oughtta get out, you know," she said. Let's Try Being Cheerful. "See a movie or something. A coupla kids are going out this weekend and–"

"Look, I can't, awright? Besides, they don't want me. You don't want me. You're just being nice to make yourself feel good." He swirled creamed teeth.

"That's not true."

"Yeah, it is. You think you're doing good to be a better person, like it's gonna get you brownie points."

"Joey, please," she whispered. "Play along. It'll feel better."

He stared up to meet her pretty face. "Look, I was there, okay? I was there. I didn't do anything."

"I know."

"You don't know. I didn't do anything to stop it."

"You couldn't have." She dropped her voice to a whisper. Kids in all directions were listening.

"I just want to help you get back into things. Maybe I could help you study, or we could just go for a walk. Talk."

"Thanks, I really appreciate it." He got up.

"Well, I want to be here for you. Just let me know if you change your mind."

"Okay." He dropped his tray on a belt that led to the churning waters of a huge stainless steel washing machine. The woman operating it was rumored to be attempting to lose a hundred pounds. From the look of her, she could still take on Buddha Martinez, no problem.

Change my mind. One hypothalamoose to go.

Despite his brushing her off, just talking to someone made him feel better. He started walking with his head up, looking back, defying the stares. He even said Hi to someone.

But then he got more than a Hi back.

"It's Joey 'the Killer' Netchie."

Brandon Miller, the basketball player he barely knew, stood cocky, confident, bracketed by two of his huge buddies. Joseph felt hurt at first, as if he could just walk away, around them, or even dart under them. He could do that.

He turned around, faced the Basketball Wall. "What did you say?" A couple of kids on the sides of the hall froze, smelling trouble.

Miller's eyebrows darted up, impressed. "You heard me. Killer. Whadja do, getcher Mafia friends to pay off the cops? Didn't help your boyfriend, did it. I heard Khors's gettin' gang-banged in juvey."

Another goon. "Ha. And lovin' it."

On the mat, he had never broken the rules. He'd never shoved an opponent, never used his skills to intentionally hurt another boy. He'd never felt the surge of violence he'd seen other wrestlers use in matches. He was as pure as the sport itself. He'd always shaken hands after every bout, happy to be a good boy.

Happy was out. Technique was on deck.

Since Miller looked to be about forty pounds and one foot above him, he figured a surprise move would be best. Joseph dove low for a double leg takedown. It took a long, arcing moment to get him down, like felling a tree. Once they crashed to the floor, he crawled up, grabbed Miller's arm, a neat nelson, tied him in a pretzel bundle, squeezing Miller until he bleated.

Miller's face turned red as Joseph tightened his grip. Miller's free hand grabbed at anything, Joseph's hair, his shoulder, his eyes. As Miller randomly punched his face, he felt his flesh move and tear, felt bone underneath, squeezed Miller's neck tighter, pressed down on his chest. Some blood dripped, liquifying the fury in Joseph, the blanked outrage, to finally do this, after so long, after being so contained, not using his skills for anything but sport, fun, the excuse to touch. Like his father's best wrench, he clamped Miller's rage shut, turning the neck of his willing, obstinate and entirely unworthy foe purplish, veiny, constricted. He felt the charge in him rise bigger than this white bread Aryan Youth Group asshole who acted like he owned the place, hurt him the way they wanted him to

179

hurt Anthony, or Dink or anybody. The screaming around him was familiar enough, but there was no whistle, so he kept choking, until Miller got an arm up to rip at Joseph's face again.

Other hands from behind grabbed him, pried him off Miller, plucked him up off his feet, slammed him against a locker.

He slumped down to a sideways heap.

Beside him, a pair of shiny black shoes tapped the floor.

The Ass Prince had glasses, a greasy comb-over, diplomas on the wall. He resembled a marshmallow in a suit. Outside was the principal's office. The Ass Prince had a smaller office, a smaller desk, but a bigger nameplate: Assistant Principal Mr. Schieffe.

Miller had already yakked a while. As he'd walked out, holding a compress to his face, he glared down while Joseph sat in a waiting room chair. Miller knifed his own throat with a finger, then pointed to Joseph, as if they had a future appointment.

"Mister Netchie?" The Ass Prince stood in the doorway.

He listened to Schieffe rattle out some rules, regulations about school insurance, regulatory bla bla. He expected a scolding, but then he heard "suspension."

"What?"

"This is, merely a, regulation that's school policy. Anyone who is suspended is automatically prohibited, from athletic activity, if they are, participating at the time of the incident that—"

"Then don't suspend me."

"The rules are very clear about fighting in school—"

"What, like he's not getting suspended? He said things that were . . . I was defending myself."

"Did you hit him first." It wasn't a question.

"I didn't hit him, I got him in a double leg takedown."

"You see, this is what I'm talking about. You're a weapon, young man, and we can't have weapons in our school."

"What?"

"We don't fight in this school. Maybe in Newark, or in Catholic schools, you boys like to rough it out, but not on school property."

That burned. He had never gotten in trouble, not until he moved to this suburban paradise. The Ass Prince argued, "The Miller boy could have gotten a concussion from falling. He has a game tomorrow night."

"And I got a match in three days, against Nutley, which our team has successfully defeated for the last consecutive six years."

"Boy, Cleshun really knows how to stoke you boys up."

"I found it in the library." Brett Shiver had found it, actually.

"Are you on steroids, young man?"

"Excuse me, sir?"

"Do you take drugs?"

"No."

"Good. I believe you." Liar. "I know you're a good kid in spite of all this." Liar. "You have good grades, but we're concerned for you as well." Double shit liar. "Take a break. Cool off. Think about your future. Look, I'm going to have to suspend you both from athletic activities for now."

Scholarships. Planes and hotels. NCAA. Meeting Les Gutches. Crashed and burned, thank you very much. He didn't even try to explain. The problem wasn't wrestling. Not wrestling was.

"I'm sorry, son. That's the uh. You're welcome to have your parents write a letter to the school board."

"That's okay. I'll do it myself, sir. I got a B in typing." Pretty good for a delinquent, huh, StayPuf?

He needed to see him alone, so he faked a need for grief counseling in the middle of last period. Instead of going to the nurse's office, he walked softly, quickly, to the gym.

Fiasole sat in the office, writing. Coach Cleshun wouldn't arrive until the bell ending his last period chemistry class. He had to go begging. He had to ask.

"Mister Nicci," Assistant Coach Fiasole said, surprised. "They just told me in the office. I . . . I'm really sorry."

"I just wanted to talk to you. I had to. . . the Assistant Principal said I gotta write to the school board to ask to be put back on the team, but I had to know if you'd—would you—"

"I'd like to, I really would, but I can't say anything, Joe. I already got in trouble for saying—I'm—my job's on the line, man."

"I'm sorry."

"Sorry. I know. I look at you. . . you know how much I see him in you?"

He nodded. "I just wish it was all last year so I coulda made it not happen."

"I know." Fiasole eyes kept scanning the door. He seemed nervous being alone with him. He'd never been nervous.

"I just need to know," he asked. "Could you. . . would you let me just come to practice?"

181

"Of course," he said, in the way kids need to hear lies. "It's just out of our hands. Understand?"

"I think so." Joseph stared down, digging his thumb along the edge of the coach's desk, trying to push off the quivers. He was very good at not crying in school, but this wasn't like school. It was private, a special place. At one time he'd felt himself lost among every guy on the team, comfortable enough not to worry about himself.

But that wasn't happening. He felt shudders, stammers escaping him, felt Fiasole move toward him, hugging him, a rush of tears, warmth. He gripped the man tightly, not wanting to let go, rocking side to side, feeling big hands on his back. He pressed hard into the man's chest, the clean sweatshirt, feeling his chest muscles tighten, backing away as Joseph's erection pressed against his leg.

Joseph pulled back a little, looking up into Fiasole's reddened eyes, arched his face up, just to see if he could kiss him, but Fiasole's chin got in the way. He was so tall, his lips so far away. "No, please."

"But I thought–"

"Don't. Look, let's just talk."

His handsome coach used words like "survivor's guilt," "grief," "questioning sexuality." The man told him things that would help, but then other guys starting coming in, and most of it evaded Joseph, except the basic underlying No way ever, kid.

On his way out, he banged his fist against the metal wall, scraping a finger against the pushed-out slats. He had to stop in the hall, suck his finger to stop the sliver of blood.

He ran from the school, left his gym bag in his locker. His arms felt naked without the bundle over a shoulder weighing him down, keeping him tied to the earth.

The streets were quiet, softened. He could cry all he wanted while he reconstructed what he wished could happen with Fiasole for the nights to come, the nights in bed where in dreams they would touch slowly, differently.

The house was locked. He didn't want to go next door to Mrs. DeStefano's. He walked around, looking for a way in, until he tried the side garage door, shoved it open.

The old pick-up lay unused in the garage. Yet another engine problem had consigned it to dormant status. His father had been getting rides or walking to his nearby office, riding in company trucks to construction sites. Sometimes he took the Bronco, but his mother more often had an errand that took priority.

Joseph ran his hand over the cold metal front door where his father had painted over Nicci Plumbing, followed by their old phone number. The letters still pressed out in script-shaped bumps. Joseph opened the door, hiked himself up in the driver's seat. Pens, a dusty notebook, old billing sheets, a soda lid cluttered the floor. Joseph lay on the seat, unbuckled his pants, held himself.

purplish darkness where he and Dink floated amid burning votive candles in the engine room of the Starship Nosedive, looking up dolefully at Muscue Larry, played by a naked Assistant Coach Fiasole, who was strung up on some girders, just trying to smile. Hunter and Bennie lay in alien sleep cribs with plastic on top and red sirens going off and they looked totally dead and Anthony floated around in space outside the window, saying without moving his lips, "Come on." Joseph floated through the cabin until the pressure busted, the window breaking into splinters, and he and Dink and the candles and the sleep cribs hurled out into a star-clustered abyss of

The garage door rumbled open. He jolted up, caught himself in the truck's rear view mirror. The seat left him with a strange face print. He decided to play it calm as his mother and Sophia got out of the Bronco.

"What are you doing in here?"

"I got locked out."

"Why didn't you go to Irene's?"

Sophia scampered around him, into the truck, calling out, "Sleepyhead."

"I forgot." He sat, unmoving.

"What. What happened?" She noticed Joseph eying Sophia, then sent her inside.

He told her, his voice groggy. His mother stood by him, listened.

"So, I'm off the team an' I gotta stay home the next three school days. I can call in my homework assignments, but I forgot to bring my books home."

"We'll take care of that later. I'm gonna call the school."

"No, don't."

"I'm gonna call the school and talk very patiently with this, what is his name?"

"Staypuf."

"What?"

"Shrike. Some pig name."

"Joey." She leaned in to hug him. Her touch hit the button on his bawl machine. He started up again, embarrassed.

"Why am I so bad? Why is this all happening?"

"Shhh. Shhh. You're not bad. It'll be okay."

He wanted his father to be upset, to scream at him, to shove him around, flatten him. But at the same time, he felt a calmness. He knew once he explained why he did it, how he knocked the Miller kid down, his father might be a little proud. He was.

He waited in his room, tried to draw. But it was too warm in his room. His mother had been blasting the heat all winter. It was dry, not like the practice room, the heat from bodies.

He put on some extra sweats, turned on his cassette player, plugged his earphones in, descended the stairs.

"Where are you going?" His father called out.

"Just outside."

"Good. Maybe you might wanna get some of that ice offa the driveway while you're out there."

"Okay."

But he just sat shivering on the porch, headphones humming away in his ears, blocking out the street silence, what the choir at the Christmas assembly had sung about, a winter wonderland.

Through the trees, he imagined distances. To his left was the school, about a five-minute run. Behind him, the woods, seven minutes. Somewhere north, that way, Totowa. He considered running it, figured it would be a good twenty minutes. But it would be under highways he didn't know. He'd get lost. As much as he considered intentionally getting hit by a truck, he would have preferred to do it in his good running shoes.

Joseph dropped his head, hunched down low. By the porch, the little orange sign, HOME of a COLT!, inched out from the shrubs. He plucked it from the snow, almost tossed it in the garbage can, but instead hid it in a pile of gardening tools.

He heard them "discussing" inside, more about his mother not consulting his father before doing anything. But it was still about him. It started to get a little loud, but then it stopped, short. Joseph heard the back door. He peeked around the house, saw his father walk out into the yard. A cloud of smoke rose from his head, then he turned back with a cigarette in his hand, the first one in years.

Joseph spent his first day of suspension staying up late, crept down to the living room, switched on the tube, volume low, then into the kitchen for some potato chips. He also fixed a cold meatball sandwich from the leftovers.

He flipped channels, having missed the end of any music videos, shows, infomercials. Nobody'd bought or rented a video since New Year's. He'd never seen half the groups on MTV, so he didn't know who was cool.

The Spanish channel featured a cute guy, but trying to understand it got tiring. After late boring news, down to the sports, he knew he'd missed anything that might be about Anthony, something else to add.

He found an old rerun of some show with tacky little sets. Charlie Sheen's dad was in it, about twenty, not all crazed like in *Apocalypse Now*, which he and Dink had watched one night. This Charlie Sheen's dad was doubtful, like Father Scanlon, one of many teachers Joseph remembered affectionately. Wearing a tight turtleneck, then a priest's collar, Sheen's eyes burned with a holy intensity.

He had to laugh with his mother the next day after they both realized how silly it sounded, Joseph asking if he could please go to confession. When she stopped laughing, she hugged him.

"I'm sorry honey, but it's just–"

"I know, but I really think it would be good for me."

"I'll drive you in one hour. Then we got half an hour to pick up Soph at day care, then I gotta get a roast for tomorrow. Yeah, that'll work."

While he waited in his room, he tried out a new prayer. In practice he'd felt his body toughen up, as if every hold were his best, every bruise and sore spot made holy, like muscular stigmata. He wished his soul could be so tough.

"Our Father, who art in heaven, please let me back on the team and I will wrestle for Jesus."

The doddering old usher who sat in front of him nodding his head to everything, the priest's rock star portable microphone, the way Sophia deliberately repeated all the Amens just a moment too late so she could hear her own little cherub voice echo through the church, not even the woman who rushed in late during the homily, scattering the contents of her purse on the pew near him; nothing would sway him from attempting a direct link.

185

He tried to hear where to put his voice during the hymns, but it came out tinny as always.

He sat in his good pants and button-down shirt, feeling sure one of the pins was still stuck in it, knowing he wouldn't move, even if punctured.

He stood silently, muttered the right prayers, knelt while Mike and Sophie fidgeted. Up, down. Between the padres and the saints. Ready for take-off.

He crossed himself, walked forward. His stomach rumbled as the wine landed in his empty stomach. He wondered if Dink was having breakfast right then in Passaic, if he got to sleep in on Sundays. Were Bennie and Hunter sitting in their cells, plotting revenge on him?

Inside him, the wafer softened on his tongue. He tried. He really tried. But he knew. None of it meant anything to him anymore. His was a new faith; Anthonianity. Anthonism. He couldn't decide.

9

At first Miss Pooley didn't understand Joseph's sudden interest in her computer, until he "got an idea" since he had to write a letter and would she help him, maybe?

"Why don't you let me type it," Miss Pooley said, sipping from her big coffee mug that read DAMN, I'M GOOD. "I type a lot."

"That's okay, but I was. . ."

"Come on." She sat him down on a little chair beside her computer. Joseph saw pictures on the wall above it, little snapshots next to a Kathy cartoon, pictures beside the baby photos Joseph's mother had fawned over, a vacation shot of Miss Pooley in the sun with her glasses off, smiling, wearing a life preserver with some other women in a raft.

Miss Pooley looked over the page from Joseph's spiral-bound notebook. His squared-off lettering wobbled up and down a few times, but was legible. "Now, how do you start the heading, Joseph, you remember? You must have seen enough formal letters recently."

"Yeah, right, uh, tab left, the heading, the address."

"And you have that?"

"Yeah."

"Yeah, what?"

"Yes, Ma'am."

Miss Pooley clacked away, her hooped earrings making a tiny chime sound.

Dear school board members,
You are possibly familiar with my name in

"What do I say there, 'in the death of'? That's gross."

"In the recent unfortunate events?" Miss Pooley suggested, her fingers hovering over the keyboard, waiting.

"Yeah, put that."

in the recent unfortunate events surrounding the death of my teammate Anthony Lambros. I was also suspended recently for being involved in a fight which actually began by an incident of verbal bigotry by another classmate but I want to apologize for those events and I did. What I am trying to do is convey my apologies for disrupting the peaceful educational environment that has come to be my school at Little Falls. My family had a lot of adjustments to make since we moved here.

I would like to ask that I be allowed back on the Colts Wrestling Team to return to my athletic endeavors. Wrestling is very important to me and I also feel that in light of the recent crisis the team is very short of athletes who can also help bring more fans to matches and bring up school spirit. I hope you read this and let me know as soon as you can about your decision.

Joseph leaned into the screen. "Can you print it out?"

"Just let me fix a few parts, okay? But you gotta mail it yourself. They're real touchy about the postal meter."

Like hibernating animals, in winter most people eat more. The process had been reversed for his sport. He'd had to train, keep his weight within the borders of a few pounds, the rise and fall of numbers sinking low just before, jumping back up the day after each match. His energy and tension, attention span and fatigue, fluctuated.

Most days at home, he did neck-ups and stretches. He sporadically pumped up at the school gym, where Walt, the Shivers, some other jocks hung out, but that led to conversations which led to them inviting him to a prayer group, and Joseph reminding them he had plenty of that but in a different flavor.

Without wrestling, moving up in weight didn't concern him. He ate, no matter what his mother's, or her cooking's, condition. This calmed her, which calmed everybody else in the family, which made her cooking better.

He put on more pounds, filling out, thickening. It gave him a feeling of solidity, something he always felt he lacked, being so small. It was a strange feeling at first, but he ate; pasta, roast beef sandwiches, big glasses of milk that made him burp, fruit, crackers with lots of funny leftover Christmas cheese with nuts on top. He ate a whole box of Oreos in one afternoon, watching shows, hoping to see a little bit of himself on the screen. Sometimes it happened.

But the court proceedings against Bennie and Hunter had been delayed. People were mad, particularly the family and friends of Anthony. Mrs. Lambros had admitted her son was small, not perfect, but that it was no reason "to go and kill a boy."

"To make a donation to the family, that number again . . ."

Joseph didn't tape that show.

He would become a perfect student. He would become a strong athlete, again. He would volunteer for the Catholic Youth League. He filled every minute of his days with behaving properly, following the rules, holding his tongue, working out, waiting for people to figure out how to act with him. Nights were briefly met with measured time for some silent crying. He would remember to air out the pillow cases.

He began to awake at dawn without the help of his alarm clock, as if he were on patrol. Sleeping in on weekends or non-school days had been next to impossible in Newark, even on snow days, which they hadn't had so much anymore, or teacher's strikes, which they'd had more often.

There were no sounds to wake him, no dawn three-alarm fires, no off-ramp humming, no invisible Bottle Man rattling his shopping cart down the alley behind all the row houses. Sometimes, though, the quiet woke him up, the empty sound, pierced only by birds who stayed through winter.

He stood at the sink, peed, watching his morning hardon soften in the bathroom mirror. He flushed the unused toilet, then ran faucet water.

Downstairs, he drank some juice, but didn't want to make any food. He wanted to enjoy the quiet.

Outside, the town woke up, people, dogs, but there was so much more space between sounds. Joseph parted the curtain of the sliding glass door to the back yard. He pressed his face and body close to the glass, feeling the dawn chill push forward, his breath appearing and disappearing, blurring the view. He made a nose print.

To walk outside, feel the crunch of frozen grass breaking softly under his feet, was possible. He could. He could go out, keep walking, past the Whatsit's tarp-covered swimming pool, past Mrs. DeStefano's shrouded rose bushes, past the salt-stained streets, out into those woods, the branches like gray sponges, a model of a town.

He wondered if guys who never got married always got to have mornings like this, or if he could wake up with a boyfriend still in bed, and a dog, in some far off place. Portland, maybe.

10

Irene's "boat," a mint green Chrysler New Yorker with crushed velvet seats and little lights in the back that Irene DeStefano let Mike turn on and off and on until Joseph put him in a brief headlock, ambled through the few blocks back home after Mass.

"Boys," their mother scolded. "She's trying to drive."

Patches of greyish sludge clotted the streets. They felt impenetrable in the boat. Outside the windows, other cars looked puny.

"Why weren't you singing, Joseph?" His mother looked back.

"I can't sing. You know I can't sing."

"You should try."

"You want me to try?" He grinned. "Okay," then blurted out an hallelujah in the key of aluminum foil.

"Awright, awright!" She gave in, shaking her head. Mike and Soph cautiously unplugged their fingers from their ears.

"He proved his point," Irene said.

When they returned, his dad lay on the couch in sweat pants and a faded Pipe Fitters Union sweatshirt. The house smelled of coffee. The kitchen table was laden with plates of eggs, toast, and sausage. The Lord said to rest on Sunday. His dad cooked.

"You kids, I told you, change first before you eat."

Mike and Sophia altered their flight plan around the kitchen table back through the living room, where they dropped their coats on their way up the stairs.

There had been a time when Joseph sprawled out on the floor, fishing through *The Bergen Record*, *The Star Ledger*, cutting out pictures, comics, art museum stuff, wrestling, if any.

Still half-asleep in his suit, Joseph sank down into the big chair with just the Metro sections.

"Nothing today," his father sighed.

"Oh."

He checked anyway.

After a few minutes, Mike came hurtling downstairs, his shirt on backward, bare feet and an old pair of Joseph's jams hanging below his knees like a skirt.

"Come and eat," his mother said.

"In a minute."

He trod upstairs, peeled off the suit, hanging it carefully, since he didn't know when they were going to call him to court next, for an adjudication, or a preliminary counsel, a hearing.

He pulled on some jeans and a St. Augustine's sweatshirt as if they were old skin.

In the kitchen he piled his plate with a bit of everything, a Flintstones glass of orange juice, rechecked the listings, got a tape, inserted it in the VCR, then asked to turn on a show. His dad nodded a befuddled, cautious yes.

Joseph flipped the remote. Commercials, then some stunt show. *America's Most Amazing Explosions.* Joseph switched again.

"–rrific I'm sure, but don't you think there ought to be random drug tests or locker searches, I mean, getting to the root of it, who sells them things, that is what is going to help."

The camera cut to a sportscaster with what Dino called "some very technologically-enhanced hair."

Rick Rodden's Sunday talk show, *Sports Beat*, usually featured highlights and interviews with millionaire pro ball guys with necks thick as bulls. But this time, it was wrestling. The coaches were from other Jersey teams.

"We're discussing violence in sports. In light of the recent events, Coach O'Malley, do you think there's too much emphasis placed on aggression in high school sports?"

Joseph sat back, watched his father take notice. It had almost become a bit of a friendly competition, each of them seeing if they could find anything else about it all, "spin-offs," Dino called them, like the week-long special all about steroids, drug abuse in –where else?– high schools.

How could he ever explain the deadening shock of having images of Benjamin Skaal, Joseph's secret sadistic nightmare, reduced to mere stock footage?

"Well, I don't know about wrestling," the coach said, "but in basketball, the emphasis is placed on team playing, on discipline, but also on enjoying the game. I don't encourage an atmosphere of aggression, no."

Rodden turned to his other guest, a guy Joseph remembered from an invitational back in Newark. "Coach Garcia, you've had some real champions come out of your tutelage. Some have gone into world class competitions. Do you think there's an atmosphere of aggression that could lead to the events at Little Falls?"

"No. First of all, let me say that I think the coaches at Little Falls probably did their very best to keep the team playing in a good friendly atmosphere in the practice and at matches. This area has produced some of the finest athletes in this sport for decades. I understand the boys who were actually charged with these particular crimes had outside problems; alcohol, abusive families. . ."

"Gee, the guy really knows me," Joseph joked. A piece of toast checked him in the shoulder.

"Secondly, wrestling is the oldest sport in history. It has been refined though the ages and is not at all about violence."

Joseph felt better.

"It's about helping athletes achieve their very best, especially here in New Jersey, where our programs are doing great, but we still need support. It's people who associate the more violent, and staged, I might add, versions of wrestling, like the WWF, which is not really wrestling at all, but more of a show, and people don't. . ."

Joseph clapped his hands. "Awright. You tell 'em!"

His father sat up by then, his plate set aside on the coffee table.

Rodden interrupted. "Whoa, we don't want Andre the Giant coming and showing us a lesson, do we?" Forced laughter.

They watched the men debate his sport, all the way up to his comments at the end about "bad players that oughtta be kicked out of the game."

"It's not a game, it's a match, you pissant."

"Joe," his father growled.

"Sorry, Dad." They glanced to the kitchen. His mother hadn't heard it.

Rodden sure enjoyed covering fights at hockey games, pileups and punch-outs on baseball diamonds. Let it happen in a sport where they didn't even know the rules, and they were playing judge. Joseph wanted to do something, call them, write a letter, but he just steamed.

"We have some footage from a recent game. . ."

"That's match," Garcia corrected.

"Right. A 'match' of the Colts team, a kind of opening warm-ups. Can we roll that?"

Not again.

"Oh, Jesus."

"Joseph Sebastian Nicci!" All the way from the kitchen that time. She was listening.

This time the video was just the warm ups, the "Down you go." Joseph actually liked seeing it again, but from a different angle than Cleshun's or Mr. Khors' tapes, and he was glad he'd remembered to tape it. He tried not to be scared when they showed his face. It was from far away, and just with the rest of the team. Still, people knew him. This was just a personal rerun.

Rick Rodent then started talking about the song, and recited the lyrics like Church Lady: Isn't that in-teresting.

"'Down you go. Sin make me strong?' Now, you all have these opening kind of things sometimes, don't you?"

"Yes," Coach Garcia said. "Not all groups use music, but–"

"Do you think the coach knew what was in this song?"

"Well, I really don't think that it, I mean, kids have music they like, if it helps. I had a coach who liked to have us come out whistling 'Bridge on the River Kwai,' and he was a Marine."

The men laughed.

"But we never blew up any bridges."

They howled. He had 'em begging for it.

11

Miss Pooley had called to say it would be a good idea if he did his best to look good. Accordingly, Marie bought him a new tie. The tie would become a talisman, one not to be worn again. The tie forever after said, You wore me the day you died a coward's death.

Because of the "sensitivity" of the case, there were few spectators, just the parents of the accused, parents of the victim, no cameras allowed. They perched outside.

He had to tell it all again, and listen to the others in the closed courtroom. There were a few members of the press allowed, including that damn Latino guy who was responsible for the Digital Joey look. He recognized the lacquer-haired woman from the other station. She smiled at him, once.

Miss Pooley provided a legal pad to write down any comments or requests, just so nobody could overhear anything while they watched, but Joseph kept doodling, making hard angular shapes like boxed-up Escher blocks, his pen digging down three or four layers into the pad. Miss Pooley kept taking the pads away. Joseph wondered where they went, if maybe she would sell them at an auction someday. Delinquent Gallery.

Who would play him in the movie version? Somebody, one of the lawyers had joked about that. Why not? Why not play himself? Naw, too much like that creepy ice skater. She would do that.

Miss Pooley's hand lightly touched Joseph's arm, silently saying, Pay attention. This is your life evaporating under these fluorescent lights.

After a lot of moving of papers, writing things, his name was called.

A top-down version of a confession box, the witness stand was larger than he'd imagined. The carpet under the chair had some dust around the edges. The microphone was thin as a pencil. There was no echo, like a rock concert mike, so he didn't know if he was speaking too loud. It was all going into some tape recorder somewhere maybe or into the headphone of the lady who typed into the steno thing. He was just glad the Soto guy couldn't bring his Robocam inside, and that *Court TV* had been shut out for the day. He didn't want to be famous anymore.

He was distracted from the questioning. Ten feet away in the first row behind Bennie and Hunter's families and lawyers, in a suit made for funerals, bookended by parents, sat the runty love of his life.

The defense woman started ruffling her papers.

After some hemming and hawing during which everybody just sort of forgot everything for a few minutes, debating some stuff, moving papers, the defense lawyer stood up, a thin woman who looked as if she worried a lot, but wasn't worried now.

"Before the events of January first, did you consider Benjamin to be a friend?"

"Yes."

"You even went to see a movie with him, is that right?"

"Yes."

"What was the movie?"

"Uh, *Demolition Man.*"

The defense lady turned a moment, fighting a grin, eyed the room to silence. She turned back to Joseph.

"Did you like it?"

"Yeah, it was funny."

"Who taught you the ankle ride?"

"Benjamin."

"Level changing?"

"Hunter, and Coach, uh, Coach Cleshun."

"Who always helped you with pull-ups?"

"Benjamin. And Din-Din-Donald. Donald really helped me the most."

"So they all helped you become a better athlete, didn't they?"

"Yeah, but–"

"Thank you."

"When we weren't smashing windows."

"Thank you."

The defense lawyer gave him a look that drained him. She went back to her desk while Joseph contemplated the idea of helping send Bennie to jail. He stole a glance at Bennie, who seemed already strait-jacketed into his suit.

From her table, the prosecuting attorney heaved a long, exhausted sigh, stood and approached him.

Joseph wiped his face of sweat.

"You mentioned, in your testimony, that you were afraid of the defendants. Was there ever a time when any of them said things to you, threats or violent remarks addressed to you?"

"Well, when they smashed the window or–"

"I mean to you. Did they ever say, I'm going to beat you up, or–"

"Objection. This is really inappropriate to–"

"I'll have to agree."

"Tell us when Andrew ever said anything threatening."

Hunter sang a Pearl Jam song to me. That would sound stupid. "No. Not ever, really."

"Thank you. I'd like to talk about the night of Anthony's death."

Joseph shot a glance at each piece of the posse. The three of them looked around the room, dodging his glance.

"What did Benjamin say while you drove from the scene?"

"He would eat us alive if we narced, but I couldn't hear the other stuff."

"Why was that?"

Joseph blushed. "My head. . . I was on the floor, because I was still sick, and Donald held my head down, just in case."

"Was Donald trying to hide you?"

"I don't think so. I think he just wanted to keep me down if I got sick again."

"Did Donald say anything?"

"Yes."

"What did he say?"

"The Hail Mary."

"And how did you respond?"

"I started saying it, too."

"Did Benjamin say anything?"

"Yes. He was praying, too."

"Did Andrew say anything?"

"No. I don't think he knew the words."

"Why did you say the Hail Mary?"

"It was, it's like we were praying for Anthony's soul, and our own."

"So you knew he was dead?"

"No."

"Did you see Anthony before you left?"

"I was. . . no."

"How did you feel when they took you home?"

"I was scared. Sick. Thought the cops were gonna pop out any minute. I thought all kinds a sh. . . stuff. I thought. . . I thought they were gonna get me next."

"Why did you think that?"

"Because I knew."

"You knew what?"

"I knew. . . why. . . that he did all that, Bennie, Benjamin, and I'm not the kind of guy to. . . I was gonna tell anyway."

"Tell what?"

"About the other things we done. Did."

"Before the. . . death of Anthony?"

"Yes."

"I understand you were supposed to meet the next day?"

"Yes. Sunday."

"What happened then?"

195

"Bennie was going to call, but I don't think he did. If he did, I wouldn't have gone out anyway. I was grounded because I came home drunk, so I wouldn't have gotten the call anyway."

"You were grounded?"

"Yes."

"And your parents don't let you take calls when you're grounded?"

"Course not."

A laugh in the courtroom was cut off by the prosecuting attorney's remark. "I commend your parents for their strength." Then she sort of turned toward the other half of the room, where Bennie's foster parents sat. "If only more parents controlled their children, these sort of things wouldn't happen."

"Counselor."

"Sorry, your honor. Now, about your teammates. Did you want to meet with them?"

"I didn't wanna see these guys. I mean, except Donald. He, I mean, he didn't do–"

"We were discussing Benjamin and Andrew?"

"Yeah. It was them, Bennie and Hunt– Andrew. I thought for sure they were gonna kill me, because I thought they knew I was . . . that I was. . . "

"Yes?"

"Well, like gonna tell. I mean the point is they, and me, but they, they were being that way because Anthony is gay. Was."

"Excuse me?"

"Gay."

"A homosexual?"

"Yes."

Joseph heard a gasp amid the cluster of parents. It was definitely his mom, because his dad muttered something to quiet her, then glared at Joseph.

The first time he'd wrestled at St. Augustine's, he was thirteen. Some kid from Jersey City basically flipped him in a half-assed Greco move, high up in the air and down to the ground in the first five seconds. From the mat, he remembered hearing his mother make the same gasp. She'd sworn off coming to matches after that.

"Go on."

"Um, and that I told everything the night when the police showed up. And I thought if they found out, they might go for me next."

Dink bowed his head, brought his hands up, covered his face, shook his head, slowly.

"Joseph? Joseph?"

"Yes."

"We were talking about Andrew and Benjamin. You were implying that they were intentionally trying to harm Anthony, in your opinion."

"I was not implying. I said it."

"And you were saying why?"

"Why they killed him."

"Because he was gay."

"Yes."

"And how do you know this?"

"Um. . ."

"Who told you? How do you know this?"

Joseph could only see the top of Dink's lowered head, his father rubbing his shoulder, comforting him.

The judge said, "Joseph?"

"How do you know this?"

Bennie met his gaze, finally, stunned.

Hunter just smirked.

"We had an understanding."

Papers were pushed back, forth, adjournments until bla bla bla. He sat down again with his parents, five rows behind the buzzcut.

12

Musty incense, red velvet, stories of apparitions in tiny towns in the Alps, faces set in stained glass; these were what he'd grown up believing held the magic of his faith. They gave him a comfort he could smell in the wood. He believed in the goodness of the Church by loving its physical beauty and majesty, the layers of stories, lives, stars of suffering. He needed cool marble to give him gravity for what he had to face.

Instead, St. Dominic's felt warm, to be sure. Blond wood in long slats swept along the side walls. Swift in design, large chunks of colored glass blocked light more in the design of a starship than a church. Was it the paneling, having seen Anthony's funeral there?

His confessions were functional but apparently not satisfying. He was invited for a few talks with Brother Brian. They were calming, friendly but a bit remote, usually ending in a sales pitch for activities run by the Sisters. Teen Catholic Jamborees. He went. They got him points in his case file.

When his mother made plans to spend the weekend in Newark with Grandmama, he asked to tag along. He needed urban, noisy, gothic.

Once they were back on familiar turf, or at least the interstate, he noticed his mother relax. They talked nonstop about everything, almost.

Grandmama welcomed him with open frail arms, feeding them immediately. He listened to the women talk, three generations of recipes, rumor, wisdom, with Sophia playing nearby, soaking it in.

He hadn't been back since Christmas, and then, St. Augustine's was filled to overflowing with joy and singing.

The Saturday afternoon he entered the church, two elderly ladies sat at opposite sides of the main aisle, small lumps in the rows of shiny wooden pews. Joey looked toward his family's usual place, to the left and near the back, by the daycare room. He walked up the left aisle, passing the flickering electric red plastic candles around the statues of the Virgin and St. Augustine. But what caught his eye, and held it, was his favorite, the Stations of the Cross, the stone relief sculptures high up along the walls. Joey stopped before the station with Jesus being torn of his garments, then through a side door, down a hallway to a tall doorway.

"Well, Mister Nicci. It's been too long. How the heck are ya?"

Father Scanlon stood from behind his large wooden desk, lit up with joy, hand extended. His graying hair only further distinguished him in his black clothing and white divot of a collar. His black eye patch looked as dramatic and foreboding as ever, but beneath the worn face of a man in his sixties shone a constant lightness. He patted Joseph's shoulder, sat him down in one of the immense red cushioned chairs Joseph had only had the pleasure of sitting on twice; once to discuss his first communion, the second time to discuss why he'd broken Jimmy Cianfotti's glasses. He was ten at the time. Even he didn't know why. He only then realized it was just because Jimmy was so darn cute.

"I'm glad you could see me, Father."

"Of course. Always time for one of my favorite students. It was nice of your mother to call."

198

Joseph blushed, smiled. Unlike a few others from his days there, Father Scanlon never had a bad word to say, at least in class. When Joseph wanted to ask a silly question, he'd be able to ask Father Scanlon, such as, How old are angels? What's heaven made of?

"So, your mother tells me you're recovering quite well from all the . . . unpleasantness."

"Yeah, well, I suppose so."

"I'm sure it's been very difficult for you. I think you've also been a little difficult with your parents."

"Yes, and for that I am truly sorry. Are we–should I do the–"

"Oh, no, no. I'll take your confession, but let's just talk. You said you had some questions."

"Yes, Father."

"Some questions of faith, now that you've suffered the trials of public school."

"That's one problem, yes, sir. I got a few tough ones this time."

"Yes, well?"

"Um. Theological question first."

"Okay."

"How does someone become a saint?"

"Excuse me?"

"I was thinking of. . . Somebody made a joke about Anthony. Anthony Lambros. They called him Saint Anthony." Joseph did not say that the joke was his own. "I was wondering if it might be possible to have somebody from now, like these days, be elected or nominated to be a saint. I mean I heard about the Vietnamese woman who was–"

"Just a minute, Joseph. I think–"

"Sorry."

"No, no. It's a valid question. The problem is, a person's suffering, it has to be for the faith, for the good of the Mother Church, for Our Lord. First, they have to be beatified."

"Oh."

"But it's not just suffering. Now, I'm sure you're aware about your, um, teammate's death being problematic. Of course, since he was so brutally murdered, of course he will ascend to heaven."

"But if like he was gay or something."

The priest's eye blinked. He waited. He coughed. "That's different. It's . . . that is not . . . God does not like it when we willfully sin, and if someone lives a less than saintly life . . ."

"Right. So?"

"So, that would pose a problem with the sainthood proposition."

"I guess so." He wanted to ask, why then did the saints voluntarily suffer, lay on beds of rocks, allow themselves to be burned and whipped? And if they were heretics then, wouldn't somebody who disagreed with the church now be the same kind of person? Someone like Anthony?

"You have to think of it this way," Father Scanlon continued. "Think of the Pope and the Mother Church as your grandfather or your grandmother. Now, we know how wonderful your great grandmother is. I think she was even at my first communion," he joked. "But they're very set in their ways, you know, being their age, and well, they're just not quite ready for some of the new ideas you kids have got going. D'ya understand?"

"Sort of."

"Good."

"But what about the thing that. . . See, Anthony, he, um, well, you read it in the papers–"

"Saw it on the news. Yes."

"And I was, like thinking. Would God not let Anthony into heaven because he was gay?"

Nothing. Father Scanlon's eye didn't even blink.

Joseph let the silence fill the room. He knew the impact his words would have. He knew the soft warmth of the room would daunt him, the leaded glass, the books, the curtains, all the cool curving columns would charm him back to submission. That was why he'd practiced his questions. He knew that one word would blow away a lot of dust.

"Joseph, my boy. You're on the wrestling team."

"Well, that's–"

"Think of it this way. You have a set of rules. You don't cheat when you compete, do you? Or when the ref blows the whistle."

"Right."

"So, when we. . . misbehave, or cheat, or don't play by the rules, we can't play the game, right?"

"But what about if Anthony loved somebody and really really felt a closeness and wanted to only be with that person. I mean, what if he just wanted to–"

"Joseph, are we talking about Anthony or you?"

"Both."

"Well, then, I suggest you consider playing by the rules."

"I don't like those rules anymore."

"Well, that, my boy, is a problem."

"Why can't the rules change? Wrestling rules change all the time."

"We don't work so fast here, as you may recall."

They both forced out smiles, tried to find a way back. Back was not an option.

"Do you think it's evil, Father?"

"What is?"

"You know. Being, like. . ."

"Joseph. You know what sin is. You know what damage it wreaks. Look at those boys. See what their lives have become. Thank your parents for raising you honorably, to tell the truth, in Anthony's memory."

"Yeah, but where's Anthony going? Seems to me like he keeps hanging around me."

"You're just feeling sad about his death."

"And plus I'm thinking that the church is like booting him out for being, what is that, intrinsically evil."

"You don't know–"

"Yes, I do. I do, Father. I knew Anthony and I know what the church says about it and I'm thinking I can't agree."

"Now, don't get in a dander."

"The Pope said that, he said, 'Intrinsically evil.' What's intrinsically?"

"Well, it means, well, by nature, that by nature, the act, um, not you yourself–" His words faltered, became a jumble. Joseph looked away. He wasn't going to find an answer. He knew the answer. It was the same with Assistant Coach Fiasole, the same with the Ass Prince, the same with Miller and everybody else.

"I know you're tryin' to be nice to me an' all since I like suffered all this. But, ya see I'm really having a problem seeing this the way it's told to me like I gotta be somebody else or dead before I'm gonna get some slack."

"I see."

"I'm not . . . I . . .already . . . I know what I am. I mean, I'm not gonna go march in a parade." Yet. "But I gotta be honest with myself, right?"

"Yes, if that's what you call it."

"Because it's what everybody's thinking. It's what everybody's saying behind my back. I turned both cheeks and then some."

The priest waited for Joseph to say more, but when he said nothing, Father Scanlon started again. "If you want to be what you say you are–"

"Want. What is to want?"

"You are settin' yerself up for a lot of problems, suffering and humiliation. Think of your family."

"Sir, I am, but see, there's this other family. This family I can't see."

"I don't getcha, Joey."

"Um . . ."

"Well, would you care to explain it to me?"

He wanted to talk about the other Joeys. He wanted to say how some of this suffering should come to some good, as he imagined, or had imagined any saint's life to be worthy of. But all he could see was more suffering. He wanted to be home, wherever that was, or outside, breathing the cold spring air. He needed a little bus exhaust, some more of Grandmama's lasagna, spiraling DNA balloons in all colors taking flight.

Sunday afternoon, Marie nodded as she drove by their old house. "There it was," she sighed.

He gazed through the car window at the house, the worn slats of aluminum siding, the windows and doors, a box of memories, one-eyed photographs.

After leaving Grandmama, who loaded them down with food to take home, Marie and Joseph visited Marie's old high school pal Angelina, who had been their neighbor in Newark, but had moved down the block to a better building and kept meaning to come up to Little Falls to visit.

After Angelina asked a third just-curious question about "the tragedy," Marie asked if her son could leave the room and watch some television. "Oh, sure. I'm so sorry!"

As the women talked over coffee in the kitchen above him, he channel-surfed in the basement den, found a re-run of *Saved By the Bell's Hawaiian Holiday*, with one scene of Mario Lopez in a Hawaiian skirt and nothing else.

That time, he used his own sock.

13

The pasta maker, exiled to the cabinet, was replaced by economy bags of the dry stick version. Sauce arrived in bulk cans. The lasagna became more frequently black around the edges. Lopsided chunks of carrot sunk down into bogs of dressing. Take-out menus began to fill the napkin rack.

When Marie Nicci had become pregnant with Mike, then Sophia, her own health shifts and eating habits had taught him more than the basic birds and bees, but also how to gauge his mother's mood by her cooking.

"Why don't you clean the basement?"

He'd been hovering in that way that usually got her talking, got them talking about it, whatever It was. But now It was not up for discussion.

"The basement?" What, have her lock the door? Keep him in the cellar? It could lock. He'd done it to Mike twice. "Okay."

"I just think since you've been hanging around the house so much you could do a little more. I'm very busy right now."

"I said okay."

"Well, I'm sorry. Perhaps I can make an appointment with your counselor to 'access your needs.'"

She was on medium peeved mode, sort of waiting for the conversational match to ignite her. "Whatever I did today or yesterday or tomorrow, I'm sorry, awright?"

Her eyes started welling up, which made Joseph think that was just a scream or a shout being held back. "All I could think is this, in the middle of all these problems, when your father told me. . ." The hand to the face, the wiping away. Joseph held fast. "All I could think was, my first born son is never gonna get married."

Joseph found himself in her arms, comforting her, just swaying in the kitchen with her, dancing slowly.

They pulled apart when he joked, muffled into her arm, "You just want a big wedding."

She acted shocked, pulled away, wiping her face. "You. . ."

"Well, don't worry. Ya got two more chances. Besides, if that thing in Hawaii ever happens, maybe I will be a honeymooner."

"What? What are you talking about?"

"That, um, lawsuit. They got like a lawsuit to try to get married, these, people, these, these gay people."

"Oh," she said, looking around her kitchen, as if searching for the place where the word stuck, so she could wipe it off. "And?"

"And, well. . ." He didn't understand how only a moment ago they were a Hallmark card, and now he was on trial again. "I mean it would be a good thing, right?"

"To another boy?"

"That's what I was saying."

His mother heaved a sigh, put her hands on her hips, then crossed her arms. It was as if she were trying to learn how to talk to him differently.

"You know, your father is having a tough time. I am, too. Sophia's teacher says she might be dyslexic. The other day at recess your brother bit the head off a worm to show off. We are all having a tough time. I think you have to think about other people a little, okay?"

"Okay."

Laundry first. He started by shoving all the wet clothes from the washer into the dryer. He plucked white sheets, towels, socks, his father's T-shirts, underwear, his underwear, his mother's bras from an overflowing basket into the washer. She didn't want him ruining anything. He'd received more detailed instructions than in the weeks preceding his Confirmation.

He dropped in Dink's sock. To avoid losing it he'd kept it hidden, made a little mark on the inside with a permanent magic marker for washing. As much as he wanted to savor the memory of Dink, it had begun to smell like a dead fish.

The double churning hum of the machines comforted him, as did the oily feeling on his fingertips after pulling out a strip of fabric softener.

With a dust mop Joseph swirled the webs of dryer lint clustered behind the machine, around the ducts to the high windows where spiders lived. "Cotton Candy for the Dead," he joked to himself.

He remembered the toads, wondered if they were happy, then went to check on them. They both sat in the terrarium, still except for the movement of their gullets oscillating. He wanted to find a bug to feed them, tried to pick up boxes quickly, find some silverfish to smash. There weren't any.

Looking up to the basement window, now nearly blocked with

snow, he wondered what it would be like to freeze to death. The once-fun snow had became a chore to be pushed around in the driveway, off steps.

To compensate for the chill, or the grief, or the discomfort of having a son they no longer knew, his mother had begun to pray more, buy more little items: rosaries, ceramic praying hands, decorative devotional objects to fill the undecided spaces of their new home. His father bought equipment for projects that were soon abandoned, or delayed: furnace filters, drainage pipes, garage wall shelving, caulking kits.

The plaque still hung over his father's workbench. Tools hung neatly on beaverboard pegs above the wooden table. A hundred strange metal secrets lay clumped in its drawers. Joseph toyed with his father's power drill, wondering if maybe Freddy Kreuger could just stop in for a visit and screw a hole through his skull.

No, too messy. They'd never get it cleaned up. They'd have to abandon the basement, have the laundry sent out, sell the house amid clouds of rumors.

He found a can of lubricant, began wiping his father's tools, giving them a shine, smoothing away bits of rust or sawdust. He toyed with wooden handles of saws, nubbled tips of rubber-handled pliers, a heavy crescent wrench.

He walked over to the boxes, some still unpacked, or repacked with toys, games that had too soon proved boring, or were out of season. Mike's (now Sophia's) Big Wheel, Joey's (now Mike's) Mousetrap game, nobody's broken Speak n' Spell.

Toys made him feel old. Everybody kept saying he had to think about the future, that he had a full life ahead of him. He felt like a little old man. With Dink, the memories were soft, sweet, every moment from their brief few hours crystallized into glorious dreams.

He wondered why Bennie'd chosen Anthony to wipe out and not him. He felt very guilty about that, and about the wildly elaborate sexual stuff about Bennie, being forced to do things. That stuff was strange. He had to put it away. Yanking off to it usually did the trick.

He shoved boxes around, found a cluster of half-burned votive candles that had been placed in windows or bathrooms, above the fridge, back in Newark. Marie liked to call them "decorative," until they moved to Little Falls. They looked stupid in the new house, so she'd put them away. Maybe she used to believe they actually did something. Maybe they could. Even if they didn't, they'd look nice all lit up if he turned the lights off.

He returned to his father's workbench, rooted around for it. Near the solder gun, or maybe the acetylene torch. There. Matches.

Before he lit the first candle he hauled out the little fire extinguisher, just in case.

Carefully extracting a dozen votives, he arranged them in a circle, almost lit the candles, but something was missing.

Tunes.

But when he got to the top of the basement stairs, he was afraid to enter the kitchen, so he just cracked it open. Seeing no one, he reached his hand around, turned the handle, locking himself inside. He flicked the light off, felt his way back down. He'd have to settle for singing in his head.

He lit the candles, saying the name of each member of the team, the twelve chosen, the lost one.

Standing in the middle, then crouching, then kneeling, one hand dug into his sweat pants, Joseph prayed for the souls of Anthony, himself, the coaches, even his friends in jail, that everybody still on the team would have a good season, not get hurt or killed, or in two cases, out on bail.

To feel them again, smell them, some more than others, he wanted to hurt in his muscles, not in his head or guts. He longed for the good pain, somebody on him, pressing him down, forcing him to push up for survival. During some moments, his hips rising off the floor, he grappled with Dink or Fiasole. It was the circle he was making love to, not any one guy, but the space between them, what connected them.

He felt a surge, pressed his dick down to keep it from rising up in him. Rolling on his back, the basement floor was too hard for a bridge. He settled back up on his forelegs, humping air, riding an invisible partner. He didn't want to spill all over himself, or the dirty floor, so he stood up, looking for something to contain it.

In a box of his old toys, he found a tiny white football helmet, one he bought for a quarter at the Woolworth's in Newark on Market at Broad. Or was it the Gristede's? He couldn't remember.

When he'd first heard the name of his new school's mascot, the next day, he'd popped a quarter in the machine and this Indianapolis Colts helmet tumbled out in a plastic bubble.

Putting the helmet on the head pinched his dick. He twitched, held the helmet upside down, clutched himself more, spurted into it, offered it up, slurped. It tasted like sweetened snot.

"What the hell are you doing?" His mother looked afraid to even descend the stairs.

When he heard the basement door jiggle, then again, then open, he had just enough time to pull up his sweat pants, blow out a few candles, give up on that, hide his dick between crossed legs.

"Praying."

"You pray in church."

"I wanted to pray now."

"What is this? Are you some kind of . . . ? Are those my candles? I'm calling ya father."

"No. I'll clean it up."

"You betcher ass you will."

"I already cleaned everything else up."

His mother scanned the basement. Aside from the strange glowing circle of votives, everything was more orderly. Even her husband's tool bench seemed to shine.

Spaghetti, sausage with extra onions, extra sauce, extra silence. No "Joey cleaned the basement." Not even "Joey started his own religion today."

He couldn't explain what he'd been doing. It just felt right. He needed spooky, sacred, secret. At least his mother hadn't told on him, yet.

After doing the dishes, responding to questions with only a few grunts from his father, who let Sophia ramble on about where rain comes from which she learned in pre-school, he holed up in his room, looking at page 156 of his Math book for about two hours, the same way he'd spent an hour a day staring at the empty desk where Dink should have been.

While drafting his own version of an encounter between Spidey and Wolverine, he couldn't decide which parts of Spidey's tights should get shredded. Dink's music mix blasted from his headphones. "Disappointed a few people. Well, isn't that what friends are for?"

Mike's feet appeared at his side. He jumped to cover up the drawing, which had become less than subtle.

"What?" Joseph plucked the phones off, annoyed.

Mike held his finger to his lips, quieting Joseph, led him to the top of the stairs, where they heard parental voices back in the kitchen.

His dad. "The counselor said it would be a bad idea to move him again. He needs stability."

"He needs discipline, order. I told you he shoulda stayed-"

"Marie, we agreed before-"

"That was a long time ago-"

"Not even a year ago-"

"You know what I mean."

Mike whispered, "They're gonna send you to boot camp."

"No, they're not. Shut up."

"I don't have to shut up."

"Shut it!"

His mother's voice: "Joseph, are you listening?"

The boys froze.

His father's voice: "Come down here, young man."

Not a word was uttered until he sat, both his parents hovering about the sofa, not sure where they were supposed to stand.

His dad looked up the stairs. "Michael, go."

Joseph heard the ceiling creak as Mike padded off to his room, shut the door.

His mother's arms were crossed tight across her, then not crossed, her fingers picking a piece of something off the top of a new chair. "We think it's best if you go back to parochial school."

"I already graduated," he shot back.

His dad charged toward him but stopped, satisfied with just a good flinch from his son.

Marie countered, "There's other Catholic schools."

"You're gonna transfer me?"

"We're still discussing it," his father gritted through his teeth. Joseph wasn't sure, but Dino seemed more upset with Marie than him.

"Well, I am against it," Joseph tossed in. "That's my discussion. I won't go."

"Excuse me, but you are still my son and not even able to drive a car-"

"Yeah, but when I do-" he stopped.

"Yes?" his father asked. "You'll what? What are you gonna do? Tell me now what is in that thick head of yours," his father's hand loomed, ready to smack. Joseph didn't even raise his arm to defend. "Because I'd much rather-"

"Dino."

"-know right now than have to come and pick you up again at the-"

"I'll kill myself," the boy muttered.

"Do you know what I have had to go through-"

"Dino! I am talking here!"

He was silent, but by the look in his father's eye, Joseph figured things were going to be very noisy in their room that night. Then she'd go back to Newark for a few days. That's right, it's Friday, Joseph remembered. Pizza night, or what was pizza night.

Marie adjusted herself into the next-to-the-sofa chair while Dino stood silent, arms crossed. "We think it would be a good thing for you, to get away from everything that happened, those boys picking on you. We think not having some more closely watched supervision, but also, listen, listen, we just don't think public school is good enough for you."

"But." He waited for silence, a nod, permission to speak. Then he said, slowly, softly, "Please. . . don't. . . do this. Don't just make me disappear. I done that."

"You can make new friends," she said, switching gears with a hint of fake hopefulness.

"I got friends already."

"They're in jail," his father popped. Joseph glared back, dropped it, but noticed his mother wasn't pleased with his dad for interrupting her nice approach.

"It seems like the right thing to do," she said.

"But they don't have wrestling at St. Dominic's anymore."

"Well, maybe that's something you'll have to give up for a while."

He stared at his mother as if she were a complete stranger.

"Ma. It's not wrestling that made this happen. It's not wrestling that got me in trouble-"

"I'm not saying that-"

"Marie-"

"I just think you ought to have friends outside-"

"Who, Ma? *Girl*-friends? Is that what you're talking about? Huh? Some church lady's blind daughter?"

"That's enough." His father that time.

Joseph waited, then softly, "I got good grades. I promise ya, please, please don't, don't do this. It's. . .it's. . ." A Miss Pooley word. He couldn't find it. "I am very stressed now, okay?"

"It's not having any faith that did this," she muttered to herself.

"Did what? Did what, Ma?"

She could accuse, but wouldn't name it.

"Ma. I'll go to Mass. I'll go every Sunday. I promise. I'll light a candle for Anthony every day and pray for his soul, awright?" He considered going down on his knees, but that would have been overdoing it.

The seriousness of his pose lost its import when his father said, "It's two blocks closer than the public school. Figured you'd wanna go for a change."

His mom was about to start up again, but his father must have given her some secret look. "If you promise to be more responsible."

"I promise. I'll clean my room. I'll do the dishes. I'll take out the garbage."

"You already do that," his mother reminded him.

"I'll do it better."

"You promise?"

"Promise."

They looked at each other, at him, at the walls.

14

Whatever he did in the basement, it worked.

A letter from the school board arrived, saying that after a review, it was decided he would be allowed back on the wrestling team, on a probationary period.

They impersonated Back to Normal very convincingly. It was a team effort.

Practices had moved on, but the team wasn't its former self. Assistant Coach Fiasole never spoke about the little incident of "misguided affection." Fiasole rarely spoke to him, and never alone.

Coach Cleshun kept up the drills, coaching with an intensity bent on eradicating any misbehavior. Still, the team had a consistent losing streak.

Some people still came to the home matches, out of a morbid curiosity, perhaps, but a losing team, no matter how notorious, is still a losing team.

But by Advent, the blocks and "oops" trips were getting to him. Every night before bed, what felt like a knife in his knee, or his elbow twinging, or that damn knuckle that Troy really didn't mean to step on, or even more annoying, just a sliver of pain from where he chewed a nail too short; every tiny arrow accumulated, throbbed.

After one too many falls from helping Ricky Ponzell practice an ankle ride, Joseph fell on his back, stayed there.

It did not take many by surprise. Ricky apologized immediately, remaining by his side. He waited for Coach Fiasole to tend to him. Cleshun approached instead.

"What is it?"

"The neck." He couldn't move it without jabs from what felt like a swallowed fork.

Icepacks were produced. He was assisted to a corner, eased to a soft wall.

Joseph winced as Ricky helped him sit up.

"I'm sorry."

"No prob."

Cleshun said, "Is this the same. . ."

"Yeah."

"How long have you been in pain?"

Joseph smirked. "Good question, sir."

Walt stood up on a bench, pulling his pants up, casually said, "So, ya hear from Dink?"

"Huh?"

"Heard he's livin' with his dad in Passaic."

"Oh yeah," Joseph bluffed. "Um, actually, yeah, he called me."

"How's he doin'?"

"Pretty good."

Walt nodded back.

"Considering he's livin' in Passaic."

Walt laughed. So did Joseph.

"Hey, Neech, are you okay?"

He regarded Walt, shirtless, his muscles so perfect, his intentions so sincerely clueless. "Breathin', dude."

The neck put him out for a week that time. He still had lunch with a few guys. It was still mostly Walt, The Shivers, Troy, some other jocks. Since the court proceedings, Joseph was interesting again.

He figured a couple of them as half-queer. Ever since losing Dink he began to remember his lines, his hints. Joseph began to see clues; earrings, lisps, looks, T-shirts. He saw girls who didn't seem like the dating type. He saw everything differently. Everyone was a candidate for love or treachery.

He also saw the difference between himself, his family, others in this new town that he learned to be cautious of. This was not like Newark street fear. These were mostly richer kids than his family. Some of them had big houses, houses his father worked in, people Dino worked for.

That topic, strangely enough, came up out of the blue.

"So, Neech, what does your father do?"

Joseph chewed a big hunk of a thing the school menu called Wiener Winks; to him, lousy cheesedogs.

He noticed everybody on Jock Row. Most of them had cars, stacks of abandoned video games, college plans. They leaned in, watching him chew, waiting for his response.

Raul mentioned something else to change the topic, but a little muttered comment about his dad "layin' pipe" from Troy cut Raul off, then Troy said, "Don't blow chunks, man."

Giggles, snorts, smirks continued as Joseph held the food in his mouth, slowly swallowed it down, wondering how much longer he was going to be able to keep from opting for a projectile food fight, until the laughter died down. He kept on grinning like a fool, blushing, waiting, just like Grampa telling the funniest, big-laugh story to end Christmas dinner so everybody could get up from the table, relax, have some coffee, relocate. Joseph waited, knowing they would laugh, not with him, but at him, so he delayed the inevitable humiliation, then, in a deft Grover impersonation Sophia always went wild for, Joseph, not only to brush off their attempts at ridicule, but demean them, diss them right back for their childishness, chirped, "My daddy is a plumber."

Everybody exploded with laughter, except Joseph.

Troy nagged him to tell the nun and the priest and the camel joke again, but he only smiled, nodded no.

Besides, nobody was drinking milk.

15

By mid-March, practices were geared toward regional finals, a competition Joseph knew was out of his reach. It had been, in the words of Coach Cleshun, "a difficult season."

He didn't move as fast, what with his collective injuries, other guys' elbows, heads, shoes beginning to collide more often with his body. It wasn't anything on purpose. Guys were just wrestling. It was either Joseph trying to overdo it, or not at all, wavering.

Practice was only an hour, just a review of what Coach Cleshun hoped the boys would remember for the Belleview match that night. Everybody was a bit edgy.

In the practice room, Troy told just the punch line of some joke Joseph didn't get. "What?" Troy said, "Nothing," to which Raul Klein added, "It was at the Passaic match."

"So, tell it."

"You had to be there," Troy shrugged it off, as if he wasn't worth explaining it to. "And you been outta commission."

"What? What is wrong?" Joseph was getting sick of their distance. "What the hell is with you guys?"

"It's not you, man," Raul said, trying to soothe him. Joseph had passed beyond Dink's old weight, moved up to Troy's slot at 135. That bit of information had been common knowledge for a week. Raul seemed relieved at first that he might be bumped down, but Troy was different.

"It's just. . ."

Joseph had asked to be adjusted in weight class. Coach Cleshun had said, in front of several other boys, that they would have to compete for it.

Troy puffed his chest up, claiming turf. "It's just that you remind us of a ghost." Troy stared. The other guys stretched out, but listened, ears alert for a fight.

Joseph almost backed down. "Why don't you just leave it alone, man. He's dead."

"Yeah, just a dead fag." Troy thwapped Joseph's chest with a finger. "Just like you. Soon. And you know, I don't think we oughtta have to share a locker with your kind."

"What?"

"Homo. Thalo. Moose."

"You're a confident little Christian."

"Call 'em as I see 'em."

"Call yourself challenged."

It was, to say the least, brutal as a holy war, but with two armies of one. Not the sort of match some people care to watch. It was a good thing that it happened in the practice room, under watchful, if not refereed, supervision. It would have been a good warm-up if it hadn't nearly killed him.

213

Dizzy, exhausted, throbbing with pain, tied with Troy after an overtime, he refused to give up, and would have lost, but Troy tripped, Joseph grabbed his leg, yanked, jumped, pinned.

That night, Joseph Nicci moved up to 135. Troy was cast down to manning the video camera. Assistant Coach Fiasole gave a little talk about "fairness" for the length of the bus ride.

Joseph was not pumped because he had a fresh buzzcut, or that it was their last duals match of the season. He was not pumped because he had gulped a double caff capp, nor because he enjoyed scoping a certain member of his team pop a half-chubby in the showers.

He was pumped because although he had beaten Troy off the record, nobody would ever forget why.

The Belleview Patriots came barreling out of their locker room with a rush and a thunder of blue and white, fans clapping and stomping to the tune of "Eye of the Tiger."

"How original," Lamar muttered.

Among the few dozen Little Falls family members sat Dino Nicci, his Colts Boosters jacket matched a few other errant fathers amid the rest of the Pumpkin Squad, a tiny cluster of orange and black amid the Belleview sea of patriotic blue and white regional championship banners in just about everything except wrestling.

So when Dustin got his first pin, it wasn't just for him they cheered, but themselves, for the team, or its ragged endurance.

Joseph's opponent was a squat pimply-faced Asian kid, Something-Pak. The back of his sweatshirt read PAK-MAN. He appeared to be Belleview's hot dog. When they shook hands, he smiled like an old friend. As he moved in on the mat, the smile disintegrated into a snarl.

Joseph suffered a contusion to his temple that made his ear bloat up. His headgear slipped off twice. He re-strained his neck injury, which required an ice pack. He got so nauseous after the match that he hurled. Nothing came up.

But he won.

Afterward, his dad hugged him, talked with other parents, all of whom had come to the match.

Joseph felt himself relax as his father passionately armchair-described the moment when, five points behind, he'd merely waited for the right moment, grabbed the boy's hand, yanked, flipped him on his back and pressed.

As the icepack numbed his neck, he remembered it as reacting to some pretty awful hits, grabbing at anything, ignoring all pain, just plain refusing to lose.

But that wasn't the victory that mattered to Joseph. His occurred afterward. Troy was bent over, fumbling with extension cords, the team equipment that had strangely gone "out of whack" during Joseph's toughest match. He stood over Troy, out of earshot from anyone else, muttered, "Pretty good for a dead fag, huh?"

"Don't open it," his mom said. "It's not done re-heating."

Joseph and his dad checked the oven as the lasagna cooked. Just the smell alone made him feel better.

He trotted out of the kitchen as if nothing were wrong that day, as if he were just going off to the tub to take a bath, maybe get some chores done for "gimme some slack" points. He'd held out through the season, needed to hibernate, lick some wounds.

But Marie cut them off at the stairs.

"Michael came home with a black eye today."

"Just one?"

"He got in a fight. Why do you think he got in a fight?"

Dino and Joseph exchanged glances, shrugs. "I blame Professional Wrestling."

"It was about your other son," Marie scolded. "Some boys were saying he. . . They were calling him names and talking about him and Mike just started swinging. I had to go to St. Dominic's today, walk down there and why doesn't that secretary in your office tell me where you are when I call?"

Dino put a reassuring arm on his wife's shoulder. "They only got two cell phones. I gave the other one to the foreman on the site."

"Why didn't you call home before you went to his match? I had to go to that school with Soph. Irene's not home."

Joseph scooted out of range, but his mother caught him with a "Wait a minute."

"What?"

"Did you hear what I said?"

"What part?"

"Don't get smart."

He stood still, holding back a grin, his arm up, holding his icepack.

"I want. . . I want to know what to tell your brother."

"Tell him to try an arm bar next time."

215

Dino laughed at that one.

"Hey!"

"What, Marie?"

"I want to know what to tell him."

"Tell him his big brother just won his last match of the season, awright?"

"Not that."

"About what?"

"About you," she said.

What was her problem, Joseph wondered. What had he done this time?

And then he got it. About you, the Household Homosexual. "Oh, man," He turned away to leave the kitchen.

"Well, he asked me and I thought I should–" The phone rang. His mother didn't answer it.

"Oh, great, I'm sure what you'd tell him would make him think–"

But she stopped, waving him away. He retreated into the kitchen while she stood by the phone, listening to his father fend off another intruder. He wondered if that included members of the Khors family.

His mother returned to the kitchen.

"Who was that?" he asked.

"No one."

They looked at each other. She opened the oven, withdrew the pan of lasagna. He saw his mother looking, or sensing the space outside the house, as if someone were waiting.

"I'll talk to him," he said.

"Your father's first. Listen, I don't think you should–"

"I'll talk to him, awright?"

"Eat first." He sat. She scooped out lasagna, set his father's plate on the table.

"Don't tell him those things that people like you–"

"Whaddaya mean, like me?" His voice had a tendency to squeak when raised. "You think I'm, what, a freak or something? You think I'm out struttin' around, tellin' everybody?" He shoveled in lasagna, determined to eat her excellent food, no matter how much she wanted to argue.

"You did in the court room."

"Igh was ebivence!"

"Eat. Chew. Then talk."

He swallowed. "Whaddaya think I been gettin' at school? At least, at least at Little Falls I know who my enemies are there. Every day, I'm like waiting for it. Every day."

"Awright. just . . . calm down, awright?"

"Awright."

She watched him eat. He scowled.

"Where's Soph?"

"Asleep."

He wiped his plate with a slice of bread.

"You want more?"

He nodded.

"Gimme a hug first."

He stood, his fork still in his hand. It was formal, cold, but they did it. The pain was not soothed. It was amputated.

Dino entered, sat at the table, ate and retold Joseph's match in proud proportions. But Joseph wasn't proud at all. It had been his worst match. The guy had hit him, scraped him, cheated. He'd been all angles and jabs. In defense, Joseph had used rage instead of technique.

"Where's Mikey?"

"In his room."

After starting some hot tub water, he knocked on Mike's door. "Hey."

Mike sat on the floor in his pajamas, amid a pile of dinosaur toys. Among them shone, in its new presence, the thing, the horse, the monster; Evil Pegasaurus, in the house.

Mike looked up. A bluish mark below his left eye resembled a smudge. Marie must have gotten the toy to make him feel better.

"Hey, look what you got."

Mike turned away.

"Wonder what you get for a broken arm."

More silence.

"Heard you beat up the whole school today."

"Nobody beat me up. Mark Piselli said you were a fag and I hit him. This is from his elbow."

"Gotta watch those elbows."

"Brother Brian whacked me. In front of everybody."

"Bummer." Joseph sat on Mike's bed, slowly to avoid another neck twinge.

"Is it true?" Mike asked without turning to face him.

"What?"

"Are you a fag?"

Joseph looked around his little brother's room. Action figures, puzzle pieces, every toy he ever abandoned for wrestling. Mike had moved the toads up to his room. They sat silent, nearly invisible in their terrarium behind rocks half underwater, a little dead branch planted like a tree.

"Look, I don't know, okay?"

"How can you not know if you're a fag?" Mike turned around.

"Look, you. Don't say that again. That's a really bad word. Look, I'm really happy you stood up for me and all, but don't tell Ma I said that."

"Okay." Mike sort of smiled. "But are you?"

"Uh, see, what. . . oh, man." As he knelt down on the floor, his knees made a crunching sound. His shoulder twinged. His neck throbbed. He had to get to the tub before he stiffened to Tin Man status. "What I am is none of their business, okay? Anybody starts making cracks about me, you tell them to try sayin' it to my face, awright?"

"But are you?"

He remembered the time when he was Mike's age. Even then he looked at men differently, touching his father's hands, seeing other boys on the playground of St. Augustine's, in ties, white shirts, watching their soft profiles in classrooms, not knowing what to do with them, so full of feelings. "Yeah. I am."

Mike waited, took it in, then said, "Well, you shouldn't be."

"Well, I got no choice. So get over it."

"Brother Brian says you're going to hell, even if you confess a million times, you're sinning by your evil desires."

"Since when did you start believing what Brother Brian says?"

"Since he whacked me."

"Well, remember who's your family and who loves you and who gave you all his old toys without you even having to ask and I nevah hit you. Not once."

"I don't want your old toys. I don't want anything from you. I wish you were dead."

"Fine."

Joseph walked to his room, grabbed a towel on the way, stripped down to it, picked ZONE OUT, popped it in the little box, clamped it on, went to the bathroom, sank in the water, suds up to his neck, knowing it was ridiculous to even imagine electrocuting himself on two AA batteries.

16
DRUNKEN SPREE ON HIGHWAY
ATHLETE DESCRIBES SCENE

He considered throwing away his clippings about The Varsity Posse. Ever since one paper coined the phrase, it stuck.

His parents kept saying it was going to be okay. They didn't have to see the faces turn away in the halls the day after he appeared in court. They didn't have to pretend the looks didn't sting.

But then he figured they did. At work his father must have been getting hassled. Would he be fired? Could his mother write a check without being recognized at D'Agostino's?

Talking about things should have helped, but she didn't talk to him. Mrs. DeStefano visited, enjoying being needed, helping his mother cry, worry, wonder aloud what to do, what the neighbors would think.

He wanted to go downstairs, but he couldn't stand the women's stares, the accusing glances, the way they watched his every move.

He dug into his closet where his new and old Asics lay tumbled together with his gear in his wrestling bag. A jock strap tangled around a plastic bag, the extra instant cold compress Coach Cleshun had given him for his neck. It wobbled like a water balloon. One slap and it would be freezing. Somebody said the stuff inside was toxic. He read the back of the bag.

"WARNING! May be harmful if swallowed. If accidentally swallowed, give one or two glasses of milk or water and induce vomiting." It went on, in Spanish too. Joseph tried to read the words, but gave up after "el vomito," shoved all his old gear back into the closet.

Another check in the hall. He didn't hear voices, but then low whispering.

It was about Anthony again. Checking stories before commissioning the shrine or some stuff about the school and the police.

"She said the assistant coach came to her door to apologize for something. . ."

A clink of coffee cup. *Live at Five* blathered away.

"Now it's like, everybody knows. . .I don't know what to do. He refuses to talk about it. I don't know what to say."

"He hasn't found the right girl."

"He's never had a date."

That they would continue this wasn't what made him bolt. He wanted to hear more about Anthony. Him and Fiasole? No way. If it were true, more power to Anthony. At least he didn't die a virgin. He wanted to go talk to Anthony, blue-faced or not.

The only way to make a quick escape was to dash down the stairs, turn right through the dining room, then the kitchen, porch, yard, air, silence.

He breezed by them, but his coat whipped around the banister.

"Where are you going?"

"Out."

"Don't get in any trouble. You have to go back to court tomorrow."

"I'm just going for a walk!"

"Joseph!"

He went anyway, out the back door.

"You cannot run away from this!"

Through the neighbor's yard, pulling on his coat, then finally running, he almost heard one last call of his name, but knew his mother wouldn't shout like she could in Newark, not here with all the cute hedge rows, driveways, listening lawns.

He ran to a chunk of woods in the back part of town he'd gone to explore with Mike. His knee began to hurt, so he had to slow down, then walk. He considered turning around, going back toward Totowa. He wanted to find the headstone, then changed his mind. He just found a part of the other woods, a small acreage, coated in mushy clusters of leaves that hadn't fully rotted from the winter snow. He walked until the rumble of the highway receded. The woods were silent except for his footfalls and panting.

By the time he got to the place it would be easier to cry, he found that he couldn't. He had almost come to like the feel of his tears. He always felt a little better afterward. Now it was only sweat. He watched as the drops soaked into his gloves while his breath snaked up in wisps.

About a year B. S. A. (Before Saint Anthony), when everything was okay, his father had let him drive the truck. Even though it was in a parking lot, he felt as if he could handle it.

But where would go if he took the truck? There weren't any cliffs handy, except maybe an overpass on the turnpike, or the Palisades. He didn't think he'd be able to push the truck through the stone barricades along the sides. He'd seen the skid marks on roads where people had wrecked cars, glass crumbs shiny on asphalt.

But messing it up, just getting injured, ripping a leg off, being a cripple, a vegetable; no, there was no sure way to do it. He'd get away with people thinking it was a mistake, but that wasn't what he wanted to do. He had to atone, make God understand, then Jesus would take him under his arms. Anthony would be there to welcome him, forgive him.

"Bullshit."

The sound of his own voice was sucked into the woods. "Bullshit, bullshit, bullshit!" He growled aloud, then screamed, a wordless noise that made birds flutter away, then echoed out, absorbed again by the ragged blanket of snow. He was still alone, but his throat hurt.

Joseph wondered what Dink was doing in Passaic at that moment. Miss Pooley told him he could write to Dink, but what would he say? "Sorry I narced on you, but gee, maybe we can still be friends." How about, "I'd like to have another date, if you aren't too busy getting your ass plowed by drug dealers and bank robbers."

They'd never done anything like hiking or going to the city together. Dink was due to get his driver's license, but that wasn't going to happen until December, if ever.

Joseph dug into his pants, tried to push off the sad feelings with sex feelings. Heat pushed out from his body, warmed his hand like a small brush fire. He recalled how Grampa had told stories in their musty apartment in Newark, how his Grampa's father had fought in the war, how cold it must have been, how they stayed warm by huddling close together. He felt both heartened and guilty for imagining himself a soldier, hugging close to his buddy to stay alive, bumping helmets.

17

Grandmama Nicci drove Joey and Mikey to a theme park in a fake desert with booths and souvenir shops where the dinosaurs weren't out but he could hear them or maybe it was coming out of those little speakers in the bushes but he couldn't tell since it got dark and Grandmama said she was tired and Joey had to drive from the back seat then found his way up the front seat until they got lost and had to ask directions at a takeout place where Joey asked how far it was to the exit. "Do you mean with raptors or without?" the speaker box said. Off to the side Joseph saw his posse standing with the earth crumbling away under Hunter then Bennie like one of his father's Yes albums which looked cool but then Dink started losing his footing as the ground under his wrestling shoes got all mucky like Easter grass and marshmallows combined and Dink fell away too and he wanted to follow but found himself in a warm room with boxes of adhesive tape lining a wall and Assistant Coach Fiasole leaning over him to look at a leg muscle that spasmed but Fiasole wore only a jock strap and glasses.

By morning, he couldn't remember the rest, except for waking up with a boner and his gastrocnemius in spasm from running to the woods the day before. He got up, ran a hot shower, took care of business.

The decision about Bennie was supposed to be in the paper, but there was some kind of delay. Joseph had slept all afternoon. By nightfall, with everybody asleep, he was restless in bed until about four in the morning, then quietly slipped downstairs, lay on the sofa.

He'd been up this early a few times to catch buses for tournaments, but that was different. A queasy nervousness kept him awake, kept him from really seeing the sky, a blurry fatigue born of too much sleep.

Sitting, then lying, then standing silent in the living room, imagining himself as a piece of lifeless furniture, Joseph overcame the urge to switch on the tube, to eat, to move.

They were starting to hone in on Bennie, making him out like a Born-again nut, Waco Boy. At St. Dominic's, Brother Brian had told him that a Catholic must feel sorry for sinners, even murderers, even for a guy who shoots up a dozen people in a McDonald's. Especially them, he'd said. Maybe Bennie was that bad, needed extra prayers.

But then he wondered—and was glad he didn't ever have the opportunity to make the grave mistake of asking it aloud—weren't people like Bennie supposed to go to hell?

Looking out the window, he listened for stray cars whooshing by on the busier road down from their street. The whole town slept, except for a few people driving, maybe tired workers off their shift at a donut shop.

He found his old sneakers, padded out onto the back porch. Already a glint of light had surprised him, filling the sky like a slate.

The porch and yard were coated in a light dew, making the grass glisten in the weak light. He heard a twitter of a few arguing birds.

A slat of purple, then orange, appeared in the sky. He'd never seen the sun come up, wanted very much to go out to a high hill, just see the world. There was supposed to be a great view up on the hill in Laurel Grove Cemetery. He vowed to go to that place, where Anthony was buried. He wanted to see what was out there, the faraway buildings in Manhattan where all those gay men were supposed to live, the ocean, where people didn't care who he was, or what he hadn't done. A mourning dove hooed like a wood flute. A garage door rumbled open down the block. He pulled back into the house, crept back up to his room.

Hey Don!

Greetings from purgatory! I got your dad's address of where you're at from your mother who was very nice. I guess she didn't remember to send you the other letter I sent.

hoping you're doing well. I'm thinking it's better for us to be apart for now. I keep thinking that. the ass prince kicked me off the team and suspended me for three days after I got in a fight with brandon miller the b-ball goon who basically was a creep and deserved it. you would be happy, Dink. I finally fought back. I'm also 135 now and I beat Heil Ass out of his slot at least for the last duals.

it's raining a lot here but I guess it does where you are too. I hope things are going okay and they are beating you I mean treating you nice. I have basically been grounded for the rest of my life but I know it's nothing like what you are going through. the Colts really were losing bad which shows how good we were huh? Maybe enough of us will get our act together to go all-county tourney. Did you get on the team there? guess not. Maybe I'll see you there. I am hoping you are still my friend. I wish you had just looked at me in court. I saw you all those times you were on and the other guys. I even taped some of it which you might think is crazy but I miss you and wish everything hadn't happened. I wish you were still my friend that you knew how much I miss you and when you get out we could go do stuff but legal stuff if that's okay with you.

I listen to your music tapes a lot and it helps. I hope you can write to me or call me. We got a new number. I don't know what they let you do now.

Joe

What with his "difficult season," Joseph didn't qualify for Group 4 District Finals. Even so, he went with some other guys on the team to root for Walt and the Shiver brothers, who did qualify.

The Passaic County Finals were held in Paterson, but a different school than their Washington match. The gym was enormous and modern, like the students.

Little Falls had the least amount of wrestlers competing among bigger teams like Clifton, Hackensack, Bergen, Wayne. Mrs. Shiver brought lots of food, which the boys wolfed down as they parked themselves a few rows up on the bleachers, thus allowing them more space for lounging and swearing.

Between the stands and the mats, the gymnasium was divided in half, the WRESTLERS ONLY half cut off from the families by a very familiar long yellow plastic tape.

It had been four months, and still things like that could chill him. Joseph spaced, not watching the matches for a while, until Raul nudged him about some ace move that everybody was cheering over all of a sudden.

Occasionally, Joseph wandered around, low-fiving guys he recognized, or had wrestled. He felt the whispers follow him like a shadow. "He's the guy who. . ." ". . .I swear, that's him. . ." He grew wary of the attention, of playing cool. Because asking the Passaic coach made him nervous, Joseph checked the roster. No D. Khors.

Coach Cleshun stopped by, but stayed out on the floor with Walt and the Shiver brothers mostly.

Scanning the bleachers, fading in and out of interest with Walt and the Shivers' matches, he trotted off into the locker room to pee. He stood at a urinal, walked by the showers, blocked a few thoughts, memories, desires.

Then he saw something that looked slightly out of place.

A square-shaped black gym bag, the side of it webbed, sat unguarded on a locker room bench. He'd wanted to get one like it, to store stinky workout clothes away from his other stuff, but used a plastic bag instead. For a moment, he considered stealing the bag, but an internal leash reminded him of Miss Pooley, his parents, all those people he'd face if he did anything else wrong.

Then he noticed something about the bag.

It had a sound.

Joseph stepped silently toward the bag, peeled back the zipper, his heart pumping up under his ribs in great gulping thuds, as he saw, nestled in towels, a small video camera.

It was running.

The webbed side of the bag faced the entrance to the shower room, where, in a few minutes, dozens of boys would be walking by.

Panicking, understanding, wondering who, but not why, he wanted to wait to let it capture what he saw daily, knew as a treasure, but a private one.

He'd felt them nearby at matches. This was just one more step closer, too close. He felt a shiver of disgust, envy, contemplated what to do, what not to do.

Walt got third in his weight. Brett got fourth. His brother Jeff lost after his second bout. Out of nine teams, Little Falls came in ninth.

Some guys won. Some guys lost. One guy at 130 from Hoboken thought he'd won, but the scorekeeper on the lighted wall tally was off from the official score at the table. The boy raised his arms in victory. When the ref held up the other guy's arm, he literally shouted "What?" stormed off.

"Aw, man, that is so embarrassing," Jeff Shiver cracked. Everybody laughed. "Dude, if that happened to me, I would just die."

Joseph waited a moment, just long enough to catch Jeff off guard, get his attention, grinned, "Would you? Would you really?"

Jeff's eyebrows furled. He pulled back. "Chill, man. C'mon, Neech. It was a joke."

"Right."

He chilled, scanned the bleachers, dramas and victories played out before him in an arena.

Mrs. Shiver gave the boys a party afterward. It was very creative. She had set up little WWF paper napkins that matched the paper WWF tablecloth in the yard, where an array of chips, sodas, cookies were descended upon by the boys, who refused to reveal to her what was so darn funny. They were speculating on the story that one boy from Fort Lee had told about having found parts of a smashed video camera in each of the locker room toilets.

Then they all played a few video games.

Not ones with guns, the maze type.

18

When Joseph heard it, he almost laughed. Pinned in Paterson. Finally.

He watched Sotorama, trying to feel good. He was supposed to be happy. It was supposed to be over.

The flood of cameras and reporters crowded around Bennie and his lawyer as they shoved their way down a hallway.

"Are you going to appeal?"

"What did you think of the decision?"

"Do you have anything to say?"

Bennie turned his face toward a camera. For a moment the bright light burned his face white as a small meteor, then jolted to his side, revealing some splotches of acne on his cheek. He spoke with a cold conviction. "We are persecuted, but not forsaken, cast down but not destroyed."

His lawyer shoved him through the throng, out again through the doors of the Hall of Justice. The cluster of light, sound, wire followed them.

He'd spoken directly to Joseph. It creeped him. Joseph imagined Bennie being walked into a real prison, eventually getting what he feared most, being surrounded by thugs, told what to do every minute, possibly raped. He said to the television, "Looks like you don't get to eat the world this time, big bad wolf."

"Joey, who are you talking to?"

"Nobody."

His mother descended the stairs, walked into the kitchen, where warm, meaty smells, sizzling sounds made his stomach growl.

"Hey, was there any mail for me?"

"No," she said.

"Oh."

Joseph hoped he'd gotten Dink's address right.

"That was your father on the phone."

"Huh?"

"Your father."

"What's wrong?"

"Nothing is wrong. He wants to take you to a movie."

"I thought I was grounded till the end of time."

"We let you go to finals, didn't we?"

"Yes."

"He just called to tell you to stay here until he gets home."

"Oh, like I'm goin' somewhere?"

She sighed. "He's working late on some new house somebody's remodeling. Could you just put on some real clothes and behave yourself?"

Joseph looked down at his baggy sweats. He did look like a slob, but so what? "You gonna hold dinner?"

"Yes. Can you stand waiting?"

"Sure." He didn't want to start a fight again. It was too tiring.

On the way to the movie, his father brought up the news story about Bennie, which got them talking about the other news story, the St. Patrick's Day Parade. About a hundred gays and lesbians had been arrested on Fifth Avenue in Manhattan for trying to march.

"Do you understand why they were protesting?"

"Yeah, sure," he said as he fidgeted under the seat belt. He kept leaning forward to change the radio station. The belt kept yanking him back.

"Would you want to do that?"

"I don't wanna march in some drunken Irish parade."

"But do you understand why they did it?"

"Sure, it's like black people with Martin Luther King and Malcolm X, like they were protesting the prejudice."

"I'm jus' tryin' to help."

"I know, Dad."

The radio talked for a while.

"You know, even though the way they teach us stuff in school, which totally ignores things that are all over the tube, I got an idea about things. I mean, I've done stupid things, but I'm not stupid."

"I'm not saying that." His father shut off the radio.

"Then why are you taking me to this movie about some gay guys with AIDS?"

"Because I want you to see what'll happen if you aren't careful."

"Dad, I'm. . .practically a virgin."

"I thought you said–"

"I'm nearly immaculate!"

"Joker. I shoulda taken you out of Catholic school a long time ago."

"No, you shouldn't. I learned stuff. I mean, I dunno about the

Pope being infallible or some things. I mean, I pray and stuff, and I believe in Jesus and the saints. I think they protect me and I know you don't believe that but I don't care anymore. I mean maybe sometimes Jesus looks like the old pictures. Maybe angels don't have wings. Maybe Anthony won't have asthma in heaven."

His father said, "I don't want you to feel forced to go, or not go because I don't. I think you oughtta give it a chance, but give it some perspective."

"I am, I just. . .you know, feeling a spiritual crisis or something."

"Okay."

"So let's not go see that depressing AIDS movie, okay? I'm really not up for it, but I appreciate your helping."

"Awright. Ya wanna go get some ice cream or something?"

"What, cheer me up with sugar?"

"No, it's. . . It's your day. Whatever you want."

"Okay. Cookie Puss."

His father kept asking him if he had questions. He asked them, but it was just about plans they made. If he got in trouble again, if he was called as a witness, what he should say. But he had unanswerable questions. Would Bennie really get raped? Which was worse, hoping for it or getting turned on by imagining it? Could Hunter's brother come and get him? Would he just get a stray bullet someday, like in *Goodfellas,* how you don't know when?

Streets glistened in the wash of a brief morning rain. The Bronco gleamed after the downpour. Through the drive, Joseph watched a few pink flower petals, some caught in the wipers, loosened one at a time, flew off the windshield.

The kids were allowed to open the windows, letting spring whoosh in. They glided into the church parking lot with ease. Girls smiled, beamed in their buttercup skirts, delicate hats. Boys became angular cartoons of themselves, their hair shiny with gel, slanted one way or the other. Parents, old people, all smiled, shook hands, greeting each other with extra friendliness.

The pews were packed with families he'd never seen before. Lilies exploded in clusters along the aisles, white ribbons hung up along the sides. The priest's speeches, prayers were filled with goodness. Joseph listened to every word. Sunlight shot through the blocks of glass in beautiful shafts of color.

The Easter egg hunt on the church lawn afterwards was pleasant, cordial. Cakes, cookies, desserts lay out on a table whose skirt of a paper tablecloth kept blowing up. Joseph got to pig out while his parents talked to other parents about anything but him, he hoped.

"Hey, Netchie, how ya doin'?" Marty Bonfiglio and Terry German-something, a couple of Mike's friends, approached.

"Pretty good. Happy Eastah."

"Ask him," Terry whispered.

"Hey," Marty said. "We was thinkin' of askin' you to show us how you flattened Miller. You know, like lessons."

"Sorry, boys. You can't afford the fee." Joseph grinned wide, then shoved a forkful of cake into his mouth. The boys retreated, piled stuff on their plates, dealt with, dispensed. Nobody was going to get to him today. His face beamed, no frowns, no smiles, though. He imagined himself blank, unreadable, like the scribbled drawing the news artist had made of him, sitting upright, no facial features, like the picture of the angel in *My Mass Book*, the Young Catholic Missal Mike received before his First Communion. Even Mrs. Lambros said hello. He didn't even mind wearing the suit, since his mom had put a little flower in his lapel like he had a date with Jesus. Everybody was good, nice. Really nice.

"Irene wants us over for coffee," his mother announced as she strapped in her seat belt, careful of her corsage.

"How many us's?" his dad asked.

"Just us, us." She turned back in her seat, "Kids, can you all be good for a little while longer?"

Joseph thought she meant the two cherubs on either side of him. He'd let them have the windows. He was a wall to put between them, even if they were being good.

"Yes, Ma," Mike and Sophia said in unison.

But then Marie looked at Joseph. Dino's eyes glinted in the rearview a moment, like every other guy that scared or comforted him; Bennie, Mr. Khors, the cops.

"What, me?" he blurted. "I been good all year."

"Okay." She turned back.

"I'll be extra good all day!"

"How long is till midnight?" Sophia asked.

"Why? You stayin' up?"

"I wanna know how long we have to be good for."

Everybody laughed, like a little party just blasted into the car, but then they had to explain to Soph the difference between "laughing at" and "laughing with."

His mother put her sunglasses on to walk across the driveway as she did whenever they left the courthouse. It could have had something to do with the occasional van parked near their house.

Dino had stripped off his suit, jumped into his Sunday jeans, sneakers, an old Mets sweatshirt in record time despite Marie's protests. They looked funny, she still in her Sunday best like Jackie O., while he was ready for the sofa.

"I think our host might want to cook for us again," his father whispered.

Joey mimed choking his own throat. His dad whacked him once on the butt, just playing, but it sort of jolted him.

Mike darted to the basement, inspecting his dead thing collection. He'd had to throw it out when his mother found a desiccated toad Mike was "drying out" so he could paint it. The other appeared forlorn but surviving, but it was hard to tell with toads.

"Jo-eee! I'm hiding and you can't find me!"

"Bet I can!"

At first Joseph tried to figure out some way to get Sophia to fall asleep. More candy would do it. One bump up, she'd crash like a zombie. Sofia's fourth birthday had been a month before, but she still had yet to stay awake through most movies.

"Watch it with me, Joee-oo." Sophia laid out their collective Easter booty; marshmallow bunnies, jelly beans. Joseph traded his chocolate bunny for Sophia's malted milk balls, each peppered with pinks and blue.

"Soph-ioo, you see da sprinkles?"

"Yup."

"How do dey do dat?" he said, holding one egg extra close to Sophia before popping it in his mouth.

"Da movie!"

"Yeah, it's on. First we gotta read about our little friends. See those letters?"

"F.B.I."

"Very good."

"Yay!" Her little hands clapped. "Sing the songs with me!"

He didn't know why he did it. He couldn't explain it to his mother when she burst in, but they started watching the movie, Joseph was just, not happy, for sure, but relieved or giddy, not in the mood for crying again, so he just started waving his hands a little during the opening song, and Sophia kept laughing, so he stood up when Aladdin came in and started doing the actions he saw, singing, thinking how cute the guy was, especially when his voice cracked, wondering if it was weird for him to want to have sex with a cartoon. He picked Sophia up, carrying her around like Abu, sitting on the sofa with her in his arms – "one skip ahead a my doom" – jumping up and carrying her while she laughed, then spinning around as their mother appeared out of nowhere and yelled something and he fell down with Sophia in his arms, and that was why she started howling, not because of anything he did.

"I don't believe you! I leave you for one minute!"

"But, Ma. I didn't–"

"Give her to me."

He stood over his crouching mother while Sophia bawled, a loud piercing scream. Her face was a red mushy bump, tears dribbling down with her drool. Joseph stood, tried to reach out his hand, but his mother stormed up the stairs, carrying his sister away.

He didn't turn the movie off, but his mother did a while later.

"She wanted to watch this," he said.

She said each word carefully, as if picking up glass. "Don't. . . do that. . . ever again."

As if summoned by the banging pots, his father popped his head through the kitchen door. "Hey, Marie. You comin' back or what?"

"Get in here."

No trip to Chez DeStefano. Burnt ziti again.

19

"What I'm saying is," Miss Pooley explained during what she called his Final Report, since he was no longer considered a PINS. "You're a very smart kid. Your aptitude tests are well above average. I know you've had problems in school, but believe me, it'll pass. And since you have no previous record, you're very lucky, and very fortunate things turned out the way they have."

Terrific, then how come I've acquired the habit of chewing my fingernails to stumps?

"How is your family doing?"

My mother keeps waiting for the Virgin Mary to appear over the dining room table and convert me to a heterosexual. My dad's smoking again. My brother thinks I'm an alien. Sophia still likes me, but that's only because I can imitate Grover. "Fine."

231

"Now, do you have any plans for a summer job?"

"Yeah, making johns."

"Excuse me?"

"Plumbing. Ceramics department."

"Oh, well, that sounds like an. . . interesting choice."

"Yeah, but I think the word is 'appropriate.'"

"Why's that?"

"Because my life's in the terlet."

Miss Pooley sighed.

"That's a joke."

"I'm laughing inside," she said.

"Okay."

"Joseph, let me remind you of a few things. You have two parents, a very rare thing with the kids I see. You have a home. You have a brain. You aren't strung out on drugs. I hope."

Joseph rolled his eyes, told himself an inside joke about being piss-approved.

"On top of that, you're white."

"I'm Italian."

"Okay, European-American, but that's white to a judge and a potential employer. You have it easier."

"I guess."

"Are you sexually active?"

"What?"

"Your father told me you had a sexual relationship."

"Oh jeez, whad he say?"

"There are services available. Do you know how to use a condom?"

"I think that's a personal question."

"I'm sorry. I just want you to be careful."

All the guys he wanted to make out with were locked up. How more careful could he be? "Yes, Ma'am."

"Did you read those pamphlets I gave you?"

"Yes. My parents gave me. Yes. Yes."

"All right."

"And no, even though it's none of your business. I'm. . . I haven't done that." He figured she didn't understand specifically what he meant, but he wasn't going to explain.

"Well, you want to make sure it's someone you love, that you're careful."

"Yes, Ma'am."

232

"How about we just finish these annoying little forms and call it a day so you can get out of here. I'm sure your father's very tired of the selection from our candy machine."

"Okay, but, um. . ."

"Yes?"

"This is gonna sound kinda sick, but, I don't know what it was, but, I miss them."

"Who?"

"Bennie and Hunter. Dink especially. Once, I had just ridden shotgun with Bennie, because, you know, me and Dink always sat in the back, but even so, that one time, Bennie was cool to me, and there were so many good times we had together."

"Yes, I'm sure there were many good times."

"It was weird, I felt. . . like finally I belonged, like they weren't gonna tease me anymore. Before all this, it was something good, ya know? I was really never a part of the group. Does that sound weird to you?"

Miss Pooley walked him to the door. "Lemme tell you about a few cases I worked on. Ten years ago in Middlesex, a bomb blew up a house and killed two people. The bomber was their son. Now, don't get any ideas. Coupla years ago in Rahway an escaped juvenile lived for two years in a PATH station before being discovered. A month ago in Camden a baby was found on the highway, alive. The mother is a crack addict who thinks the child is possessed. Last week in Jersey City a woman was attacked by a herd of rats outside a Kentucky Fried Chicken."

"Wow."

"Well, I didn't work on that one. I read that in the newspaper."

"Oh."

"That's a joke, Joseph. You can laugh."

"I'm laughing inside."

Riding home from Miss Pooley's office for the last time, Joseph felt an odd familiarity with a certain corner, then noticed in just a flash a wall he'd painted.

Awesome.

The wedge of brick disappeared.

His father said, "What?"

"Huh?"

"You see something?"

"No."

His dad was supposed to be fixing the garage door, but he kept putting it off, enjoying his Saturday. Ever since the funeral and everything, Dino decided he ought to "spend more quality time at home." Babysit the PINS was more like it.

Some baseball highlights game rambled on and on. Commercials alternately blasted beer, trucks, beer, trucks. Joseph fidgeted in his seat, fighting off the urge to just lie on top of his dad as he'd done as a boy. As if sensing Joseph's thought, his father got up. "You want a soda?"

He shook his head.

"This is boring." His father flicked off the box. The room was silent.

"What, are we doing some grief counseling now?"

"I just want to talk."

"So Mom clears out so we can shout, or me bawl my eyes out, is that it?"

Marie had taken the kids down to Newark for the weekend to visit Grandmama, she said, who wasn't feeling well, she said. Just a visit, good for the kids, good for Grandmama, good for something, but Joseph knew.

She didn't trust him alone with his own brother or sister. It was up to his father to deal with him, talk to him, maybe get him to straighten up.

"Whyncha go pick a record?"

"What, from your stuff?"

"Yeah, I think there's something there you like."

He went into the dining room, crouched down to open the cabinet, flipped through the Springsteens, Madonnas, Crosby, Stills, Nashes, picked out a Beatles album with all the funeral flowers on it. He put it on, sat on the dining room floor, looking at the record cover, listening to the music. He could feel it coming, another "chat," wanted to avoid it by not returning to the living room, but then his dad parked himself down on the dining room floor next to him, said, "That's the second one of those I got. The first one had all these posters and stuff. Shoulda saved 'em. Coulda made a lot of money selling those old records."

"What, like how much?"

"Oh, vintage, hundred-fifty dollars, maybe more."

"For an old record?"

"People put a lot of value in old things. I know you don't get

234

that, but it's true."

"Did you ever see them?" He held the album.

"Oh no, they broke up when I was about ten years old. Used to watch them on Ed Sullivan when I was about Soph's age."

"Did you get stoned?"

"Not at her age!" His father's eyes sort of bugged out jokingly. He covered his mouth with his hand while stroking his mustache. "Well, kids were doin' a lot of stuff in those days. It wasn't such a big deal then, to get it, and . . ."

"So did you?"

"Yeah."

"Did Ma?"

"A few times, with me, but she didn't like it. It messes with your head. It. . . I mean, she would be asleep and I'd wanna go out dancing or . . . get romantic. We always ended up on opposite sides."

"Like now?"

His dad's forced grin dropped. "Look. She is having a hard time with all this."

"She hates me."

"She does not hate you."

"Some kid in school said people who do drugs have babies that come out deformed."

"That is not why you are. . . Look, your mother loves you. Actually, she's afraid of you. For you."

"Me? What, does she think I'm just gonna. . . Doesn't she believe I didn't do anything?"

"Your. . . You have really gotten angry all of a sudden and I know it's from all. . . the trial and Anthony but don't take it out on her, okay?"

It was funny seeing his father sitting on the floor. Joseph imagined him at a party, young as himself, sharing a joint, being stupid. Under that mustache, Dino was just a big boy, a boy-man.

Joseph looked at the record again, at the picture of the Beatles. "The one that died, John Lennon."

"Yayugh."

Joseph looked up at that sound. "Why are you crying?"

"That puts me in another place that was very sad, when they shot him. Your grandfather got sick, although you were a baby at the time. Grampa spent his first time in the hospital and I was very sad. We went to the city, to Strawberry Fields in Central Park. We were

235

doing some Christmas shopping and I said 'Come on, let's go,' and she understood, I think."

"Did you take me?" Joseph remembered the trip to New York to see big balloons on Thanksgiving. He'd sat on his father's shoulders all afternoon, watched his breath fly up to meet the Spider-Man balloon.

"Oh yeah, had the little backpack, the papoose." It lay hidden up in the attic, along with a lot of other baby stuff they'd used for him, then Mike and Sophia.

He saw his father's squinted eyes tear. Joseph stood transfixed a moment, felt a longing for his father, but at the same time wondered why such a happy memory for him was so upsetting.

"You're not. . . smokin' pot, are ya?"

"No, Da. Just used to get drunk with the guys, go out beating up homos, just good all-American fun."

His dad sighed. "I only wish you'd come to me before things got out of hand."

"I know. I'm sorry."

"Just, just talk to me, about anything, anytime, okay?"

"Okay."

"Now, how 'bout helping me with that garage door?"

"That's okay."

"How 'bout we toss a football."

"Dad. I don't do football."

"Awright. You don't 'do' football." He stood, then crouched. "Rassle?"

"No. I don't . . . I'm totally outta shape."

"I'll go easy on ya." Dino went for Joseph's head, but he ducked his father's swat. Then he stood to go, but as his dad wrapped his arms around him, he banged his hip against the dining room table trying to escape.

"Stop it!" Touching his dad wasn't like touching Dink or a guy on the team.

"Come on."

"No, goddammit!"

"Joey!"

"I do not wrestle anymore. They hate me 'cause I'm a fag just like Anthony!"

He ran up to his room to be alone, but the names were everywhere, the pictures, the trophies, the ribbons, the plaques.

Naturally, he wrecked the place.

First he found the worst, loudest Nirvana song, blasted it, then shoved his bed against the door so his dad couldn't shove it open. He went for the shrine first. With double fists he punched up from the lowest shelf. They flew over his head. Medals, ribbons shot out behind him. He turned to survey the damage. A broken trophy part stuck into the wall.

He dug in the closet, grabbed his new Asics, tried to rip them, but he only managed to break an orange shoestring. He grabbed his drawing pads, flung them down, but before ripping them, he stopped. No, not them. Not yet.

His desk knocked over, the lamp broken, alarm clock nearly thrown out the window, re-aimed at the door at the last moment, he felt pretty stupid all of a sudden. It felt good to have knocked it all down, but a little while later he figured he was too embarrassed to really cry, so he lay still on the bed until the tape ran out.

He nearly jumped a minute later when he heard his father's voice on the other side of the door.

"You done?"

Joseph pressed his hand against the door. "Yeah."

"We'll talk after you've cleaned everything up. I don't even wanna see what you did."

"Okay."

He felt the door shift as his father stood up to walk downstairs. He waited.

The footsteps backtracked.

"J'ever think that God wanted you to be there so they would get caught? Huh, Joe? J'ever think of that?"

20/20

The camera loved Bennie. Bennie brooded. Bennie "looked pensive." Bennie got prime time. Bennie got fan mail.

Joseph wondered if they gave acne medicine to murderers. Bennie'd lost weight, too, that was obvious. His neck didn't bulge out of his suit as it had in his senior portrait, which they used whenever they described him as "an accomplished athlete but a troubled teen, torn by a broken home." Joseph had only been in the driveway, so he couldn't verify that.

"Still unknown is why the defense again tried to dismiss the testimony of the other teammate, who was at the scene of the crime, but is considered a witness. The minor was recently suspended from Little Falls High School for fighting with another classmate."

PAUSE. FF.

"Oh, bite me, Betty Boop. You don't know what you're talking about."

PLAY. A grassy field, with trees, that Soto guy walking to the camera. "But as the ordeal ends, and the legal process continues, slowly, there is still one ritual that remains."

"Sweeps Week." He wanted to tape over it, erase the segment.

REW. Instead, he watched it again. The camera panned to the headstone, flowers piled high, almost covering the name.

"Earlier today, Eugenia Lambros brought fresh flowers to remember her son's birthday. In Little Falls, this is John Soto."

STOP.

He heard a sound. He wanted to go see, but at the same time figured ducking under the coffee table might be a good idea, especially if whoever was out there had a gun, which could include both Hunter and Lambros brothers, he'd been told.

The stairs creaked. He scooted from on the floor to under the table, practicing.

"Any good chewing gum under there?" his father's feet appeared besides him.

He slid out, embarrassed.

"I was doing pull-ups."

"Sure. Do you know what time it is?"

"No." He sat up.

238

"Who were you talkin' to?" Dino's hair was disheveled, his bathrobe barely covering his body. Even though his eyes were puffy little slits, his hair stuck out in places.

"What are you doin' up this late?" He watched Joseph retreat to the sofa.

"Can't sleep."

"You're watchin' the news again. I tole ya not to." His dad flicked off the tube. The VCR lights were still on. He had to remember to grab the tape before going to bed or Mike might record something over it, on purpose.

"It'll just get you upset. Ya gotta let it run its course."

"Dad, you don't know. . ."

"I know you aren't sleepin' right, you're eatin' too much, you haven't been out."

"I know, but–"

His father sat beside him, his arm around him. "Sit up. Look. It's . . .This is not easy. Just try to get over it. I dunno what to say. Ya jus' gotta forgive yourself."

"Have you ever seen anybody that's dead?"

"Yes, actually."

"Like, Anthony's still a very popular guy in my head, now. If only I'd. . ."

"Stop." He grabbed his son's arms. "You can't keep reliving that. Now, you asked me a question. Yes, I seen people dead. I seen people die, too. And one of 'em was your grandfather. He punished himself all his life for something he wasn't responsible for. The man smoked and drank himself to death. It wasn't just a heart attack."

Joseph had to turn away when his father's eyes welled up. He felt his dad pat him, say, "I don't want you to do that, okay? Don't do that. It wasn't your fault."

His father looked around the silent living room. "Ya gotta think about your future, not a hundred years from now, some other place, heaven, hell, but stickin' with school. You gotta think about Joe and what he's gonna do to feel better about himself."

He felt cloudy, spent, in the middle of so much. "Are you and Ma gonna get a divorce?"

His father's "No, not at all," would have been more reassuring if he hadn't taken that extra moment to say it.

The next week, Dino took Marie out to dinner, almost to prove something. To honor this, he swore that he would be good.

"We're sending the little ones to Irene's tonight." She was dressed up in a way she hadn't been in a long time, her hair done up in what Mike mimicked as "Mah-velluss."

In a suit, his father's hair all slicked back, Joseph figured a cigar would finish off the Guido Supreme look nicely. "Woah!"

"You like? Haven't worn it since. . ." He must have just shaved too, because his usual five o'clock shadow was trimmed back to eight a.m.

Then it hit him. His parents had already remembered, waited for his reaction.

"Oh. Right." He reassured them. "Hey, I'm okay."

"You sure you're okay? Irene can bring the kids back over." Marie fiddled with her earrings, checking herself in the hall mirror.

"That's okay. I'll go rent a video."

His mother's smile dropped. But then his father said, to her, "It's four blocks," to him, "Only if you promise. You come right home. No trouble, okay, or I make you wear that awful boosters jacket."

"No. I promise."

"And the cap."

"Never. Cross my heart and hope to–"

"Enough!"

She almost didn't want to go, but then Dino stood at the door, yanking his tie again, leading her out.

"Don't you kids stay out too late."

He looked in the fridge, half-nibbled some leftover ziti, then went upstairs to the bathroom. His father's beard stubble coated the sink. He touched a few bristles, brought his hand to his face, contemplated shaving, turned on the shower water, letting the bathroom fog with steam. He stripped, pranced around the upstairs naked, humped his parents' bed, got bored with that, took a shower, shaved his chin, upper lip and for the first time, the back of his neck. Not that it needed it.

Drying himself, he picked out some jeans, socks, clean underwear, a blue T-shirt, jacket –not his varsity jacket– walked four blocks to the bus stop on the street he remembered led to the other pieces of a trail that led him to the closest version of what he needed most that he could find at the moment.

ADULT

Blinking lights swirled around in neon big enough for anyone as far back as the highway to see. He walked by it once, just pretending he wasn't going in, kept his eyes to the side, noticing the cars in the lot, a man going in. Would there be cops? Would they card him? Would anyone recognize him? By the third time around the block, he didn't care.

The lights were harsh. Whoever worked behind the tall counter had gone away for a minute. It was momentarily devoid of people, slightly scary, like arriving at a party before anybody'd shown up. A big boombox chained behind the counter played a new song about "girls who want boys who like boys who dig girls who do boys like they're girls who dig girls but they're boys. . ."

Joseph scanned the store, the walls of videotapes, another wall of magazines, video boxes, more magazines stacked on tables, paperback books on circular racks.

A guy with a mustache looked at him, but averted his eyes every time Joseph looked back. A chubby guy emerged from some other area with a turnstile in it, adjusting his fly as he left. There were funny sounds coming from behind the doorway.

Joseph tried to move slowly, be invisible, but the pictures surrounding him were glossy, hard. There were guys with women, women with women, black guys with Asian chicks, big-bosomed white women with herds of guys, huge fake cocks in display cases, funny straps, lotions, the magazines, there, further back, a whole section of them, all of them guys, some with their faces shoved, distorted, the skin bumping out, cheeks puffed up with shoved-in cocks, some guys even wrestling, which made him smirk.

Most were just naked, though, dripping with wet stuff, spit or something shoved in mouths, asses. He felt sick, wanted to laugh at the same time. Some pictures were gross, some were just stupid, fake, forced, someone else's idea of Sexy. Guys with their mouths open, their legs spread, hands gripping enormous boners, most of them not like his, but some of them, their foreskins pulled back, or halfway, or all the way down, some dripping with goo, some with the stuff caught mid-air.

His hands were already quivering. His heart thudded.

Agita attack. I'm gonna pass out, die here. That will be his revenge. But he found the nerve to continue slowly looking, taking it all in, long enough to adjust his pants, try to move his boner upright, so it wouldn't stick out so much.

He looked closer at a rack of shiny magazines with proud, big super-muscular guys, some smiling so nice, some mean, tough, all of them beyond gorgeous. One looked familiar, almost like his father; the same mustache, the same heavy shadow of a beard, but the smile was different, the eyes blue instead of brown, the face differently-shaped, thicker, more muscled. The name was Italian. Another was a dead ringer for Bennie, except he was uncircumsized and had a goatee.

But what made him almost laugh out loud was the name on the poster, on each magazine.

Colt.

Young buff guys stood naked and amazingly stiff enough to hang a coat on. Others featured drawings, perfectly formed cartoons of superhero bodies, men lounging, wrestling naked, with equally super cocks, butts, a masterful achievement, what he'd had all along been trying to do with his drawings.

He had to have one. Even if he had to steal it, he had to have one.

Holding it in his quivering hand as he approached the counter, he felt it nearly slip out, his hand was so sweaty, the paper so slick. Behind the counter, a skinny guy with a ponytail emerged by the sign that read: 'Proof of age is required for purchase,' said, "Help you?" The guy smiled, not as mean as he looked at first.

Joseph put the magazine on the counter. The guy wouldn't stop smiling.

"You eighteen?"

"Sure."

"You got ID?"

He felt in his pocket, took out his wallet, pretended to look for the driver's license he wouldn't get until September. Even then, he would only be sixteen. He should have swiped it, kept his cool. He had to have this now, but he'd suddenly grown a mustache of sweat.

"I forgot it."

"Sorry."

"I got money."

"Sorry. No can do. We got closed down last year. Things are a bit tight. You understand." The guy took the magazine. It disappeared behind the counter. "Hey, try *Details* or *Men's Workout*. They got lotsa nice underwear ads. You can get one of those muscle magazines in the grocery. I know how ya feel, dude."

Racing out in a flurry, flushed with embarrassment, sweat

242

suddenly coated the layer between his T-shirt and his back. He turned away into the lot, hid out behind the building a minute, pacing, burning with anger, frustration as the last bits of purple and magenta bled from the dusk sky.

A car pulled up, its lights glaring at him, past him.

At the other end of the parking lot, the mustache guy from inside walked toward his car with a slim brown bag in his hand. He stopped, half-waved with his hand.

A very different sort of panic filled Joseph, a good fear, like before a match, like jumping off a cliff when you know there's warm water waiting. He crossed the lot.

"I couldn't help but notice your little problem in there."

"Yeah, well, whatever."

"Would you like some of mine?"

"What?"

The guy held up his paper bag.

"Lemme see."

The guy looked around. Darkness crept in, but they were still visible.

"Come on." He clicked the alarm on his key ring. The car blurted an electronic fart. The guy opened his car door, sat inside. Joe went around to the passenger side, heard the bing, bing as he sat down, the guy clicking his ignition key on to play some music, some geeky Lite FM.

"Take your pick."

The magazines he'd wanted fell onto his lap.

"Um, thanks."

"Anything for you, Adonis."

"Who?"

The guy wasn't bad-looking. His face was nice enough, not too handsome, but harmless. His jeans were loose. He didn't seem to have a great body, not that his body would be the point of it.

Wild with thoughts, his breath grew shallow as he heard his heartbeat thump in his ears, felt his blood race down to his cock as the guy put a hand on his thigh. Then the man leaned over, kissed him. He tasted like toothpaste, like he'd expected to kiss someone.

"You are so beautiful," he muttered as his fingers trailed up Joseph's chest, pawing him lightly, tugging up his jacket and T-shirt. His heart punched at his ribs, then the guy's mouth was on his belly, his wet tongue, mustache bristles tickling. He cringed, his stomach muscles contracting. He worried the guy would stop, but he kept on, catching the little ripples, thrusts.

The guy's hand fumbled with his pants. He tried to pull them down, but Joseph wanted to keep his pants up in case he wanted to run, but he knew he wouldn't run, knew he wanted to see his own dick in somebody's mouth again. He unzipped his pants, letting the guy feel the hard ridge under his shorts, then released his cock, which bapped up against his belly.

He heard the guy gasp, as if coming up from swimming. He whispered, "Beautiful. Uncut. I love that."

"Whatever."

The guy remained in his lap, licking around it, stretching it with his tongue. As much as he loved Dink, this guy was a lot better at it.

After only a few minutes, the guy pulled his head back, yanked it with his fist. A pearl of it flew up onto the dashboard, another glop stretched out on Joseph's jeans, on his thigh, like an arrow, saying, This Way Out. He quivered, closed his eyes, shot again, felt it all, thought, how nice that something so gross could feel so good.

Then the guy fished out his own cock, touching it, pumping it, as if he was late for something, said, "You wanna?"

"Um. . ."

"You don't have to."

"No, um, lemme. Just once."

The guy's cock was reddish, like his face, somewhat gross, but at the same time he wanted it, wanted to see if it fit. He opened his mouth, the guy shoved his pants down. The smell was clean, a soap smell caught in the hairs tickling his nose. The guy started shoving his hips up into his face. Joseph choked, but held onto it, more to use his hands to keep the guy from banging his cock too far up, since his head kept hitting the steering wheel. Then he had to swat the guy's hand away, which was creeping down toward his butt.

He heard slick sounds as the guy grabbed his own cock, pumping. He kept rubbing the back of his neck. It was nice, but then he knew the guy wanted him to do more. He wanted to, but only because he closed his eyes, pretending it was Dink, Fiasole, Cleshun, Bennie, Hunter, Marky Mark, anybody else, that he would do this again someday, just not in a car.

He pulled back. Like those few times with girls, where he kissed them, pretended, he leaned in, kissed his mustache, yanked it with him. He closed his eyes again, suddenly enjoyed it more, twirled his tongue around inside the guy's mouth, how he would have kissed Max Fiasole if he'd had the chance.

He moaned a little into the guy's mouth, then he felt wetness burst into his hand. He pulled harder, faster, until the guy grabbed his wrist, instinctively yanked his hand away, throbbed, relaxed.

A wrist hold. Could have wrapped him like a pretzel.

"Wow," the guy said, looking at a glob of sperm dangling from the dashboard like wet tinsel. "I'll never wash my car again."

"You're crazy."

"Not really."

Adjusting pants, zipping up, the guy said, "So, I could give you a ride home."

"That's okay."

"Can I buy you a soda?"

"Naw."

"Right."

His throat was all gooey. He asked to roll down the window, then spat.

The overpass hummed a ways off, the skimming tops of cars and trucks gliding on a cement river in the sky.

21

SHOPPING, the note on the fridge said, which explained the whereabouts of his mother and possibly Sophia so early in the afternoon. His father? At work. Mike? Who knew? Dissecting roadkill, probably.

Joseph downed five cookies with a glass of milk, sat silent at the dining room table, his books sprawled out in the convincing illusion of study. No tube. No music. Not until everybody was home and he needed something to block them out. Just be silent.

He took out his drawing, his first B-minus after years of art class A's. They were supposed to draw their families for a display to go in the lobby at school. Some PTA thing. "Where are you?" Mrs. Bridges had asked. Joseph immediately made a joke about him sitting on a hill painting his family on a picnic. That hadn't satisfied her. It was only later that he realized he'd put himself out of the picture.

He was supposed to give it to his mother. As if. She looked horrible in the drawing, her neck gangly, her hair wrong, her eyes too dark. Forget it. His dad had been enlarged to more muscular proportions, looking more like a bad sketch of a skinny Wolverine.

Mike held his toad in one hand like a prize watch. He'd probably think Joseph was making some kind of "comment." Joseph had Sophie with one toe extended, smiling, sprite-like. She'd like that.

He slipped the drawing inside his book, then took it out, nearly ripping it into little pieces, but he thought he heard another creepy sound, was ready to hide under the coffee table again, but it was the middle of the afternoon.

He heard steps retreating from the porch, cautiously got up, went to the door.

A manila envelope lay in the ghost square where the welcome mat used to be. He saw the photographer kid across the street, walking briskly.

"Hey!"

The photographer turned, caught.

Joseph waved him back.

He turned away, then turned back, walked all the way up the driveway, to the door. Joseph stood in his sweats and a ragged T-shirt, felt suddenly self-conscious that the kid would see his belly. Tom, that was his name.

"Sorry," Tom sputtered. "I didn't know if anybody was home." He stood at the bottom of the porch steps.

"What are you doin' around here?"

"I just wanted to stop by and give you that." Tom pointed to the manila envelope. "If you read the note, um, we were clearing out files for the yearbook, and I just thought you might want these."

Joseph crossed his arms, not retrieving it. "You the one that's been snoopin' around my house?"

"No. They're those wrestling pictures. I never got a chance to— What, somebody's following you?"

"Never mind."

"I just—well, you never talk in school. It's like you're trying to be invisible."

Joseph shrugged. "Yeah, tryin'."

Tom said nothing. He looked out to the clean lawns across the street to see if any neighbors were watching. "Come on up," Joseph said. Tom cautiously walked up the stairs, picked up the envelope.

They stood for a moment, not saying anything, until Joseph blurted out, "You know what pisses me off, more than him dying? It's like everybody's back the way it was, just like it never happened. And we're like—"

"Yeah, I know."

"You know?"

"He was my friend, too. You're not the only one that hurts."

"I never saw you with him."

"Well, neither did anybody else."

Joseph blushed, trying to take it in. Anthony and Tom. "No way."

"Way."

They both tried to laugh.

He wanted to say anything that would make Tom feel better. "I'm sorry. I'm very sorry."

"He was always talking about you. He liked you so much."

Joseph choked off a sob, reached out to hug Tom, but only touched his arm slightly, hesitant.

A car glinted down the street. He heard the garage door rumble itself open.

"Oh shit." He grabbed Tom, pulled him down behind the porch. The two boys lay low. Joseph muttered, "You gotta go. You gotta go."

"What, is that your–"

"Please. I'll talk to you in school. I promise." They heard his mother's car pass the porch, disappear into the garage. If she had groceries, he had about twenty seconds to hightail it out of hearing range.

"Well, um, we can talk in school, okay?" Tom sort of begged.

"Sure."

"Oh, here, here." Tom pushed the manila envelope at Joey.

Like he needed pictures of himself, who he used to be. Joseph clutched it as he backed inside. "Thanks. See ya on Monday, okay?"

"Okay . . ." Tom walked down the stairs slowly, too slowly. Joseph half-waved before closing the door just as he heard the kitchen door. He flew up the stairs in four leaps, closed his bedroom door, opened the envelope, took a quick scan, breathed.

Him and Dink. Anthony, Hunter, Bennie. The whole happy fucked-up family twisting around on the mat. The team picture. Everybody smiling, proud. Bip. Bip. Bip; the sound of his tears falling on photographs.

"Joey? Come and get groceries."

Be a man now. Deal with this.

"Joey?"

"Be down in a second." He wiped his face with the belly of his T-shirt, hid the pictures in the secret place with the magazines, trotted

247

slowly down the stairs, pretending his heart wasn't racing.

"Where were you?" His mother stood behind two brown bags.

"Sleeping."

"You're sleeping too much. Why don't you go out, get some exercise?"

"Yeah."

"Get the other bags." His mother looked around herself for a moment. "Oh, and my purse."

His socked feet left sweat prints on the garage floor. The trunk lay open, with two bags full of food; English muffins, Flavorpops, Cheese Doodles, Honeynut Cheerios.

He remembered the commercial where, in response to "What's for breakfast?" a cowboy says. "Nut'n, honey!" The other cowboys draw their guns to the guy's head.

Even cereal commercials told him to die.

He went to the front seat, figuring he'd strap his mother's purse on his shoulder, like he used to do with his wrestling bag.

But first he looked inside. Money, pictures of the family, credit cards, a Little Mermaid doll head, tissues, half a pack of Dentyne, two Tampax, a tiny phone book, a little bottle half-full of pills.

Go tonight. Anthony wants to wrestle.

He put the less-full bottle back in her purse, brought in the bags of groceries.

22

Mrs. Khors didn't look quite so perky. She wore a loose sweater, jeans, two different-colored socks. "Oh, Joey. Um, look, I'm really–"

"Can I come in?"

"Um, well. . . All right."

The house smelled like nothing. There were blank spots on the wall where he remembered some scribbly pictures. A few empty boxes sat forlornly along a wall. Was she moving? How could she abandon this place, the shrine where he and Dink had come together in a holy bond of goo and sweat?

"I was just actually, I had to wait for a very important phone call, so if you, well you may have to wait for a few. . . Um, can I get you something?"

Your first-born, please. "No, thank you."

248

She mumbled, running her words together, not really talking to him, but to the sofa, the wall, the tube, anything nearby. She could not stop moving, so he didn't sit down.

"I wanted to know how Di-Donnie was."

"Donnie?" she said, pretending surprise. "Oh, Donnie's fine. He's doing his best. He. . . we're trying to get the panel, or board, people, advisers, these sharp pointy-headed people with lots of forms, anyway, they're saying maybe summer, or if he gets in another fight, three years. He'll be visiting. I'm sure he'd like to see you. You know, I was just watching one of his favorite shows, with that poor boy who died."

"Who?"

"Oh you know, that Cuban boy."

"Oh. Right." Pedro died?

"Um. I'm sorry. I didn't mean to–"

"Oh, no, that's okay. It's okay."

She swooped toward him, gave him the shortest hug, too fast for him to even think about getting his arms around her.

Mrs. Khors seemed suddenly embarrassed by the display. Her eyes met his. "Do your parents know you're here?"

Pedro died?

"They're out now. My dad's at work. Actually I was just selling raffle tickets for–"

"What is it?"

"Raffle tickets. For the Catholic League Raffle? We got prizes and you don't have to be in the church to win? But the money goes for the victims of a drought in Zaire." He was goaded into another of the Sisters' activities by his mother to 'take his mind off his own problems.'

"Oh, I'd be happy to, Can you just wait one minute while I get my checkbook?"

"Sure."

He stood, tying himself to the door, fending off the urge to just race up the stairs, into that room again, just to smell it or steal something.

Pedro died? He hadn't even seen the show yet.

"So, how's Donnie?"

"You haven't talked to Don's father? Is that–"

"Mrs. Khors, please, I just–"

She kept looking at him, or near him, waiting. She fished around in her purse, but at the mention of Donnie, her eyes were upon him.

She must have been like his mother, medicated.

"I . . . Mrs. Khors, I was wondering . . . I just want to talk to him. Can you– Do you know if he got my letter? I got the right address, but I never heard from him. You do have his, your, Mister Khors, I mean the address, right?"

Mrs. Khors sort of cocked her head, fished around on a table for something. She lit up a cigarette. "Maybe he needs to be away on his own for a while."

"Whaddayou mean? He's in Passaic. How much more away do you–"

"He's living with his father. He won't be going to Little Falls anymore."

"I know, but–"

"What I'm saying, Joey. . ."

It seemed time to leave.

"This has been really hard for all of us–"

"I just wanna know he's okay."

"Sure."

"Can you tell him?"

"Sure."

"Okay."

"I still think we should call your parents. Just let them know you're okay." She was already walking to a phone.

"No, I'll go now."

"Wait, I'm buying raffle tickets. Remember?"

"Oh."

She stopped. "Joey, you have to understand something. I want him back, too. But everything's different now. If it means he can't go to school here, or anything else, I'm going to do it, because he is my son."

"Yeah."

"Now, who do I make this check out to?"

He traced the eleven blocks toward home. A lawn sprinkler darkened a wedge of sidewalk at his feet. Trees bloomed with lime-tinted buds. Birds sang. Everything was perfect.

23

The heater rumbled warm air through the grates. Then it stopped, as if finished breathing for the season.

He went to the bathroom, leaving the light off, took a last piss, then almost hit himself in the head when he opened the medicine cabinet. He took the aspirin bottle, careful not to let the white discs inside clatter.

Someone stood in the hall.

"What are you doing?" Mike appeared in his Gargoyles pajamas, groggy from sleep.

"Nothin'. Go back to bed."

We always kiss goodbye.

He must have been too tired to react. As Joey's lips brushed his cheek, Mike just blinked and blinked.

Joseph watched him pad back down the hall, look back once before retreating to his room. He returned to his own room, quietly pushed his desk chair to his closet door, fished high up for the drawings, took them down from their hiding place.

His varsity jacket fell silently off the hangar. He slipped it on.

He knelt. Deep inside his gym bag, he felt for the rustle of the plastic compress. In the kitchen, he found some matches, then stuffed them and the bottle of aspirin in a coat pocket. He pushed the stool to the cabinet where his father had hidden the whiskey bottle, took that down. He took a gulp, gasping at the burn, then poured water into the bottle. He took the remaining Valiums at the sink, stuffed them in his mouth, washing them down with the whiskey, water, stuffed the bottle in his pocket.

He opened the back door slowly. A rush of cold air swept into the kitchen. A spring storm bit with tiny drops of half-rain, sleet. Then he was awash in it, stepping down off the porch, out into the purplish glowing night.

"Shit," he muttered, already blurry from the first gulp of whiskey.

Tunes.

Creeping through receding piles of shoveled road snow, mucky lawns, his poisons rattled in his pockets, sloshed in his gut.

Where to?

Purgatory, maybe, the blue-skinned beauty queen in *Beetlejuice*, the nun's explanation, waiting on the Dean's bench, forever.

The Valiums were beginning to blur synapse function, Joey's ability to say the word. He decided singing along to AUURGH, then figured as his limbs grew queasy that the music in hell would probably be Easy Listening.

He felt drunk, only less liquid, as if he were thickening inside.

The woods closed in. Occasionally, a branch lashed his neck or face.

He stumbled around a small pile of rocks where some kids had made a fire. He gulped aspirin while guzzling watered-down whiskey. It still burned his throat, but he had to eat them all. That was what he had to do. His chest rumbled with hiccups. He grabbed a bit of puddled water, lapping it off his hand, the grit of rotten leaves, earth mixed in.

He had trouble pushing the rocks up to make a better windbreak. He lit the drawings on the fourth try, but they sputtered out. He tossed some sticks, whiskey on it, the paper whooshed into a little ball of flame, flying up. One sheet, half-eaten by flames, rode up a few feet like a kite, lighting him, warming him for a tiny moment. He found the knife, stabbed the cold compress bag, sucked the fluid out. It was bitter, burned like road salt or how he imagined antifreeze would taste. He managed to gulp down one blast of it, but had to toss the bag aside, coughing. He remembered the punch line of a joke about a Lambrusco on the Rocks, except he forgot the rocks.

His limbs grew numb as he stumbled in the mucky earth. What he had known so deeply, his own body, all its sensations, drifted away. His head grew cloudy. He fell down, then lay, a cluster of soggy leaves under his head. Stars hovered through the trees, like distant unseeing eyes. He felt his heart, which he'd fed on passionate moments, falling away as the thud in his ears grew slower, then turned to ringing. Somebody was calling his name. He felt himself floating, sinking at the same time. The trees' branches covered the sky like a spidery canopy. Bits of charred paper and black flakes floated up to meet them.

A gurgling interrupted his expected epiphany.

"Wait a fuckin' minute." The gurgling found a partner, multiplied, shifted upward, demanded swift exit.

El Vomito Grande.

24

"A priest and a nun are in the desert on a camel."

Joseph was telling the joke, trying to make a rather hunky dude from Cedar Grove laugh as they sat on the mat in cross-legged groups. The dude snubbed him, so he feigned fascination with a small feather, from a pigeon, perhaps, that had fallen from the gym rafters. He stuck it in his sock.

He was still getting over the embarrassment of the previous weekend, having trudged home, keeping the whole thing a secret until the bottle was found missing. He'd cried. It didn't take much, he was so hung over. He said he'd drunk some and tossed the rest, which was true, in a way.

So when Coach Cleshun, then Raul Klein, called, and he said that he wanted to finally get back into something other than being miserable, his parents practically shoved him out the door. A wrestling clinic. Go. Live a little.

Joseph was trying to repolish the tiny bits of social skills he still had by telling the joke. He didn't get to finish it. A coach for the local school led them in warm-ups.

The great wrestler held a clinic and boys from many schools had come to a gymnasium on a Saturday morning for that day-long clinic. It would give all the boys an edge, they were told.

The great wrestler had won awards, trophies, medals. Coaches and parents sat back on the bleachers, watched as he showed the boys moves they had never tried, or been allowed to try. Wrestling season was over, but wrestling season, in a sense, is never over.

Dustin, Raul and a few other boys Joseph knew by face or weight, but not name, squatted in a circle and watched as the great wrestler grabbed and pushed and shoved and kicked the boys in various ways that had made him a champion and left the boys rubbing parts of their bodies in slight yet inspirational pain. He showed them the way of wrestling outside polite competition. This was the way it was. This was what it took to be a champion.

In the midst of his teaching, he occasionally let slip a few comments that at first merely gave the coaches and parents cause for bemused smirks.

The great wrestler, to be honest, had a dirty mouth.

This did not shock Joseph. He was dealing with the hunky dude totally snubbing him. There was a bit of turf action going on.

When the great wrestler broke them up to do drills, they kept it light. Raul partnered with Joseph. Raul had continued his athletic endeavors on the track team. He tried to get Joseph to join so they would have something new in common, become closer friends, maybe new best friends. Joseph shrugged it off. "I don't like running."

Raul let it slide. It was an off day all around.

The great wrestler, at a late hour in the long day of practicing fireman's carries and bow-and-arrows and Russian arm bars, found himself at a loss for words to describe the swift hopping motion that was required to accomplish a certain move.

As he showed it, he made mention of how this swiftness should be accomplished, "like a, like a fairy, like a little fairy."

He smirked. Many of the boys smirked. A few chuckled.

That they didn't even know who they were laughing at brought him to his feet.

Ignoring it would have been easier for weaker boys. They laugh along.

Joseph, however, was long past laughing along.

He felt his blood drop, as if someone had pressed the elevator button, punched him, put a bag over his head, pressed DOWN. He realized that yes, he had heard that from the great wrestler and yes, it was an insult and yes, it was his right to be offended.

It is difficult to say when the exact moment of Joseph's resolve to die for Anthony came about. It was certainly a cumulative vision, but this moment should suffice.

It occurred on a Saturday, in a suburban area, in a school gymnasium among a few dozen bright-eyed boys and a few older men. The boys were shown the various positions for the man on the bottom, the arms and legs moving like a clock with extra limbs. Here is the hour of defense, the hour of our victory, the hour of our death.

When Joseph failed to respond to yet another joke of questionable taste, the great wrestler singled him out and asked him if he was bored.

"No."

"No what?"

"No. I'm not bored."

"Come here."

It occurred on a Saturday, when Joseph chose a happy death. He was invited with a single finger to assist in showing a move. He was told not to resist. For a fifteen-year-old boy to resist, or by being in the wrong place and resisting, particularly under a man with a fifty pound, twenty-year, 247-pin advantage, was to risk serious injury.

"What?"

"Did you want to volunteer?"

"You asked for a fairy."

"Joe. Don't," Raul muttered.

The circle of boys fell back slightly, some suppressing bursts of astonishment, disgust, bewilderment.

Raul dropped his head, covered his face. Dustin stared, amazed.

On his way through the cluster of parting legs, and again, with his back to the mat, his neck suddenly in a very wrong position, the boy looked up.

Perched high on the girders of the gymnasium ceiling, crouched like a thoughtful monkey, in a white singlet and whiter wrestling shoes, His pristine wings fluttering, His skin blue as a dolphin, His holy power ready to defend the only member of His faith, Saint Anthony of Totowa prepared to swoop down.

"I'm not saying I'm better than any other person. You just get to the stage where your pain threshold must be higher than the average person's. You learn to live with pain that would generally disable someone else."

Ian Roberts
rugby player

1

Neither Hell nor Heaven had ever been described to him as pine-scented. His nose told him he'd missed the other-worldly bus.

The beeping sounds and annoyed announcements confirmed it. His insides had been scraped out and shoved back down his throat. He tried to move, but with a tube in his nose and another one sticking out of his arm, and about four feet of steel cables suspending his head in a sort of geodome of wires and supports, even blinking hurt.

Everything ached.

Something beeped behind his head.

Something beeped inside his head.

A rumpled dress made of paper choked his neck and bunched up under the sheets.

He couldn't move, but half-saw, by moving his eyes sideways until even that exhausted him, his mother curled up in a chair.

A curtain skirted the other side of his bed. He banged his hand on a metal bar at his side. In the drug haze of immobility, laughing inside, thinking that if he was paralyzed and he had to piss there was only one way, he did, without moving.

Before falling back to sleep for another week, he muttered, to no one in particular, "You fag."

1.5

"Ma, he woke up."

She hovered close from the other side.

"Feelin' better?"

"Awg."

"You're alive."

"Mnhn."

"You died for a whole minute!" Mike barked.

The experiment was a success! He wanted to shout. But the river of silk in his veins heavied his lips. "Jhyugh."

His mother took his other hand. "Michael. Go sit outside a minute. Let me talk to your brother."

Mike scowled. "You gonna feed him?"

He had to watch the perimeter of his brother's actions, as the metal work surrounding him prevented him from looking up. He feared for his toes in Mike's presence, felt his legs move, was thankful, relieved.

"No, my love, but I will smack you if you don't behave. Don't go peekin' in other people's rooms."

He heard Mike leave, and watched his mother park herself beside his face. He kept darting his eyes sideways, until it hurt. He held up a hand, and she took it, but started crying, then stopped crying enough to hold him.

"Where's Da?"

"Downstairs."

"Smokin'?"

"Well, you made us very scared. They had to . . . the things they did. Then you, you were gonna die. . . ." Her face scrunched up with tears, her hands covered her eyes.

"Sorry. . . Sorry."

"I . . . know."

"He said," and she stumbled over it, ". . .that it would take a while, maybe a few months, but you're gonna be okay. I know you will."

". . . know. . ."

"Yes, you will!"

"I said. . . I know. . . not no."

"Oh. Okay. You want I should get you a pen and pad?"

"Can we . . . later?"

"Of course."

"Can. . .you get. . ."

"Yes, dear, what can I get you? You want some water?"

"The mylar. . . balloons. They hurt my eyes."

"Okay. Anything else?"

"Dad."

"You want I should go find him?"

"Yeah."

"You'll be awright?"

"Promise. . . won't jump out a window."

He imagined a plane with huge beds. The drugs they gave him rocked so much he didn't care if he'd ever be fine.

He crept a hand up to feel the metal whatever-it-was around his head. He must have broken his neck. Finally. That was why he died. Almost. He even smiled imagining the scene he caused.

His proud smile dropped as his fingers felt the parts of the brace pressed against his skull.

No, not against.

In.

Drilled into his head in a circle were six metal pins.

2

Three hours or days later, in the dark, his father sat beside his bed without saying a word, holding the boy's hand.

"Wha' time. . .? What the . . .?"

"It's late. Your mother went home. Easy."

"Get 'em out. Get these things outta my head, Dad. Please."

He then had a bit of a panic attack, bumped things, until his dad pressed down, shushing him.

His dad's beard stubble scraped his cheek. He smelled sweat, coffee. Dino's flannel shirt warmed him. He held on, but couldn't keep the awkward position.

"Here," he patted his own stomach.

His father nestled on his belly like a dog.

Dr. Behn, his surgeon, visited him. She answered questions, had others. She seemed amazed by his rapid healing, despite her excellent work. They talked about the equipment, vertebrae, nerves, fusion. They'd even made a video of his operation. That viewing would have to wait, not that he didn't want to see it. His hospital room didn't have a VCR.

Although nurses, visitors, drug people, clean-up people, flower people came and went, the one that Joe liked best, aside from the cute guys who came and went, was Irene DeStefano.

It was only then that he really got to know her. He couldn't always see his visitors, but Joe could smell her cigarettes and perfume. Her voice was raspy, but she cheered him up when she told him how worse things were in her day. She told stories, brought food, reassured, read to him. "You should be happy you're alive."

"I am," he said, still frequently touching the two-and-a-half-inch titanium pins connected to a two-pound head brace called a halo. "I dunno why, but even though I am in so much pain, I've never been happier."

He'd have been happier if a few of the cuter male orderlies paid more attention, but Irene's voice had a quality that healed the time, passed the afternoons, giving his parents some time off, since the drive was almost an hour.

They'd moved him to a hospital that specialized in neck injuries. It also helped them avoid the cameras, which had hounded them to the emergency ward after the accident.

But then an opening at the best Children's Hospital in the state suddenly turned up. Rico Nicci wasn't in hospital management for nothing. They'd even flown in for a visit he still barely recalled. He just remembered his uncle and aunt standing over him.

Maybe he had died and this was the waiting room.

Whatever it was, Irene was there, and knitting up a storm as she talked. "I mean, you would not believe the things that people go through, and survive and manage to live wonderful lives. One gentleman on this floor, seventy-five, just in for a slight heart problem, found the girl of his dreams, get this, at a high school reunion. At sixty, finally got her. So, I say, if you're gonna dream, you should dream, you know what I'm saying?"

A full minute, Dr. Xing, his other doctor, had said, confirming Mike's point of fascination. After the accident, he had flatlined. Dr. Xing told him some guy had given him mouth to mouth.

261

"Which guy?" Joe asked.

"A medic."

Dr. Xing made a note to lower his dosage when the patient couldn't stop laughing at his own joke, "Is he married?"

Plants, red roses, crayon anenomes from Sophia, cards from school, from Newark, several coaches, other teams, and of course his own team, or its remaining members, filled his room, even though with the position of his neck brace, he couldn't see it all very well. He asked them to tape some to the ceiling, but the orderlies said no. They adjusted his bed to tilt, when he was ready. A mirror was brought in, but he asked them to take it away. He did not want to see himself. Looking at the puncture permanent made him nauseous.

Grandmama visited, all the aunts, two by two. They held his hand, hovered over his face like moons. They brought flowers, plants, candles. They cried, prayed. He loved it.

His parents traded off shifts of staying with him, refusing to leave him alone until he assured them he was okay. Teachers, administrators, came in suited pairs. A lawyer visited. He seemed very enthusiastic.

Even Miss Pooley visited. Somehow the flower idea had been squelched in favor of drawing pens, paper, his textbooks.

He requested tunes, comics, music mixes. The guys on the team ruled that department. They came in posses.

The view outside his new window faced east, he discovered on his first day upright. On days when they sat him up, he could almost see the tips of Manhattan skyscrapers over the green hills.

In what was called a "miraculous recovery," crediting the marvelous microsurgery of Dr. Behn, he became mobile, with the brace carefully limiting his movements. On the ward, he was referred to as Iron Man, Robowrestler.

He still had visits and massive entertainments of painkillers. On a Sunday afternoon, while returning from the rest room, he knocked over a tray, which woke his father, who lay slouched in a chair under a slat of morning sun.

"What?" Dino Nicci squinted, sleepy-eyed. "You okay?" his father blurted. He was tired. He'd been getting up early to go to Mass, visiting or calling every day, back to church on Sunday, Saturday and Wednesday, lighting candles, devotionals, the whole nine yards.

"You want anything?"

Yeah, Dad, could you please call my boyfriend and find out why he has yet to get his lazy ass here to see me? "Mmmn, food? There anything?"

"I don't know, um, wait."

Dino foraged in the cooler, usually packed with sandwiches, cold pasta, now running low. "Hold on." He left, returning with a bottled juice, two candy bars, three peanut butter cheese cracker packs from a vending machine somewhere down the hall.

Dino helped his son eat the snacks, washed down with tepid water from a plastic pitcher with a straw.

"Um, I'm tired. Can you help?"

Dino jumped up, eased his son down onto the mattress.

"The lawyer called. They're going to pay."

"You can't. Dad. It's my fault."

"Don't, don't, don't start. Don't get upset. You move when you get upset. We discuss, slowly, awright."

"But I wasn't–"

"Okay. Okay. You think we won't love you 'cause maybe you're never gonna get married, or because you think that it's your fault Anthony died, that your friends are in jail?"

"Well, that . . . wraps it up."

"You didn't. You tried to, and maybe you fucked up. You know what? Everybody fucks up. If I hadn't fucked up, we never woulda had you."

"Woulda been better."

His father gripped his arm, hard. Under Dino's grip, the little plastic hospital band dug into his wrist. It read: Joseph S. Nicci, followed by numbers he couldn't read.

"No. Never. You are my boy. Y'unnastand? Now, I love your mother, and Soph an' your brother, but I'm gonna tell you until you understand."

"Yeah?"

"That I love you more than anything. You are my son. You are my blood. My firstborn. I only. . ." Dino choked, but forced it out. "I only hope that, even if you really think that you're. . . Nothing you can do. . .will. . ."

"Okay, Dad. Stop it."

"Okay."

They held hands, since hugging was still dangerous.

"Ma says you're still smokin'."

263

His father pulled back, wiped his eyes. "Yeah, well, I did the same thing every time she was in the hospital havin' you kids."

"That stuff'll kill ya." They laughed, sort of. "Jus' let me keep makin' jokes like that an' I think I'll be okay."

"Not in fronta your mother."

"No hangin' from the roof?"

"No."

"No hunting trips?"

"Enough."

Priests and nuns arrived. Cameras crews arrived.

The nuns were not turned away.

After the first few dozen visits, Joe noticed the same broken neck jokes worked, made them all laugh, more comfortable. They told him they were praying for his recovery at both St. Dominic's and St. Augustine's. "A double dose!" Sister Bernadine called it.

Most never visited twice. His mother told him that folks often came by to make themselves feel better, and just visiting once was enough.

Except Raul, who said he felt guilty about not stopping Joe from getting up. Joe forgave him, asked questions about the team, which led to his life, which led around why Raul wasn't dating, then back to religion, them having a lot in common there, just different names and stories.

Raul and Dustin would visit, talk about wrestling, watch the tube with him, gossip about the other guys, make shadow puppets on the ceiling do battle to save the universe.

He'd never really noticed how beautiful they were, his little tribal brothers. When Dustin asked to touch him, feel what Raul had jokingly called his "Frankenspikes," he felt a tingle, a healing, the lightest caress.

Some nights with his family, they ate together in his room as if it were an extension of the house. Marie brought dinner that night, or maybe a week later. He couldn't tell for a while. Out in the hall, beeps, clattering carts distracted them. He'd been off saline, other things for weeks, but every now and then rubbed over the scar, the arm plug. On the tube, Doug Savant was being stalked by an ex-boyfriend.

"How old were you when I was born?"

"Eighteen," she said.

"Were you still in high school?"

"Just out."

"Was I a prom baby?"

"You were born in September. Add it up."

He couldn't.

Marie said, "January. You weren't the only one who got out of control during Christmas break."

He tried to smile. "Everybody. They all married so young."

"That's the way it works out sometimes."

"I'm really glad Dad never had to go to war."

"Me too. I think you done all the fightin' for all of us."

"Yeah."

"So how 'bout it? Ya gonna come home from the war, Giuseppe?"

They sat for a while, listening to the beeps and sounds of the hospital intercom out in the hall.

She finally spoke again, as if, as always, there was just one more thing. "How could you ever think we wouldn't still love you?"

"I don't know."

"About. . .your being. . ."

"Yeah."

"It's your pal Donnie, right?"

Unable to nod, he instead smiled.

"I could tell. I mean aside from those other boys he was your only real friend you brought over for us to meet, but if you'd only let us get to know them and be a part of your life, it wouldn't have hurt to. . ."

As she continued talking, he listened, part of him still lingering on the 'only real friend' part, trying to ignore the 'was' part.

"Huh?"

"You love him?"

He said, after about a minute, "Lemme put it this way, Marie."

"Okay, Joe," she smirked.

"I knocked him out, but I'm gonna marry him anyway."

3

Another doctor gave him another final examination. His hands worked so quickly Joe didn't even have time to worry about getting a boner. The first time he came in his name tag looked like it said Risen.

Dr. Rosen asked what other medications Joe had been taking. He didn't smile when informed of El Vomito.

Marie and Dino had a meeting with Dr. Rosen. The next time he visited, Joe received another prescription.

"You take them at breakfast, dinner, after eating, not before."

"What is it?"

"An anti-depressant."

"Not that stuff they gave George Bush."

"Why?"

"You ever hear of the Gulf War?"

The doctor didn't laugh, just let his lips shift upward a little.

"I want you to be a bit more careful with your pill-taking, young man. You need to be more careful about your health. I've recommended a very good, very un-scary psychologist. Would you be interested in something like that." It wasn't a question.

"Sure."

"It doesn't mean you're crazy or anything."

"I know."

Joe could have told him he understood. In addition to his neck, temporarily fucking up his liver with the pills and whiskey, he also had a weight problem, tendonitis in both knees, the remnants of a skin fungus, a stress fracture in his collar bone, and excess cartilage deposits in his ears.

"Your parents told you about the therapy options?"

"Yeah, someone else to report to."

"I'm serious. You have only one life, so enjoy the rest of it, you hear me?"

"Yeah."

"Okay." They shook hands, and Dr. Rosen left while flipping through his chart.

Around dusk that night, or another night, his mother called about some problem with the garage door or the car. He said he was

266

okay and would see them when they got there.

They kept telling him to rest, but he had to start moving again.

He fingered two quarters out of his bathrobe pocket, wheeled into the waiting room.

The tube hung from the ceiling. Across the room, the double-bypass lady sat dozing on a chair, her IV hanging beside her. It was said that she kept showing up in different places on the floor, claiming her room was haunted.

A news story continued, hosted by a familiar face, that chubby news guy standing behind a podium, holding an award, a piece of plastic. He talked amid camera flashes. What he was talking about wasn't clear, the volume was too low. The reporter was, to Joe, an old friend he'd never met.

Joe didn't want to wake the lady, so he wheeled close, but a foot rest clanged against the snack dispenser. She nearly jumped out of her seat to spy a disheveled creature with a spiral of metal around his head backlit by a soda sign.

"Sorry."

She stood, wheeled her IV over, helped him get his soda. They watched the news together for a while. A reporter stood outside a school yard. Some boy in some high school had tried to kill a classmate, but missed and shot a substitute teacher instead.

". . .that the only trace of rage will be felt in the hallways of this school, and the memory of its fear."

Then the show returned to the studio anchors, each sort of half-smiling, as if they'd tasted some lousy cooking and were pretending to love it. The lady: "Coming up, a Tri-state springtime holiday. . ."

The anchor guy: "And more on the baseball strike with Rock–"

"Enough." Joe hit OFF. Double bypass lady didn't complain, having already left the room.

4

Fortified by his family's love, and a lengthy prescription of what became known as "the happy pills," Joe returned home to spend the rest of May being doted upon. The last week of classes, he returned for finals.

He did surprisingly well, having been quite the captive audience for homework once the scary prospect of being a sophomore all over again sunk in.

His story was by then mythic, his return to school beatific, yet still embarrassing. With the neck brace and the remaining dot-shaped scars on his forehead, he continued to be easily identified. Fearful of an unseen collision, he found helpful bodyguards in former teammates. Occasionally, in turning, he got a ghost of a twinge, like the time he waited for his ride home outside the school, heard what sounded like a junky Mustang rumbling around a corner.

What arrived instead was Mrs. DeStefano's Boat, or the Bronco, this time driven by his mom. She talked cheerily about some plans for that evening. He reminded her of an obligation.

"I don't want you hangin' around with a bunch of other kids who could be a bad influence," she argued.

"It's in a church."

"A Methodist church."

"So?"

"So, it's not your church."

"Well, it's got the St. Dominic's seal of approval, 'cause Sister Bernadine told me about it. It's other kids like me who got problems."

"And your parents can't help you with that?"

"Ma, I love you. But there's some things you just can't talk about with your parents. Remember, you wanted this."

"It still wouldn't hurt to go back to Mass with me. Go to confession. It may not do anything for you, but I think you'll feel better."

"Ma, I went to confession. Been there, shaved that."

"If you hadn't messed with those boys–"

"Ma."

"That Khors boy–"

"Ma. Chill."

"This is what they teach you at that group? To talk back to your mother?"

"Ma," he said, softly. "I learned it myself. When I died."

"I'm going to forgive you for saying that."

Her silence followed them into the kitchen, where she began the pot and pan drum solo before dinner. He knew he'd have to apologize later. He felt better knowing he wanted to live, even if it took a fuss to do it. Besides, knowing his mother disapproved made it a bit more fun.

TEENS

Taped to the door of a little side room in the United Methodist Church, a curved slab building of gray brick that looked like a giant crab shell, the sign almost scared him off. It felt good to go, how the team used to feel, but it was a different circle altogether. Nobody else was a wrestler, but everybody had apparently done the "Down you go."

Six other kids and a counselor sat in folding chairs; Consuela, a Puerto Rican girl with a crewcut; Todd, a skinny nearly invisible kid with glasses, his arm in a cast; Malcolm, a chubby black kid who could have given Buddha Martinez some competition; Heather, a sullen girl with green and red dyed hair shaved on one side with a matching Morrisey T-shirt who always ended her sentences with a question? and Alan, a long-haired blond kid whose pimples made up most of his features.

But what relieved and embarrassed him was the presence of Tom, the photographer. It seemed Tom had gone through some similar experiences, post-Anthony. Just sitting next to him flooded Joe's head with a sea of if-onlys. He always sat by Tom. There was so much catching up to do.

At first, Joe wondered how they'd all done it, tried to kill themselves. Or were they all queer, too? He figured at least he still looked okay, the way they were looking at him, but he'd hoped to meet a guy like Dink, somebody he could be buddies with.

An older guy, Richard, the counselor, who was very patient, wore jeans, a denim shirt, didn't seem too scary.

Alan, the skinny blond very gay-acting kid, kept talking about Kurt Cobain. Alan had earrings on both sides, rings on his fingers. His every word made Joe squirm.

"When he did it, I just thought, why not? I mean, not like I wanted like I would be famous or anything. I just saw it as an option."

Heather added, "There's so much glorification of it in music? I think I was really negatively influenced by that? But I'm not going to like start listening to Michael Bolton to make myself feel better." Heather and Alan laughed. They had inside jokes. They'd already become friends.

"Crazy," Joe muttered.

"Joe, let's not be judgmental," Richard said. "We're here to support each other."

I'm here to support them, he wondered. When was it all going to be over? When could he forget?

Tom spoke up. "I think um, Joe and I have . . . it's about just always wishing we could go back, bring Anthony back. It was everywhere, and people were supportive, but they didn't understand."

Even his parents had gone to therapy, Tuesdays at seven, after dropping him off at Chez DeStefano. They'd changed, gotten so odd, as if they were behaving the way somebody else told them to act, with a forced politeness. They'd even watched a few movies, "only no dancing," his mother had said. Joe called them Forced Family Fridays, as if they all just sat together, doing things together, then the rest of the world would go away, they'd all be happy. It sometimes felt good, but he didn't like to admit that. Mostly he felt as if he was posing for a commercial.

"I know you think it's crazy," Alan said, waving his arms around, reading Joe in a 'sharing' way. "But look, you probably never got beat up for wearing the wrong T-shirt, or getting your ears pierced, being out like me. I mean, I don't have the things you have, okay? It's like a totally different experience being openly gay. There is a freedom, but there's a lot of hassles."

Heather gave one snap up.

"Heather," Richard warned.

Joe sputtered, "I'm out. . . enough. But I don't think I have to tell everybody, you know, like goin' and wearin' a button, like Hi, Blow Me. . . because I don't think it's anybody's business what I do and it totally fuc- messed me up when it got out."

"But wasn't that part of it?" Consuela said.

"No. I didn't. . ." They were all sitting there waiting, looking. Justify yourself. "I let everybody down. I couldn't deal with having to. . . well, Jeez, you all know. You all know about it. Tom knows. Everybody knows about it, even though nobody used my name. It was like I was already ripped apart. Getting hurt, it was just. . . finishing the job."

Malcolm adjusted himself in his seat. His butt spread out on both sides of the chair. Todd, the silent one, coughed and pushed his glasses back. Richard started talking, in his reasoned counselor voice, which sort of annoyed Joe but made him feel better, like the pills they'd given him, which his mother kept hidden, doling them out once a day. Sometimes they made him want to jump around or be silly, but mostly they made him slightly hyper. He wondered what would happen when they ran out.

"You've all felt pressures from outside," Richard said.

"Unbearable pressures, from peers, from family, from all around you. What I'd like you each to do, okay, for next week, is think more about your own reactions, your own feelings, and not so much about what people would think, okay? I'm not saying you should do anything you want, like rob a bank or steal a car."

That got a few chuckles and smiles, especially from Todd, who'd stolen his mother's car and smashed it into a tree. Todd was twelve.

The meeting finished. Kids folded the chairs.

Joe fought an edgy feeling inside as Alan walked up.

"So, um, you go to Little Falls?"

"Yeah, between CAT scans."

Alan laughed too hard. "Um, well, if you're allowed, we could go to a movie or something."

Joe faced him. Alan was not cute in the way he desired guys, seemed a total fag. But that was his problem, not Alan's. "This isn't like a date."

"No, no, no, oh no. Heather and Tom'll come too, if you like, but, oh no. We're sisters." Alan patted Joe's arm.

"Okay, but I have to ask my parents."

"Right." Alan turned, then sort of whirled around, saying, "Besides, I don't go for jocks."

5

Joe got off work about five-thirty, depending on how many shoes needed to be reshelved. Fake refs raked in $4.55 an hour at the Willowbrook Foot Locker.

After three weeks he found the nerve to ask his manager if they would consider carrying wrestling shoes. The manager hemmed, hawed, saying coaches always bought from the catalogs, until Joe told him he knew a few people. A few weeks and twenty sales later, Joe moved to $5.25 an hour.

Before movies, he'd met his mom or dad, or both, or Tom and Alan for dinner and a movie at the mall. Things were pretty contained for a while.

With Tom, their silences sometimes made him nervous with sexual tension, mixed with the unsaid things about Anthony. Sex wasn't really an option, since Tom had unloaded some "too much information" about a bit of childhood abuse that Joe was not prepared for, in addition to his "bisexual" claims. Joe also wasn't really attracted to him, anyway, so they talked around sex and

271

school and the whole Anthony thing, but not much about it. Still, they stayed friends, as survivors of any calamitous event often do.

Having Alan around provided a buffer. Joe learned to like Alan as a resource. He just didn't know how to mix him in with the rest of his life. Tom was nice, and Joe eventually got used to hanging with them, even though he sometimes felt embarrassed, like the day they stood in line at a movie and Troy Hilas and two of his non-wrestler friends spotted them while Alan re-enacted a scene from a John Waters movie. They all kept their distance. It seemed the polite thing to do.

Over sodas and pizzas, Alan told them about gay bars, some nearby, even the one where Hunter had smashed the windshield. Joe didn't tell them about that incident. He didn't feel like being "read" again, but waited patiently for that night's parental pick-up.

A gay bar. He didn't even have a fake ID. They'd never let Joe in, even if he remembered how to get there. Dink would have. He'd have gotten in on charm alone.

Joe entered the living room in music and darkness, then little sounds coming from above. He heard his parents creeping upstairs, his mother giggling.

He walked audibly into the kitchen, gave them some time alone, and lay on the couch, listening to the stack of albums they'd put on for their little private time. No doubt the kids were next door.

His mother's scarf and his father's suit jacket lay on the floor by the stairs, but before he hung them up in the hall closet, he pressed his face to each one, feeling the soft fabric of his mother's scarf, secret pockets of his father's jacket, smelling the difference, two perfumes, tiny particles that one day had merged to make him.

He lay on the sofa in the dark living room, listened to the bed creak above him, felt happy. Maybe they'd make another baby, maybe another girl this time. He thought their music was funny; old stuff, but it put his parents in a good mood. He wondered how he was going to feel when he was thirty or forty, listening to Nirvana someday, thinking, oh boy, those were the good old days.

As if.

He heard the steps creaking and saw his father startled, standing in boxer shorts. Unlike Joe's magazine studs, he had a thinner torso, a bit of a gut, but it was him, a part of Joe, the body a man gets from working, not working out.

"What are you doing in the dark?" his father muttered.

272

"Listening to your music."

"Not like your stuff, huh?"

"No, but it's nice."

"Gettin' some water." His dad padded quietly into the kitchen. The refrigerator light splayed across the ceiling, half-blocked by his father's shadow. He heard gulps, saw the fridge light disappear, returning the house to darkness.

"You enjoy your movie?"

"Yeah."

"You getting along with those boys?"

"Oh, yeah."

"So, how ya doin'?"

"Really good." He didn't know how to explain it to his father, but he did feel better, hopeful. In addition to his neck, somewhere in himself, fusion had occurred.

"Good. That's good." Dino stood, rubbing his belly. "Well, I spose I oughtta call Irene, go get the kids."

"I'll do it." He sat up. "I'll go next door. I'm dressed. You go on up."

"You sure?"

His father started for the steps, until Joe called out, softly, "Da?"

"Yeah?"

"Use a glass next time."

"If you stop pissing in the sink."

"I never–"

His dad waved him off and headed up.

"Da?"

He figured he'd ask now. He'd never catch him in a better mood.

6

"A no-load fee."

"A what?"

Ed Khors' condo was nice, but a bit over-decorated in a way that made Dino seem slightly uncomfortable.

Ed Khors was talking about investing in mutual funds, but when Dino was supposed to say something equally erudite, he just gave a quick glance over to Joe that said, 'Sheesh.'

The two men drank sodas, even though it seemed they would just as soon have beers if the boys weren't there. Joe hoped Dino and Ed Khors would get along to the point of being friends who had beers together. Friends of the family. In-laws. Joe caught himself doing what Richard from the youth group had called "projecting." Joe found himself doing that a lot.

Dino took Ed Khors by the arm. "Whyncha show me the property? Let the boys here spend some time together."

"Oh," Mr. Khors said, getting it. This was more of a chaperoned date.

The two fathers ambled out to the back porch, within earshot, but far enough away so that Joe and Donnie talked softly, on the sofa.

"So, how ya doin?"

Donnie shrugged. He wore a blank green T-shirt, denim pants, sneakers that looked big on his feet. He'd gotten thicker, said he was working out, but in his face, with the scraggly attempt at a goatee, Joe saw fatigue, circles under his eyes. He'd caved in on the inside but then fixed himself.

"How was juvey?"

"Food sucks," Donnie said.

"I figured."

"Actually, it was okay. We had these sessions where we talked. Kinda like confession, only we talk about moving on, y'know, making goals."

"Yeah, I go to a group like that for. . . for kids that, you know—"

"Near-death experience?"

"No. How'd you know?"

"Your dad told my dad."

"Oh. You get my letter?"

"Yeah. Like a month late. I'm sorry. Mom's all weirded out. She's not dealing with this very well. I think I'm gonna stay with Dad." Donnie looked at him, shrugging, like, *It's out of my hands.*

"Maybe you could commute. Your dad could move back."

"I dunno."

Donnie's hand picked at a loose thread in the knee of his jeans.

They shared Parade of Authority Figures jokes. Joe told him about the other kids in his group, how funny some of them were, sad at the same time. Donnie told him about some of the characters in the detention center. After defending himself in a fight with a few simple takedowns, Donnie had achieved a sort of elevated status, which he'd tried to shake off, yet it kept him safe in a way. Joe did not completely understand, but he nodded, smiled, vibrating inside just to be near him, just to hear his voice again. His hand reached out. They held on.

"It's weird. Everything's so. . .weird."

"Yeah," Joe said. "I ain't seen you in months, man. 'Cept on tape."

"Yeah. Weird." Donnie sighed, then became enthused. "But one thing. We did this Outward Bound thing, like camp. They took us to this place with, you know climb the walls and climb rope over a pit."

"Like *American Gladiators?*"

"Yeah, right. Supposed to be for our 'self-esteem. Creating goals.'"

"Hmm."

"So, what else ya been doin' with yourself?" Donnie asked.

He told some of it, enhanced gruesome medical details. Donnie just took it in, like he was soaking up the image of Joe's face to save for later.

"I did it with another guy." Joe figured he should at least tell him the good news, even if he hadn't had a good time.

"Really?"

Joe nodded.

"No sainthood for you."

"Guess not."

"So?"

"So what?"

"So how was it?"

"Jeez. . . It wasn't. . ."

"What? You're not queer after all?"

"I was . . . It wasn't right." Joe felt the inside of his throat thickening. "I wish it woulda been you."

Donnie looked at him, half-smiled, shrugged. "Well, we both got a lotta woulda beens."

"Yeah."

The boys looked away from each other. Outside, their fathers laughed at something. Donnie asked, "Was he cute?"

"Donnie. . ."

"Come on. It's me. I get lonely. I need somethin' to think about at night. I mean, I'm like totally porno-free. We get these counselors comin' in all the time inspecting the house 'cause he's—"

"What?"

275

"You know. Divorced. Single. Hello?"

"What?"

Donnie shrugged, then sang that line again, "What more can I say, everyone is–"

"He better not tell my dad."

"Bro, get over it, okay? That's his deal."

"Okay. I'm. . . I'm sorry. I'm just. . ."

"I know. So, ya got laid. Didja fuck?"

"What?"

"Your big second time."

"No, we didn't– It was in a car, okay!"

"Chill. I just. . . Well, then you're actually still a virgin."

"Says who?"

"Says me." Donnie grinned in a mischievous way that reminded him of that first distracting day. "You know I love you, like a brother."

"Already got a brother."

"Okay then, I love you like more than a brother. And when we get back on the mat, I'll show you a thing or two."

"Yeah, right."

"You're gettin' fat." Donnie poked his stomach. "Whassa matter? You don't work out no more?"

"I. . . Season's over."

"Whaddayou now, one-forty?"

"Somethin' like that." He'd also grown two inches in height since having his neck remodeled.

"You wrestle my class?"

"Yeah, and I'll pound ya."

"Dream on."

They half-laughed, avoiding each other's eyes.

"Aw, man, what am I saying?" Donnie muttered.

"Yeah, what happened, You wrestle any?"

"Couldn't deal. Just grades were hard enough. Besides, I don't need that bullshit to touch guys anymore."

Joe had to let that one sink in. "Hey, they don't letcha, ya still got me."

"Thanks."

"No, I'm serious. You come over. We train, whatever."

"Yeah, I think it's the 'whatever' our parents are worried about."

They were silent, until Donnie said, "Do you forgive me?"

Joe exaggerated his shock, thinking it would help prove his

feelings. "What are you, crazy? Hey, man, it's over, what happened, you know, I mean, I still wish we could–"

"Well, you know, maybe, it's just. . . Do you forgive me?"

Joe stared at him, wanting to tell him what he knew he'd seen, or dreamt, a flap of wings, a jolt of light. If anyone on earth would believe it, this boy would.

Instead, he switched to Sven the Laps Catholic voice. "Of course I forgeeve you! You are my brudder!"

They laughed, hugged, didn't let go, kissed.

Donnie looked back to the porch, then to Joe. "Let's go to my room." Donnie's eyes sparked.

They snuck to his room, stood kissing, grabbing, licking. Joe had a hand down inside his shorts when Ed Kohrs appeared in the doorway.

"Oops."

Donnie's father closed his eyes, pursed his lips, then said, before leaving, "Five minutes."

"Okay."

"And the pants stay on."

"Right."

Joe stared at Donnie, amazed.

"Yeah, um. Now, where were we?"

"Five minutes."

Their fathers were waiting outside by the driveway, even more awkward than before.

"Well. . ."

"Call me."

"Yeah. I'll do that. That would be nice. I'm sposed to get every third weekend or something with my mom, but she's like really touchy about her quality time. Call my dad."

"Good. Great."

Misty eyes. Lawn sprinklers a block away. They grappled, which became a mock tie-up, which was stopped because of "the neck," then allowed, but only in the slow motion form of a hug.

peat moss
trim to match den paneling
garage door opener part
filter for AC
chips
bbq sauce
videos

Forced Family Friday usually meant errands before home, hunting down the evening's entertainment and food. Joe was allowed to drive, under supervision, in a parking lot.

After he'd parked successfully, Dino congratulated him. "Pick something for everybody," he said as they entered the video store.

Joe picked *The World According to Garp*.

"I don't think so," Dino said.

"Why not? It's about wrestling."

"It's not just . . . Fine, for later, after your brother and sister are asleep. Now pick a G-rated one, for everybody, like that shrunken kids thing."

"We saw that."

Joe wandered away from his dad. He scanned the shelves, irritated that he had to think for everybody. It was like being a small dad. Anything with guns his mother refused. If it was a cartoon Mike would say it was too baby-ish. Was this what it would be like, he wondered, if he liked girls and had kids?

He met up with his dad at the science fiction aisle. They agreed on aliens. Even though he'd already seen it, Joe wanted to see the one with Steve Guttenberg getting his rocks off in a pool.

His father picked a different one.

"That's got monsters in it," Joe countered. "Soph'll get nightmares."

Dino glanced at him a moment, surprised, amused.

"What?"

"Just lookin' at my son."

Joe reconsidered. "If we tell her they're just Muppets, she'll be okay."

It was a responsibility, like his new job, which was tiring, but in a new way. On days like this one, he could just relax after working for the family, working on his home.

278

Weekends in June offered ample time for Dino's "projects." Between digging and rooting, they trekked from True Value to Gardenz-r-Us to some new taco place in three hours.

Still coated with soot, he slammed the truck door closed as he and his father walked up the driveway. His eyes a bit crusted, his jeans caked in dust, he resembled an immigrant marble worker.

Mike crouched near a tree, looked up from some insect he'd just caught in a jar. "You got company."

Joe and his dad found Coach Cleshun sitting in the living room talking with his mother. Cleshun's voice and manner were strained, like a minister coming to visit. It gave Joe a strange sense of power, watching the man court his parents' favor, especially when he had a snowball's chance of getting it.

"I just want you to know that I hope, when you come back to school, that you'll consider coming back to the team. I know there's a lot of water under the bridge, but you've got a lot of potential."

Marie took the ball, handed it to Joe.

"I'm up to one-forty now."

"Not a lot of muscle, I'm sure. We'll get you down to wrestling weight quick enough. You'll have to move up a class. I wanna see you at the track, doin' some running, you hear?"

"I . . . I'll think about it."

"I want you to do that."

Marie said, as they rose, "Well, like I said, it's up to the doctors."

Dino added, "He's very busy working now, too."

"My physical therapist said I should swim."

"Yeah? Well, that's good. Cross-training."

"No. Instead of wrestling."

"Oh." Coach Cleshun laughed, a forced laugh, then started to get up, as if to leave. Joe felt a small rip inside himself, as if this one connection, or possible connection to the world he lost were too frail, and he wanted to test it.

I told Coach, and he is all right with it.

"Um, can you guys excuse us a minute, please?"

"Oh, why sure." Marie and Dino awkwardly retreated to the kitchen.

Joe waited, then walked his coach to the door. "You know, um, one of the things goin' on is, well, you know, I'm. . . I like guys. I'm like dating . . . a guy."

Coach blinked, twice. "That's not really any of my–"

279

"So if you don't want me on the team because of that I'll understand but um I think I'm gonna go out for swimming because of my neck and all."

"I know you got this lawsuit thing goin' on. I'm not tryin' to, believe me. That's not my business. That's between you and your parents."

"And my case worker and my shrink and my group counselor–"

"Yeah, okay."

He wanted to say more, but Cleshun seemed to get it.

"You remember the times you guys razzed me about that geeky team picture I got on the wall? When you come back to school, we'll play a little game, but you don't tell anybody else, okay? You have to pick out the guy who never dated girls, the one who's goin' to those Gay Olympics in New York."

"Really?"

"Really."

"Oh, um. . ." He didn't want to make it so obvious, the connection, so he pretended to be changing topics. "Is um, Fiasole gonna be at school next year?"

"No. He graduated. Got a job at Montclair State."

"Oh. Cool," Joe grinned. So much for choosing a college. He imagined himself and Fiasole together having a beer sometime after Joe graduated in 2000 something.

He held the door closed, watched through the glass as his coach walked down the steps and along the sidewalk, didn't tell Cleshun he'd gotten the name of Gay Games wrong. Joe'd already found out when wrestling would be at the NYU gym, and asked for those days off from work.

Figuring out how to ask his dad to take him, since they'd never let him go into Manhattan alone, wasn't so much of a problem, but he was worried for his dad. How would Dino react if there were drag queen cheerleaders, or guys kissing? How would he react if Joe liked it?

He was still trying to figure out how to properly ask Mr. Khors if he could spring Donnie for a day. Maybe he'd like to go, too. Joe wanted to create Father-Son days, like a corny commercial. He had a picture of them all in the Bronco, driving home at sunset, the sky a brilliant orange and pink behind the George Washington Bridge, dads up front talking, boys in the back, holding hands, everybody seatbelted, safe. Safer.

It could happen. Heather told him positive imagery was very helpful. Maybe he was dreaming. Maybe it was time to cut back on the happy pills.

The kitchen smelled oddly dormant. Then he remembered: pizza night. He grabbed a sandwich, but felt anxious. He had to move. "Ma, where are my clean sweat pants?"

"The team ones or the blue ones?" she shouted back from somewhere in the house.

"Whichever!"

"In your drawer!"

"Thanks!"

"You're welcome!"

He found them, changed, stepped off the porch and under the warm baked air of a June day bouqueted with little fluffy clouds.

Spread out on his lawn, breathing, he rolled and flexed. His body greeted him with tiny rips and tears hello as he stretched quadriceps, hamstrings, snortissimus dorsi.